SECOND GRAVE ON THE LEFT

"Jones perfectly balances humor and suspense in [this] paranormal thriller featuring grim reaper, PI, and 'all-around badass' Charley Davidson . . . It's the distinctive characters, dead and alive, and the almost constant laughs that will leave readers eager for the next installment."
—*Publishers Weekly* (starred review)

"This is an amazing book and a fantastic series! In a lot of ways it is similar to Janet Evanovich's Stephanie Plum series, only ten times better!" —*Night Owl Reviews*

"A saucy sequel . . . Readers will be captivated by Charley's near-death adventures." —Associated Press

"Four and a half stars. Snarky, sassy Charley is back and taking no guff in Jones's action-packed new offering . . . There is murder and mystery aplenty . . . fun."
—*RT Book Reviews*

FIRST GRAVE ON THE RIGHT

"Sexy, sassy . . . Jones's characters, both living and dead, are colorful and endearing. . . . Cheeky charm . . . sarcastic wit." —Associated Press

"Jones's wickedly witty debut will delight aficionados of such humorous paranormals as Casey Daniels's Pepper Martin Mysteries and Dakota Cassidy's Accidental series." —*Booklist* (starred review)

"Jones skillfully establishes the novel's setting and keeps up the pace with plenty of action. And let's be honest—the sex is pretty hot, too. Fans of Sherrilyn Kenyon and other authors of paranormal romance will love this series debut." —*Library Journal* (starred review)

Also by Darynda Jones

The Dirt on Ninth Grave

Darynda Jones

St. Martin's Paperbacks

This is a work of fiction. All of the characters, organizations, and events portrayed in this novel are either products of the author's imagination or are used fictitiously.

THE DIRT ON NINTH GRAVE

Copyright © 2015 by Darynda Jones.
Excerpt from *The Curse of Tenth Grave* copyright © 2016 by Darynda Jones.

For information address St. Martin's Press, 175 Fifth Avenue, New York, NY 10010.

ISBN: 978-1-250-07449-2

Our books may be purchased in bulk for promotional, educational, or business use. Please contact your local bookseller or the Macmillan Corporate and Premium Sales Department at 1-800-221-7945, ext. 5442, or by e-mail at MacmillanSpecialMarkets@macmillan.com.

Printed in the United States of America

St. Martin's Press hardcover edition / January 2016
St. Martin's Paperbacks edition / June 2016

St. Martin's Paperbacks are published by St. Martin's Press, 175 Fifth Avenue, New York, NY 10010.

10 9 8 7 6 5 4 3 2 1

For Lorelei,

Whose official titles include
but are not limited to:

The Duchess of Dialogue

The Empress of Intonation

The Virtuoso of Voice

The Siren of Speech

The Ninja of Narration

Superwoman

The Baroness of Bard

The Femme Fatale of Fiction

The Enchantress of Elocution

Hot Lips*

Thank you for lending your immense talent
to this series!

....

* Does not denote ennoblement under the sovereign laws of peerage and
is not a hereditary title. It must be earned.

Acknowledgments

A special thanks to the following people, without whom this book would suck. Seriously. On several agonizing levels.

Thank-yous go out to:

Alexandra Machinist, whose initials actually stand for Awe-inspiring Marvel.

Jennifer Enderlin for being such an incredible editor and cheerleader.

Anna Boatman for the support and much-appreciated enthusiasm.

India Cooper for the wonderful copyedits.

Mr. Jones, the undeniable love of my life, and the beautiful creatures named Jerrdan and Casey, aka the Mighty, Mighty Jones Boys.

The rest of my family. Even the ones who don't claim me.

The fabulous people at Heroes and Heartbreakers.

Sarah Wendell for the brilliant band name, and everyone at Smart Bitches, Trashy Books.

Dana and Netters, who do everything for the books but write them.

Quentin Lynn for answering my 17,835 questions about the running of a restaurant.

Margie Lawson for the intervention addressing, specifically, my "as" addiction, which is a separate matter entirely from my "ass" addiction. And for Bobert. I am eternally grateful for Bobert.

Six Chicks and a Pocket Rooster. Best week ever!

Marika Gailman: Translator Extraordinaire. *Merci!*

Theresa Rogers for the notes. For the *Jeopardy!* quote. For the shoulder and the camaraderie.

Kit for your incredible insight and your willingness to answer my multiple calls to arms.

Jowanna and Rhianna for the betas.

Robyn Peterman and Donna McDonald for being awesome and letting me write with you.

Everyone in LERA, the NM chapter of RWA.

My gorgeous Ruby sisters.

The Grimlets! For being Grimlets!

And, as always, thank YOU, dear wonderful amazing reader, for loving Charley and Reyes as much as I do.

XOX! ~D~

1

Remember, it's never too late to give LSD a shot.
—T-SHIRT

I stood beside the booth and poured coffee into a beige cup that had the words FIRELIGHT GRILL written across it, wondering if I should tell my customer, Mr. Pettigrew, about the dead stripper sitting next to him. It wasn't every day a dead stripper accosted one of my regulars, but telling Mr. P about her might not be a good idea. He could react the way I did the first time I saw a walking corpse a little over a month ago. I screamed like a twelve-year-old girl and locked myself in the bathroom.

For seven hours.

I admired the rascally old man, a decorated war veteran and retired NYPD detective. He'd seen more action than most. And with it, more atrocity. More depravity and desperation and degradation. He was a tough-as-nails, real-life superhero, and I couldn't picture any situation in which

Mr. P would scream like a twelve-year-old girl and lock himself in a bathroom.

For seven hours.

In my own defense, the first dead guy I saw had fallen to his death at a construction site in Kalamazoo. Thanks to a hundred-foot drop and an unfortunate placement of rebar, I had another image to add to my things-I-can-never-unsee collection. Silver linings, baby.

I pulled three creamers out of my apron pocket where I stashed them, mostly because keeping creamers in my jeans pocket never ended well. I placed them on the table beside him.

"Thanks, Janey." He gave me a saucy wink and doctored his coffee, an elixir I'd grown to love more than air. And French fries. And hygiene, but only when I woke up late and was faced with the heart-wrenching decision of either making a cup of the key to life itself or taking a shower. Strangely enough, coffee won. Every. Single. Time.

Mr. P was a regular, and I liked regulars. Whenever one walked into the café I felt a little less lost, a little less broken, as though family had come to visit. As fucked up as it sounded, they were all I had.

A little over a month ago, I woke up in an alley, soaked to the marrow of my bones with freezing rain pelting my face and no memory of who I was. Or where I was. Or when I was. I had nothing but the clothes on my back, a honking big diamond on my ring finger, and a blinding headache. The headache disappeared fairly quickly. Thankfully the clothes and the wedding ring did not. But if I were married, where was my husband? Why had he not come for me?

I'd been waiting since that first day. Day One, I'd called

it. I'd been waiting for four weeks, three days, seventeen hours, and twelve minutes. Waiting for him to find me. For anyone to find me.

Surely I had family. I mean, everyone has family, right? Or, at the very least, friends. It would seem, however, that I had neither. No one in Sleepy Hollow—or the entire state of New York—knew who I was.

But that didn't stop me from digging in my raggedly bitten nails and clinging to the knowledge that almost everyone on the planet had someone, and my someone was out there. Somewhere. Searching for me. Scouring the galaxy night and day.

That was my hope, anyway. To be found. To be known. The spiderweb cracks in the shell holding me together were splintering, bleeding into one another, creeping and crackling along the fragile surface. I didn't know how much longer it would hold. How much longer until the pressure inside me exploded. Until it shattered and catapulted the pieces of my psyche into space; to the farthest reaches of the universe. Until I vanished.

It could happen.

The doctors told me I had amnesia.

Right?

Apparently that shit's real. Who knew?

While waiting for Mr. P to scan the menu he knew by heart, I looked out the plate-glass windows of the café at the two worlds before me. I'd realized very soon after waking up that I could see things others couldn't. Dead people, for one thing, but also their realm. Their dimension. And their dimension defined the word *cray-cray*.

Most people saw only the tangible world. The world in which the wind didn't pass through them but bombarded them, its icy grip only metaphorically slicing through to their bones, because their physical bodies would only let it penetrate so far.

But there was another world all around us. An intangible one where the winds did not go around us but passed through us like searing smoke through air made visible only by a ray of light.

On this particular day, the tangible forecast was partly cloudy with an 80 percent chance of precipitation. The intangible forecast, however, was angry, billowing clouds with a 100 percent chance of thunderous lightning storms and fiery tornadoes swirling in an endless dance over the landscape.

And the colors. The colors were stunning. Oranges and reds and purples, the likes of which were not found in the tangible world, glistened around me, whirled and melded together with each reaction of the capricious weather, as though battling for dominance. Shadows were not gray there but blue and lavender with hints of copper and gold. Water was not blue but variegated shades of orchid and violet and emerald and turquoise.

The clouds parted a few blocks away, and a brilliant light shot down to welcome another soul, to embrace the fortunate spirit that had reached the expiration date of its corporeal form.

That happened fairly often, even in a town the size of Sleepy Hollow. What happened less often, thank goodness, was the opposite. When the ground cracked and parted to reveal a cavernous chasm, to deliver a less fortunate soul—a less deserving one—into darkness.

But not just any darkness. An endless, blinding void a thousand times blacker than the darkest night and a million times deeper.

And the doctors swear there is nothing wrong with me. They can't see what I see. Feel what I feel. Even in my state of absolute amnesia, I knew the world before me was unreal. Unearthly. Unnatural. And I knew to keep it to myself. Self-preservation was a powerful motive.

Either I had some kind of extrasensory perception or I'd done a lot of LSD in my youth.

"He's a doll," the stripper said, her sultry voice dragging me away from the fierce world that raged around me.

She leaned her voluptuous body into him. I wanted to point out the fact that he was old enough to be her father. I could only hope he wasn't.

"His name is Bernard," she said, running a finger down the side of his face, a spaghetti strap slipping down a scraped-up shoulder.

I actually had no idea what she'd done for a living, but from the looks of it, she was either a stripper or a prostitute. She'd caked on enough blue eye shadow to paint the Chrysler Building, and her little black dress revealed more curves than a Slinky. I was only leaning toward stripper because the front of her dress was being held together with Velcro.

I had a thing for Velcro.

Sadly, I couldn't talk to her in front of Mr. P, which was unfortunate. I wanted to know who'd killed her.

I knew how she'd died. She'd been strangled. Black and purple splotches circled her neckline, and the capillaries in her eyes had burst, turning the whites bright red. Not her best look. But I was curious about the situation. How it had evolved. If she'd seen the assailant. If she'd known him. Clearly I had a morbid streak, but I felt this tug at my insides to help her.

Then again, she was dead. As a doornail. In winter. What could I do?

My motto since Day One was to keep my head down and my nose clean. It was none of my business. I didn't want to know how they died. Who they left behind. How lonely they felt. For the most part the departed were like wasps. I didn't bother them. They didn't bother me. And that was how I liked it.

But sometimes I felt a tug, a knee-jerk reaction, when I saw a departed. A visceral desire to do what I could for them. It was instinctual and deep-seated and horridly annoying, so I crawled into a cup of coffee and looked the other way.

"Bernard," she repeated. "Isn't that the cutest name?" Her gaze landed on me in question.

I gave her the barest hint of a nod as Mr. P said, "I guess I'll have the usual, Janey."

He always had the usual for breakfast. Two eggs, bacon, hash browns, and whole-wheat toast.

"You got it, hon." I took the menu from him and walked back to the server's station, where I punched in Mr. P's order even though Sumi, the line cook, was about five feet from me, standing on the other side of the pass-out window, looking slightly annoyed that I didn't just tell her the order since she was about five feet from me, standing on the other side of the pass-out window, looking slightly annoyed.

But there was a protocol in place. A strict set of guidelines I had to follow. My boss, a sassy redhead named Dixie, was only slightly less procedural than a brigadier general.

The stripper giggled at something Mr. P read on his phone. I finished up the order so I could move on to other vexations.

Vexations like LSD, Slinkys, and capillaries. How was

it I could remember words like *capillaries* and *brigadier* and, hell, *vexations* and not remember my own name? It made no sense. I'd been going through the alphabet, wracking my brain for a candidate, but I was running out of letters. After *S,* I had only seven left.

I sought out my coffee cup and picked up where I left off.

Sheila? No.

Shelby? Nope.

Sherry? Not even close.

Nothing felt right. Nothing fit. I just knew if I heard my name, *my real name,* I'd recognize it instantly and all of my memories would come flooding back in a shimmering tidal wave of recollection. So far the only tidal wave in my life resided in my stomach. It did flip-flops every time a certain regular walked in. A tall, dark regular with jet black hair and an aura to match.

The sound of my coworker's voice brought me back to the present.

"Lost in thought again, sweetie?" She walked up to stand beside me and gave my hip a little nudge. She did that.

Cookie had started working at the café two days after I did. She'd taken the morning shift with me. Started at 7:00 a.m. By 7:02, we were friends. Mostly because we had a lot in common. We were both recent transplants. Both friendless. Both new to the restaurant business and unaccustomed to having people yell at us because their food was too hot or their coffee was too cold.

Okay, cold coffee I understood.

I glanced around my section to make sure I hadn't abandoned any of my customers in their time of need. All two of said customers—three if I included the dead one—seemed pretty content. Especially the stripper. We were smack-dab in the middle of the midmorning lull. It wouldn't last long, however. The lunch crowd would be arriving soon.

"Sorry," I said, busying myself with wiping down the counter.

"What did you say?" She glowered playfully before stuffing a bottle of ketchup into her apron and grabbing two plates off the pass-out window. Her thick black hair had been teased and tugged into a spiky masterpiece that only feigned disorder, but her clothes were another matter altogether. Unless she liked colors bright enough to blind her customers. There was no way to tell, really.

"You have nothing to be sorry for," she said in her stern mommy voice. Which made sense. She was a mother, though I had yet to meet her daughter. She was staying with Cookie's ex while Cookie and her new husband, Robert, got settled into their new digs. "We talked about this, remember? The whole apology thing?"

"Right. Sor—" I stopped mid-sorry, catching myself before I could complete the thought and incur her wrath.

Her scowl turned semi-serious, anyway. One more "sorry" out of me and she'd turn downright nettled.

She bumped a generous hip against mine again and took her customers their lunch. Like me, she had two living customers and one dead one, since the departed man in the corner booth was technically in her section.

It would do him little good. Cookie couldn't see dead people like I could. From what I'd gathered over the recent weeks, no one could see dead people like I could. Seemed like that was my superpower. Seeing dead people and the strange world they lived in. As far as superpowers went, if a vengeful madman hopped up on 24-Hour

Sudafed and wielding a broadsword named Thor's Morning Wood ever attacked us, we were screwed. Six ways to Sunday.

I took Mr. P his order while watching Cookie refill her customers' water glasses. They must've been new to the world of Cookie Kowalski-Davidson. She wasn't the most graceful server. That fact became exceedingly evident when the woman reached over Cookie's arm to grab a French fry off her beau's plate. Big mistake. The movement surprised Cookie, and a second later a wall of cold water splashed out of the pitcher and onto the guy's lap.

When the icy liquid landed, he bolted upright and shot out of the booth. "Holy shit," he said, his voice cracking, the sudden chill to his twigs and berries taking his breath away.

The horrified look on Cookie's face was worth the price of admission. "I'm so sorry," she said, trying to right the situation by blotting the large wet spot at his crotch.

She repeated her apologies, frantic as she poured all of her energy into drying the man's nether regions. Either that or she was serving off the menu.

The woman opposite him began to giggle, hiding behind a napkin shyly at first, then more openly when she saw her boyfriend's shocked expression. Her giggles turned into deep belly laughs. She fell across the seat of the booth, her shoulders shaking as she watched Cookie see to her boyfriend's needs.

Yep, they were definitely new. Most of our customers learned early on not to make any quick movements around Cookie. Of course, most wouldn't laugh when a waitress tried to service their lunch date either. I liked her.

After several painfully entertaining moments in which my guileless friend changed her technique from dabbing to outright scrubbing, Cookie finally realized she was polishing her customer's erector set.

She stilled, her face hovering inches from the man's vitals before she straightened, offered the couple a final apology, and returned to the prep area, her back two-by-four straight, her face Heinz-ketchup red.

I used all my energy to hold back the laughter threatening to burst from my chest like a baby alien, but inside I lay in a fetal position, teary and aching from the spasms racking my body. I sobered when she got close. Cleared my throat. Offered her my condolences.

"You know, if you have to keep buying your customers' meals, you're going to end up paying the café to work here instead of vice versa."

She offered a smile made of steel wool. "I am well aware of that, thank you." To suffer her mortification alone, she called out to Sumi, letting her know she was taking a break, then headed to the back.

I adored that woman. She was fun and open and absolutely genuine. And, for some unfathomable reason, she cared for me. Deeply.

My one female customer, a shabby-chic blonde with a bag big enough to sleep in, paid out and left. About two minutes later, Mr. P wandered to the register, ticket in hand, his face infused with a soft pink, his eyes watering with humor. Cookie had entertained the whole place. The stripper followed him. He thumbed through some bills, shaking his head, still amused with Cookie's antics. The stripper took advantage of the moment to explain.

"He saved my life," she said from beside him. She'd wrapped her arm in his, but every time he moved, her incorporeal limb slipped through. She linked her arm again and continued. "About a year ago. I'd . . . had a rough night." She brushed her fingertips over her right cheek, giving me the impression her rough night involved at least one punch to her face.

My emotions did a one-eighty. My chest tightened. I fought the concern edging to the surface. Tamped it down. Ignored it the best that I could.

"I'd been roughed up pretty bad," she said, oblivious to my disinterest. "He came to the hospital to take my statement. A detective. A detective had come to see me. To ask me questions. I figured I'd be lucky to get a patrol officer, considering . . . considering my lifestyle."

"Here you go, hon," Mr. P said, passing me a twenty. He folded up the rest of his bills and pocketed them as I punched a few buttons on the cash register, then began pulling out his change.

"It was the way he talked to me. Like I was somebody. Like I mattered, you know?"

I closed my eyes and swallowed. I did know. I had become acutely aware of the nuances of human behavior and the effect they had on those around them. The smallest act of kindness went a long way in my world. And there I was. Ignoring her.

"I cleaned up after that. Got a real job."

She'd probably been ignored her whole life.

She laughed to herself softly. "Not a real job like yours. I started stripping. The place was a dive, but it got me off the streets, and the tips were pretty good. I could finally put my son in a private school. A cheap private school, but a private school nonetheless. This man just—" She stopped and gazed at him with that loving expression she'd had since she'd popped in. "He just treated me real nice."

My breath hitched, and I swallowed again. When I tried to hand Mr. P his change, he shook his head.

"You keep it, hon."

I blinked back to him. "You had coffee and ate two bites of your breakfast," I said, surprised.

"Best cup I've had all morning. And they were big bites."

"You gave me a twenty."

"Smallest bill I had," he said defensively, lying through his teeth.

I pressed my mouth together. "I saw several singles in that stash of yours."

"I can't give you those. I'm hitting the strip club later." When I laughed, he leaned in and asked, "Want to join me? You'd make a killing."

"Oh, honey, he's right," the stripper said, nodding in complete seriousness.

I let a smile sneak across my face. "I think I'll stick to waiting tables."

"Suit yourself," he said, his grin infectious.

"See you tomorrow?"

"Yes, you will. If not sooner."

He started toward the exit, but the stripper stayed behind. "See what I mean?"

Since no one was paying attention, I finally talked to her. Or, well, whispered. "I do."

"My son is with his grandma now, but guess where he's going to school?"

"Where?" I asked, intrigued.

"That private school, thanks to Detective Bernard Pettigrew."

My jaw dropped a little. "He's paying for your son to go to school?"

She nodded, gratitude shimmering in her eyes. "Nobody knows. My mama doesn't even know. But he's paying for my son's schooling."

The tightness around my heart increased threefold as she wiggled her fingers and hurried after him, her high heels eerily silent on the tile floor.

I watched her go, giving Mr. P one last glance before he turned the corner, wondering for the thousandth time if I should tell him about the demon coiled inside his chest.

2

Alex, I'll take The Slightly Less Traumatic Life for $400.
—*JEOPARDY!* CONTESTANT

It was thick and shiny and dark, the creature inside Mr. P, with razor-sharp teeth and claws that could rip through a chest in a microsecond. A niggling of recognition tingled at the back of my neck. I'd seen something similar before, but I didn't know what it was. Not really. I only called it a demon for lack of a better explanation. What else would enter a human body and lie dormant? As though waiting to be awakened? As though waiting for its call to arms? And what would happen to Mr. P when that call came through? My only reference was the fact that I knew, probably from movies or literature, that demons could possess people.

Mr. P didn't seem particularly possessed. Then again, how would I know? Maybe demons were really smart and knew how to behave themselves in the human world. But the one inside Mr. P seemed to be sleeping. It lay coiled around his heart, its spine undulating, flexing every so often as though stretching. And I thought tapeworms were horrifying.

I checked on Cookie's customers, explained that anytime a patron is accosted in the Firelight Grill, their lunch is on the house, then went to check on her. But not before one last scan of the area outside. The billowing clouds from the otherworld, as I called the second dimension, were roiling and churning. A storm was coming, another one like the night I woke up, all fierce and savage, but that wasn't what I was looking for.

As pathetic as it sounded, I was looking for tall, dark, and deadly. Another force that was fierce and savage. He came in every morning for breakfast as well as every day for lunch. And, apparently, for dinner as well. Every time I'd come to the café in the evening—because I had no life—he was here, too. A bona fide three-meal-a-dayer.

We had several three-meal-a-dayers, actually, and we had some drop-dead lookers in the bunch, but the regular I both feared and salivated to see was named Reyes Farrow. I only knew that because Cookie ran his card one day and I peeked at the name on it. Where others exuded aggression, deception, and insecurity, he literally dripped confidence, sex, and power. Mostly sex.

Admiration was not my immediate reaction to him, however. The first time I saw him and realized he was something else, something dark and powerful and about as human as a fruit basket, I fought the urge to make my fingers into a cross and say, "I think you're at the wrong address, buddy. You're looking for 666 Highway to Hell Avenue. It's a little farther south."

Thankfully, I didn't, because in the very next instant,

when my gaze wandered up his lean hips, over his wide shoulders, and landed on his face, I was dumbstruck by his unusual beauty. Then I was all, "I think you're at the wrong address, buddy. You're looking for 1707 Howard Street. It's two blocks over. Key's under the rock. Clothing is optional."

Thankfully, I didn't do that either. I tried not to give out my address, as a rule. But he had a prowess about him, a feral bearing that tugged at my insides any time he was near. I kept my distance. Mostly because he was bathed in fire and a billowing darkness. The kind that sent tiny shudders of unease through my body. The kind that kept me from getting too close for fear of being burned alive.

Of course, it helped that he never sat in my section. Ever. Probably a good thing, but I was starting to get a complex.

He hadn't come in that morning, though, and that fact had me a little more down than usual. Tormenting Cookie would lift my spirits. It always did.

I spotted Kevin, one of our busboys, through the pass-out window and asked if he could keep an eye on things for me while I took five. He waved, his mouth full of Sumi's incredible banana pancakes, then went back to his phone.

Grabbing my jacket on the way out, I found Cookie in the alley behind the café, very close to the spot where I woke up. The Firelight Grill sat on a corner lot on Beekman Avenue, in an old brick building with dark inlays intricately placed to create gorgeous arches and carvings, to the utter delight of the tourists. It had a very Victorian feel.

Right next door sat an antiques store, with a dry-cleaning

business beyond that. A white delivery van had backed up to the cleaners, and Cookie was busy watching the men haul boxes out.

"Hey, you," I said, walking to stand beside her.

She smiled and wrapped an arm in mine to pull me closer. Our breaths misted in the chilly air. We huddled together, shivering as I scanned the area for the disturbance I'd felt the moment I stepped outside. A smattering of unease rippled in the air around us. A strong emotional dissonance. A pain.

At first, I thought it was coming from Cookie. Thank goodness it wasn't. That couple clearly did not take offense. No need to worry about the incident overmuch. But now I was curious about the source.

"How are you doing, sweetie?" Cookie asked.

I refocused on the closest thing to family I had. "I'm more worried about you."

She chuckled. "I guess if that's the worst thing I do today, it will be a pretty good day."

"I agree. On the bright side, after the way you saw to that customer, I see a promising career on a street corner for you. You got skill, girl. We have to work with what God gave us."

Completely ignoring what I said, she leveled a bright cerulean gaze on me. "And?"

It was almost like she was used to inappropriate, X-rated ribbing. Weird. I nudged a rock with the toe of my ankle boot. They were my very first score with my very first paycheck, and I'd quickly realized another truth about myself. I had a thing for boots.

"I'm good," I said with a noncommittal shrug. When she narrowed that arresting gaze on me, I added, "I promise. All is right with the world. Seriously, though, you need to at least consider selling your body for profit. I can be your pimp. I'd be a freaking awesome pimp."

Though she didn't quite believe me—the I'm-good thing, not the pimp thing—she dropped it. Or pretended to. She oozed concern. After everything that had happened to her, she was still worried about me. I could tell. No, I could *feel* her concern, her desire for me to be well and happy. And I was grateful. Really I was, but there were times when I could feel deception swell out of her as well. It snaked into our conversations. A microsecond later she would change the subject. Yet I could tell she genuinely cared about me.

Then again, lots of people cared about me. From the moment I'd woken up in the alley behind the café a month ago with no recollection of how I got there, many of the residents of Sleepy Hollow, New York, had banded together to help me out. A total stranger. Some dropped off clothes while I was at the hospital. Some gave me gift cards to this store or that.

The outpouring of goodwill had waned after a couple of weeks—a fact for which I was also grateful—but people still stopped in to check on me. To see how I was doing. To find out the latest. Did the cops have any leads? Did I remember anything? Did anyone claim me?

No, no, and no.

Just like with Cookie, I felt their concern, but I felt something else from them that I didn't feel from Cookie, nor from several of my other regulars: a freakish curiosity. A blistering desire to know who I was. If I'd really lost my memory. If I was faking it.

The doctors found nothing wrong with me. According to them, I was perfectly fine. Perfectly normal. But normal? Seriously? What would they think about my ability to see into a supernatural dimension? Was that fine? Was that normal?

But maybe they were right. Maybe the only thing wrong with me was psychological. If I couldn't remember anything about my life pre-alley-awakening, was it me? Was I blocking my own memories? If so, what the hell had happened that was so awful? What made me not want to remember my own past? My own name? And did I really want to know?

Yes, I suppose I did. The struggle, the constant tug-of-war, the pull of wanting to know was stronger than the bliss of ignorance. In the meantime, there were people like Cookie who stood by me and kept me semi-sane.

There were the skeptics, of course. Not everyone believed I had retrograde amnesia, and I knew it. I felt doubt leach out of the occasional customer. I felt disbelief hemorrhage out of a random passerby, and with it, a revulsion.

For most, however, it was just a small suspicion. They wondered not only if I was faking it but why. And they were right. Why? Why would I fake something as horrific and agonizing as amnesia? For the attention? For the money? There were easier ways to get attention, and the money sucked. I now had a gazillion dollars' worth of debt thanks to the hospitals and doctors and endless tests.

So my fifteen minutes were proving costly. I lived tip jar to tip jar. I could never pay all the bills I'd accumulated, not unless I got that major book deal I'd been angling for. At least, that was one theory floating around. According to some more aggressive skeptics, I had an angle that would lead to a huge payoff. Sadly, I didn't. But their doubt, their certainty that I was faking it, kinda sucked. As far as I knew, I'd never faked it.

But that brought me to my second superpower. I could *feel* things. It was awesome.

No. It was *beyond* awesome!

If a deranged serial killer who uses control-top panty-hose to strangle brunettes ever attacked me, I'd be able to *feel* how much he wanted me dead.

Okay, it wasn't that bad. It did have its perks. Like, I knew when anyone lied to me. I absolutely could-bet-my-life-on-it knew. No matter how good they were. No matter what tricks they'd adopted to conceal their deception, I knew. So there was that.

But along with the perk came the drawback. I felt other things as well. Otherworldly things. Sometimes I felt like I was being watched. Hunted. I felt the cold gaze of a stalker I couldn't see. The hot breath of a predator fan across the back of my neck. The searing touch of a stranger's mouth brush across mine. Of course, I only felt those things after my seventh cup of pre-noon coffee. The moment my customers' faces started to blur, I switched to half-caff.

"Cold enough yet?" I asked her just as Dixie, the owner of the café and my savior—in the nonreligious sense—stuck her head out the door. Her hair was very much like Cookie's only a bright, almost neon, red. Though I had yet to confirm my suspicions, I was pretty sure it glowed in the dark. It made her pale skin look vibrant and youthful despite the fact that she had to be in her late forties.

She raised her brows at us. "You two planning on waiting tables today?"

Cookie drew in a deep breath, preparing to face the music. Probably disco. Disco seemed more penitential than other forms of music. Except maybe thrash metal.

I decided to practice for my new calling in life as we

turned to walk in. Whispering under my breath, I said, "Where's my money, bitch?"

"I'm not going to be a streetwalker."

I rounded my eyes in innocence. "I'm just practicing. You know, in case you change your mind."

"I won't."

"Damn it." I wilted beside her, all my hopes and dreams of being a pimp dashed against the cruel rocks of reality. And an unwilling ho.

Then the pain hit me again. A wave of it. It stemmed from somewhere close, but I couldn't pinpoint the location. I turned in a circle, but saw no one.

"You okay, hon?" Cookie asked me, taking my arm again. And again the concern she felt welled up inside her. I didn't quite understand her. Why she felt so strongly about me. Why she was so caring.

"You're always so nice to me," I said. Out loud. A little surprised by that fact.

She squeezed my hand. "We're besties, remember? Of course I'm nice to you. Otherwise, I'd be the suckiest BFF ever."

I chuckled softly for show, but she meant it when she said we were besties. With every fiber of her being. And that niggling suspicion was back stronger than ever. We'd only known each other a month. Damn it. She was clearly one of those needy psycho chicks who boiled rabbits on the stoves of her enemies.

Oh, well. I'd enjoy her friendship while it lasted. But I mentally crossed bunnies off my shopping list.

When we walked back into the café, we had several new customers. We'd only been out for, like, thirty seconds. Weird how quickly they accumulated.

I had just hung up my coat when Dixie called out to me.

"We have a couple of deliveries. Just waiting on fries for one."

She wore a grin that stretched from multi-pierced earlobe to multi-pierced earlobe.

"You seem chipper."

"I had a very productive morning." Her face flushed and an excitement rushed through her as she packed up one of the orders.

"Clearly. I was wondering where you were." She'd been gone all morning. Now I wanted to know why.

"I hired a new cook," she said, her eyes a-twinkle. "He starts tomorrow. First shift."

"What?" Sumi's tiny head popped up, the pass-out window framing it almost perfectly, except she was too short so we couldn't quite see the bottom half of her face.. "I'm first-shift cook. You can't do this to me." She waved a spatula. "I'll sue!" Pretty brows slid fiercely over almond-shaped eyes, her wrath thoroughly incurred.

I never let my guard down around Sumi. The fact that she was vertically challenged meant nothing. She could kick my ass in a heartbeat. That woman had a temper. And she was quick. Limber. Horrifyingly good with knives.

"Oh, hush," Dixie said, clearly not as fond of her faculties as I was of mine. "He's going to be more of a"—she folded the top of the bag and stapled a ticket to it—"I don't know, a specialty cook."

"Cool," I said, more interested in our customer base. One of our three-meal-a-dayers had shown up right on schedule, but with the eleven o'clock hour came our second-shift tag team, and my section was now officially split in half.

Francie and Erin were already busy taking orders.

I only had one customer in my section so far. I glanced at him. He was one of them. One of the three. They came every day like clockwork. Morning, noon, and night. Cookie and I had started referring to them as the Three Musketeers, for lack of a better descriptor. Though that would imply a friendship among them, and as far as I knew, they'd never even spoken.

The first one, a handsome ex-military type with fantastic biceps, always sat in my section. In the same booth when possible, but always in my section. He wore a khaki jacket that complemented his burnished mahogany skin and close-cut black hair. His eyes were silvery gray. Sharp. Capable of amazing things.

Garrett settled into his usual booth, then glanced up at me, offered me a whisper of a smile, opened a copy of the latest Steve Berry, and began to read.

"Looks like you're up, sweetie."

I leaned toward Cookie, and we both took a moment to admire the view.

"He looks like he'd have great abs," I said, deep in thought. "Doesn't he look like he'd have great abs?"

She let a slow breath slide in through her teeth, and we watched for the sheer pleasure of watching, the way you would a sunrise or the first pot of coffee brewing for the day.

"He certainly does," she said at last.

I grabbed the carafe and headed toward him.

As though on cue, Musketeer Number Two walked in. A rascal named Osh. He was young, perhaps nineteen or twenty, with shoulder-length hair the color of sunlit ink, though it was perpetually sheltered by the charming tilt of a top hat. He tipped it toward me before taking it off and finding a seat. Never one to sit in the same place twice, he decided to take a seat at the counter and flirt with Francie a bit.

I could hardly blame him. Francie was a cute redhead who liked to paint her nails and take selfies. I would take selfies, too, if I had someone to send them to. I used to send them to Cookie, but she had to ask me to stop when they got a little too risqué for her taste. It was probably for the best.

Osh flashed Francie one of his dazzling smiles, causing her to almost drop the plates she'd just taken from the pass-out window. The little shit.

The first time he came in, he ordered a dark soda. When Cookie asked which one and listed what we had, he shook his head and said, "Any dark soda will do."

From that moment on, we mixed it up for him, gave him a variety of drinks even between refills, a game he seemed to enjoy. Though not as much as flustering the servers.

Francie giggled and rushed past him with her order. At least she was semi-nice to me. Erin, on the other hand, hated me with a fiery passion. According to gossip, she'd asked for extra shifts, but when yours truly showed up, frozen and homeless, Dixie's generosity turned into a hardship for Erin and her husband. I'd basically taken any hope she had of extra shifts, and with it, any hope of friendship.

Garrett's shimmering eyes held me captive as I walked toward him, the silver shards sparkling atop the deep gray of his irises. They were warm and genuine and . . . welcome. I shook out of his hold and offered my best dollar ninety-nine smile.

"Anything besides coffee, hon?" I asked as I poured a cup without asking. He always wanted coffee. Hot and black. There was something fascinating about a man who drank his coffee hot and black.

He pulled the cup toward him. "Just water. How you doin' today, Janey?"

"Fantastic as ever. How about you?"

"Can't complain."

A man I didn't recognize spoke from the next booth over. I could feel impatience wafting off him. "Hey, honey," he said, jerking his head up to get my attention. "Can we get some of that over here? Or is that asking too much?"

A spark of anger erupted in my current customer, but on the outside, Garrett's expression remained impassive. It held no hint of the slightest concern.

Definitely military. Probably special ops.

"Sure thing," I said. The tight-lipped smile I offered the jackass and his friend hid my grinding teeth. I poured two cups as they leered at me, taking in every curve I had to offer. "I'll get you some menus."

Technically, they were in Cookie's section, but I didn't want her to have to deal with them. She'd had a hard enough day. When she started over, I shook my head and nodded toward another couple in her section who looked ready to order.

"I just want a cheeseburger and fries, sweet cheeks," the first one said. "He'll have the same."

Apparently all the guy's friend could do was leer.

"Rare," he continued. "And no rabbit food."

"You got it," I said.

"You gonna write that down?"

"I think I can remember. I have an excellent memory." Ironically, I did. When it came to orders, anyway.

"You get it wrong, and Hershel is not going to be happy."

I could only assume his friend was Hershel. Either that or he referred to himself in the third person, which would make him even more of a douche. But the name embroidered on his oil-stained shirt read MARK.

His friend's shirt had the same logo and read HERSHEL. They worked at the same trucking company. Truckers were usually the nicest lot, but every barrel had its bad apples. Judging from the dark oil stains they shared and the thick odor of diesel wafting off them, they were probably mechanics.

I stepped back over to Garrett. "What'll you have, hon?"

He was seething underneath his *GQ* exterior but graced me with a smile nonetheless. "I'll have the special."

"Good choice."

I took his menu, trying my best to show him that I was unaffected by the little truckers that could. I couldn't help but notice the knife he had sheathed at his belt. I didn't know what he did exactly, but I knew it had something to do with the law. Not a cop, per se, but something similar.

The last thing I wanted was trouble, however. No one needed to risk his safety for me. No one needed to defend my honor. In all honesty, I wasn't sure I had any. I had forgotten my life for a reason. What if that reason was bad? What if it was unthinkable? Heinous? Evil?

A wave of nausea washed over me. I hurried to the service station and tapped in their orders, but a familiar feeling, one I could only describe as a panic attack, had already hit me square in the gut. I'd been having similar attacks off and on since Day One. It was the sensation of loss, an utter and devastating loss, that brought them on. That tightened around my chest until my lungs seized. That burned my eyes until I went blind.

Shaking uncontrollably, I dug my nails into the counter, leveraged my weight against it, scraped and clawed against the black veil that kept my past hidden. Something was behind the curtain. Something I had to get to.

A feeling of urgency spread like wildfire. I had forgotten. I had left something behind. My most prized possession, only I had no idea what it was.

My teeth welded together and my lids slammed shut as I fought to get through the veil, determination and desperation pushing me to remember. Driving me forward.

The room spun, and I could hear my own heartbeat carpet-bombing my rib cage, my own blood flooding my veins until even the edges of my mind darkened and closed in on me.

"You okay, sweetie?"

Startled, I lifted my lids to see Cookie, my brows cemented together, my breaths coming in quick, short bursts. I felt the dampness of the attack slicken my skin, and my wet palms slipped off the counter.

"Charley!"

Five.

"Come here," she said, hauling me to the storeroom in the back.

I didn't miss the fact that she'd called me Charley. She'd done it before. Four times, actually. It was either a term of endearment where she was from, or she was accidentally calling me by the name of someone else she knew. Probably her dog.

She sat me on the cot I'd slept on for over a week before I found an apartment I could afford. This was my home away from home away from home. Wherever that third home was.

She wet a towel and pressed it against my forehead, over

my cheeks and mouth, and down my neck. "You're okay," she said, her tone soothing, her voice so familiar.

The spinning slowed, and my heart rate decelerated to a normal speed. A normal rhythm.

"You're going to be fine." She wet the towel again to cool it off, then placed it on the back of my neck. "You haven't had one of those in a while."

I nodded.

"Can you tell me what started it?"

"I don't know," I said, my voice hoarse. Then I looked up at her. I wanted her to understand, to be completely aware of what she was getting herself into. "I don't think I'm a very good person, Cook."

She knelt in front of me. "Of course you are. Why would you say that?"

"I think I'm being punished."

"Punished?" My statement shocked her. "Punished for what?"

"I've forgotten something."

She placed a comforting hand on my shoulder. "You mean, besides your entire life up until a month ago?"

"Yes. I mean, no. No, this is something . . . something much more important. I feel like I went on a long trip and I left my most precious possession behind. I abandoned it." Tears stung the backs of my eyes, the evidence slipping past my lashes and down one cheek.

"Oh, sweetheart." She pulled me into a hug. The soft warmth of her body was a welcome reprieve from the sandpaper world around me. "You have amnesia. Nothing you did could have caused it." She sat me at arm's length. "You remember what the doctors said, right?"

"No. I—I have amnesia."

After chastising me with a pursed mouth—that'd show

me—she said, "You remember exactly what they said. This could have been caused by any number of things. You just have to give it time. This did not happen because of anything you did."

She couldn't possibly understand how wrong she was, but it wasn't her fault. What I did was on me. I would have to figure it out and make things right. I had to.

3

You can't make someone love you.
You can only stalk them and hope for the best.
—INTERNET MEME

The storeroom door opened and Erin stood on the other side, her aura a dark shade of red. Not that I needed to see her aura to know she was angry. It hit me like a heat wave. "You both have customers."

"Sorry," I said, rising unsteadily to my feet, but she was gone before I got the whole word out. I helped Cookie up, then went to the utility sink and splashed water on my face before checking my watch.

"He should be in any minute now," Cookie said, brushing herself off.

I turned back to her. "Who?" When she offered me a sympathetic smile, I said, "Doesn't matter, anyway. He never sits in my section. He always sits in yours. Or Francie's." I tamped down the jealousy that bucked inside me. I had no right to be jealous. It wasn't as though he ever talked to me. Or looked at me. Or, hell, acknowledged my existence in any way whatsoever.

"Maybe he's just shy," Cookie offered. "Maybe he likes you so much he's afraid to make the first move."

I snorted, dismissing the notion entirely. He didn't strike me as the shy type. "Anyway, how do you know that's who I'm waiting on?"

"Hon, every female in the café is waiting for him."

My skin flushed again. Francie was so hot for him, her adrenaline spiked tenfold every time he walked in. Her aura turned red as well. A pinkish red. And for a very different reason.

"True. But he's so angry all the time."

"Angry?" She tugged at the stray wisps of chestnut hair that had escaped my hair clip, placing them just so. "What makes you say that?"

"He glares at me."

"He glares at everyone."

That was true, too, and it made me happy inside.

"His middle name is Alexander, by the way." She said it as though it were a test of some kind. As though she expected a reaction out of me.

And boy, did she get one. I couldn't have fought back the telltale signs of surprise if I'd had an Uzi at my disposal. Or a rocket launcher.

Reyes Alexander Farrow. I liked it.

"How do you know his middle name?"

"I saw his driver's license."

Her answer caught me off guard, and I flinched. Not because she'd managed to see Reyes Farrow's license, a fact I was a tad jealous of. I flinched because she'd just lied to me. Why would she lie about something so mundane? What did it matter how she found out Reyes's middle name?

"Do you think it's odd how many great-looking guys come into this place?" she asked, changing the subject as she always did when she was being less than 100 percent. Almost as though she knew I could sense her deception and thought that veering off topic would dilute it.

Either that or my guilty conscience was getting the better of me. It was wrong to spy on people, and reading their emotions was tantamount to spying. But they were just so *there*. People's emotions. So in my face. It was impossible *not* to read them.

"Odd? Maybe. But a slew of great-looking guys walking in pretty as you please? Hell, yes. And then some."

She chuckled and ushered me out. "You have an excellent point."

Before I got two steps into the café, Dixie waved me to a stop. "Can you take this over, Janey?" she asked, shoving a to-go order into my hands. The ticket had the name Vandenberg written on it. "Erin ran the other order to Mrs. Udesky."

"Um, okay." No idea who Mrs. Udesky was.

"I'll cover for you." She nudged me toward the exit, her gaze wandering to Garrett until she lost all control of the grin she was trying to suppress.

"But just so you know," I said in warning, "stalking is a crime."

She gaped at me. "I'm not stalking him. I'm waiting on him. And if our conversation happens to turn toward the romantic variety, who am I to argue?" She leveled another lustful gaze his way. "The things I could do to that man given half a chance."

I giggled and started for the front exit.

"Hey, sugar," Osh said from behind the counter, his flirtatious grin transmissible. His hair hung in a shining mass to his shoulders, the cut blunt, the color so black it almost looked blue against his pale, perfect skin. I wondered what he was. Mostly because he had no soul. The color that did surround him, though soulless so not really an aura, was a smokier version of the unique bronze of his irises.

I found it mesmerizing. I found him mesmerizing. So much so, I stopped and stared for several awkward seconds. Awkward to me, anyway. I got the feeling from the playful tilt of his mouth he was quite used to that kind of captive attention. The key word being *captive*.

"Hey, back," I said.

His expression toppled dangerously close to vulgarity, diluted only by the appreciation glittering in his eyes. As comely as the kid was, he only pretended to be arrogant. He was not. Far from it, in fact.

I'd figured out fairly early there were two kinds of beings in this world: those that belonged and those that did not. Garrett, for example, was the former. He was human through and through. As was Mr. P, which brought up the question of why the demon was inside him. Osh, however, was a different story.

He had a fierceness to him that belied his youthful appearance, a devil-may-care attitude. He was only part human. The rest was all manner of beast, the two sides held together with an otherworldly energy, hence the color that surrounded him. It wasn't a soul like that of a human but a power, as though his life force originated from something other than human necessity. In other words, I wondered if he survived on the food he ordered from the café every day or if he had another form of sustenance.

"Need any help?" he asked, his gaze a little too wolfish.

I leaned into him. "I'm old enough to be your . . . much older sister."

I actually had no idea how old I was. The doctors put me somewhere between twenty-five and twenty-nine. Close enough for now. They wanted to run more tests, to involve more body parts than just my ailing brain. I wouldn't let them. For one thing, each test hemorrhaged more money than I made in a year. They were worried I'd been assaulted in some way. I assured them I hadn't been. I had no bruises. No scrapes other than the ones I'd sustained after waking up in that alley.

He raked a hand through his hair, revealing the alluring angles of his almost too-perfect face, then let it cascade back into place before leaning in, too. "I love older women."

I had a feeling he knew way more than his age would suggest. And that he was teasing as much as I was. I could test it. See how far the little shit would go. But the customers were piling up, and I had a sandwich—several, in fact—to deliver.

He broke the spell with a shake of his head, chuckled softly, then sat back and, with a forlorn sigh, said, "And all good things must come to an end."

Before I could ask what he meant, the door opened, the room quieted, and I knew who'd come for lunch. With the precision of a German infantryman—always in formation, always showing up third out of the three—Reyes Farrow walked in, thus completing the trio of Musketeers, and the world around me fell away.

As did all sense of logic.

Reyes Farrow was an enigma. He was his own energy source. Drowning in a perpetual darkness. Baptized in fire. It licked across his skin, the heat radiating out in blistering waves.

Before I'd realized that heat was coming from him, I thought I'd entered menopause early. I kept having hot flashes out of the blue. But then I saw him for the first time, saw the fire that bathed him, that rushed over his skin in bright oranges and yellows, that created the billowing smoke. He wore it like a robe. It cascaded over his wide shoulders, over his sinuous arms, and down his back to pool on the ground at his feet.

Even with the darkness that surrounded him, the unease I felt anytime he walked in, I welcomed his visits. I craved them the way an addict craved heroin. I often came back in the evenings, timing my dinner with his. A girl had to eat, after all. I told myself I went back to the café because of the familiarity of the place. The hominess. But if I were honest—something I rarely tried to be—it was because of him.

Like Osh, he was only part human. The other part, the questionable part, was still a mystery. He was like nothing I'd ever encountered. Not among the folks in Sleepy Hollow, anyway. His presence made the air crackle with electricity, mostly because of all the spontaneous ovulating going on when he walked in.

I'd slowed to an almost complete stop. Snapping out of my stupor, I picked up the pace to hurry past him. The closer I got, the more I saw, both physically and otherworldly. The molecules of his makeup seemed denser than those of a human, his DNA somehow wound tighter. He exuded a rare kind of power, as if he could command the seas and the stars alike. As if he could bend the universe to his will.

I looked past the fires that engulfed him to his slim hips that tapered up to wide shoulders. His arms, corded with muscle and sinew. His smooth biceps. Shadows undulated over them with even the slightest effort as the valleys between flesh and tendon shifted.

My gaze rose to the strong set of his chin, forever darkened with a day's growth, but only a day's worth. His mouth was truly one of his most spectacular accomplishments. It had the gentle fullness of passion, as though he'd just made love. As though he'd just satisfied some fortuitous woman's deepest desires. I continued my perusal to the straight line of his nose, neither too thin nor too wide with a tilt at the very tip.

But the most startling aspect of the entire encounter? His eyes. He often wore dark shades that hid one of his best features. When he didn't, the effect was breathtaking. He had gold flecks in his deep brown irises that sparkled beneath impossibly long lashes. They complemented his sculpted mouth and the hard set of his jaw to perfection.

Not that I was obsessed with his looks or anything.

Stepping so close to him was comparable to being within the reach of a jaguar's jaws. It was exhilarating and terrifying. I had no idea what he was exactly, but he was damned sure not dating material, no matter how tightly his molecules were wound.

Thankfully, he rarely looked at me. The sideways glances he did grace me with were mostly filled with anger and a seething kind of resentment. I had yet to discover what that was all about, because despite his acrimonious scowls, he was interested in me. I felt it leap out of him when our eyes met. Like now.

It was such a rare event, it caught me off guard. Our gazes locked for the briefest of seconds as I walked past. His nearness seized my lungs. Sent tiny shivers up my spine. Scorched my skin. And his interest shot straight to my very pinkest parts.

Our shirtsleeves brushed as I hurried by him, and I tried not to let the fact that he sat, once again, in Francie's section bother me. I'd never felt that spike of interest when he looked at her. Or anyone, for that matter, including the menfolk, thank goodness.

But why the animosity? Why the searing glares and seething ire? What had I ever done to him? Probably not nearly as much as I'd like to.

Again, confusion where Mr. Cranky Pants was concerned gripped me. I bolted out the front door and headed toward Mr. Vandenberg's store, fighting the desire to look back inside the café for another peek.

Cool air wisped around me. It was a welcome refresher after being burned alive. But in my haste to get past him, I'd forgotten my coat. It was worth it, though. We'd almost touched. My shoulder almost brushed across his, and I realized he hadn't been wearing a jacket either.

This time, anger shot through me. What was he thinking? It had to be thirty below out. Or thirty above. Either way, it was freaking cold. But he shows up in a light rust-colored T-shirt, one that fit snugly across his broad chest and tapered down to accentuate his lean stomach, and jeans, loose across his hips but tight enough to show the exquisite definition of his shapely ass.

Another thing I'd figured out about myself pretty early: I had a thing for asses.

He'd catch his death, especially since his hair was slightly damp. He'd just showered, his scent clean and earthy like lightning in a rainstorm.

I fanned cold air over my face, waved at a store owner

across the street, then almost stumbled when I got to the entrance of Mr. Vandenberg's antiques shop. I took hold of the handle and let the pain I felt—the same pain I'd felt earlier—wash over me. The sensation was not a welcome one. It clenched my stomach. Spun my head. Weakened my knees. And it was coming from inside the shop.

I peeked in the window, raising a hand to shield the sun, to make sure the coast was clear. It looked clear. Mr. V stood at the register, his shoulders tense, his gaze a thousand miles away. Behind him sat a man I didn't recognize. He was thumbing through a magazine, his booted feet propped on the counter, aka, clue number one that something was amiss.

That counter was over a hundred years old. Mr. V treated it like it was family. He was very particular about food and drink in his store in general, but nothing, absolutely nothing edible was allowed on that counter. And there sat a brute of a man with muddy boots flung on top of it.

I squeezed the door handle and fought the urge to turn tail and run. It was none of my business. Whatever Mr. V had going on was none of my concern. I couldn't get involved with others' problems just because I could sense them. Or the effects of them. Even if I did get involved, what could I do? I didn't even know my own name. How could I help others when I couldn't help myself?

I couldn't. Involvement of any kind was out of the question. I'd deliver the sandwiches and call it good.

I raised a barrier around my heart, pushed open the door, and entered as nonchalantly as possible.

When he glanced up, the weight of Mr. Vandenberg's stress, of his agonizing emotional pain, hit me like a brick wall. It ripped into me. Punched me until I almost doubled over.

I set my jaw and forced one foot in front of the other. "Hey, Mr. V," I said, my voice a husky shell.

"Hey, Janey. What do I owe you?"

I couldn't help it. I had to test him. After a quick survey of the brutish man sitting behind him, I put the bag on the counter. The counter on which no food was allowed to sit.

Mr. V said nothing. Nor did he do anything besides open the register. His normal response would have been to snatch the bag off the counter posthaste for fear of an oil spot. Instead, the brute stood and opened the bag to rummage through it. He took out a sandwich, then closed it again, never even glancing my way.

"Janey?" Mr. V asked.

"Sorry, twenty-seven even."

He nodded and dipped shaking fingers into the till.

Another man walked in from a back room, spotted me, and almost turned around. The brute barked at him.

"What did I tell you?" he asked. In Farsi, his Middle Eastern accent thick.

Seven. Farsi was the seventh language I knew, counting English. As tourists from all over the world came into the café, I would listen to their conversations, and every single time I understood them. I had yet to hear a language I didn't know—but I remembered nothing of my past. How was that even possible?

The other man wore coveralls, the knees and elbows dirty as if he'd been digging, and he had an ax in his hand. He eyed me from underneath thick eyebrows that knotted in suspicion, his too-lean features stark in the low light.

"We are through," the man said, his Farsi hinting at a northern Iraqi upbringing. "We will need the plasma cutter tonight." He said the words *plasma cutter* in English, and the brute's gaze snapped toward me to see if I was paying attention. I'd already taken the opportunity to take an extreme interest in an antique necklace Mr. V had in a display case beside the register. I sighed longingly.

Appeased, he tossed the bag to his partner and jerked his head in a silent order to leave. The brute, who was not so much tall as beefy, then turned his attention to his own sandwich.

Mr. Vandenberg handed me two twenties, trying hard to control his shaking fingers. He was one of those middle-aged guys who seemed much older, mostly because he was thin with slightly graying hair. The fact that he wore outdated wire-rimmed glasses and a bow tie didn't help either. He lived for all things nostalgic.

"Keep the change," he said, his gaze suddenly pleading. He wanted me out of there and quick.

"Thanks."

More voices wafted over from the back room. They were muffled, so I had a hard time making out what they were saying. All I caught was something about a support beam. It needed to be restrengthened? Reinforced. It needed to be reinforced. Another spoke about a metal pipe. There seemed to be something blocking a route.

The brute took note of my lingering presence. I had no choice but to leave. Just as I turned, another woman came in. I'd waited on her at the café. A part-time hairdresser and full-time busybody with more gumption than sense.

Mr. V's adrenaline shot through the roof.

"This is pretty," I said, pointing to the necklace so I could hang around a bit longer.

"Hi, William."

"Good morning, Ellen. I have your lamp boxed up and ready to go." He cast a quick gaze at the brute as though asking permission, then shuffled to a shelf in the back to get the box.

"I'm so excited," she said, oblivious. Or not. "It's going to look great in my foyer. Oh, Natalie missed her hair appointment. I hope everything is okay." She was fishing. Must've been running low on scandal.

"Oh, yes, I'm sorry." Mr. V walked back to the counter, box in hand. "We had a family emergency. She and the kids had to go to my mother's for a few days."

Lie.

"Oh, goodness." Intrigue drew her closer as the melody of fresh gossip slid inside her ears. "I hope everything is okay."

'Nother lie.

"Yes. Yes." He pushed his glasses up the bridge of his aquiline nose. "It's fine. My mother fell and bruised her hip, so Natalie is staying with her this week."

She took the box, her razor-sharp gaze raking over him. Did she know he was lying? She let a calculated smile widen across her face. "Well, you give her a big hello when you talk to her. And tell your mother to get better soon. I'll be expecting more of that fabulous zucchini casserole before too long."

He forced a soft laugh, but I felt fear radiate out of him. A fear that was so genuine, so dire, it pulled the air from the room.

Having gained nothing terribly gossip-worthy, the hairdresser waved a saucy good-bye and left with her lamp. Mr. V cleared his throat when he realized I was still waiting. Dug into a pocket. Dropped several coins on the floor but ignored them to rummage through the small bills he'd freed.

"Janey, sorry, what's the damage?"

It took me a moment to realize he was so distraught he was trying to pay me again.

"It was twenty-seven." I waited a second as he counted out the bills and another nice tip before adding, "But you already paid me."

When his blue gaze crested the gold rim of his glasses, he flushed. "I did, didn't I?"

I gave him a sympathetic nod.

"Sorry." He stuffed the bills back into his pocket. "Did you want to look at something?"

I didn't figure "The back room?" would go over well. My only question at the moment—besides the one involving the letters *W-T-F*—revolved around how much English the brute knew. I couldn't risk talking to Mr. V in case the man was as fluent in my native tongue as I was in his, and I didn't know enough about the situation to try to signal the anxious store owner.

"Nothing I can afford," I said with a teasing grin. "Have a good day."

He took off his glasses and began to clean them. "Yes. Absolutely. You, too."

The brute had bitten through half the sandwich and was glued to the magazine again, but I doubted very seriously he had any interest in Mr. V's copy of *Antiques & Fine Art*.

I'd had zero intention of getting involved when I walked in. By the time I left, I had zero intention of leaving it alone. Mr. V was in such a state of distress, I was impressed he could even speak. But how much longer would he be able to keep up the charade? He was cracking inch by inch. Whatever his new friends were up to, there were at least four involved. That bag held four sandwiches, none of which Mr. V could eat. He was allergic to eggs, yet he'd specifically ordered mayo on all four.

I opened the door and listened to the cheery chime of the bell, so at odds with the climate inside. This time the frigid air served only as a reminder that I was not dressed for the frozen tundra. But a picture caught my eye just as I was leaving. It was on a shelf, meant to display one of the antique frames that were for sale. It had a sign by it with a child's writing that read, *For sale: Frame $50. Parents $49.95 OBO*.

I let the door close behind me and fought a shiver. To display the frame, Mr. V had put a picture of himself and his family in it. I knew that family; I just didn't know they'd belonged to Mr. V. They came into the café a couple of times a week. His wife, Natalie, was gorgeous. She looked like an islander with exotic coloring and thick black hair. Her children were a combination of the blond-haired, blue-eyed Mr. V and the rich dark colors of his wife.

Their names were Joseph and Jasmine. Joseph was around ten, and Jasmine a few years younger, six or seven perhaps. I remembered them so vividly from our very first meeting partly because of the combination of dark hair on both of them and crystalline blue eyes.

"You're really bright," Jasmine had said to me as I took their order.

"Well, thank you."

"Are you an angel?"

Joseph elbowed her without taking his eyes off his phone.

I laughed softly. "Not usually."

"Sorry," Natalie said. "Jasmine thinks she can see auras."

"Wow." I turned to her. "That's a cool ability."

"You don't have an aura," she said, in awe. "You *are* one."

"Aw, that's so sweet. Thanks." I winked at her and asked Joseph what he wanted to drink.

"Coffee. Black."

Knowing he couldn't be more than ten, I looked to his mother for assurance.

She lifted a shoulder. "It's his only vice," she explained.

At his age, I should hope so. When I poured him a cup, he took out a chocolate bar from his coat pocket and dropped a square into the coffee.

"His only vice?" I asked Natalie.

She smirked. "Does that count as two?"

Ever since that first meeting, I automatically took Joseph a cup of coffee and added the caveat "Drink responsibly." He would laugh from behind the cup or give me a thumbs-up while Jasmine studied me, tilting her head this way and that, looking for my wings. I'd fallen head over heels for them.

I leaned back against the brick wall of the building. Were they involved somehow? Were they in trouble? Once the cold got to be too much—about nine seconds later—I pushed off the building and headed back, playing out the hundred scenarios that might explain the bizarre events in Mr. V's store. The men were digging near the west wall. The only thing beside the shop was a dry-cleaning business. Why would a group of Middle Easterners tunnel into a dry-cleaning business?

I stopped and glanced back at the cleaners. Everything appeared normal. It looked, well, like a dry-cleaning business. What could it possibly have that would convince a group of what seemed like perfectly sane men to tunnel into it?

I looked past the cleaners. The next building was

vacant, and there was a wine shop beyond that. It was a very popular store. Tourists loved wine.

Who was I kidding? I loved wine. Who didn't love wine?

Seeing as how the men were risking so much to tunnel into a dry-cleaning business in the middle of the day when they could be spotted and/or heard, there had to be something pretty spectacular in that building. But my mind spun with a thousand questions.

Why dig during the day? Why not wait until night? The noise, perhaps? The lights? Unusual activity could draw unwanted attention faster than if Mr. V just happened to be doing renovations. But why not use the vacant building to tunnel in from instead of essentially taking a man hostage? Maybe what they were after was closer to Mr. V's shop? That made no sense either. Once they were in the building, they could go anywhere they wanted. Then again, why tunnel? Why not just break in?

None of the situation made any sense. Not that it mattered. All that mattered was getting Mr. V safely back to his family. If he were being held hostage—

I stopped at the entrance to the café and considered the magnitude of fear I'd felt radiating out of him. It was one thing to be afraid for your life, but could Mr. V's entire family be at risk? Were his wife and kids hostages, too?

I had to report my suspicions, but what if a cop started poking around and got Mr. V killed? Or worse, his entire family? The situation demanded delicacy. A cavalry galloping to the rescue with lights flashing and guns blazing was not the answer. Sadly, I didn't know what was.

A blast of arctic air urged me inside. I stepped into the gentle roar of a full house, and my gaze instantly shot to

Reyes. His back was to me. Probably a good thing since I couldn't think clearly when I looked at his face. Or his shoulders. Or his thick, unkempt hair.

I took out the money Mr. V gave me and headed toward the register to ring it in. Sweet Mr. V and his lovely family. Who could I go to with this? I needed someone high up in the law enforcement food chain, like a detective or even the police chief. I'd gotten to know a couple of the cops, but again, the situation demanded kid gloves, not boxing gloves, and the cops I'd met so far did not inspire that kind of confidence.

But that brought me to problem number two: What would I tell the person I did go to? I saw these Middle Eastern guys and got a bad feeling? Racist much?

I glanced at Garrett as I walked by and considered asking him. He did something coplike, though I wasn't sure what. There was Mr. Pettigrew as well. He was a former detective. Maybe I could talk to him, but again, what would I tell him? And how much could I count on him what with that demon lurking in his innards?

I spotted Cookie looking at me with a huge smile on her face. An appreciative smile. Like a really big one. I slowed as she walked toward me. Her arms opened, and I half expected her to plant a big wet one on me. Instead, she planted one on her husband, which made more sense. He'd walked in right behind me.

"Hi, Janey," he said when Cookie stopped accosting him. Weren't there laws against X-rated PDA?

Robert, or Bobert as I liked to call him, but that was Cookie's fault, had warm eyes and a charming, full-mustached smile. He seemed to like me almost as much as Cookie did. They were always inviting me over for dinner or to a movie. At first, I found their enthusiasm a bit intimidating. But once I got to know them—and realized they weren't swingers—I was grateful for it. They were a grounding force in my antigravitational life. A cord that kept me tethered to earth.

"Hey, Bobert. How's it hanging?"

"Little to the left. You?"

He pulled me into a giant bear hug, swallowing me in his arms. It felt wonderful despite our conversation about the trajectory of his manly parts. Some might have seen that as awkward.

I had a thing for awkward.

"Same," I said when he released me. "Your wife tried to service another customer today."

He glanced at Cookie, his expression sympathetic. Her cheeks flushed a soft pink. They'd only been married a couple of months and were the cutest newlyweds on the planet. I was certain of it. Especially Bobert. To be so old, so elderly and decrepit, practically on his last legs, to find love where he least expected it, at a rave in the Mohave. At least that was what Cookie told me. She'd been lying when she said it, though. If she lied about meeting her future husband at a rave, she had to believe that the truth would sound worse. The truth must have sucked. They probably met at a strip club. Or a human sacrifice. Or a tractor pull.

Bobert took a table near the drinks station, while Cookie and I decided to do what we were paid to do. Weird how that was expected of us.

I rang up Mr. V's order, feeling much better about the whole situation. A solution had come to me the moment I'd walked in out of the cold. Bobert. I could ask Bobert what to do. Cookie said he was a detective of some sort in New Mexico. I didn't know what they called detectives in Latin

American countries, but he spoke English really well. Surely he'd know who I could talk to. Who I *should* talk to.

And he didn't have any ties here. He wouldn't send the cavalry in and risk Mr. Vandenberg's life. I could ask him who in the department would be the most likely to take my concerns seriously and keep the investigation under the radar.

Bobert normally stayed for the better part of an hour. He hung around until Cookie had a break and could eat with him. It was so sweet. Hopefully by then, the café would've cleared out a little and I could talk to him in semi-private.

I couldn't decide if I should bring Cookie into it. He might be the type of officer that kept his professional and personal lives completely separate. He might not want Cookie involved in any of his investigations for her own safety. I'd try to approach him about it before Cookie took her break.

I glanced toward Reyes. He sat at a booth, eating a sub and reading on his phone. He was doing the same about five seconds later. Five seconds after that, he took another bite, then started reading again. Approximately five seconds later—

Francie sauntered up to him with the dessert plate we used to tempt unwitting customers into ordering just a bit more than they could safely stuff into their stomachs and asked him if he saw anything that he liked.

She was not talking about the dessert. She'd undone the top two buttons of her blouse and leaned in to give him a better view.

I so could've done that. I had fantastic boobs.

But Francie was laying it on thicker than usual, becoming more desperate. It was sad.

It was even sadder when Reyes took note, causing me to almost drop a plate of spaghetti in a customer's lap.

After a pause that had Francie and me both in breathless anticipation, he said, "I'm good for now."

Disappointment washed over Francie. Triumph rocketed through me. Triumph mixed with a sweet shot of euphoria. I rarely heard him talk. His voice was like being bathed in warm caramel. Not appealing to some. Scary appealing to me.

"What do you think of that one?" Dixie asked me, nodding toward the issuer of my future restraining order.

"Who?" I asked, all innocence and myrrh. "Oh, Reyes?"

"Mm-hm," she said, refilling my customer's iced tea.

"He seems . . . nice."

A grin as wicked as my darkest fantasies spread across her face. "I think so, too."

Saucy minx. Dixie made the rounds, often gravitating toward either Garrett or Reyes, which would explain why she was making the rounds at all. She rarely waited tables.

I started taking orders, beginning with a table of thirty-somethings. All female. All dressed to the nines. All salads and lemon water. Poor things. I took the orders of two more tables and two booths. All female. All dressed to the nines. Thankfully, not all salads and lemon water.

I wound my way back to the server's station to put their orders in and ran into my oldest and dearest friend. Cookie was busy tapping in orders, too, her nails clicking on the screen. As far as rush hours went, this was a doozy. And they seemed to be getting doozier every day. I would've thought December a far cry from tourist season. Apparently not.

"Is it just me, or are there a lot of women in here?" Cookie asked, closing out her order.

I scanned the area and concurred. There were a lot of customers in general, and they all seemed exclusively focused on one customer. The tables of women. A couple of tables of men. Even a businessman sitting alone pretending not to be interested in tall, dark, and delicious. I couldn't blame any of them, but it did up the competition.

Not that I was competing. Reyes was evil. And he hated me. I would never entertain the idea of us hooking up. Of him following me to the storeroom, pressing his body into mine, pulling my skirt up and my panties down so he could bury himself inside me.

Nope. All that was more of a . . . a caveat for something I most definitely did *not* want to happen. He was like a panther in the wild. Beautiful to look at. Far too dangerous to approach.

Cookie took off to do God knew what. I entered orders. Erin, the server who despised the fact that I dared to breathe air, and Francie, the server who pretended not to despise the fact that I dared to breathe air but who I suspected was right there with Erin, hurried past me for this or that, and the lunch crew behaved like a well-oiled machine. A well-oiled machine with one tiny clink: a loose cog named Cookie. Other than the occasional hiccup, however, we performed like a pit crew at the Indianapolis 500 despite our differences.

Cookie walked up to grab a couple of plates off the pass-out shelf.

"Do you see that?" I asked her, nodding toward Reyes.

A velvety fire licked over his skin, the undulating waves mesmerizing. That was nothing new. The fire he left on the table was. While he scanned his phone with one hand, the other rested absently beside his plate, his fingertips drawing lazily on the smooth surface. His touch left a trail of soft flames in its wake, as though he were igniting the wood beneath his hand.

No one but me seemed to notice. Still, I had to be sure we weren't all about to be burned alive. Maybe he was a pyromancer. A supernatural arsonist.

By the time Cookie turned for a look-see, her arms full of plates, he'd shifted and put his hand down. Yet the table was still on fire where it had been.

"I do indeed," she said, her tone appreciative.

"You do?" I asked, surprised.

The flames slowly died away, leaving wisps of smoke drifting heavenward.

She smirked. "Honey, I'm married. Not dead. How could any woman not see that?"

I scooped coffee into the basket, remembered it needed a filter, poured the granules back out, and started over. "True. But do you see anything out of the ordinary? Anything—I don't know—hot?"

"Sweetheart, that is the definition of hot."

"No. Well, yes, but do you see anything unusual?"

"You mean the way he sits?" she asked, her voice growing husky. "His legs always slightly parted with one hand resting on his thigh. How can any man make something so mundane as sitting so damned sexy?"

She clearly did not see the fire.

Before she took off again, she asked, "Is it wrong that every time he comes in I want to straddle him?"

"Only if you act on your desires. In front of your husband."

She chuckled, narrowly escaped a head-on with Erin, then took her customers their lunch.

But she was right. So very, very right. The guy defined the hyphenated euphemism *sex-on-a-stick,* and I had to get the fuck over it. Dating him would be like playing Spin the Bottle in a nuclear reactor. He should've been wearing a biohazard sign, because I was so not tapping that. I had no intention of going anywhere near it. One hundred percent off-limits. Soooooooo not happening.

I grabbed the water pitcher to see if he needed a refill, which was not so much me going near him but me doing what I was paid for. I had a job to do, damn it. And I lived in a constant state of denial.

Actually, the reasons for my approach were threefold. One, I wanted a closer look at the table. Did he really burn it? Two, I wanted to test a theory I'd had for a long time. Every time he walked into the café, the entire area seemed to grow warmer. It made sense, him being made of fire and all, but was he really causing my hot flashes? I was way too young for menopause, so I had my fingers crossed on that one. And three, how close could I get? If he really was hot and he touched me, would I burn like the table? Would he set me on fire—in the nonmetaphorical sense? Would his touch blister as much as his presence?

I walked toward him with purposeful steps but slowed as I got closer. Cookie stopped what she was doing to watch me, surprise evident on her face. Francie had a similar reaction when she spotted me heading for her customer. Not that it was all that unusual. We each saw to all the customers as needed, and this one was most definitely in need. The poor guy was on fire, for crap's sake. If anyone needed water . . .

Twenty feet. I was now about twenty feet away and closing fast. Ish. The heat that I felt whenever he walked in increased exponentially with every step I took until it became almost unbearable by the time I stood beside his table. Standing next to him was like being too close to a blazing furnace. His heat radiated out in white-hot waves.

"Can I top this off for you?" I asked, my voice only a little wobbly.

He didn't look up at me right away. He'd seemed to sense my approach, though. His sparkling gaze landed on my lower extremities as I'd walked up, but he didn't move then and he wasn't moving now. What was moving was the fire that forever sheathed him. It sparked to life. Swelled. Consumed him completely until his muscles contracted beneath it. His jawline sharpened. His forearms corded, hardened to the density of tempered steel as though he were fighting something inside him. As though he were fighting for control.

I took a minuscule step back. After a few seconds, the fire died down to the soft glow of his everyday armor.

I waited a moment longer, a moment that seemed to stretch forever, before taking the hint. He really did hate me. His emotions were so dense, so tightly packed, I couldn't distinguish any one in particular, but I was certain at the middle of it all lay a seething kind of hatred.

Embarrassment rocketed through me, and I prayed for a sinkhole to appear beneath my feet. On the bright side, no one knew who I was. Including me. I could leave town anytime and all this would be forgotten.

I'd have to change my name. Janey Doerr—because Jane Doe was so last week—would become nothing but a memory. And I didn't have many of those. I could use a few more.

Mortified, I started to step away, but then slowly, methodically, he lifted his lashes. His gaze raked up my body, leaving heat trails everywhere it touched until it met mine. The effect of that meeting was like being hit by a freight train, his presence was so powerful. So raw.

He nodded, the movement barely perceptible, and I'd almost forgotten the question. The cold pitcher in my hands reminded me. I swallowed hard. Tore my focus off him. Bent forward to top off his water.

He monitored my every move, studied me with the intensity of a hungry jaguar, and I suddenly felt like prey. Like I'd fallen for the oldest trick in the book and had been lured into a trap by the deadliest of predators.

My hand started shaking. Embarrassed once again, I pulled it back and tried to ignore the heat spreading over my cheeks.

Then I noticed the entire café had grown quiet. I glanced around to realize we'd somehow become the center of attention. The spotlight flustered me even more, and the pitcher slipped from my hands. It didn't go far. Reyes caught it, his movement too fast for my mind to comprehend.

He held it for me, waited until I had a good grip on it. Once I did, he stood. I stepped back but still had to crane my neck. He towered over me in the best—and most frightening—way possible.

And then he spoke the very first words he'd ever spoken to me. His deep, rich voice dissolved my bones. I almost responded with "Of course I'll have sex with you before you sacrifice me to your gods." Then I realized he'd asked me where the restroom was.

I cleared my throat and pointed. "It's just down that hall and to the right."

That could've been embarrassing.

His gaze swallowed me a moment longer, his expression almost unreadable if not for the faintest hint of sadness. Or perhaps . . . disappointment? Before I could grasp the emotion exactly, he stepped around me and headed to the back.

I filled my lungs at last. With cool air this time, realizing just then how his presence scalded me both inside and out. Talk about things that go bump in the night. Metaphorically and literally. I also realized that the onlookers were no longer paying attention to me. Every head turned toward Reyes as he walked past.

"You okay, sweetie?" Cookie asked from beside me.

But something I'd seen in my peripheral vision pulled my gaze back to the table. There, branded into the wood, was a word written in an ancient Celtic language. A language that was no longer used. It was a word that referred to the people and culture of the Netherlands. In a literal and modern-day translation, however, he'd written the word *Dutch*.

4

*Being an adult means never having to show your
work on math problems.*
—T-SHIRT

Cookie glanced at the table and back at me. "What is it,
hon?"

She couldn't see it. He'd seared the wood, but not in the
tangible world. How was that even possible?

Another realization hit me. I knew a Celtic language, a
dead one, and there was only one possible explanation. I
faced Cookie with eyes rounded. "I think I know what
I am."

"You do?"

"Cookie, I am a genius."

She chuckled. "You are?"

"I am." She followed me back to the prep area. "I'm
smart. But not just smart." I took a quick sip of my coffee
before explaining. "I'm, like, stupid smart. I'm probably a
prodigy of some kind."

"You think?" she asked, clearing Osh's plate off the counter.

"What kind of prodigy?" Osh asked.

I was still reeling from the possibilities of it all. And the fact that Reyes had talked to me. "I don't know, but I'm freaking smart. I know shit."

"Like your name?" he teased.

My face did a deadpan thing. "Fine, I don't know my name, but I know other stuff."

"I'm sure you do," Cookie said as though talking to a child. I was glad she was wiping down the counter; otherwise she probably would have patted my head.

"I'm serious. I think I'm a savant. I might be an astronomer. Or a mathematician. Or that guy who invented Friendbook."

Cookie handed me a plate for immediate delivery while she balanced the other three on her left arm. She was getting really good. "I'm pretty sure you're not the guy who invented Friendbook."

"How do you know?"

"He has short curly red hair."

"And," Osh added as Cookie and I rounded the counter, "a cock."

"Osh," I scolded, glancing around for kids. Thankfully the only one in the whole café was out of earshot.

"It's okay," he said, all grins. "You can have mine if you want."

I rolled my eyes. The little shit. We delivered Cookie's order. When we got back, Lewis, another of our busboys, was leaning his head through the pass-out window, summoning me with a psst. A very loud psst. Not sure who he thought he was fooling.

The café was beginning to clear out, and I glanced back

to make sure Bobert was sticking around. I wanted to catch him before he left. He was such a sweetheart. Always checking on Cookie. Waiting for things to slow down so they could eat together. Picking her up from work so she wouldn't have to walk. Either that or he was a controlling ass. It was hard to tell at this juncture.

Lewis, a prime customer for those big and tall men's clothing stores, jerked his head to urge me closer. He was in his early twenties with rich olive skin, neatly trimmed brown hair, and eyes the shade of wet moss. The effect was quite stunning, but many girls, including the one he was pining over, would never see past his large waistline. Then again, he played bass in a metal band called Something Like a Dude. I couldn't imagine he had much trouble with the opposite sex. And yet his heart was set on the one girl who didn't know he existed: Francie.

"Is everything set for tomorrow?" I asked him. I could feel the reservations he was having as clearly as I felt the draft coming from the open back door.

Lionel, the prep cook, had probably propped it open again. Sumi was going to stab him in the face one of these days.

"Yeah. But, I mean, are you sure about this?"

"Positive. Until Francie sees you in another light, she is not going to give you the time of day."

He still seemed unconvinced. And it was his idea!

Okay, it was my idea, but he contributed.

"Dude, look, your cousin comes in during the afternoon lull, pretends to rob me, you rush up, clock him, and he runs off with no one the wiser. What could go wrong?"

He lifted an unconvinced shoulder.

"I'm not saying you'll get the girl, Lewis, but until you

do something to get her attention, she'll never give you the time of day."

Though I would have preferred Lewis find someone who saw him for who he was, the poor schmuck was in love with Francie. She was a cutie with shoulder-length red hair and an adorable pug nose, but she had the arrogance to match her looks. I was certain she'd grow up someday, but at this point, she saw only Lewis's size. Not how wonderful he was. Or talented. Or dashingly handsome.

Then again, who was I to argue? I was attracted to evil incarnate. Our libidos didn't always take the safest paths. And if I was completely honest with myself—again, something of a rarity—I wanted Francie's eyes as far away from Reyes as I could get them. Not that her lack of interest would give me a snowball's chance, but in my warped brain—the same brain that screamed for me to run in the opposite direction every time Reyes was near—it would up my odds that he would notice me. The heart wasn't the most logical organ. The spleen, however . . .

What Lewis didn't know was that, while I was going along with his plan to win Francie, I was secretly placing stimuli, kind of like those ads that used subliminal messages to get consumers to buy their products. Only I wasn't quite as subtle.

"So, I heard Shayla was at your concert this weekend."

"Really?" he said absently. "I didn't see her."

One of our third-shift servers, a tiny, elf-like creature named Shayla who looked about fourteen but was actually almost twenty-one, was just as much as in love with Lewis as he was with Francie. No, she was more in love. Lewis was simply infatuated. Shayla truly cared for him, so much so, she wanted him to have what he wanted, aka Francie.

She knew he had a thing for her, and instead of flirting or asking Lewis out, she stood back and gave Francie every chance possible to see the wonderful man in front of her.

That was true love. So what I had for Reyes wasn't so much true love as, well, stark raving obsession. Which, oddly enough, worked for me.

Erin rushed past with a tray full of drinks, reminding me I should probably get back to work. Or not. Everyone in my section was eating happily. Who was I to interrupt?

When we'd first come up with *The Plan*, as we were calling it, it was in direct response to a certain redhead falling head over heels for a certain raven-haired, preternatural regular. Her infatuation with Reyes had left Lewis miserable.

"Who am I kidding, Janey?" he'd said one afternoon, confiding in me, trusting me with his most precious secret.

As fate would have it, thanks to a spider bite and a headless picture that went viral of a man who'd dropped his jeans at a Chevelle concert, I knew his most precious secret, and it had nothing to do with Francie. The man in the picture became known as the Anaconda, and I knew it was Lewis because, again thanks to a spider bite and Lewis's fear that he was going to lose his leg after he got one on the inside of his thigh, I'd seen the skull tattoo on his hip. It was exactly like the infamous Anaconda's, right down to the words COLOR IS A LIE underneath the skulls.

Most guys would love for a photo of their little friend to go viral, but I suspected Lewis's unwillingness to step forward into the spotlight had to do with his deep respect for his mother. He was a good guy. Who, for some reason, dropped his pants at a Chevelle concert.

Kids these days.

"She'll never go out with me," he'd said, drowning his

sorrows, and a glazed doughnut, in a cup of joe. "Not when there are men like that on the earth." He'd indicated Reyes with a nod.

"You're right," I said. When he gaped at me, I added, "Hey, I'm on your side. It's just, the guy's freakishly hot." We glanced at Reyes again, my glance lingering a bit longer than Lewis's. "She has to notice you. *Really* notice you."

My mind raced, and I was busy nibbling my bottom lip when it hit me. *The Plan.* It was like a lightning bolt, and I was like a metal rod mounted on top of an elevated structure, electrically bonded with a wire conductor to interface with the ground and safely conduct the lightning to the earth. Excited, I turned to him, but my expression gave him pause.

"What?" he asked, suspicion in his voice.

"You need to save her."

"From what? That guy would kick my ass."

"Not from Reyes. Could you imagine?" I accidentally snorted as I laughed, the thought was so preposterous.

He stared at me with nary a hint of amusement in his moss green eyes.

I sobered. "Sorry, but you could save her from, I don't know, like a robber or something."

He turned dubious. "Sounds kind of dangerous. And where are we going to find a robber, exactly?"

"No, not a real robber. Do you have any friends who could pose as a robber? And we need a gun."

"A gun? Look, Janey, I appreciate the sentiment—"

"You're right," I said, deflating. "I mean, she'll take note of how awesome you are someday, right? Maybe in twenty years? Because girls like her always appreciate the good guys. After they've taken a dip in the bad end of the pool. Over and over. For several decades."

Somewhere deep down inside I knew the unfavorable description of women I'd just given him applied to me most of all, but I'd take one for the team. This was Lewis. He deserved a shot at happiness.

He let out a resigned sigh. "Okay. Let's do this."

And thus *The Plan* was born. He was going to have his cousin pretend to rob the place, aka yours truly, while Francie looked on in horror. Lewis would save us by punching him out—they might need to practice that move—then his cousin would run before the cops got there.

Sadly, we wouldn't be able to identify the robber. It was all going to happen so fast, Francie wouldn't have a chance to be too scared, but once she saw Lewis in action, once she saw how wonderful he was, she'd have to fall for him. Or at least, realize he was alive.

"Your cousin knows what to do, right?" I asked him.

He nodded.

"Then this goes down tomorrow. It'll suck if Francie calls in sick." When he cast me a horrified look, I dismissed the thought with a wave of my hand. "She won't. Don't worry. That woman is as healthy as a horse." And she wouldn't dare miss an opportunity to see Reyes.

Speaking of whom, it had been several minutes since he'd gone to the restroom, and he had yet to come out. I gave Lewis a thumbs-up and wandered that way, feigning my own need to make pee-pee. When I entered the hall, I heard voices coming from inside the men's room.

I'd noticed Garrett wasn't at his table. Maybe that was who Reyes was talking to. Their voices were muffled, but I could feel strong emotion coming from inside. Like torrential strength emotion.

I bit my bottom lip and eased closer.

"Gemma said not to push her," a male voice said.

The wall shook with a loud thud, startling me, but I wasn't about to give up my ringside seat. I inched even closer.

"The only one I'm pushing is you." That came from Reyes. I'd know that bourbon-rich voice anywhere.

And the other was definitely Garrett. I had no idea they knew each other. They never spoke. Never said hi. Never called each other bitch, as men were wont to do.

Garrett said something else, but his voice sounded oddly strained, so I couldn't make it out.

"What's going on?" another male voice said from beside me. Right beside me.

I swung around and jumped with a humiliating squeak before offering Osh my best glare. It was good, too. So good, I'd thought about naming it. But that might seem weird.

"Osh, what the hell?"

That Cheshire grin spread across his face. He looked past me toward the door. "What are you doing?"

I fought the urge to follow his gaze. "Nothing."

"Eavesdropping?" he asked, as though repeating what I'd said.

He stepped closer. So close I had no choice but to back up. I kept backing until I hit the door, but I stood my ground from there. I raised my chin and dared him to try to force me farther. Would. Not. Happen. Unless one of them opened the door.

"Anything interesting?" he asked.

I wasn't born yesterday. He didn't want me to overhear what was going on in that room, and it had me very curious as to why that might be. "Not as interesting as this," I countered.

"Yeah?" He arched a brow, and before I knew what he

was doing, he raised an arm over my shoulder, leaned closer, and slammed his palm into the door.

It opened instantly, and I stumbled, yep, right into Reyes's arms.

Utter mortification washed over me. I pushed away from him, away from the blistering heat of his hold, the fierce strength of it. Darting around Osh, I rushed out of the restroom and back to the station, wondering one thing and one thing only: How did they know each other, and what were they arguing about?

Okay, that was two things. Perhaps I wasn't a mathematician after all.

5

I don't think I could ever complete anyone.
But driving someone insane sounds doable.
—INTERNET MEME

The men came out a couple of minutes after I did. Garrett paid and stalked out, his anger leaving me winded, but Osh and Reyes stayed behind. Osh took Garrett's booth, while Reyes went back to his own. They didn't look at each other. Didn't speak. But I suddenly had the feeling that was all for show.

Yet, what show? Why would I care if they knew each other?

Unless . . .

I narrowed my lashes and looked at them through the menacing slits created by my lids. Maybe I was really the daughter of a billionaire and they were planning to kidnap me for ransom. Two of the three would-be abductors were only part human. They probably had really bad ethics.

"He lives at the Hometown Motel."

I turned to Francie, then grabbed a wet towel to wipe down the prep station.

She pressed her lips together in amusement, her pale skin luminous beneath her bouncy red hair, and followed me. She was holding a phone and scrolling through pictures as she spoke. "Reyes. He lives at the Hometown. You know, that motel on Howard? It's a couple of blocks over."

I knew it. I walked by it at least twice a day to and from work. It was right down the street from my apartment. It wasn't exactly the Waldorf, but what did I care? He was a strapping young man with a menacing scowl. He'd be fine.

I knew better than to ask. I knew it was what she wanted, but my curiosity got the better of me. "How do you know where he's staying?"

She grinned and leaned into me as though we'd been best friends since grade school. "Wouldn't you like to know." The implications were crystal clear, and yet I wasn't sure I believed her. She seemed a little too desperate for my reaction. When she got none, she added, "His room has navy carpet and a blue-and-gold bedspread. It's all very manly."

That time I flinched. What made it worse was that she saw.

Erin walked up then, her long blond hair pulled up into a messy bun. She didn't want to be that close to me, but apparently the phone in Francie's hand was hers.

"She is so cute, Erin," Francie said, scrolling through more pictures. "Isn't she cute?"

Much to Erin's chagrin, Francie held out the phone for me to see. I knew she'd recently had a baby, but that was about it.

I leaned over to look at the phone and a jolt of shock

rocketed through me. I gasped and threw a hand over my mouth before catching myself. They were playing a prank, and I'd fallen for it like a drunk with vertigo.

But they weren't laughing. If anything, Erin was ready to scratch my eyes out. Even Francie was appalled. The scowl on her face could scrub the ring off a toilet.

Erin jerked the phone away from Francie and stalked off. Francie shot razors at me before leaning in and saying softly, "You're a bitch."

I blinked, utterly confused. My heart was still racing. I didn't get it. What they showed me was not a picture of a baby but a picture of a decomposing elderly woman, her toothless mouth open as though she were screaming into the phone, her eyes solid white, almost glowing.

What the bloody hell?

And what made matters worse was the fact that my dramatics attracted the attention of one Mr. Reyes Farrow. He eyed me from underneath his lashes, his brows drawn in concern.

"Hey," Lewis said from the pass-out window. "What was that about?"

Embarrassed for the twelve hundredth time that day, I picked up the coffeepot. "I have no idea," I said under my breath, just before stalking off. It was trending, after all.

After filling the cups of several customers, I made my way toward Cookie's husband. Unfortunately, I had to deal with Mark and Hershel along the way. They were still there.

"Can I get you anything else?" I asked them.

"I wouldn't mind a piece of that ass," Mark said.

"Really? There are actually people like you in the world? For reals?"

"Oh, I'm real, sweetheart."

I jutted out a hip and slapped my palm onto it. "This is unbelievable. I mean, I've heard stories, but I just thought you guys were an urban legend. You know, like that one where the couple is making out in the woods and they hear a sound and the guy gets out to check and the girl is all alone and she hears this drip and she looks and it's the blood of her boyfriend dripping from a tree branch overhead and she screams and gets back in the car and races away and when she gets home the cops find a bloody hook stuck in the door handle." How the fuck could I remember shit like that and I couldn't remember my own name? It was so wrong.

My soliloquy didn't faze him. "You got the legend part right."

Out of all that, that's what he came away with. "Can I take your picture? I have to post this on one of those sites that has photos of UFOs and Sasquatch. Otherwise no one will believe me."

"You done being a smartass?" he asked me. It was a legitimate question.

I thought about it. Shook my head. "Prolly not. Can I get you some more coffee?"

He grunted.

I filled their cups and pretended not to notice the scent of alcohol wafting off them. They must've brought their own stash. The Firelight Grill didn't serve alcohol.

Apparently Mark considered it his civic duty to give me a hard time. A girl could only take so many hateful digs filled with sexual innuendo before she snapped. I doubted Dixie would appreciate a lawsuit brought on by my dumping coffee on her customers' heads.

After wishing them a good day, I moved on to Cookie's husband, Bobert. Bobert's real name was Robert, but the first time he'd come into the café, Cookie grew super nervous as she pointed him out. No idea why.

"His name is Bob . . . ert," she'd said, turning away from me.

"Your husband's name is Bobert?"

She turned back, laughing softly. Nervously. "Robert. I meant to say Robert, though a lot of people on the force called him Bob. I didn't. Still don't. Nope, he's just plain old Robert to me. Except at home. Sometimes I call him Bob at home."

That was a lot of explanation, but it didn't allay the disappointment I felt at not knowing someone named Bobert. "Can I call him Bobert?"

A nervous laugh spilled out of her. "You can call him whatever you want. I have a feeling you'll have him wrapped around your little finger in no time."

Why would she say that? I decided to ask. "Why would you say that?"

"Because you, Janey Doerr, are a charmer."

My spine straightened. A charmer. I'd take it.

"You could probably call him Pudding and he'd be fine with it. He's going to adore you."

I'd raised my chin in pride. "Really? You think he'll adore me?" After tilting my head this way and that as he scooted into a booth, I added, "I mean, he is kinda hot."

Her sweet expression Houdinied into thin air. "I don't think you two would work out that way."

"Oh, right, on account of you guys being married and all."

"That's one take on it, yes."

Married people were so possessive.

That was a little over a month ago, and she'd been right. We became friends the moment we met.

"Can I talk to you a minute?" I asked him. As usual, he wore his short brown hair slicked down and kept his mustache thick and well groomed. I couldn't decide if he was a product of the eighties or just really nerdy.

And, just as Cookie had predicted, he'd taken to me almost as well as she had. I figured he'd felt sorry for the amnesiac the way you do for a carnival attraction. But whatever the reason, he seemed to genuinely like me. There was a shortage of that today.

"Please." He folded the paper he was reading and gestured for me to sit down.

"Thanks." After putting the carafe on the next table, I sat across from him.

"What's up, pumpkin?"

I almost giggled, the term of endearment a welcome respite from the maddening crowd. "I kind of have a situation, and I'm not sure who to talk to about it. I'm hoping you might be able to point me in the right direction."

"Oh." He squared his shoulders. "What kind of a situation? Are you okay? Did something happen?"

"No. No, I'm fine." His concern made me warm and mushy inside. "It's more of a legal thing, and I wasn't sure if you'd want me to get Cookie involved, so—"

"A legal thing, how?"

I didn't know how much to tell him. I couldn't put Mr. Vandenberg or his family in danger. Then again, they were already in danger. Serious danger, from what I could tell. "Okay, what if, hypothetically, I knew about a man who was possibly being held hostage against his will. Along with his entire family."

His pulse sped up, but just barely. He'd probably seen it all. Probably had amnesiacs filing preposterous reports all the time. "Do you know of such a person?" he asked, his tone taking on a sharp edge.

"What? Pfft. No. Maybe. I don't think so. No. Absolutely not." I drew in a deep breath. "I might."

"Then you need to report it to the police."

"I know. I really do. It's just—I'm worried that if I go to the police and they rush over there with sirens blaring, my friend will get hurt. Or even if dispatch sends a uniform to check it out, the hostage takers will get spooked and kill him. Kill his entire family."

He nodded, beginning to understand what I was getting at. Flooded with relief, I waited as Bobert took out a notepad and pen. Once a detective, always a detective.

Unfortunately, Cookie walked up. "And just what are you two talking about?" she asked as she scooted into the booth beside her husband. She gave him a quick peck.

When I hesitated, it took him a moment to figure out why. "Oh, it's okay, hon. Cookie helps us with cases all the time."

"Us?"

"Cases?" Cookie asked, surprised. "We have a case?" Bobert gave her shoulders a squeeze, and they exchanged a pointed glance. A little too pointed. She nodded after a moment. Cleared her throat. Started over. "Yes. Yes, I do help with cases. It's more of a hobby, really."

Bobert nodded, too, and added his own "Yes, a hobby."

I waited for them to elaborate, but they just stared at me, their smiles forced. They did that sometimes.

"And who is 'us'?"

Cookie raised her brows at her husband. "Well, that's . . . It's—"

"The Albuquerque Police Department," Bobert cut in, relief flooding him. For a detective, he wasn't the best liar I'd ever met.

"Cookie helps the Albuquerque Police Department with cases?"

Bobert's gaze didn't waver. "Yes. Yes, she does."

"Yes, I do." She continued to nod. Patted Bobert's hand. Glanced out the window. "Yes, indeedy."

Oddly enough, they weren't lying. They just weren't telling me everything. I got the feeling, as I did often from those two, that they were leaving out the best part. I mean, what did Cookie bring to the table? What could she do to help the police?

Then it hit me, and my entire perception of her changed in an instant.

Cookie was psychic!

It was the only explanation. Okay, probably not the *only* one, but it made perfect sense. And she certainly looked like a psychic. Or how I imagined a psychic might look. She had spiky black hair and sparkly blue eyes. She wore flowing, brightly colored clothes that never quite matched. And she added a little extra vertical lift to the concept of flighty.

Oh, yeah. She was psychic. This rocked so hard.

"Okay, well, if you don't mind," I said, pretending I didn't know the truth. Then again, she was psychic. Would she know that I knew? I told Bobert and Cookie about the *hypothetical* man and his *hypothetical* family. She didn't fall for it. Damn her and her psychic abilities. I'd have to watch what I said around her.

No!

I'd have to watch what I *thought* around her. Crap, this was going to be hard.

"What makes you think this man is being held hostage?" Bobert asked.

I didn't know how much to tell him. He was still a cop. Would he go to the police anyway? I couldn't risk it, not until I knew more.

"I don't, really. It's just a hunch," I said, ashamed I couldn't elaborate. But I didn't want to end up in a padded cell when I mentioned how I could feel Mr. V's pain. His fear. "I don't have anything concrete. Yet."

"Do you know where the family is being held?"

That was the million-dollar question and next on my list of things to check out. Cookie and I got off at three. I planned on finding out where Mr. Vandenberg lived and checking out his house. Incognito style, of course. If the family was there, I could go to whomever Bobert suggested and tell them everything I knew. I could tell for certain if it was a hostage situation or not.

"I don't know that either," I told him. "Can you find out who I'd talk to? Who would treat this with discretion?"

He let out a lengthy sigh and sat back. "It's going to be hard going to the authorities without a plausible explanation as to how you came by this information. Trust me. I've been down this road before."

Of course he had. How could he tell others about his wife's psychic visions? He'd have to make something up, like maybe he got the information via an anonymous tip or something equally as lame.

I wondered if that was how they'd met. She'd walked into his office with a tip, tears glistening like the finest ice in her baby blues as she begged for his help. He razzed her. Called her a crazy dame. Told her to beat it and not to come back, but the big palooka just couldn't get her out of his head. He'd fallen for that cat's pajamas, and how.

Twenty-four hours and three bottles of shine later, he was rapping his knuckles on any door he could find, searching for the dish who'd stolen his ticker, vowing to get hand-cuffed to the doll if it was the last thing he did.

It could happen.

"I thought about calling in with an anonymous tip, but—"

"—but the first thing they'll do is send in a uniform," he finished for me.

I was beyond thrilled that he understood. Heck, I was thrilled he was even listening to me.

"Let me see what I can find out," he said. "I have a few contacts in the area, just not this town in particular."

I nodded and stood. "Thanks so much. I really appreciate it."

But he stopped me with a hard glare. Or, hard-ish. "Just don't do anything stupid before I check around."

"Like what?" I asked, my expression completely innocent.

"Like what you're thinking right now."

That was totally eerie. It was like he knew me or something. "I would never."

I grabbed the carafe and started for the drinks station. Cookie gave Bobert a quick kiss and followed me.

"I think the customer at thirteen needs a refill," she said, adding a wink.

I turned. Took in the alarmingly alluring form of Reyes Farrow. Tried to pretend I wouldn't be willing to trade non-essential organs for a night with him.

"Go talk to him," she said, urging me that way.

I gathered a plate and bowl off a table as we strode past. She took it from me and cleared the rest of it, erasing my excuse to go to the back instead of toward a certain brooding ball of fire.

"I can't talk to him," I whispered.

"Sure you can."

How could I tell Cookie what I saw? The darkness that enshrouded him. The eternal fire that bathed him.

"Just ask him how he's doing."

"I better not," I said, shaking out of it. "Besides, I'm going to marry Denzel Washington. I watched one of his movies last night. There are no words."

"That's kind of sudden. Have you told Denzel?"

"No."

She straightened with her load. "Have you told Denzel's wife?"

"No. But I did name my mattress after him."

"Well, there you go. You're practically engaged."

"You cuttin' us off, sweetheart?" Mark grabbed my elbow from his seat behind me, his fingers biting into the tendons much harder than necessary to get my attention.

I tried to jerk out of his grasp. Instead of freeing myself, though, I sloshed coffee over the rim of the carafe. It splashed to the ground and onto my boots. My new suede boots with a topside zipper.

A wall of heat hit me from behind, but I simply stood in shock at first. That anyone would just grab me. That anyone would feel he had a right to. Ignoring the heat that swirled around me in an angry mass, I raised my lashes and focused first on the large hand that still had a vise grip on my arm, then on the asshole it was attached to. The diesel mechanic was laughing at me for spilling coffee. They both were. And a spark of anger flared to life inside me.

Oddly enough, nature chose that exact moment to grace

us with an earthquake. I'd never been in an earthquake, not that I knew of, so the novelty should have shaken me out of my stupor.

It didn't.

Anger arced around me like electricity even as the earthquake grew stronger. A couple of the patrons screamed. In my peripheral vision I saw some grab for the edges of their tables while others dived under them. Dishes rattled. A glass fell and shattered. A woman cried out for help. But still my ire rose.

Mark's eyes were saucers. He let go of my arm and grabbed his table as well. Hershel did the same, but I suddenly and quite surprisingly wanted their necks to snap.

I heard a soft voice in the distance. Felt a light touch.

"Charley," it said.

Six.

"Sweetheart, are you okay?"

I ignored her. Cookie. She'd placed a hand on my shoulder. It didn't help. I could practically hear their necks snapping, I wanted it so bad. Could feel the sharp cracks as their vertebrae were wrenched apart.

Their heads twisted in unison on their shoulders just as a bolt of lightning flashed in front of me. Startled, I glanced out the window, unable to tell if it had come from this world or the other. But the fluttering of wings was most definitely from the other.

They were huge, the wings. Massive, spanning at least six feet on either side. Startlingly white on the edges and soft gray underneath. And they did not belong to a bird. They flared out, and a bright figure swirled around to face me, its image a blur in the winds of the otherworld. It darted forward as though to tackle me. I sucked in a sharp breath, and everything went black.

I heard Cookie again as I blinked, trying to focus.

"Janey," she repeated, squeezing my shoulder softly. "Are you okay?"

I looked down. I'd dropped the carafe, but it hadn't broken. Laughter and sighs of relief swirled around me.

"It's over," someone said. A woman. "Oh my God."

A quick glance ensured me that, indeed, the earthquake was over. Another glance, a deeper glance, told me the winged being was gone.

"I've never been in a real earthquake." I knew the voice. Lewis.

"Me neither." Erin. "I have to call home." While I felt relief from almost everyone else, I felt fear spike in her. Fear for her baby.

"Are you okay?" Lewis again.

"I'm—I'm fine. I think." I turned just in time to see Francie check her hair.

That's when I saw the darkness beside me. Reyes stood on my other side, and I realized he had Mark's hand in a brutal hold. The man cried out, his face plastered against the table, a picture of pain.

Hershel bolted upright as though to challenge Reyes, but one look from the supernatural being, a look fairly glittering with rage, convinced him to leave instead. He tucked his chin and left without looking back.

Reyes dragged Mark out of the booth, then let go. The man didn't need any more encouragement. He rushed out the front door, his tail tucked between his legs, and the only thing I could think to say was "He didn't pay yet."

"Is everyone okay?" Dixie asked, winded and worried.

The workers and patrons alike nodded, their shock still evident. We clearly didn't have any customers from California in the bunch.

"She's okay," Erin said, relief flooding her cells at last. She had a phone pressed to one ear and a hand pressed to her chest, her smile a radiant beam. "Hannah's fine. They didn't even feel it at the house."

I realized then that Cookie had dropped the plates she'd picked up, but she was more concerned with me. She still had a hand on my shoulder as though to keep me anchored.

Dixie gave Erin a hug, then said, "I guess we have a few messes to clean up."

Sirens wailed in the distance, and people made their way out of stores across the street. They looked stunned as they surveyed the landscape. Questioned each other. Embraced.

Bobert rushed to Cookie and pulled her into a hug before turning to check on me, but my attention was still on the man standing so close. So startlingly and dangerously close.

Reyes had yet to move. Again, his emotions were so tightly packed, I had a tough time figuring out what he was thinking, but I did feel concern behind the hard expression he'd leveled on me. Then his gaze slid to where the otherworldly being had been, and I stilled.

Had he seen it, too?

The fire that forever engulfed him surged, the heat blistering. It licked over my skin and caused the most explicit sensation. All thoughts of the being fell away as a tendril of desire coiled inside me.

When he turned back to me, his expression was still granite hard. It bit into me, tugged at my overheated core. His burnished irises dropped to my mouth, and he took a minuscule step closer. If Bobert hadn't interrupted, I would have jumped his bones right then and there.

Yes, *near me* was a dangerous place for Reyes to be.

"Are you okay, pumpkin?"

I tore my gaze off the object of my most humiliating fantasies and melted into Bobert's embrace. Cookie joined us for a threesome. Score!

"That was crazy," I said, suddenly realizing we'd just survived an earthquake.

"Yes, it was."

I pulled back. "Have you ever been in an earthquake before?"

They exchanged glances, hedged a little, and then Bobert said, "Yeah, in a way."

Cookie nodded. "A couple. You know, little ones here and there. Nothing major."

"Well, screw that." I took the carafe and headed for the coffeepot. "I, for one, am never moving to California."

Erin and Cookie swept up broken glass as several of the customers went outside to assess the damage there. Fire trucks pulled up, but there didn't seem to be any smoke. Francie cashed out a couple of customers, then went to help Dixie with a stack of files that had fallen over in her office.

Stepping out of the circle of warmth created by Reyes's presence, I started for the kitchen to see if I could help with anything there. A departed woman stepped into my path, drawing me up short. The top of her head barely reached my chin. She had on a plain blue dress and a gray sweater. Her graying hair was mostly hidden by a floral headscarf, and deep grooves lined her soft brown eyes. I looked back to see if Reyes saw her, too. He gave no indication that he did. His unwavering focus was still on me, so I couldn't talk to her there.

"You are the light," she said. In Portuguese! I knew *another* language. What were the odds?

I nodded toward the restroom and had every intention

of going there in hopes that she would follow me. Instead, she stepped forward as though she were going to go through me. I didn't have time to tell her she couldn't do that. I was solid to the departed, and they were solid to me. Or they had been up until that moment, because instead of bumping into me and bouncing back, she passed right through. That was new.

I'd assumed it would be like when a departed passed through any one else. She would just pass through me as though I weren't there. But that didn't happen. When she stepped forward, something magical happened. I saw a light swallow her just before she disappeared. And then I saw . . . everything.

Her childhood. Her death. I saw everything. I felt everything. All at once. All of the emotion. All of the heartbreak and triumph. All of the joys and sorrow. They hit me like a tidal wave.

Air disappeared. The world fell away. And Ana's life literally flashed before my eyes.

She was from Barrancos, a small village that lay on the border between Portugal and Spain, where they had their own language, Barranquenho. She knew five languages, in fact, even though she grew up very poor.

Her mother was a seamstress, and Ana followed in her footsteps. It was how she met her husband, a famous *cavaleiro*, a horseman bullfighter, Benito Matias. He'd been knifed in a bar fight in her small village one night. When they found the medical clinic closed, his friends had taken him to her, begged her to stitch him up so his father wouldn't find out.

She did, and it was her memory of him that drowned me. That intoxicated me. He was the most beautiful thing she'd ever seen. And judging from the way he'd gazed at her that night, Benito felt much the same way. They fell in love, and she found herself in the middle of a real-life Cinderella story.

He took her to his family's estate, where she ended up designing all of his mother's clothes as well as many of the other family members'. She became famous in her own right. They had three sons and one daughter. Then a wave of heartache punched me in the gut. Knocked the air from my lungs. They lost their youngest son to scarlet fever. The agony of that loss ripped through me, the wound still fresh somehow, as though the concept of time became meaningless in this place. We were floating in the space between dreams and reality, between memories and emotion. Sorrow choked me. Clawed at my heart until we slid past the heartache to more jubilant times.

Her other three children grew up healthy and happy. There were bad spells, of course, but her love for Benito never wavered. That was why she didn't cross when she'd died of breast cancer three years earlier. She was waiting for the love of her life, Benito. He'd died just moments before she sought me out.

And then I understood. I was a portal of some kind, and Ana knew it. She literally crossed through me to where Benito—to where her whole family—awaited her. How was such a thing even possible?

When the world materialized around me again, it was spinning much faster than it had been before. The floor tilted, rocketed toward me, and I lost my balance. Either we were having another earthquake or I was about to face-plant.

A microsecond before I played tonsil hockey with a square of cracked linoleum, steely arms encircled my waist and plucked me out of the tumbling air. Fire rushed over me. Heat enveloped me. Unable to stop the world from spinning at dizzying speeds, my head fell back against a wide shoulder. Darkness began to settle around me, and as though from a distance, I heard my savior's deep voice say one word: *Dutch*.

6

I have seen things.
Awful things.
Empty coffee cup things.
—T-SHIRT

Voices. Angry voices. That was the first thing I heard when I swam back to the glittering edge of consciousness. One voice belonged to tall, dark, and deadly. I'd recognize that smooth tenor anywhere. Surprising since I'd only heard it a few times. I couldn't place the other's, but it seemed familiar.

"She could have destroyed the entire block—" the male voice I didn't recognize said.

"She could have destroyed the entire planet," Reyes countered.

"—but she didn't," the other one continued. Osh, perhaps? "This doesn't change anything. We stick to the plan."

Someone else spoke then. Another male, but younger. Hispanic. "*Aye, dios mío.*" Angel. He was the first departed I'd actually talked to after Day One, and I only talked to him because he wouldn't leave me alone until I did. I was in denial at the time, and pretending he didn't exist kept me in my happy place. But he harped on and on about how he could give me the best night of my life and swearing that once I went cold, sex never got old.

Seriously. He was thirteen. He told me. I told him I had a really strong gag reflex. He pretended to be offended but continued to hit on me every chance he got. I wondered if exorcists charged by the hour. If I saved up my tips . . .

"You two are like cheerleaders," he said, "fighting over the quarterback."

There was a silence that I suspected was filled with glares before Angel continued.

"*Mira,* I get it. You're afraid she'll ascend. Scared she'll come to her senses and leave your ass."

I heard a scuffle, then a tight "What is your point?" from Reyes.

When Angel spoke again, his voice was slightly higher than before. "You don't get it, *pendejo.* Maybe she just wants to be normal for a little while."

Another pause.

Angel coughed and Reyes asked, "What do you mean?"

"Maybe, I don't know . . . Maybe she just needs a break from all the bullshit. It's controlled her life since the day she born."

"Kid has a point," Osh may or may not have said. Still wasn't sure.

"Fuckin' A, I have a point. A razor-sharp one, *cabrón.*"

Overall, this was a really unusual dream. Most of my dreams were filled with utter nonsense and questions like what color scythe would go best with my sweater. No idea. But this one had no pictures. Just darkness. And voices.

And a hand on my arm. But it wasn't until I felt the tongue slide up my face that realization sank in.

I'd fainted! My lids flew open, and humiliation surged through me. I was such a dorknado. Not only had I fainted, I'd done it in the arms of Reyes Farrow. I groaned and slapped a hand over my eyes. No telling what he thought of me now.

Artemis, the departed Rottweiler I'd met after waking up in the alley, whined and scooched closer, almost pushing me off the cot. I gave her a quick hug, then replaced my hand.

"Hey, sweetheart," a male voice said, but it was not a voice I particularly wanted to hear.

Artemis growled. I only knew her name because her collar had a tag on it, but she'd stuck with me through thick and thin. Mostly thin. She also had an affinity for showers, but only while I was taking one, and cooking, but only while I was in the kitchen. She could materialize anywhere, including on the countertop where I prepared food, which wasn't as bad as it sounded. She was departed, after all. How germy could she be?

I pried open my lids one at a time and focused through my fingers. Officer Ian Jeffries sat on the cot beside me in his police uniform, his blond hair cut military short, his jaw freshly shaven.

He'd been the responding officer that first night when I woke up in the alley and walked into the café with exactly zero memories. Since then, he'd taken it upon himself to check up on me almost daily. Sometimes several times a day.

He was sweet for the most part and very nice looking, but I got a strange vibe off him, a possessiveness, as though he felt he had dibs on me because he'd helped me that first night. He'd gone with me to the hospital and stuck around when a detective questioned me. When Dixie showed up and offered me a place to stay and a job until I got my head screwed back on straight—her words—he'd insisted on driving me back to the café, to what would become my accommodations for the next two weeks.

I glanced around. I'd lived in this storeroom until I found an apartment. Thankfully, Dixie had connections and convinced my current landlord I was a good egg—again, her words—and that he should rent to me despite my lack of credit history. Or any history, for that matter.

I was hoping to see Reyes and whomever he'd been arguing with. Instead, I got Ian. I tried not to get rankled by his use of the too-familiar colloquialism. His sweetheart I was not, but rankled wasn't my best look.

"I heard you took quite a spill." He drew tiny circles on my arm with his thumb. Tiny, possessive circles that sent shivers lacing up my spine. I didn't want to seem ungrateful for everything he'd done, but he was a cop. Responding to a call. Wasn't that, like, his job?

I lowered my hand. "I barely remember what happened," I croaked. Literally. Suddenly thankful Reyes wasn't within earshot.

And I'd lied. I remembered everything about Ana and her life, but it was just too much to process at the moment. Too impossible. Too unbelievable.

"I'm just glad you're okay. I'll drive you home when you're ready."

I eased onto my elbows as an excuse to get his hand off me. Artemis took that as her cue to dive-bomb me. Air whooshed out of my lungs, then again when she used my stomach as a launchpad to bigger and better things, dis-appearing into the otherworld.

"That's okay," I said, my voice tight as I fought a groan of agony. "I still have some work to do."

He chuckled. "I think Dixie will let you off this once."

I didn't want to tell him about the *other* work I needed to get to that had nothing to do with Dixie or the café.

Fortunately, Cookie came in with a bottle of water and a washcloth.

"You're awake," she said, relief evident as though she let out a breath she'd been holding.

"That I am."

She gave Ian a harsh glare and shooed him out. "She needs rest," she said, and while I didn't, I was not about to argue.

The minute she waved the washcloth, encouraging him to leave, a spike of anger shot out of him. It made my own ire rise in reflex.

"I'm fine, Ian."

"I'll wait for you out here."

"She already has a ride," Cookie said. She seriously didn't like the guy. It cracked me up.

But another spike of anger set me on edge, and this time I was the one who leveled a heated glare on him. He was about to argue when he got a call on the handheld at his shoulder. He gave me a curt nod, then left.

"That man," Cookie said as she pulled up a box and sat down beside me. She arranged the cloth on my head. It felt heavenly. Next, she forced the water bottle into my hand and watched with toes tapping until I downed at least half.

"You're dehydrated," she said, and she was right. I se-riously needed to cut back to ten cups of coffee a day.

"What time is it?" I asked.

"It's almost four thirty."

I bolted upright. "I've been out for hours."

She patted my shoulder, then took my hand into hers. "We were going to call an ambulance—"

"No!" I said with more aggression than I meant. I took another sip of water and forced myself to calm down. "No, it's all good. Thanks for that. I have enough bills to last me a lifetime."

"I wouldn't worry about that, honey."

Clearly she hadn't seen the paper mountain growing in my apartment.

"Can you tell me what happened?"

To my surprise, I wanted to tell her. I wanted to trust her, but I couldn't be certain she wouldn't try to have me committed.

And how could I explain the things I saw? The things I experienced? Truth was, even though I'd only known her for a month, I loved Cookie. A lot. A really, really lot. I didn't want to taint her opinion of me. I didn't want her to look at me with anything other than admiration. Or befuddlement, depending.

"I'm fine. I just got light-headed."

"Good. But are you okay okay? With everything? We haven't really talked about your . . . situation in a while. Maybe, you know, the stress—?"

Ah. Was I okay with being the local amnesia chick? "I think I'm okay. I mean, I look at everyone who walks into the café to see if there's any resemblance, but I'm dealing with it."

She nodded, her sympathy genuine. "Have you thought about therapy?"

"Yes, I have. And as soon as I sell that kidney I listed on eBay, I'll be able to afford it."

"They have programs."

"Right? Those things are great. I watched a zombie program last night, and tonight I'm going to watch this one about a blond chick who controls dragons. And there's this sexy short guy who's drunk all the time."

"Not those kinds of programs." She admonished me with a withering stare. It almost worked. "There are clinics."

I scooted back and leaned against the wall. I didn't know much, but I did know if I told a counselor about my interactions with dead people, she'd lock me up and throw away the access code. I just wasn't ready for a life of padded rooms and pudding.

"I don't think therapy is the answer."

"I couldn't agree more." She shifted excitedly. "You need hypnosis."

I blinked. Squinted. Crinkled my brows.

"Think about it. You could learn about your current life and your past ones."

"There is that."

"I'm pretty sure I was Cleopatra in a past life."

She was serious. I tried not to giggle.

"Or a vacuum cleaner salesman. My arches fell."

I didn't ask. "I'm not sure I'm ready for a padded cell." Pudding, however . . .

"No way. What could you possibly say that would convince a therapist you needed to be committed?"

If she only knew.

"No, really," she continued. "You can tell me anything. You know that, right?"

I rose, and she helped me stand. After I knew for certain I wasn't going to snog the linoleum again, I said, "Can I ask you something instead?"

"Of course!" She followed me out.

The café was glaringly bright compared to the storeroom. Reyes was gone, as were most of our customers. The dinner crowd wouldn't start showing up for another hour. And thankfully Ian was gone, too. One less headache I had to deal with.

I called out to Frazier, one of the third-shift cooks, and ordered two sandwiches to go. Cookie had grown used to my order and didn't question it. The sun loomed low across the cloudy sky in preparation for the inevitable sunset, and the air outside looked frozen. My walk home was going to suck.

I turned back to Cookie. Now was as good a time as any to ask her about something that had been niggling at me, but I had to surprise her. To get her true reaction before she tried to cover it up.

I grabbed a takeout bag and opened it while slipping in a casual "Who's Charley?"

Cookie gaped at me a minute as I read her every reaction.

When she didn't say anything, I decided to explain. "You've called me Charley at least six times lately."

At first, I thought she might actually know me, but Charley didn't fit any better than any other name I'd tried. Not to mention the fact that I looked nothing like a Charley.

"I—I'm sorry," she said. "That just slips out occasionally because it's what I call Robert at home. I'm just so used to saying it."

That was a bald-faced lie. And the mystery deepened. "You call your husband Charley?"

"Yes." She nodded for emphasis. "Yes, I do. Because that's his name. Charles Robert Davidson." She tossed the towel she'd been carrying and took off her apron. "Everybody back home calls him Charley. So I still call him that most of the time."

"I thought you said everybody back home called him Bob."

She blinked. Did her darnedest to recover. "Yes, they did. They called him Charley . . . Bob."

I coughed to keep a giggle from erupting. "Charley Bob?"

"Charley Bob."

The second she said it, Bobert walked in, his timing impeccable.

A rush of sheer panic washed over Cookie, but she recovered and waved to him a little too enthusiastically. "Hey, Charley Bob!"

He slowed, a frown creasing his brows as he got closer. "Hey, Cookie Butt."

She laughed out loud and waved a dismissive hand. "It's not his favorite nickname. But I have to tease him every once in a while to remind him of his past."

He stepped closer and gave her a quick squeeze before settling his attention on me. "Are you okay, pumpkin?"

People asked me that so often. "I'm good," I said as he pulled me into a hug. I breathed in the scent of his drugstore cologne and the barest hint of a cheap cigar. He smelled wonderful.

It was odd how when Cookie and Bobert called me things like sweetheart and pumpkin, I wanted to drown in their embraces. But when Ian did the very same thing, my skin crawled. Clearly my skin was trying to tell me something. Either that or I was a meth kingpin and had a

natural aversion to cops. I didn't think so, though. I had
fantastic teeth.

Cookie chuckled again. For no reason. "I was just telling Janey that your nickname back home was Charley Bob
and that I call you Charley sometimes. At home. When
we're alone."

He set me at arm's length. "Ah."

"So, can I call you Charley Bob?" I asked, ever so
hopeful.

"No."

He sat in a booth close to the station. Cookie scooted
in next to him and I sat across from them, completely uninvited. 'Cause that's how I roll.

"Okay, I have to be honest. I do this thing and—" I
wasn't sure how to tell them, so I decided to skip the hows
and get right down to the whats. "I can tell when someone
isn't being completely forthcoming. And I know that your
name is not really Charley Bob. Thank God, because
damn."

Totally busted, Cookie wrapped an arm in Bobert's and
sighed. "I'm sorry. I didn't want to bring it up. It's very
painful."

Okay, she wasn't lying that time.

"It's just . . . I recently lost my best friend and her name
was Charley and I keep slipping and calling you Charley
and it's just wrong. I—I apologize."

Bobert covered her hand with his and squeezed.

I cringed and prayed for a freak hurricane to shatter the
glass and cut me into tiny pieces. "Cookie, I am so, so
sorry."

"It's okay," she said, hurrying to console me.

"No, it's not. Why didn't you tell me? What happened?"

After a quick glance at her husband, she said, "We don't

really know what happened. We lost her a few weeks back."

"She died?"

"No, she just . . . vanished. But we're hoping she finds her way back to us."

Every word she said was the truth, and I felt like dog excrement after a jogger stepped on it and ground it into the dirt. I sucked ass.

The bell dinged. Frazier had finished my sandwiches, and I had work to do.

"Cook, I don't know what to say."

"Janey," she said, taking my hand into both of hers, "don't you dare feel bad. I should have told you."

"No. It was none of my business. I shouldn't have forced it out of you."

"We'll give you a ride home, pumpkin," Bobert said.

A sadness had settled over both of them, and suddenly my dog-excrement analogy seemed too light-hearted.

"That's okay. I have to do a couple more things before I leave."

Bobert's interest was piqued. "You aren't going to do what you said you wouldn't, right?"

"No way. Speaking of which, did you find anything out?"

"I'm meeting with a guy tonight. He's with the local FBI."

The FBI? Wow.

"You just have to stay out of trouble until then, *capisce*?"

"Got it. If there's anything I can do, it's stay out of trouble."

I hurried to get the sandwiches, paid for them with my tip money, then headed out the front door and straight toward trouble.

* * *

Mr. Vandenberg's door was locked, and the sign had been turned to CLOSED a few minutes earlier than he normally quit for the day. I cupped my hand and peered in the glass door. The store was empty, and all the lights were out. Alarm and a sickening sense of dread rose inside me. What if they were finished with him? What if they didn't need him or his family anymore? Would they kill them?

I had no choice. I was going to have to bring Ian into this. To tell him what was going on. He might not believe the whys or hows, but he would have to report it to his superior officers. I'd just drive home ad nauseam the fact that they could not go rushing in without knowing the whereabouts of Mr. V's family first. If they were being held captive and someone tipped off their captors . . .

I shuddered with the thought and turned my immediate attention to the dry-cleaning business next door—and grew more confused than ever. If the men in Mr. V's shop were tunneling in that direction, maybe it had nothing to do with the business. Maybe there was hidden treasure under the shop. It was an antiques place, after all. It could have pirate loot underneath it. Because why on planet Earth would anyone dig a tunnel into a dry-cleaning business? What could they possibly hope to gain? A dinner jacket? A prom dress, maybe? Window treatments?

I decided to go deep. I'd pose as a customer and check it out. Get a feel for the place.

By the time I walked the fifteen feet to the store entrance, I was already shivering. The jacket I had, the only one I owned, was an old army jacket, and while it was plenty warm most days, today was not most days. The wind crept through the pores of the fabric and sliced into me like razor blades, cutting the marrow of my bones. The wet air hung thickly, and the threat of a freezing rain loomed close by.

I'd have to hurry if I planned on making it home before I froze to death, but more importantly, in time to borrow Mable's car. She was my neighbor, and she hadn't had an actual license in over a decade, but she'd kept her husband's car to drive to church twice a week. Unfortunately, she went to bed early, and once that woman was asleep, there was no waking her up.

After checking the dry cleaner's hours, I pushed open the door. No bell chimed to announce my visit, so I cased the joint while I had the chance. It looked completely legit. Then again, so did that Louis Vuitton I bought off a man named Scooter in the Walmart parking lot. Not to mention the Rolex.

Plastic-covered clothes hung on an automated rack behind the front desk. Not a lot, but enough to look believable. A cash register with tickets piled beside it sat on the desk along with a cup for pens. A framed business license hung on the wall to my right, and a huge man sat in a padded red chair on my left.

I jumped when I noticed him, wondering why he wasn't the first thing I noticed when I walked in. He had biceps the size of my waist.

He folded a paper he was reading and stood. His muscles were so big, he was unable to drop his arms at his sides, and I wondered how on earth he wiped after going number two. It was wrong of me, but still . . .

He walked around the desk and pinned me with a set of cool gray eyes. We stood in uncomfortable silence for, like, ever. The dark hair that had been sheared short all over his head topped off a rather menacing look, mostly because he was glaring at me from underneath it.

Just as I was about to speak, he asked in a thick Russian accent, "Vy you are here?"

Odd way to greet a potential customer. If his attitude didn't change lickety-split, I was so giving this place a negative review on Yelp.

"I—I need something dry-cleaned."

A woman came up then, older than the man and a lot shorter though no less stout. "Vy you are here?" she asked me in the same thick accent.

What the hell? I glanced around again just to make sure I'd come into an actual business. Yep. They had a sign and everything. I turned back to her. "I need something dry-cleaned."

"Vat?" she asked, shooing the man aside. But I hadn't thought that far ahead. I needed something to dry-clean and fast, but the only thing I could take off without making Schwarzenegger think I was desperate for a man was my coat. My warm, plush coat that a nice homeless lady gave me when I offered her a lap dance.

It wasn't as bad as it sounded. I was looking for a second job and needed an opinion.

A cold wind rushed up my backside as two men walked in. They stood behind me, speaking softly to one another. I chanced a glance over my shoulder. They wore expensive charcoal suits, and one carried a leather briefcase and a ticket stub. He nodded to his comrade, then spoke to the woman, his tone brusque, and I fought to keep my eyes from rounding.

He spoke in Russian. Russian! And I understood every word, which was basically "Vy she is here?"

I stood stunned. Eight. I knew eight languages. I was a freaking genius. I couldn't wait to tell Cookie. Seriously, who speaks eight languages? I suddenly wondered if I knew more. Maybe I knew Icelandic or Arabic or Swahili.

I turned to the man and asked, "Do you speak Swahili?"

He glared. I took that as a no and faced the woman again.

"Let me have," she said, snapping her fingers at me.

With a heavy sigh, I peeled off the coat and handed it to her. She took it and looked it over, then asked, "You need mending?"

I most definitely needed mending. My coat, not so much.

The men behind me were inching closer, showing their impatience by trying to intimidate me. Sadly, they didn't have to try very hard. I was ready to sprint out of there.

Instead, I stepped closer to the counter, hinting that my personal boundary was being invaded.

When they kept back, I said, "No mending. Just a cleaning."

"You are stained?" She was still studying the coat, but I was beginning to wonder if she wasn't really talking about me.

"No stains." Not visible ones, anyway.

"Today," she said, tearing off a ticket and shoving it into my hand.

"Today?" I was impressed. It was already late.

"Two day," she said louder, holding up two fingers.

"Oh, right. Okay, thanks." I turned to leave but was blocked in by the Wall Street boys. "Excuse me."

The one in front moved ever so slightly to the side, giving me just enough room to squeeze past. He spoke

Russian to his friend again, and I almost told him exactly how impudent zees Americans could be. The nerve.

The cold!

A freezing gust slapped me in the face when I walked out. Not just chilly. Not just frigid. An eighty-below gust of sleet-infused wind scraped across my exposed skin. I had a thick sweater at home that would have to hold me over until I could get my coat back. If I made it that far.

I crossed my arms over my chest, tucking the bag of sandwiches under one arm, then hurried down the sidewalk. I only lived two blocks away, but in this weather, it would be a long two blocks. And it had all been for naught. I now had neither a coat nor answers. I asked myself for the thousandth time why anyone would tunnel into a dry-cleaning business.

Just as I rounded the corner to go north to my apartment, I caught sight of the two Russian men getting into their car, a sleek black job that probably cost more than all my hospital bills combined.

But that wasn't what caught my attention. They weren't carrying any clothes. They'd had a ticket when they walked in but hadn't walked out with any clothes. Even more interesting was the fact that the briefcase was gone.

Maybe the dry-cleaning business was even less legit than Scooter's entrepreneurial adventures.

7

*I have enough money to live comfortably for the
rest of my life. If I die next Thursday.*

—T-SHIRT

The sun set completely as I walked home, abandoning me
like everyone else in my life. If that weren't bad enough, I
hadn't made it half a block before the heavens opened up
and poured buckets of ice-cold water over my head. That
was what it truly felt like. When it stopped raining for a
split second, I saw flurries of snow drift down as if they
hadn't a care in the world, and then the sleet-infused rain
started again.

By the time I hit Howard Street, I'd turned blue and lost
all feeling in my extremities, and my voice had taken on a
mind of its own. Odd, whining sounds erupted out of my
throat with no rhyme or reason. Every time a shudder took
hold, I'd wheeze out some grumblings that sounded like
profanity but lacked the true conviction of blasphemy.

My hair hung in thick clumps around my face and

shoulders, parts of it turning to ice. I realized my shirt now revealed more of my body than it hid, and this was not the best neighborhood to be peddling my wares.

I could see my apartment, or at least a small corner of it, as I forced one foot in front of the other. The wind mocked me. Taunted me. And I suddenly knew how salmon felt when they swam against the current.

I realized I was walking past the Hometown Motel. The one in which Reyes Farrow was staying. Glancing over, I saw rows of run-down blue doors and a dirty white exterior. Even after all this time, I didn't know what Reyes drove, so the cars parked out front gave me no clue as to which room was his. It was for the best. If I knew which room was his, I'd be tempted to knock on his door and beg for a ride, and I doubted he was attracted to drowned rats.

But my good fortune seemed to get gooder and gooder. The door to one of the rooms on my right opened, streaming light onto the sidewalk in front of me. I looked over as Reyes Farrow stepped into the door frame. He must have had the heat all the way up, because a warmth from heaven slid over me like a blanket. The door stood twenty feet away, so either that or his heat could penetrate even this torrential weather. Not that I cared at that moment.

Since the light shone from behind Reyes, I couldn't make out his features. I didn't need to. The harshness in his voice spoke volumes. "What are you doing?"

I slowed my pace but didn't stop. It hadn't been a question of concern but one that demonstrated his complete faith in my ineptitude. What the hell had I ever done to this guy?

"Walking home," I said, fighting the urge to wrap my arms around myself with every fiber of my being. My wet clothes clung to my skin, leaving little to the imagination, I was sure, the thin material slowly turning to ice. But the heat that now saturated me made me want to cry. I would've sold my soul for more.

The light cast a soft glow on the hills and valleys that encased his exposed forearms. Unlike the Russian's, however, Reyes's were smooth. Sinuous. Fluid. The shadows that rested in the negative spaces shifted with each movement he made as though a gorgeous painting had been brought to life. The unearthly fog that cascaded over his shoulders like a cape and pooled at his feet billowed around him, and the fire that licked across his skin glowed a soft amber in the low light. I wondered for the thousandth time what he was. I did know one thing for certain: He was not completely human. I also wondered if he knew.

He took a drink from a whiskey glass, keeping his glittering gaze locked on me as though laser guided. It was the one thing on his face I could make out clearly, his dark eyes glistening beneath thick lashes. The light rainbowed off his irises as he regarded me with what I could only assume was derision.

He lowered the glass to his side, the ice clinking— salient word: *ice*—and hooked a thumb into his jeans pocket. "Where's your coat?" He wore a white button-down with the sleeves rolled up, only the buttons weren't buttoned. The shirt hung open. The cold didn't seem to faze him. It irked.

"Where's yours?" I countered.

He ignored me. Kept his piercing stare locked on its target, its visage so arresting I stopped. As though he'd ordered me to. As though he'd willed it.

Frustrated, I said with a heavy sigh just as a gust of wind sent a chill shuddering through me, "Getting dry-cleaned." I tensed my arms, curled my hands into fists, prayed he couldn't see how cold I was. Or how blue.

"Why?"

I frowned at him. "Why what?"

"Why are you getting your coat cleaned?"

"I'm not entirely sure."

"Get in here," he said, releasing his talonlike hold at last. He turned and started inside.

I stiffened. Or I tried to. I was pretty sure I shook visibly now, and it was only partly due to the cold. That boy had no idea what he was asking. If he didn't hate me so much and he wasn't an evil supernatural being, I'd be on him like black on Cookie's toast.

That woman could not make toast.

I let go of my musings when he turned to look at me over the expanse of a powerful shoulder. When he arched a shapely brow. When he engaged his tractor beam and pulled until my feet started moving me forward. Damn it. He was an alien. I should have known. An evil, throw-me-against-a-wall-and-fuck-me alien. Aka, the worst kind.

I stepped inside the sparse motel room and almost climaxed. It was so warm, it hurt. In a hurts-so-good kind of way. My frozen skin didn't know what to think. How to react. What color to be. It tingled as if pins were pricking it, or maybe tattoo needles. I was pretty sure I knew what it felt like to get a tattoo. I had one. A little-girl grim reaper on my left shoulder blade. Just didn't remember getting it. Maybe that was where the scythe dreams were coming from.

Reyes walked out of the bathroom and handed me a towel before stepping around me to close the door to my one and only exit. I wanted to be afraid. I wanted to be very afraid, but I couldn't quite manage it, the warmth felt so good.

He walked to a small kitchenette, poured me a cup of

coffee, and doctored it without asking me how I took it. Not that it mattered. My answer would have been "Any way I can get it."

My Pavlovian response kicked in at the smell, at the sound of the spoon clinking against the ceramic cup, at the steam billowing over the sides of it, and I had to swallow my enthusiasm. I'd put the sandwiches on a rickety table and was scrubbing my hair with the towel when he handed me the mug and gestured for me to sit. He sat on the other side, then stretched his long legs out and crossed them at the ankles, his motorcycle boots making a clunking sound.

The whole thing was so casual, so everyday, it felt oddly comforting. I wasn't sure what I expected, but *everyday* did not make the list. Sadly, clandestine orgies and human sacrifice did.

"Thanks," I said, taking a sip. Then I tried not to moan. I had no idea if I succeeded, I was so lost in the moment.

He wrapped strong fingers around his glass and examined it, but only for a second before turning his attention back to me.

I cleared my throat, then asked, "How long have you been staying at a motel?"

"Few weeks."

I nodded. Took another sip. "Do you like it?"

"It's a bed."

I nodded again and looked around, mostly to keep my wayward gaze from locking on to his chest. He had clothes draped over a third chair in a corner, clothes I'd seen him wear often, simple yet exquisitely tailored. The bathroom light was on, and I saw a few manly toiletries, but nothing extravagant. And the bed looked like it had been made before someone lay across it. Before Reyes lay across it.

"How long are you planning on staying?"

"Long as it takes."

"As long as what takes?" Was he a temp of some kind? Perhaps a construction worker or professional assassin?

"My business."

"Oh." Clearly he had no intention of elaborating. "What do you think of the town? Do you like it here?"

That time, he thought about his answer more thoroughly. When he spoke, it was with a singular intensity. "I like some of the people in it."

I brightened. "Me, too. I love Cookie, the woman I work with, and her husband, Bobert." When he raised a questioning brow, I amended the name. "Robert, actually. I just call him Bobert. And I like Dixie, my boss. She's so great."

"And the cop?"

His questions surprised me. "The cop?"

He dropped his gaze back to the glass. "Your boyfriend."

"Ian?" I asked, taken aback. "He's not my boyfriend."

"You're always with him."

My eyes rolled of their own accord. "No, he is always with me. Big difference."

"Then tell him to get lost."

Who was he to tell me what to do? I stood, utterly annoyed. "I'll tell him when I'm good and ready. What do you care, anyway? You have throngs of women throwing themselves at you. Have you told any of them to get lost?"

"Throngs?" he asked, eyeing me as I picked up the sandwiches and headed for the door.

"And why did you invite me in here when you're in a relationship?"

"I'm in a relationship?"

I turned. As if he didn't know. "You're seeing Francie."

"I'm not seeing anyone. And who the hell is Francie?"

"The waitress at the café? The gorgeous redhead with legs as long as the L train?" When he continued to frown, I added, "You always sit in her section? She serves you coffee and giggles every time you look her way?"

He shook his head. "No clue."

Even though he had to be lying, his answer made me much happier than it should have. Then reality sank in. "Wait, she told me where you live. She implied that she'd visited. More than once. Described the carpet even."

"Then she's breaking and entering." He took another swig. "Would it bother you if she had visited?"

I snorted. "Not even." I'd planned on storming out, but my curiosity got the better of me. I strolled to his nightstand. Ran my fingers along a Rolex. He must have met Scooter, too, though his looked way more authentic than mine. "So, why are you living in a motel?"

I felt a slight bristle come off him.

"I was . . . seeing someone."

A soft gasp escaped me. No idea why that would surprise me. "Was?"

"She left me. No good-bye. No note. Nothing. Just vanished into thin air. I had nowhere else to go."

I sat on the side of the bed. "I'm sorry, Reyes. When did that happen?"

"A while back. I'll get over it. I have no choice. She's forgotten all about me."

"I seriously doubt that." No woman in her right mind could forget the likes of Reyes Farrow. Of that I was sure.

I glanced up at the thermostat. It read fifty-five, but it had to be at least seventy-five in the room. My bones were finally beginning to thaw. "I think your thermostat is broken."

He didn't answer. He didn't even look at it, and while

I loved the attention he showered upon me, I had places to be and people to save. Fingers crossed.

"Well, thank you for letting me warm up." I stood and tried to hand him the towel. He stood, too, but didn't take it, so I draped it over the back of the chair I'd been sitting in. "I have to get home."

"I'll drive you."

"It's one block."

"It's seven degrees."

"I'll be fine."

"You'll be frozen."

I didn't dare let him drive me home. I would attack. I knew it as surely as I knew the sun was going to rise at dawn. Being in his presence here was bad enough. But get me in a car with him, a warm one with soft music and mood lighting from the dashboard, and I'd be a goner. A goner with a criminal record once Reyes filed charges against me for assault.

It was so time to leave. I put my hand on the doorknob then turned to say good-bye. He stood right behind me.

He was so unimaginably warm. I'd never felt anything like it. Heat drifted over me, saturated my soaking-wet shirt, penetrated every pore on my body.

I started to open the door, but he reached over me and pushed it shut. Before I could question him, he took the bag of sandwiches from me and draped a jacket over my shoulders. A thick leather jacket that weighed more than I did. It swallowed me. Cocooned me in him. His warmth. His scent.

"I can't take your jacket."

"I have another," he said, turning me to face him so he could zip it up as I threaded my arms into the sleeves. I watched as his long fingers tugged at one side and fastened it. The muscles in his forearm bunched and flexed with the effort. As did the ones on his chest and stomach. It took every ounce of self-control that I had not to reach out and slide my fingertips over them. He did the same with the other side, and I realized the jacket was adjustable.

Unfortunately, it didn't help much. It still swallowed me, and I no longer had shoulders or hands, but that was okay, too. The length would keep my fingers from turning into flesh-flavored Popsicles. He curled the cuffs, but only once. They still hung past my fingertips.

After a moment, I realized he'd stopped and was staring down at me. I looked up into the glittering depths of his mahogany irises. A soft line had formed between his brows as he studied me, and I realized for the thousandth time I could not read him. Not like I could most people. I felt emotion roiling within him, but it was jumbled, chaotic, a mixture of desire and concern and regret.

His gaze dropped to my mouth, and I wondered just how many drinks he'd had. So I asked.

"Just how many drinks have you had?"

"Not enough," he said, his voice oceans deep.

"Not enough to forget her?" To forget the woman who still haunted him? The jealousy that spiked within me did nothing to boost my self-esteem.

"There isn't enough alcohol on the planet to make me forget her."

That stung. He was clearly hung up on his ex, and I was standing there like a schoolgirl hoping to be asked to prom. A foolish schoolgirl.

Humiliation burned beneath my skin. "Please excuse me," I said, grabbing the bag and jerking open the door. I rushed into the frozen air again. The jacket helped, but it wouldn't have mattered either way. I ran as fast as I could without slipping on the ice, embarrassment and a devastating sense of loss driving me forward.

I didn't realize until I locked the door to my apartment and leaned against it, panting, that my cheeks were covered in frozen tears. I was such an idiot. And my heart hurt. Bad. Every beat sent an ache rocketing through my body. I was having a heart attack. Or, more likely, my heart had just broken.

Either way, I realized my mistake—my attention was not where it should have been—when a man walked up beside me and grabbed my arm.

8

My heart lurched and lodged somewhere in my esophagus as I tried to karate-chop the intruder. Sadly, I didn't know karate. And he was very well versed in escape and evasion. He easily sidestepped my blow and ducked past the next one.

"It's me," he said, catching my arm again.

I jerked out of his grip. "What the fuck, Ian?"

"Where have you been?"

I gaped at him. He'd essentially broken into my apartment and he was grilling me? "How did you get in here?"

He dangled a key in front of my face, his watery blue eyes waterier than usual. He'd been drinking. "I was worried about you." As though that would explain away the key.

"How did you get a key to my apartment?" I asked, strolling to my cracker-box kitchen and setting the bag on the counter, thoroughly annoyed with myself. I'd forgotten to get James his sandwich, as frozen and mushed as it was.

James was a homeless guy who lived in an abandoned, partially collapsed shed across the street from me. I'd never actually seen him. I'd heard him. He always sang as I walked home from work, and I finally stopped to talk to him one day. He wouldn't come out of his cubby of boxes and blankets, but he did tell me his name was James and that he was from the planet Hazelnut. Before that, I'd had no idea there even was a planet named Hazelnut, but I totally wanted to move there. Hazelnut tasted great in coffee. I fucking loved science.

"I had one made in case of emergency," he said.

I wiped at my face furiously. This had gone too far. It was time to end it. Right after he gave me a ride back to the café. I would have borrowed Mable's car, which had actually been my plan, but it wasn't in the drive. Apparently her great-nephew had borrowed it again. That kid was such an inconvenience.

"I was worried about you," Ian continued. "You freaking passed out at work. You could have a concussion."

"I don't. Someone caught me before I hit the floor."

Emotion spiked inside him. "Who?"

"A guy. You don't know him. Wait, how did you get into my apartment again?"

When he dangled the key a second time, I swiped it out of his hand.

"What the hell?" he asked, trying to swipe it back, but I'd curled it into my fist and stuck it behind my back. If he wanted it, he was going to have to fight me for it, and I was not above swallowing it, though the key ring might present a problem. Also, I didn't particularly cherish the thought of another visit to the emergency room. That would take some explaining.

"You don't get to just make copies of people's keys, Ian. I'm pretty sure that's illegal."

"Not when they're dating."

I leveled a warning glare on him as I took off Reyes's jacket and walked back to my bathroom. I'd wanted a scorching-hot Reyes, but a scorching-hot shower would have to do. Yet I couldn't even have that with Ian here. "Ian, we're not dating. We talked about this."

"What do you call it then?"

He followed me. Into the bathroom. Unbelievable.

"We go out to eat," he argued. "We go to the movies. We watch television together."

When I looked in the mirror, I wanted to cry. I really was blue. My lips were a particularly pretty shade of violet, had they been a sweater or a sport drink. And my hair resembled a wig that had caught fire.

I ran my fingers through it and cringed. Reyes had seen me like this. I couldn't have looked worse if I'd had scales and a forked tongue.

"What do you call that?"

"Hanging," I said, dragging out the tiny travel blow-dryer I found at Goodwill. It was worth every cent of that two dollars and, sadly, not much more. It would take forever to dry my hair, so I concentrated on the roots. I yelled at Ian over the sound of the dryer. "That's what friends do, Ian. They hang." Not for much longer, though, if I had anything to say about it. This was getting downright creepy.

I rethought telling Ian about Mr. Vandenberg. He didn't seem the most stable of men. Maybe Bobert would come through and I could talk to the FBI tomorrow. Until then,

Mr. V and his family were in mortal danger. I needed to get to the café and check to see if he'd gone back to the shop. If those men were still with him. Maybe they got what they were after and left, but I doubted it. I tried to come up with a plan. If only I could slip a note to Mr. V somehow. I'd have to think on it.

"We going to dinner?" Ian asked over the hum of the dryer, dismissing the conversation we'd been having.

"If you want to eat at the café, we are."

He wilted. "I wanted to take you somewhere nice."

"I'm not dressed for nice. I look like a blue Popsicle with hair."

A smile slid across his face. He was trying to make amends. "I like Popsicles."

It didn't work. Sadly, if Reyes had said that, I would have melted into a pretty blue puddle. Ian didn't give my girly bits quite the same zing.

"Out," I said once I got my roots fairly dry and the rest of my hair pulled up into a ponytail. I pointed to the door, ordering my unwanted company out. I had to change if I was going anywhere, and the last thing I wanted to do was give Ian another reason to think there was more between us than there was by changing in front of him. That would be equivalent to throwing gasoline onto a fire.

He backed out, his slow moves evidence of his reluctance. What did he think? I'd scramble out the window? I looked toward it. It was way too small. I'd never make it.

"I'll warm up the car," he said.

I gave him a thumbs-up, then shut the door and collapsed against it. The Reyes Effect was still screaming though me, pulsing along my nerve endings, whetting my appetite for more. But it didn't matter. I had to get my hormones under control. He loved someone else, and there was nothing I could do about it. Absolutely nothing.

I changed clothes, then pulled Reyes's jacket on, breathing him in as I did so. Before I left, I said a quick good-bye to Irma.

"Hold down the fort, Irm!"

I had no idea what her name really was. She was there when I'd rented the apartment, hovering with her nose in a corner, never moving, never speaking, her toes several inches from the floor. She wore a bright floral muumuu and love beads despite her tiny stature and advanced age. She was old enough for blue hair, so I was guessing she was at least seventy.

I almost didn't rent the apartment when I saw her there, but I really needed out of that storeroom, and this was the only thing I could afford. Once I got used to her, I couldn't imagine the apartment without her.

As usual, I didn't get a reply from Irma. Ian was in his running car when I braved the cold once again. At least it had quit raining at last. I held up an index finger to tell him to give me a minute, then ran next door and knocked lightly on Mable's window. I didn't want to wake her if she was already asleep, but she called out for me to come in.

"Hey, hon," I said, dragging a frozen, wet sandwich out of the paper bag.

Mable was already in her pajamas and housecoat, getting ready to settle down for the evening. "Have you seen my brush?" she asked me. "The brown one?"

I chuckled. "Not lately. I brought your favorite, but it's kind of squished. And frozen."

"Oh, honey, squished and frozen are my middle names."

Yesterday her middle name was suppository. Long story.

She hurried over, her face the picture of glee. Surely she could roast the sandwich to dry it out a bit. Make it crunchy.

"Can I borrow the car when Stan brings it back?"

"You can borrow it now. He doesn't have it. Little shit wrecked it the other night."

Alarmed, I asked, "Is he okay?"

"He's fine. It was just a fender bender. Barely left a scratch. Nothing to write the governor about."

That woman loved to write the governor. "That's good. So it's not in the shop?"

"Nope. It's in my backyard. He doesn't get to take it anymore until he pays for the damage."

"God bless you. Kids these days." I didn't mention the fact that Stan and I were very close to the same age.

"But you can take it anytime, sweet cheeks."

"Thank you," I said, rushing around her counter to give her a squeeze.

She fought me off with a threatening wave of her spatula, but relented and let me give her a quick hug.

"Key's on the hook."

I grabbed the key to her Fiesta, wishing I'd known about the car situation beforehand. I could've avoided another evening with the cop voted most likely to be put on administrative leave pending a psych eval. It was a real award. Oh well, surveillance could begin later. It might be better if it did, in fact. I could check out Mr. V's house after bedtime when everyone had settled in for the night.

I ran outside, held up my finger again to an ever-more-agitated Ian, and sprinted across the street, only almost busting my ass on the ice once. I saw a soft glow coming from inside the shed. He must have gotten oil for his lamp.

I picked my way carefully through the brush and to the fallen structure. "James?" I called out.

He didn't like me to get too close, so I put the bag just outside what used to be the shed door.

"I'm leaving your sandwich here. I apologize for the state it's in."

After a moment, I heard a grunt and then a honk.

A honk!

Ian had honked at me. I whirled around and glared at him, though I doubted he could see me. I would not be honked at. That was absolutely the final straw. This ended tonight.

I could've just broken off our friendship right then and there and taken Mable's car, but I wanted to explain to him why we couldn't see each other anymore. And I wanted to do it in a public place. I didn't trust him. Thinking back, I'd never really trusted him. Even that first night.

We drove to the café, which took all of two minutes, in absolute silence. He knew the honking thing had set me on edge, so he wisely kept his mouth shut. His emotions, however, raged behind his stony visage, and they spoke volumes. He was pissed. At me. For being mad at him. At least that was my guess. Of all the gall. I suddenly could not wait for our relationship to come to an end.

But I'd been wrong. Once we pulled up to the café, he turned off the engine and faced me. "Whose jacket is that?"

He was just noticing? Some cop.

"It's a friend's."

"What friend? You don't have any friends."

"Well, fuck you very much," I said, turning to leave.

He grabbed my arm for the second time that evening. I did a twisty move and jerked out of his grip. For the second time that evening.

"Look, Ian, this whole friendship thing we have going on isn't really working out for me."

"Really?"

"Really. I would love to be friends with you, but you don't know where to draw the line. I see no other choice but to end our friendship altogether."

The calmness that came over him should have been a sign. An indicator of what he was truly capable of. I felt anger swell hot and fast inside him, but on the outside, he was a picture of amiable reserve, the way a nun might be at a kegger.

"I'm sorry," he said, his tone soft as though he were talking to a child. "Let's just have dinner, okay? Then we can talk about it."

"There's nothing to talk about."

He lowered his head, and I saw the shimmer of wetness gather between his lashes. But nowhere in his emotions did I pick up even a hint of remorse. "I'm so bad at this. I know. And I'm sorry, Janey. I don't want to lose you as a friend."

Praise the Lord. At least we were finally back to being friends and nothing more. That, I could live with. Maybe.

"So, we're friends, right?"

He raised a hopeful expression. "Right."

"Nothing more?"

"Nothing more. I just . . . Well, you're really special to me, and I just worry about you."

I had to admit, he was a good actor, but a coldness had settled over him. He was resting one hand on the keys still in the ignition as though waiting for my response. I had little choice but to do some character acting myself.

I smiled at him and, taking that extra step that always impresses directors, threw my arms around his neck. His anger dissipated, though not entirely, and he hugged me back.

When I pulled away, I said, "Let's eat, yes?"

For the barest fraction of a microsecond, he narrowed his lids in suspicion.

I didn't give him a chance to dwell on my sudden shift in moods very long. I bounced out of the car with a flirty "I'm starved."

He followed at a slower pace, so I wrapped an arm in his, sending him a thousand different mixed signals. But his peace of mind was hardly my priority. I just wanted to be near people. People who could call the police should the need arise.

I totally needed a phone.

Making sure to sit where I could see the alley, I scooted into a booth. Ian tried to sit next to me. After I shot him a warning glare on the dos and don'ts of friendship, he moved to the other side.

Shayla, a tiny, fairylike creature who defined the phrase *cuter than a bug's ear,* brought us some menus. "Can't get enough of us?" she asked, teasing.

"It's the excellent service."

She giggled, took our drink orders, and went to wait on another table. I was half hoping Reyes would be in. Maybe we couldn't have a relationship, but I could damned well look upon him when he presented himself to be looked upon. That wasn't so much stalking as appreciating. Like art. And porn.

We'd barely sat down when a truck pulled up behind Mr. V's antiques store. I was hoping to see more of the van Cookie and I had seen that morning behind the dry-cleaning business. It hit me some time later that most supply vans rarely carried boxes *out* of a business. Wasn't it their jobs to carry boxes of supplies inside? So what would they have been carrying out?

I'd racked my brain trying to remember which supply company the van had been with, but it just wasn't coming to me.

Cleaner Supply Warehouse.

I blinked in surprise. It popped into my head out of nowhere the moment I'd stopped trying to remember it. I saw the green lettering on the white van clear as sunshine, a commodity we'd had far too little of lately.

I jumped up, grabbed a pen off the checkout counter, and wrote the name down. I'd look the company up later. See how legit they were. For now, I focused on the truck, a red four-door Chevy I didn't recognize. Two men got out and put the tailgate down. There was some kind of equipment in the back. I leaned in, but it was just too dark to see. Also, a set of fingers began snapping in my face.

My ire rocketed to an all-time high as I scowled at Ian.

He scowled back, his patience seeming to run thin as well. His audacity was reaching new levels of stupidity by the second. Why did I ever put up with him? Because when I first showed up, I had no one and he was nice.

"Are you even on earth?" he asked.

I bit back a retort. I had him in a public place. I could end things for good here, but first I needed to get a look at the contents of the truck before they hauled their load inside.

Still, I was finished worrying about his feelings. "Order me a quesadilla."

"What? Where are you going?"

"I'll be back," I said in my best Arnold voice, the niggling at the back of my mind concerned at how I could remember a line from a movie and, again, not my own name.

I hurried to the alley exit and snuck out the door, trying to stick to the shadows and ever so grateful for Reyes's jacket. Thankfully, there was a slight discrepancy in the length of the two buildings. They were connected, but the antiques store was a couple of feet longer, which gave me the perfect barrier to hide behind.

I leaned against the brick. The two men were unloading a piece of equipment, some black duffel bags, and a couple of plain boxes that looked pretty heavy. They put all of that on the ground and went inside.

Mr. V wasn't with them, and I didn't know how to feel about that.

A male voice spoke from behind me. "What are you doing?"

It was just loud enough to get one of the men's attention. He stopped and scanned the area while I pressed a finger over Garrett Swopes's mouth. It was warm under my freezing hand, his shadow scratchy and more than a little sexy.

Removing my finger from his mouth, I repositioned it over mine, then leaned back to see if the men had taken note of us. They were busy bringing boxes out of the shop.

"What is that?" I whispered to Garrett.

He leaned over me, gave the area a once-over, then whispered back, "Plasma cutter."

I frowned. "Why would they need to cut plasma?"

He grinned down at me. "Want to tell me what you're doing?"

"No."

"Does this have anything to do with the shopkeep's current state of captivity?"

I bolted upright. "You know?" I asked, amazed and relieved I wasn't the only one.

He stepped back. "I saw the men in his shop today when I walked past. Add to that the fact that he looked really uncomfortable . . ."

"Right? I saw them, too," I said, only partially lying.

"What do you think we should do about it?"

"I . . ." I just didn't know. What if something happened to Mr. Vandenberg because of something I did? Something I said? He'd been scared shitless that morning, impatient for me to leave. I lowered my head. "Nothing."

I started for the back door to the café.

"Nothing?" he asked. He leaned back against the brick and fidgeted with a rock he'd picked up, his breath fogging in the icy air. "You sure about that?"

"Yes, I'm sure. Why?"

"I don't know. Just doesn't seem in your nature to do nothing. To sit back and let people suffer."

I winced at the implication, but Mr. Vandenberg wasn't there. I would've felt him. If I tipped off the men holding him captive, what would they do to him?

"What if someone gets hurt because I got involved? What if I make it worse for Mr. V by reporting suspicious behavior? I think they have his family."

"You're right. That's solid reasoning if I ever heard it. But if that's truly the case, why are you out here?"

I nudged at the ice beneath my feet with the toe of my boots. "Just, I don't know, curious, I guess. Gathering intel to give the authorities. If I can find where they're keeping Mr. V and his family, the cops can rescue them before the captors even know what's happening." When he only nodded, I asked, "Do you have a better idea? One that doesn't get Mr. V or his family killed? I'm very fond of his kids."

He eyed me a long moment, then said, "I think your boyfriend's getting worried about you." He nodded toward the back door, where Ian stood, his figure a silhouette against the soft light streaming out.

"What are you doing out here?"

The shadows of Garrett's face formed a soft grin. "Taking a piss."

"I was telling Garrett we have a restroom inside," I said, trying to cover.

Ian walked out to join us, flabbergasted. "You strolled outside while a man was taking a piss to offer him the use of your facilities?"

"It wasn't like tha—"

"And public urination is illegal."

Fuck. Ian was a cop. I tended to forget that little nugget of fun.

He leveled a hard gaze on Garrett, a man I was finding more intriguing by the moment, then took a step closer, waiting for a response.

"Yeah, well, I was on my way home when the urge hit." He was not helping. Especially when he matched Ian's stance and took a step closer himself. The challenge crackled in the air around us, the tension combustible.

"He wasn't actually peeing," I said, growing exasperated again. I put a hand on Ian's arm to defuse the situation. "I'll be inside in a minute."

Instead of appeasing him, however, I enraged him. "Don't patronize me," he said through gritted teeth, turning on me this time. His anger stirred the wisps of hair on my face.

Garrett took a casual step back and leaned against the brick again, where he stood assessing the situation, thank God. I didn't know what Ian was capable of, not entirely, but I could only imagine what would happen to Garrett if he assaulted a cop.

I had no choice but to bring Ian into the fold. To explain our actions. "Look, Ian, I think—I mean, there might be something going on next door."

I led him away from Garrett to give us the illusion of privacy.

"How do you know him?" he asked, completely ignoring me.

"What? Ian, I'm trying to report a crime."

"You seem to know him really well."

"Are you even listening to me? I think something is happening"—I lowered my voice even further—"at Mr. Vandenberg's store."

Frustrated, he finally asked, "What?"

"There are men over there. They have plasma cutters."

His eyes widened, mocking me. "Not plasma cutters."

"And today, Mr. Vandenberg seemed really upset. Like something was wrong."

"Of course something was wrong. His wife took the kids and left him. It's all over town."

Holy shit, that gossip chick worked fast. I wasn't going to argue with him. His mind was made up, and all he cared about was my conversation with Garrett.

"Where do you know him from? Work?"

I brightened. "Yes. I deliver lunch to him sometimes. And today, he just seemed—"

"Not Vandenberg," he said, his tone as glisteningly sharp as a chef's knife. "That guy. Swopes." I paused, taking note of the vehemence in his voice. And the fact that he called him Swopes instead of Garrett, a name I hadn't used. Had he checked up on Garrett? Why would he do that? Either way, my patience had pretty much dissipated.

"You know what? I'm going to help close up. Maybe you should go home."

He went to grab my arm, and I stepped out of his reach.

"This is over," I whispered, throwing in a little vehemence of my own.

"You're upset," he said, suddenly trying to defuse the situation himself.

"That you broke into my apartment? That you order me around? That you won't take 'I just want to be friends' seriously? Noooo," I said, my tone dripping with sarcasm.

"Are you really saying we're over?"

"Ian, we never began."

"I'll give you some time to think about it."

I wanted to throw my arms up in exasperation. "I don't need time, Ian. I need you to leave."

"You don't know what you need."

This time the anger that flared around me was my own. I felt a flash of heat wash over me as he continued.

"I was there for you when you had no one."

"And I'm grateful, Ian, but you're a cop. It was your job. It doesn't mean I owe you my life."

His scowl glittered hot. "Doesn't it?"

"What the fuck is that supposed to mean?"

He pushed away from me, gave Garrett one last glare for good measure, then strode into the café, slamming the door behind him.

"So," Garrett said, "things are good between you two? You seem really happy."

"Thank you for not trying to stand up for me." And getting yourself arrested in the process.

"Somehow I doubt you needed my help."

What a sweet thing to say.

"Crazy chicks are usually pretty tough."

Or not.

"What are you going to do about him?"

"Ian? What do you mean?"

"You don't actually think that's the end of it?"

"Well, yeah, kind of. I mean, I just told him it was."

"Because that works so well with psychopaths."

He had a point. I'd received conflicting vibes from him since Day One. He was a habitual liar, had terrible anger issues, and wore the same shirt for days at a time. He definitely had mental issues. Then again, I was standing in a dark alley with someone I hardly knew. I turned away from him, exasperated, and saw a kid standing at the end of the alley.

"Is that Osh?" I asked Garrett.

The kid stood with his hands in his pockets, his breaths fogging around him, so it was hard to see his face, but how many teens wore top hats? He glanced over his shoulder toward us, then just as quickly turned back to the street.

"Looks like it," he said.

A car pulled up then. Osh leaned over and spoke to the driver before it pulled away again.

Alarmed, I asked, "Is he selling drugs?"

"Nah, I think he's a male prostitute."

I gasped. Placed a hand over my heart. He was so young. And absolutely stunning. He had his whole life ahead of him. Why?

"It's okay," Garrett said. "He's been a whore for a long time."

My heart broke until I realized he was laughing softly.

I glared at him. "Are you teasing me?"

"Not at all. He's a manwhore. Ask him."

After crossing my arms, I said, "He's just a baby."

"Baby, my ass."

"How well do you know him?"

"I just met him today."

"Fine, I give up. I'm heading in to eat. You hungry?"

Before he answered, he looked down the street to where Osh stood. In my peripheral vision I saw Osh tip his hat like a fine gentleman, then walk away.

"I better not," Garrett said. "I have some work to do."

"Your loss," I teased, but he cast me a serious expression.

"It is indeed."

9

Without coffee, I'm just a really tall two-year-old.
—T-SHIRT

When I walked back into the café, the warm café, Shayla was just placing the plates on our table. Or, well, my table, since Ian had been invited to leave.

She glanced up nervously. "Um, your date . . ."

"Left," I finished for her. "I asked him to."

"Oh, perfect, then."

It was about that time I noticed where all the heat originated. Reyes sat at a table a few feet away, studying the menu. I slowed my pace, suddenly aware of every hair out of place. I could only hope my lips hadn't turned blue again.

I scooted into my booth as Shayla brought me some extra salsa—she knew me so well—her MedicAlert bracelet sparkling in the fluorescent light.

"Dang, girl," I said, admiring it. "You blinged-out your medical bracelet. That's cool."

She laughed and shook it so that the fake diamonds caught as much light as possible. "My dad did it for me."

"He sounds fantastic."

"He is," she said, before walking off.

I glanced at Reyes periodically as I ate, a man I could never have and yet craved so powerfully, it scared me.

He was wearing the shirt he'd had on earlier—only buttoned up—and no jacket. That fact caused a soft flood of alarm. Did he lie to me when he said he had another? No way was I taking his only jacket.

I wiped my hands, then walked over to his table. I'd left the motel rather abruptly and felt I owed him an apology. At least, that was the excuse I was going to give for my intrusion.

He'd splashed on a hint of very expensive cologne, and it wafted toward me as I got closer. Even though he only wore the button-down, he didn't seemed chilled at all. In fact, he'd rolled up the sleeves. I was beginning to realize he was his own furnace. Generated his own heat.

He watched me walk up. Had been watching me from the moment I left my booth, his gaze shimmering beneath the shadow of his lashes.

When I stopped in front of him, he raised his head. "Ms. Doerr," he said, making the name sound like a mixed drink.

"Mr. Farrow. I wanted to apologize for my—"

"No, you didn't," he interrupted, the barest hint of a smile tugging at one corner of his mouth.

"Fine." I pulled out a chair and sat across from him. "Is this your only jacket?"

"No," he said. He wasn't lying, but that didn't mean he had another jacket with him. It could still be at his ex's or something.

"You just chose not to wear one tonight? On one of the coldest nights of the year?" He didn't answer, so I continued. "Do you need your jacket back?" I started to take it off, but he held up a hand.

"Keep it. It looks better on you."

Clearly he'd never looked in a mirror. Ever. "It swallows me."

"I'd swallow you, too, if I could."

A combination of elation and bewilderment bucked inside me, and I lowered my head, embarrassed. "If you need it back, will you promise to let me know? I should have mine in a couple of days." Again he didn't answer, so I spurred him with "Promise?"

I'd placed one hand on the table. He reached over and touched his fingertips to mine. The contact was like an electrical current, and my pulse stumbled on its own beat.

"Cross my heart."

I pulled my hand away, confused. He was obviously still hung up on his ex. He made no bones about it. But he felt genuine interest in me as well. I just didn't know how to handle it. If I should steer clear until he recovered from his recent breakup or not. The last thing I wanted was to be the rebound girl. Those relationships never lasted.

Besides, I thought as I offered a quick wave before getting up to leave, I might already have a husband. What would he think of me?

"Can I get you anything else, Janey?" Shayla asked.

The café had begun to fill up with women. Odd how that happened every time Reyes showed up. Shayla seemed to be the only one immune to his charms, and I was pretty sure I knew why. The other two servers had things under control, so I asked Shayla to sit with me a minute.

Tomorrow was a big day. I wanted to give Shayla as

much of a fighting chance as Lewis, the busboy, was giving Francie. If all went as planned, Lewis's cousin was going to fake-rob us. Lewis was going to knock him out, and Francie was going to fall in love. But I had a feeling Shayla deserved his love way more than Francie did. Shayla saw Lewis when Francie didn't. I felt it every time she looked at him.

"I can sit for a sec," she said, scooting into the booth opposite me.

"So, what do you think about Lewis?"

I'd caught her off guard. She lifted her fingertips to her mouth to chew on a nail. "I think he's pretty great," she said from behind an index finger.

"I do, too."

One corner of her mouth tipped up as she thought about the man she'd been in love with for probably quite a while. "He was so nice to me in school."

"You guys went to school together?"

She nodded, her enthusiasm infectious. "Oh, yeah. He was so smart. And he was a geek, but not, like, a total nerd."

"Yeah, the Star Trek shirt he wears says it all."

"Right? It's red. Get it?"

When I frowned, she said, "It's like he's tempting fate. You know? Like he's saying, 'I'm going to wear the red shirt. Show me what you got, universe.'"

"The red shirt says all that? Impressive."

She nodded, the barest hint of a dimple appearing on her right cheek. "Most people don't get him, but in school, he was the smart kid who didn't act smart. He was nice to everyone."

I could see that about Lewis. What I couldn't see was why Shayla didn't say anything. She never even attempted to flirt with him. "Why don't you tell him how you feel?"

Her eyes became saucers. "I couldn't do that. I mean . . .
He doesn't . . . He's not—"

"How about this?" I said, stopping her before she had
a panic attack. "How about you say hi. You know, maybe
strike up a conversation about his band."

She melted a little at the mention of Lewis's band,
Something Like a Dude.

"All guys like to talk about themselves. It'll be great."

I was doing this because I had a feeling even a heroic
stunt like saving Francie's life was not going to turn her
focus off Reyes. Not for long, anyway. Shayla could be
there to pick up the pieces of his broken heart.

"At least think about it." She acquiesced with a nod.

I finished my quesadilla and decided I'd waited long
enough. I needed to surveil, to find where Mr. Vandenberg's family was being held, and to somehow get them
help. My strides were brisk as I walked home, but that
didn't keep a car from following me. It was slick black and
fancy. I pretended not to notice and kept walking. Eventually the car turned off, and I practically ran the rest of the
way home.

Since I had the keys to Mable's 1990 Ford Fiesta, I ran
straight to her backyard and started it up. It was ugly as
all get-out, but it got me from point A to point B. And,
thankfully, the heater worked really well.

I'd looked up Mr. V's address on the Internet and drove
out to Philipse Manor. He lived in a ritzier part of town
than I did. Pretty much any part of town was ritzier than
mine, but his was super ritzy. He definitely had money. I
wondered why the men didn't just take his money and go.
Maybe it wasn't that simple. Maybe he had all his income
tied up in hedge funds and shrubbery funds and biennial
cabbage funds.

I was so bad at giving investment advice.

I drove past the Vandenbergs' house, parked about half a mile away, started to walk to the house, got back in the car, drove until I was about a quarter of a mile away, then got out again. The icy wind whipped around me and slipped into any opening in my clothing it could find. Where was a supernatural furnace when I needed one?

After risking my life by scaling an iron fence with pokey things on top, I scurried to the dark house. All the curtains were closed, but it didn't look like a single light was on inside. I closed my eyes and concentrated. Reached out. But I felt no emotion of any kind. My pulse sped up. If they weren't at this house, the captors could be keeping the Vandenbergs anywhere.

"What's up, *chiquita*?"

I jumped at the sound of Angel's voice behind me and considered exorcising him. But first I had to ask him about the conversation I overheard today.

"This guy giving you a hard time?" he asked me.

"What guy?" I turned to where he'd nodded. An elderly departed man stood not two feet from me, trying to poke me with a stick. An incorporeal one. Had he died with it in his hands? His hands were shaky, so he kept missing, which worked for me.

"I'm kind of investigating something. Can you go into this house and see if anyone is inside?"

"For you, *mi amor,* anything. And then we can make out."

"Dude, you are like twelve years old. Really?"

He straightened his spine, rising to his full height. All five feet two of it. "First of all, I died when I was thirteen. But that was years ago. I'm really old now, like, I don't know, forty or something."

"I think I'll pass anyway."

He shook his head, then disappeared after tossing out a quick "You don't know what you're missing."

A shudder ran through me. I didn't care how many years he'd been dead. Kid was thirteen. Bottom line. I felt a soft poke at my rib cage and brushed the stick aside.

About thirty seconds later, Angel popped back out again. "Not a warm body in sight. What's going on?"

I started to reply, then asked him, just in case, "By warm body, you aren't insinuating that there are some cold ones in there, are you?"

"Dead people?"

I swallowed hard and nodded.

"Nope. No dead ones either. But there is a really pissed-off cat."

"Oh, no!" I brushed off another poke and turned an exasperated glower on my attacker.

He lifted the stick and tried to poke my eye. What the hell?

After brushing him off again and stepping away from the elderly version of Charles Darwin as he attempted to identify a new species, I asked Angel, "Do you think it's hungry?"

"No idea," he said, chuckling. "Want me to go ask?"

My eyes widened in awe. "You can talk to cats?"

"Fuck no, I can't talk to cats. What the hell?" His brows crinkled just under the bandanna he wore, feigning insult if the laughter sparkling in his eyes was any indication. It made him look even cuter. Even younger.

But he did dis me. No way was I taking attitude from a punkass kid with no skeletal system.

"Look, half pint," I said, curling my frozen fingers into his dirty T-shirt. I drew him closer until we stood nose to nose. "I don't know how this shit works, so stop being a little bitch, go back in there, and find me a way inside so I can save the cat." I shoved him. Admittedly, not very hard.

A slow Cheshire grin slid across his handsome face. "Damn, girl. You got a set the size of a Cadillac. And here I thought you were all shy and sweet and helpless."

When I clenched my teeth and went for his shirt again, he held up his hands in surrender.

"I'm going. I'm going."

He disappeared just as my fingertips touched his shirt. He was lucky. That time.

While Angel searched for a way inside, I checked out the exterior, which was ridiculous in the dark. I could barely see beyond the otherworld enough to put two feet in front of me, much less find a way inside a locked mansion. Especially with Darwin poking me every five seconds.

"Seriously, dude. You have to stop."

"Got it!"

I jumped and whirled around. Angel stood behind me.

"There's a doggy door. A big one. You can squeeze in through there." He fought another grin. A suspicious one.

"All right, what's the catch?"

"No catch. It's just, I don't think you'll fit with your clothes on. Probably best if you take them off." When I deadpanned him, he added, "You wouldn't want to get them dirty."

"Not. Happening."

We strolled around to the back of the house, and he showed me the doggy door. Thankfully, he was right. It was for a large-breed dog. I could actually fit if I wiggled a lot. That should make him happy.

I took off Reyes's jacket and regretted it instantly. The frigid air swallowed me like an ice-filled ocean, and I gulped a lungful of icy air. Which actually didn't help. I got onto all fours and pushed the plastic door in. "I totally need a flashlight."

"No idea why. You're like the freaking sun."

But I was busy trying to get my shoulders past the door frame. It cut into them, then into my ribs, then into my ass. When I felt something in that general area, I said, "Angel, that had better be departed Darwin poking my ass."

"It is," he said, stifling a chuckle. "I swear."

I rolled my eyes and heaved my ass through the suddenly tiny opening. It hurt. The frame scraped across my legs. I was totally going to bruise.

"Okay," I said, lying on my back to catch my breath. "Where's the cat?"

But he didn't have to answer. The cat poked its head around the corner, then pawed at my hair.

"Hey, kitty," I said a microsecond before it took a swipe at me.

Its needlelike claws took off half my face. I screamed and held on to the shredded remnants. The cat took the opportunity to purr and rub against me.

"Are you kidding?" I asked it from between gritted teeth.

It purred louder and threw in a hoarse meow every so often, twirling in dainty circles. It was fluffy. Gray. Deadly.

I looked at my hand. It was covered in blood. Or, well, one finger had a little blood on the tip. Either way, my face stung like the dickens.

I frowned at it. "All cats are evil. Just FYI."

"Are you going to play with the cat all night or help me look for food?"

"I'm helping already." I stood and brushed myself off, then started going through cabinets.

We were in the kitchen. Since Angel couldn't open cabinet doors, he just kind of walked through them, searching as he went. We decided to split up. Angel took the upstairs, and I took the bottom.

I called out to him. "We should probably look for clues as to the Vandenbergs' whereabouts while we're here, too. Maybe they're being held at a motel or something and the captors looked one up in the phone book. Do you see an open phone book?"

"I don't think other people process information the same way you do. Bad guys would not look in a phone book to find a motel."

I paused my search. "Why not?"

"They had a plasma cutter. They clearly planned this shit out. They aren't going to be looking up a motel at the last minute. A motel where a maid could walk in anytime or where the Vandenbergs could signal an SOS by tapping on the wall or something."

"You're right. Too public. Any luck yet?"

"Either they never fed their cat, or they are completely out of cat food."

"Wonderful. I'll have to go get some."

"You know what I'm curious about?" he asked.

"Why you can't get a date?"

He snorted. "No. Well, kind of, but aren't you curious about the dog?"

I rose onto my toes to see what the top row of cabinets in the laundry room had to offer. "What dog?"

"The dog that goes with the door."

I stilled. Why didn't I think of these things? I was so single-minded. I didn't have the attention span to focus on anything but the here and now.

"Did you see a dog?" I asked, glancing around warily.

"No. Where's this go?"

He'd found a door in the back of a supply closet. I stepped inside the closet. "Odd place for a door."

"It's a basement."

"Cool."

"Wait!" he yelled, but I'd already opened the door.

The stench hit me first, the pungent scent almost knocking me to my knees. I covered my mouth and stumbled back before I realized what I was smelling: death. It stung my nose, and I fought my gag reflex when a terrifying sense of dread washed over me.

"No," I whispered. My vision blurred instantly. "Please, no."

"Janey, wait!" Angel said, but I flew down the wooden stairs.

A fluorescent light must've been connected to a motion sensor, because it flickered on automatically, and I saw a mass of beautiful black and tan fur. The Vandenbergs had a German shepherd, and their captors had killed it. He lay on a cement floor with only a tiny bit of blood on his side.

I slammed my hands over my mouth. He was stunning. Magnificent. The ultimate protector. And he'd paid the ultimate price. I reached out a shaking hand to pet him. He was too still. Too quiet.

I dropped to my knees and ran my fingers through his thick fur. Nuzzled his ears. Leaned over the gorgeous beast and whispered, "You tried, didn't you, boy? I promise I'll find them."

"Janey," Angel said. He'd draped an arm over my shoulder and was tugging gently. "We have to go."

I nodded, gave the beautiful dog one last caress, then stood up. I knew now that the Vandenbergs' captors meant business and that the family was in serious danger. I had no choice but to tell the police what I knew. But if they caught me at the house, the danger the Vandenbergs were in would get lost in the fact that I broke and entered.

"Okay," I said, wiping at my face, "I'm going to call 911, grab the cat, then run. The cops will show up and find the dog. They'll know something is wrong."

"Good plan, but maybe you should grab the cat first."

True. I picked up the cat, took a few hits for the team, then asked Angel if he saw a phone.

He looked around. "Nope."

"Wonderful." We searched the house again, this time looking for a phone, with no luck. "They must not have a landline. I thought all mansions came with landlines."

The cat took another swipe as Angel said, "You'll have to go to a pay phone or something and call in an anonymous tip."

"Good idea. I just have one problem."

"Just one?" he asked, brushing his finger through the cat's nose.

The cat swiped at him, and I was surprised. It actually saw him. Maybe I wasn't crazy after all.

"How am I going to get the cat through the doggy door?"

He turned to assess the situation. "You'll have to put the cat through first."

"What if it runs off?"

"Dude, it's a cat. It can hunt the shit out of this town."

"That doesn't help. Oh, wait." I grabbed a cookie out of a jar on the kitchen counter. "This'll keep it busy."

After enticing the cat with it, I tossed the cookie out the doggy door, then shoved the cat through. I suffered a few near-fatal lacerations in the process—fucking cat—but it seemed to work. The cat stayed put as I started to shimmy through the door after it.

"You know," Angel said, standing over me, "you could just unlock the door."

"Fuck." I shimmied back inside, unlocked the door, then ran for my life. Or, well, for Mable's car. The cat was none too happy about being manhandled, but there was nothing I could do about it at the moment except do my darnedest to dodge its claws. We had to hurry. Mostly because the alarm went off the second I opened the door.

We ran past departed Darwin, and I felt bad. Like I was abandoning him. So I grabbed his arm and tried to lead him to the car. When he refused to budge, I yanked at him.

"Janey, seriously, we have to go."

"Charles!" I yelled in his face. He snapped to attention. It would be crazy if that was really his name. Or if he really was Charles Darwin. I pointed to the car. "Move it!"

He loped after us. Angel helped with Charles while I tried to get into the car holding a volatile ball of fur with razors for claws.

I finally got it inside and tossed it in the backseat. It hissed. Like literally. After Angel got Charles inside the car, I turned the ignition and sped down the street. About two more blocks away, I pulled a U-ey, then parked to watch the cops. Thankfully, we'd hightailed it out of there before they came.

Angel tapped my shoulder and pointed.

"Crap." I'd taken off without Charles. "He must not know how this works. Can you go get him?"

"What if the cops come?" he asked.

"You're invisible."

"Right." He disappeared, then reappeared beside

Charles and dragged him all the way back to the car. After wrestling him inside again, he asked, "Just what are you going to do with him?"

"The cat?"

"The dead guy."

"I'm not sure. I just feel, I don't know, obligated somehow."

"Interesting," he said, peering out the windshield.

Charles, who was now in the backseat directly behind me, poked the back of my head.

"What's interesting?"

"What?"

"What's interesting?"

"You."

"How?"

"What?"

He was totally fucking with me. "How am I interesting?"

"Well, right now, you're not. But if we both got naked—"

Charles poked me again. I turned around, and he went for the eyes again.

I dodged his twig, then glared at him. "I will rip that ghost stick out of your hands, mister. Don't make me come back there."

And when he poked me a third time, I did just that. I took it from him, broke it in half, and tossed it out the window.

Charles gaped at me—for, like, ever—before he recovered and started poking me with his finger. I tightened my grip on the steering wheel and prayed for patience. Angel was right. I had no idea what to do with him. With either of them. Thankfully, the cat was busy taking potshots at Charles's wristwatch.

"Shouldn't they be here by now?" Angel asked.

"Yes, they should." I started to grow concerned. I grew even more concerned when, twenty minutes later, no cops.

"Hold on," Angel said. He disappeared, then reappeared. "The alarm is off."

"What the hell? Don't they have to check it out?"

"Not if they called him first."

I dropped my head back onto the headrest. "They did. They must've called his number. He had no choice but to tell the company it was an accident. But that means that Mr. V is probably still alive."

"You still gonna call the cops?"

"No. The captors must be on edge now. Anything could set them off. Could convince them to cut their losses—and the Vandenbergs' throats—and run."

Charles had finally stopped poking my head with his finger. He'd graduated to phrenology, examining every inch of my head by touch.

"What are you going to do?"

I turned to Angel, thankful that while the departed were solid to me, I could still see through them for the most part. Charles was now studying the shape of my eye sockets and the size of my nostrils.

"We drive around."

"Oh, hell, yeah," he said. "We'll cruise. Chill out a little. Check out the babes."

"Do people still say babes?" I asked him, starting the car.

"What? They don't?"

"I'm going to drive around town and, well, try to *feel* him. Is that dumb?"

"Only because he's married and he's probably not in the mood to be fondled right now."

"His emotions. They were so powerful today, maybe I'll be able to pick them up."

"Are you sure it's safe to drive with Charles glued to your face?"

"Probably not."

We drove around for hours. After we stopped for cat food and a bottle of water, that is. By the time we pulled up to my apartment, the cat was snoring, we'd lost Charles somewhere around North Washington, and Angel was telling me about the time he almost got to third base with Lucinda Baca. And while his stories were riveting, I was tired and disappointed and worried. I hadn't felt anything. I'd taken every single street in both Sleepy Hollow and Tarrytown to no avail.

I parked the car in Mable's backyard, curled the cat into my arms, and walked around to the front of my house.

"I wanted to marry her," Angel said, and I snapped back to his story. His statement brought into focus everything he'd lost.

"I'm sorry, Angel. How did you die?"

A sad smile slid across his face. "It's a long story. Maybe tomorrow?"

"Okay."

He stepped back, and I'd learned that when he did that, he was about to vanish. I stopped him with a hand on his arm. "Thank you. For all your help tonight. I don't know what I would have done."

"You would have been just fine. You're always fine."

"You clearly don't know me well," I said, with a soft laugh.

I let go of him, but before he disappeared, he leaned in and kissed my cheek. Then he stepped back again, and right before he vanished, he said, "I know you better than anyone."

A soft gasp pulled cold air over my teeth and into my lungs. I lunged to grab him, but I missed. He'd said it with such confidence. Did he know me? Did he know who I was? If only I could somehow summon him back just by thinking about him. Lord knew when I'd see him again. He was as sporadic as psoriasis.

I turned to unlock my door, but something seemed out of place. I glanced inside and spotted a light on in the bedroom. A light that I knew was not on when I left my apartment, because it had burned out two days ago.

10

Signs you drink too much coffee:
You don't sweat. You percolate.
—INTERNET MEME

After sleeping in Mable's car—and longing for Denzel something fierce—I reported to work the next morning looking like something the cat dragged in, half eaten yet somehow still alive. Sadly, I didn't care. I'd finally braved my apartment that morning wielding Satana, the Vandenbergs' cat—I'd named her based on her personality—and a two-by-four named Leroy.

Whoever had been in my apartment was long gone, but by the time I screwed up the courage to go in, it was too late for me to take a shower. Not that I'd actually slept in the car. I was shivering and worried and my mind wouldn't stop, not even for a few seconds. If I couldn't find Mr. Vandenberg and his family, I would have no choice but to go to the police. They had protocols that would put the family in danger, but there was nothing I could do about that. I had high hopes that Bobert would be able to help me.

I strolled up to Cookie, pulling Reyes's jacket tighter around me. The same jacket that kept me from freezing to death. Also, Satana put out a lot of body heat.

"Did Bobert find out anything?" I asked Cookie.

She took one glance at me, then headed for the coffee-pot. I didn't have the heart to tell her I'd already had quite a bit of the dark elixir. When I couldn't sleep, I'd driven to a local convenience store and bought coffee to keep warm. Twelve times. So I was pretty psyched about the day. Other than the fact that I'd developed a tick in my left eye and slurred my *S*'s ever so little, all was good. I would find the Vandenbergs and then go to the police.

But the scent of freshly brewed java acted like one of those magnets that pick up cars at junkyards. It attached itself to my face and pulled me closer. Unable to resist, I followed Cookie to the pot before peeling off the jacket, the warm one that smelled like Reyes, that felt like him, that embraced me when he couldn't. After breathing in as much of him as I could, I draped it over my arm and took the cup Cookie offered me.

"Did you try to use the espresso machine again?" I asked her, noting the lovely brown splotches on her blouse.

"Yes. It hates me."

"I told you, it's like an Uzi. Short, controlled bursts. Otherwise it gets fussy."

"I know. I know. Did you get any sleep at all last night?" she asked.

"What makes you ask?" When she only lifted a pretty brow, I caved. "No. But I did get a lot of thinking done. And I burned a lot of calories." Shivering did that.

"That's a plus. What did you come up with?" She picked

up her own cup as Dixie—after giving me a quick once-over—went to unlock the front doors. I must've looked worse than I thought. I'd tried to tame my hair, then decided to go with my inner rock star.

"I've figured out how to cure world hunger and to travel through time."

"Good to know."

"The only hitch is we'll need to find a space freighter, a tiny bit of plutonium, and a wormhole."

"For the time travel?"

"Oh, no, that's for the world hunger. The time-travel thing is way easier. I just need a billionaire investor with loose morals."

"Don't we all."

"You know the family I told you about?"

"The one that might be held hostage?"

"Yes. Well, they aren't at their house. And I have no idea where else to look."

She gaped at me. "You went to their house?"

"Duh."

"Alone?"

"Duh." I took another sip. "So, Bobert?"

"Nothing yet. The guy he was supposed to meet with got another call last night."

Damn it. Maybe I should just call the FBI and leave an anonymous tip. I was hoping to explain the situation, but if anyone would know what I was going through, Cookie would.

I scooted in closer and lowered my voice. "What do you do when the police won't, you know, take you seriously?"

She blinked, confused.

"You know, when you *see* something and report it."

I added an air quote for emphasis. Only one, 'cause of the cup and all, but I think she got my point.

Dixie clapped her hands to spur us to life. The sharp sound rushed over my nerve endings—the same nerve endings that had been marinated in caffeine—and I had to close my eyes.

"Look alive, ladies. This is going to be a very good day."

"Is she smiling?" Cookie asked.

I looked over at her. "I think she is."

"She never smiles this early."

"Nobody smiles this early. It's illegal in seventeen states."

Dixie hurried up to us then, her grin way too wide and way too bright for her to be completely human. Damn it. She was an alien. It was the only logical explanation.

"I have some good news." She blinked. Waited for us to bite. When we took another sip instead, our movements completely in sync, she waved her hands, dismissing our impudence. "We have a new cook. He's going to be joining Sumi this morning."

"Didn't you tell us this yesterday and Sumi was a little less than thrilled?" I asked, but before she could answer, the man I least expected to see that early strolled into the café, his gait as predator-like as ever.

I gaped, watched him a few stunning seconds in which time slowed like it had been dipped in syrup. I hugged his jacket to me. He probably wanted it back. I wondered how odd it would look if I fought him for it. I wasn't afraid to pull hair.

"Reyes," Dixie said with a little too much glee. Did she know about the jacket? "I've told the girls, and everyone is so excited."

"Wait," I said, my jaw gaping. "He's the cook?"

Dixie nodded as Reyes strolled ever closer, his gaze locked on to me like a guided missile.

I noticed Cookie out of the corner of my eye. But it wasn't her behavior that captured my attention. It was her absolute lack of surprise. She knew!

I wanted to gape at her as well but decided not to take my eyes off the supernatural being standing far too close for my peace of mind.

"I'm not sure if you know everyone," Dixie continued. "This is Cookie and Janey. And in the kitchen we have Sumi and Kevin, our first-shift busboy." She elbowed me. "Reyes is an excellent cook. I think you'll be impressed."

When a silence as awkward as eighties hair fell over the place, I realized Dixie was waiting for a response.

I stammered and said, "I'm sure I will be."

"Nice jacket," Reyes said before making his way back to the kitchen.

"Can you believe it?" Dixie asked.

"Nope."

"Half the town is in love with him. He'll be great for business."

I looked through the pass-out window. Sumi, the tough-as-nails chef who could kill me with a toothpick, was just as smitten with Reyes as the rest of us. What the hell?

I looked at Dixie. "Are you sure about this?"

She graced me with a Grand Canyon grin. "Most definitely." Then she winked and leaned in. "Dude can cook."

"This just seems wrong," I said to Cookie when Dixie left. "On all kinds of levels. I mean, what do we really know about him? He could be a serial killer or a drug dealer or a—"

"Supermodel?" Cookie asked.

She had a point.

"But," I said, lowering a brow on her, "is there anything you want to tell me?"

Her lids widened, and her gaze darted to the left as though she were trying to come up with something. "I don't think so."

"You knew about this," I accused, my voice . . . accusing.

"What?" she asked, dropping her jaw. When I pursed my lips like the Church Lady, she caved. The Church Lady had that effect on people.

"All right, I did." She wilted under my harsh scrutiny, tried to look apologetic. It didn't work.

I was flabbergasted. "How? When? How?"

"Dixie told me yesterday while you were passed out on the cot."

She was lying. Partially, anyway. But I couldn't tell which parts she was lying about.

"Oh."

Pretty soon, however, it didn't matter. We turned back to watch the show. Reyes hooked an apron over his head, wrapped the ties around his waist, and folded them into a neat knot. The muscles in his forearms flexed with each movement. His biceps contracted and retracted with the minuscule effort. How could any man look as good putting on clothes as he did taking them off?

We leaned our heads together and admired the view until he turned toward us. At which point we jumped on the task at hand. That task consisted of Cookie grabbing a towel and polishing the lid of a saltshaker and me straightening napkins. Gawd, we sucked at improv. But suddenly I didn't care so much about how Cookie knew as about how it all came to be. I mean, Reyes? Here? At the café? All morning every morning?

This would be either my greatest fantasy come true or my worst nightmare.

We went about our day doing the usual. We also worked a little. Mr. P came in with stripper in tow and demon in gut like an evil embryo. I usually tried to ignore the thing inside him, but it had moved. It had turned. Just a little. Just enough to make me worry what would happen after it finished its gestation period. Would it hurt Mr. P? Was there anything I could do to help him?

One thing I did do last night while I was shivering off that fifth cup of coffee was come up with a plan about Erin. I was the only one who could see Creepy Decomposing Lady in her daughter's image, so maybe I could find out if the woman was a real threat or if she just liked photobombing. It could have been a total coincidence. But the fact that both of Erin's previous babies died suddenly put a kernel of doubt in my mind. No, more like a brigadier general of doubt.

First, I needed to get Erin's phone and check all of her images, so that was on my to-do list for the day. But I couldn't do that until she came in at eleven. My second plan was to get a message to Mr. V if he showed up for work.

A departed man, the same one that had been showing up every morning around that time, appeared in a booth in Cookie's section. He always sat at that same booth at the same time. I'd wondered about him. He had graying blond hair and a kind face, but he never spoke to me. He never even looked my way. I figured he was working shit out. I could understand that.

"Cookie, we have a breakfast order for Mr. Vandenberg next door," Dixie said. "Want to take it over?"

Already? That was awfully early for Mr. V to be ordering anything. He didn't even open until ten o'clock.

I lunged forward with my hand raised. "I'll take it!" I said. I'd panicked and shouted way more enthusiastically than I'd planned.

Reyes paused what he was doing—namely flipping the sexiest eggs I'd ever seen—and leveled a curious stare on me.

I cleared my throat. "Sorry. I can take it. I need to ask Mr. V about . . . a lamp."

Dixie took note of how many customers I had.

"I'll take care of your section," Cookie said. "I know how much that lamp means to you."

I could have kissed her, could've gone full girl-on-girl, I was so in love with her at that moment. But I held my desire in check. "Thanks, Cook. I won't be a minute."

After sliding into Reyes's jacket, I took the to-go order, then headed out, vowing to only look back once. I did. I glanced over my shoulder. Reyes was still watching me from beneath his lashes, all mysterious-like. A shudder of excitement rushed down my spine.

I hadn't walked halfway to Mr. V's store when I felt it. The stress. The anxiety. The unmitigated fear. This sucked, and I didn't know what to do.

I stood at the front entrance, working up the courage to follow through with my plan. After a moment, I pasted on my best smile, then stormed in as if I owned the place.

The man who'd sat watch on Mr. V yesterday was pulling the morning shift again today. He eyed me, and I could feel a wave of utter contempt radiate out of him. Either my hair was way worse than I'd thought or he considered me an infidel. Probably a little of both.

"Hey, Mr. V," I said, while beaming my best I-have-no-idea-that-you're-being-held-against-your-will smile.

He adjusted his glasses. "G'morning, Janey."

"Got your order. If you'll just sign this." I pushed the receipt over to him.

"Sign it?" he asked, seeming confused. Which was understandable, because he always paid in cash.

I was confused as well, because I heard a growl. A low, gravelly rumble coming from the other side of the desk.

Mr. V's hesitation drew the attention of the infidel hater. I was pretty sure he was president of the Infidel Haters and Knitting Club. He stood and walked over to us, feigning interest in the bag of food I'd brought to get a look at the receipt. Which was just a receipt. I wasn't a complete noob. My every move had to seem perfectly legit. People's lives were at stake.

But the minute he got close to Mr. V, the growling exploded into vicious barks and blood-curdling snarls. Yet both men seemed oblivious.

"Oh," I said, talking louder to be heard over the barks, "sorry, were you not going to charge today?"

When both men looked at me as if I had two heads, I became fascinated with a little antique inkwell that would look great on my mantel. If I had one.

Mr. V played along, probably to avoid any more unwanted attention. "Not today."

"Oh, alrighty then. It'll be twenty-four fifty."

As casually as I could, I let my gaze wander toward the back of the store. They must have had another man working. They'd ordered four meals this time, but none of them came to the front.

The dog calmed a bit when the president took the bag of food over to Mr. V's small desk and started going through it. I took the opportunity to do what I'd really come for.

I slipped a note from under my left palm—the one that

read 'Is everything okay?'—while keeping my right one, complete with fingernails tapping in impatience, visible to the intruder.

Mr. V paused. Fear spiked within him so fast it made me dizzy. He spared a furtive glance over his shoulder, then refocused on counting out the money. After a moment, he gave me a beseeching look accompanied by a quick shake of his head. He wasn't saying no to my question. He was pleading with me to leave it alone.

But I couldn't. Not just yet. I flipped the note over and held my breath. I had to give Mr. V kudos on not losing his composure completely. And, in the process, possibly getting us both killed.

The second note asked him if they had his family. I thought he was going to break down, his emotions were so fragile. Like eggshells in an elephant's cage.

"Twenty-three, twenty-four, and fifty cents," he said. "Oh, and four dollars for you, hon."

When he looked back up at me, he nodded, the movement so quick and subtle, I almost missed it.

I stood crestfallen, even more unsure of what to do. How to help him. They had his family. If he had been the only one in danger, I felt for certain he'd allow me to call in the troops. Sadly, that was not the case. Keeping my movements out of his captor's sight, I gave his hand a quick squeeze. Before I could release him, he squeezed back to get my attention and then shook his head again, beseeching me, once more, not to do anything.

Pressing my lips together, I offered him the same quick, curt nod that he'd given me, telling him I understood. The dog whimpered behind the counter, and then I felt a cool, wet tongue test my fingers. I didn't respond. By that point, I realized the dog must've been departed like Artemis.

"Have a good day," I said, practically bouncing out of the shop. But I'd taken a peek at the dog, now sitting in front of the desk, and a sad sense of elation washed over me. It was the German shepherd. The one from last night. If all dogs, or all animals for that matter, had spirits that could stay behind when they died, why weren't the streets filled with the ghosts of animals? I saw at least five departed everyday, but besides Artemis, the German shepherd was the only other animal I'd seen. Maybe it was because the dog had died trying to protect his owners. Maybe he stayed behind of his own accord, unwilling to shirk his duty because of a little thing like death.

And if he had crossed to the other side, was there a heaven just for them? And what would a dog heaven look like?

Too many unanswered questions. My brain overflowed with them. I left the shop with a bittersweet taste in my mouth, even more confused about how to proceed. Did I dare talk to the man Bobert was setting up a meeting with? I'd already told Ian. I'd set off the Vandenbergs' house alarm. Had I put them in even more danger?

Bottom line: I had to find his family, and I had a plan. Unfortunately, it would have to wait until that evening. Mr. V had several family photos, and they were all taken at the same cabin no matter how old his kids were when they were taken. Either he had a cabin or he knew someone with one. Maybe his captors found out and were holding them hostage there. It made perfect sense. No neighbors. Isolated spot. Well camouflaged with a plethora of trees and brush around. And easily guarded. They'd see anyone coming up the road for miles. Most of the leaves had already fallen, and though it wasn't officially winter, it sure as heck felt like it.

After that, the day progressed rather normally. If a butt-load of women with love in their eyes was any indication of normal. We were swamped. Had been swamped since we'd opened. Reyes might be good for business, but he was bad for my bunions. Or he would have been if I'd had bunions. He was damned lucky I didn't.

"Sumi," I said, trying to get her attention.

I needed the orders for booth seven pronto. It was full of giggling preteens, and I needed them out. Every time they'd look in the rock star's direction, they'd burst into a fit of giggles and discuss his expression right down to the position of his brows. The tilt of his mouth. The implication of his glances. Did he like movies? Did he play video games? Did he like them?

Uh, he would if he were a child molester.

I wanted to say it but couldn't bring myself to break their fluttering little hearts. Especially since I'd been doing the same thing all morning. Chancing quick glances. Analyzing every movement. Wondering if he liked me.

I needed to nip a sticky situation in the bud. Reyes didn't need to be investigated because a kid declaring her love was taken the wrong way by an eavesdropper. If anything could go downhill fast, it was suspicion of pedophilia. It never ended well.

After Sumi snapped out of her latest fantasy and tore her gaze off Reyes, she nodded and got me the plates I needed.

I rushed them over, filled a few drinks, then went to the storeroom for more ketchup, where I came face-to-face with a departed woman. An agitated departed woman.

"Where have you been?" she asked, walking toward me, her strides angry and aggressive.

"Stay back," I said, my voice a soft hiss as I made a

cross with my index fingers. I did not want a repeat of yesterday's fiasco.

"Oh, stop it." She slapped my hands away, her long red hair shifting soundlessly. "Rocket's really upset with you."

I could only assume Rocket was a guy. "I'm . . . sorry? Wait." I lunged forward and took hold of her shoulders. "Do you know who I am?"

"Duh. Took me forever to find your skanky ass. What the hell is up with your light? It's, like, everywhere. And Rocket is freaking out. Seriously. Like the world is about to end kind of freaking out. Something about the angels and how pissed they are. At you, naturally. And there's this god thing going on. You have to get back there and calm him down."

"Get back? Get back to where? Where am I from?"

"Oh. My. God. Would you stop already?"

I was a microsecond away from shaking her until her teeth rattled when a thick, billowing blackness rose behind her. I stumbled back. It grew out of the ground like an evil fog. Because only evil fog could be that menacing.

"Hey," the woman said, looking around, just as surprised as I was. "What the—?"

Before she could get another word out, the darkness covered her mouth. Her eyes rounded, and she looked at me as though asking for help.

I took a hesitant step forward, but the black smoke swallowed her before I could do anything. Then again, what would I have done? What could I have done? When the billowing smoke dissipated, she was gone.

"No!" I rushed forward, looking for her everywhere. In the mop bucket. Behind the storage shelves. Under the mustard.

What the hell just happened? And why did my skin

burn as though it had been scorched by something powerful? Something angry? Whatever it was, it wanted to silence that poor woman who probably hadn't hurt a soul her
entire life. Just to keep her from telling me who I was.
Where I was from.

I sank onto a box. Was something keeping me here?
Was I trapped? A prisoner?

By the time I went back into the dining area, my section had exploded. Erin and Francie had shown up and
Dixie had even called Shayla in early. Lewis was there,
too, to help bus, and Thiago, the second-shift cook, was
putting on his apron.

"What about her?" Cookie asked me as she blurred
past.

I was still trying to process the evil fog. I turned to
Reyes. He was the only person present who had black
smoke cascading off his shoulders like a cape.

Cookie rushed past again and said, "The blonde at ten."

I glanced at table ten while picking up an order from
the pass-out window. Reyes was cooking, completely
oblivious to the evil fog in the storeroom. At least he
seemed to be.

"What about her?" I called out.

The next time Cookie and I passed like ships in the
night, she paused long enough to say, "I can see a resemblance."

I snorted, sounding much like a foghorn on a ship passing in the night. "Please. She looks nothing like me. And
I rarely walk around with a stick up my butt."

"She doesn't have a stick up her butt." She gave her a
once-over, then said, "Not a big one."

I walked over as the blonde put her Louis Vuitton on the
seat beside her. She probably didn't buy hers off Scooter.

"Welcome to the Firelight."

The woman gazed up at me, her eyes glistening, and I felt a strong sense of expectation coming from her. Hope welled inside me. Could Cookie have been right?

"Hi," she said, letting a shy smile soften her face. "I'm Gemma."

"I'm Janey."

We both seemed to be waiting for something, and I realized she couldn't know me. Wouldn't she say something if she did?

"I'll be your server. Can I get you something to drink?"

"I'm here on vacation."

"Oh, nice. Welcome to Sleepy Hollow."

"I just got here. I had to clear my schedule."

"Okay, then." This conversation was quickly leaning toward strange and unexplainable. "Are you a fan of the story?"

"The story?" she asked, blinking mascaraed lashes over blue irises. "Washington Irving? 'The Legend of Sleepy Hollow'?" Mine weren't even close to blue. They were more of a golden amber.

"Oh." She laughed into a hand and cleared her throat. "Yes. The story. Big fan. Absolutely." She looked up at me again, her oceanic gaze full of expectation and . . . something else. Something warm. "You?"

"Love it," I said, having no idea if I'd ever actually read it or just saw movies about it. I might need to make a trip to the library. "Have we met?" I asked her.

"I'm not sure. You do look familiar."

I sat across from her uninvited. "Really? Do you know me?"

She leaned forward, an expectant air about her. "I don't know. Do you know me?"

I squinted and thought as hard as I could. Tried to get past the veil that had been pulled over the last few decades of my life, but I just couldn't penetrate it. After a valiant effort, I shook my head, frustrated.

"I'm sorry. I have—" I almost told her about the amnesia, but I'd learned not to tell customers. It was like they suddenly didn't trust me to know the difference between an egg and a hamburger. I stood, because it hit me where she probably knew me from. The news. I looked familiar because of the news coverage when I first woke up. "You look familiar, too. Must have one of those faces. Can I get you something to drink?"

She seemed to wilt a little. "Sure. Iced tea?"

"You got it."

I had walked to the drinks station to fill a glass of ice when I heard a loud pssst. Only one person psssted at me. I chuckled and looked through the pass-out window at Lewis.

He peeked over his shoulder, then said, "I need to talk to you about today."

Oh, holy crap. I almost forgot. Today was the big day. And it was such bad timing. We were way too busy to pull off a fake robbery.

"Number four needs a refill," Erin said, her voice full of derision. That woman hated me so.

"Thanks!" I graced her with a killer smile and sassy hair flip, wondering how I was going to lift her phone. I might have been clueless about what I did in my past life, but I felt reasonably safe in assuming I wasn't a pickpocket.

Cookie and I made it through the lunch rush relatively unscathed. I managed to get a death threat from one of the giggling preteens when she noticed Reyes watching me, so that was a first. Cookie had to buy another man his dinner when he accused her of trying to sell her wares.

Who knew a simple "Would you like to take some of my buttery cream pie home?" could be taken so metaphorically? She'd made a pie. It was buttery. She was proud.

By a quarter to two, I'd hit rock bottom. Or, well, my energy level had. A sleepless night in a freezing car did little for my self-esteem or my skin tone. Thankfully, Reyes didn't seem to mind. At least he wasn't repulsed by me.

Bobert had come in, but we were too busy for me to get a word in. I'd have to try to catch him later and explain the whole situation. I was in so far over my head, it was unreal. At the moment, we had only fifteen minutes left on our shifts. I planned on spending that time stealing and invading someone's privacy. Unfortunately, that meant venturing into the storeroom again.

I walked past Reyes, who was finally taking a break. The café wasn't dead, but the rush was over at last. I turned the knob to the storeroom, carrying a box of condiments from the delivery guy to give me an excuse to go in there. Not that I needed one. If anyone found out about the phone, I could plead innocent. Say the mustard made me do it. In the storeroom. With a candlestick. That was such a cool game, and yet I couldn't remember ever playing it.

Holding my breath, I peered around for billowing smoke. I so didn't want to be sucked into some alternate dimension where spiders were the size of elephants. Seeing no smoke of any kind, I hurried in and closed the door. Her purse hung from a hook in her locker. That she never locked. I rooted through it until I found her phone. A thud sounded outside the door. I paused. Waited. Peed a little. When no one came in, I woke it up and thanked the heavens she didn't have it code locked.

Finding her pictures was easy. They were inside an icon titled PICTURES. I thumbed through picture after picture, each one more hideous than the next. The departed woman was in every one. Creepy as ever-lovin' fuck. Her white eyes glowed, and her toothless scream showed off a gray tongue and blood-soaked gums.

I pressed the button to end the agony. I'd seen enough. But why was the woman following them around? From what I understood, Erin's babies had passed away in two different houses. One was her mother's, and one was the house she and her husband lived in before buying the one they had now. They'd moved out of each one following the heart-wrenching deaths.

I simply couldn't imagine what she'd gone through. How she'd survived.

The room began to spin with the thought. The senseless loss of life sparked a familiar feeling for the second time in as many days, and before I could stop it, panic slammed into me. Stole my breath. Ripped at my throat.

I looked down at my hands. At my arms. They were empty. They shouldn't have been. I could feel the weight of that emptiness like a boulder in my stomach. It pulled me farther down below the surface. It suffocated. I had something once, but I forgot where I put it.

I forgot. I forgot. I forgot.

It was so small. So fragile. Yet it held such power, this tiny thing that I'd promised to protect. It was like a single atom that would someday split and spark a nuclear reaction. It would set the world on fire. It would free the mentally ill.

It would ignite the fires of revolution like nothing the human race had ever seen. And I'd misplaced it. I'd lost it.

I scratched at the linoleum floor. It had to be here somewhere. It couldn't have gone far.

No. Wait. It was a dream. I was simply dreaming again. I blinked. Tried to focus on the present. Tried to get a firm grip on my sense of time and place.

When I finally kicked my way back to the surface, I shook uncontrollably. Nausea took hold, and bile scalded the back of my throat. I tried to swallow it down but choked on it instead, doubling over as it racked my body.

"Janey?"

I shook out my agony at the sound of Cookie's voice.

"Crap," I said as she rushed in and knelt beside me.

"What happened?" she asked, frantic.

"Nothing. I dropped a bottle of mustard."

"Oh, sweetheart." She wrapped her arms around me, and I remembered that she was psychic. She probably saw me coming from a mile away. Luckily, she didn't run in the opposite direction.

"I'm okay. Thanks."

When we walked out, Francie was sitting across from Reyes in the booth he'd taken. She was doing her darnedest to flirt, but he seemed preoccupied. His head down. His mouth a firm line. Until I walked past.

"What's wrong?" he asked, his voice harsh.

His question surprised me, but his tone surprised me more. "Nothing. Why?"

Francie looked back and forth between us, trying to gather as much intel as possible, to assess if I was a real threat or not.

"So, anyway," she said, apparently coming to a conclusion,

"he calls me Red. Right? Like he had the right to call me Red. It's natural, by the way."

He hadn't taken his eyes off me, and I wanted to melt into him.

"Don't you think?" Francie asked, but I had no idea what direction she'd taken in her thrilling tales of Francie in Wonderland. Then I realized she wasn't talking to me. Sadly, the one she was talking to completely ignored her.

She bit her bottom lip and stood up. "I better get back to work."

I felt bad for her. Or I did before she tried to turn me into a pillar of salt with her caustic glare. Holy crap and damn. Now they both hated me.

At least Cookie still liked me.

"I hate you," Cookie said as she checked her phone. "Just so you know."

For fuck's sake. "What'd I do?" I asked, tearing my gaze off Reyes and following her to the front register.

"This." She held out a hundred. "Someone left a hundred-dollar tip on your table."

"No way." I brightened, snatched it out of her hands, then held it up to the light to make sure it was legit. Because it would be my luck . . . "I'm rich. I can get a phone."

"You can take me to a movie," she countered.

"Deal."

"Or that mansion you want to see."

"Oooo," I said, grinning from ear to ear. "The Rockefeller Mansion. I've been dying to see it."

"We should go today. Right after our pedicures."

"We're getting pedicures?"

"We are now."

I laughed as we changed out our tips, the metal kind, for real money, the paper kind. Cookie finished before

I did. Mostly because I couldn't keep my recalcitrant gaze from wandering in Reyes's direction every few seconds.

"You should invite him," Cookie said.

"To get a pedicure with us?"

She giggled. "Men like that stuff, too, right?"

"Then why don't you invite Bobert?"

"Point taken. I have to get my jacket."

And I had to get Reyes's, but first I had to finish counting my tips. I was so bad at counting.

I was standing there wondering if I'd counted ten quarters or only nine when a guy walked into the café, strode straight up to me, and jammed a gun into my side.

Oh, for the love of crab cakes. I forgot we were doing this today.

"Open it. Now." He rammed the gun into my ribs again a little too aggressively.

I glared over my shoulder. We said to make it look real. Not *feel* real. I leaned close and whispered to him. "Chill. We have to wait for Lewis to get up here."

I looked over the sea of tables to where Lewis stood bussing a table nearby. Then I looked around for Francie. She was just walking out of the storeroom and toward us. I gave Lewis a secret thumbs-up, which was basically a thumbs-up with enthusiastic eyebrow arching thrown in.

This was it. Lewis's big day. But he shook his head at me.

Was he backing out? Now?

"I won't say it again, bitch. Open the fucking drawer."

Lewis looked shocked. And confused. And more than a little concerned. Holy crap, he was good.

He tried to mouth something to me. "He's not . . . I didn't . . ."

I had no idea what he was saying, but I did know that

he needed to give up on his dream of becoming a rock star and become an actor, because he was totally convincing.

Maybe a little too convincing.

When Lewis stayed frozen to the spot and his cousin shoved me a little harder than was necessary into the register, I realized something had gone horridly awry. Either the man holding a gun at my back wasn't Lewis's cousin or Lewis's cousin was a scene-stealing asshole. I was leaning toward the former. And wondering how I let myself get talked into these things. Though I couldn't remember any particular circumstance in which I got suckered into a ridiculous situation, the scenario did seem oddly familiar to me. Like an old sweater or a favorite pair of sweats.

I began to panic. As adrenaline took a huge dump in my nervous system, a calmness came over Lewis's face. A determination. A disregard for his life. And my life, for that matter.

He stood up, set his jaw to extra firm, and headed straight for us, his movements sure. Steady. Calculating. And I realized he'd sautéed his marbles and had eaten them with a nice Chianti.

"Stay back!" the guy yelled when he noticed Lewis. He pointed his gun at him.

Francie screamed when she realized what was happening. Shayla covered her mouth in shock. But Lewis kept walking, even with the gun pointed right at him. Right at his heart.

There was brave, then there was suicidal.

"Hurry up!" he yelled at me, keeping the gun trained on the massive, bearlike creature coming to get him.

I had to do something before Lewis got killed, but what?

Oh, wait. I'd give him the money and he'd leave. Okay. I could do that.

I took my key and opened the register. Dixie had been robbed more than once, so she insisted on using a register that required a key to get into the cash drawer.

The man grabbed my hair and shoved my face toward it. Now he was just showing off.

"Put the cash in a bag," he said.

We didn't have any bags at the register, so I opted for a takeout box. He didn't seem to mind. I took cash out by the handfuls and stuffed it into the cardboard box. The adrenaline pumping through my body was giving me hot flashes. I felt a line of perspiration along my upper lip and under my eyes. Even more so when I heard sirens in the distance.

Someone had already called the cops, and my first concern was for Mr. V and his family. What if their captors thought the authorities were coming for them? What would they do?

I was only half finished—the big bills were stashed underneath the cash bin—and Lewis was getting closer by the millisecond.

"Keep coming, bitch," the robber said to him.

The absolute determination in Lewis's expression made me groan aloud. I sped up, hurrying to get the robber out of the café.

Just as I finished and closed the takeout box, the gun went off with an earsplitting bang, and my life flashed before my eyes.

11

I was dropped as a baby.
Into a pool of awesomeness and badassery.

—T-SHIRT

Or, well, the last month of my life flashed before my eyes. It was full of regrets and bad decisions. For example, I totally should have eaten that York Peppermint Patty that fell on the floor of my apartment. The three-second rule only applied when other people were around. No one would have known it sat there for at least a minute before I noticed.

No. No. *I* would've known. *I* would've had to live with myself and—

I blinked. Squinted. Blinked again. No one was moving. No one was screaming or ducking to get away from the gunfire. In fact, no one was doing much of anything. I scanned the café, the frozen faces that swam around me. Everyone looked like posed manikins in an art exhibit on the American experience. My ears rang, probably from the blast, but it sounded like I was underwater.

Then, in a moment of absolute clarity, my jaw fell to my knees. I'd stopped time.

I really was a time traveler!

I closed my eyes. This rocked so hard.

My lids sprang open again as all the implications of such a gift paraded through my mind. I wondered what time period I was actually from. It couldn't have been that long ago. I didn't say things like thee and thou, and I'd known how to use a coffeemaker from Day One as if it were ingrained in my DNA.

But I was most definitely a time traveler. I even knew the lingo. Quantum mechanics. Hyperspace. Flux capacitor.

Hell.

Yes.

That's why no one knew me. I probably hadn't been born yet!

I wiggled my way out of the robber's hold. Finally getting a good look at him, I took note of every aspect of his face that I could. I wanted to be able to describe him to a sketch artist should the need arise.

The tip of the gun had a fiery blast of powder exploding out of it. And a few inches away, a bullet hung in midair. It seemed surreal. Enigmatic. Unfathomable.

I walked around to examine its trajectory. It was headed straight for Lewis's heart. I doubted his cousin would really shoot him, but the odds of a real robbery taking place on the same day we'd planned a fake one were astronomical. Enigmatic. Unfathomable. Clearly fate was punking us.

Unfortunately, I wasn't entirely certain what to do about any of it. It wasn't like I could stop a bullet. But maybe I didn't have to. I looked beyond Lewis. No one would be hit if the bullet just kept going. It would shatter the window and end up in the alley somewhere, but better that than the alternative.

Okay. This could work. All I needed to do was move Lewis out of the way. I stepped to his side, placed my hands on his beefy arm, and pushed. He didn't budge. Apparently things were stuck when I stopped time. When I bent it to my will.

I dug in my ankle-booted heels and tried again. He moved. Not far. Maybe an inch. But enough for me to know he could. I pushed again and again, shoving with all my might until I'd turned him and pushed him out of the way of the speeding bullet. He now stood at a forty-five-degree angle to the floor, which would be awkward when I re-started time. He would certainly fall. I could live with that.

Wait. I stilled as another conundrum hit me. How did I restart time? What if I couldn't? What if I was stuck here? Forever? Lost in an inescapable time loop until I grew old and died? I needed to watch *Back to the Future* to get pointers, but I couldn't even do that. Panic started to set in, and I had to take deep, calming breaths.

Surely, if I'd stopped it, I could restart it again. How hard could it be? But before I even attempted such a feat, I had to do something about the robber while I could. An idea hit me instantly. I took off my apron. The material became stiff. It was still malleable, but once off me, it became like a bendable piece of plastic. It defied the law of gravity and every other law I could think of.

I hurried over to the robber, molded it to his face, and tied it around his head. It would be enough to fluster him when time returned. To throw him off his game. I pried the gun out of his fingers and pushed it onto the floor beside Lewis.

Then I stood back to examine my handiwork. I brushed

my hands together at a job well done before checking out the others in the immediate vicinity.

What few customers we had sat terrified. They'd been caught in mid-scream or mid-duck, trying to scramble to safety. Cookie looked more confused than afraid. She'd been entering an order when all hell broke loose.

Oddly enough, Erin stood like a warrior princess. Her jaw jutting out. Her legs slightly apart. Her hands balled into fists at her sides. It was as though she had every intention of kicking the guy's ass. I felt an odd sense of admiration swell up in me. A camaraderie. And I suddenly wanted to be friends with her. Not like braid-each-other's-hair friends, but definitely more than just mortal enemies. Anyone who could stand up to danger like that deserved a closer look.

Shayla, the tiny wood nymph, stood at the workstation, her face the definition of shock, a hand thrown over her mouth as she looked on in horror. She'd screamed. The love of her life was in danger. I would've screamed, too.

Speaking of whom . . .

I walked over to Reyes. He still sat at the booth, his darkly handsome features full of anger, his rich brown eyes glittering with it.

Now was my chance. I sat on the edge of the bench beside him. Tucked a wayward curl behind his ear. Ran the backs of my fingers over his shadowed cheek and jaw. Then I leaned in and placed the tiniest kiss on his full mouth.

"I've loved you for a thousand years," I said, because it seemed true. To the core of my being. I was so drawn to him it hurt. I could only pray he'd get over his ex someday.

No. That was wrong. If I should pray for anything, it would be for his happiness, no matter who he ended up with. If he loved her, if he was devoted to his ex, then he deserved to have her. On the condition that she loved him back, of course.

In the distance, I heard a low rumble. I turned toward it. The earth began to quake beneath my feet. It sounded like a train. A speeding train that had every intention of crashing into the café. After a quick scan to assure myself there was no train despite the rumble growing louder and louder, I turned back to Reyes. He was gone.

Startled, I fell off the bench and landed on my ass. No one else had moved, not an inch, but Reyes had vanished.

The sound grew louder. I could feel the rumble deep in my chest. A split second before the train crashed into me, and time—yes, it was time roaring around me—bounced back into place, I saw the winged being again. In a flutter of soft white feathers and black down on the underneath, a man appeared. A stunning man with dark hair, a super-angry expression on his face, and a sword in his hand.

I scrambled back as he strode toward me, the same determination I'd seen on Lewis's face in his expression. He raised the sword when he got closer, and a scream wrenched from my throat.

I raised a hand as though to block the blow, certain that all I would accomplish was the loss of that hand. But it was a reflex. An automatic response to someone slicing me in two.

A heartbeat before he swung, the smoke appeared again. The same smoke I'd seen earlier in the storeroom. It billowed up and around the being. The angel. It had to be an angel.

The angel stopped, lowered first the sword, then his head. He kept a wary eye on the smoke. Tightened his hold on the hilt. Then, to my surprise, spoke.

The language had round vowels and soft consonants. It was ancient and graceful and untainted.

"Show yourself," he'd said, and somehow the fact that I knew a celestial language got lost in all the other crap going down.

The black fog ignored the command and continued to grow until it obscured my view of the angel completely. But I heard the clanging of swords even over the roaring train. Before I could make out what was happening, the train crashed into me. Time crashed into me. I felt like I'd jumped from a high cliff and splashed face-first into freezing cold water, the force was so jarring. It knocked my breath away, but at the last second, I remembered I was supposed to be with the robber.

I jumped to my feet and sprinted through the awakening of time. Movement that started out slow progressed quickly until, just as I slid into place beside the robber, it bounced back completely.

The bullet zinged through the glass. It didn't shatter it, but the café would now have a nice-sized hole to cover up.

Finding it impossible to get his balance, Lewis stumbled and fell back against the hard floor, but as he did, his gaze locked on to the gun that had magically appeared beside him. He lunged for it and closed his fist around the handle.

The man beside me struggled to remove the barrier on his face. In an almost comical move, he tore it off, then searched frantically for the gun. A gun that was now being held on him.

"Get down!" Lewis shouted, and everyone in the café dropped to the floor. Everyone but the robber. He stood stunned, unable to figure out what had just happened.

I stepped back as Lewis advanced.

"Get the fuck on your knees," he said, his tone suddenly menacing.

Shayla hurried toward us but stopped short to let Lewis do his thing. Left with little choice, the robber raised his hands and slowly sank to his knees in disbelief.

The only ones who didn't drop to the floor were Erin, Shayla, and Reyes.

Reyes!

He was right where I'd left him. The same hard expression on his face. The same sour disposition. His muscles tightened as I studied him. His jaw clenched. His hands curled into fists. When he lowered his arm and pressed it to his side, realization hit me. He was hurt. A dark red stain spread over his rib cage to saturate the shirt he wore.

I gasped and started toward him, but his expression hardened even further. He rose from the seat and strode out the back door. I wanted to run after him, to check on him, but I couldn't leave Lewis to take on the bad guy alone.

The sirens grew louder, and I braced myself for what was to come. Cops. News crews. Gawkers in every shape and size. The spotlight was not a place I liked to be, so I slowly sank into a chair and willed myself to become invisible. I'd let Lewis absorb the brightest rays and keep to myself as much as possible.

Two hours later, the cops had taken our statements, arrested the bad guy, and both congratulated and admonished Lewis for his bravery-slash-bullheadedness. He would've died if I hadn't stopped time.

Or had I?

Did I have anything to do with what happened? Clearly there was more to Reyes than met the eye. Even my supernaturally inclined one.

He'd managed to elude the cops. No one could say for certain he was in the café except Francie and me. And she wasn't talking. I had to give her brownie points for that. Not a lot. Maybe, like, three.

Cookie and I had been sitting together through most of the interrogations, along with Bobert, who'd stormed in after the fact. Cookie was shaken up. No doubt about it. And yet she was handling it all way better than I thought she would. She seemed more concerned about me than about herself. Come to think of it, the second Bobert found out she was okay, he seemed more concerned about me as well.

I wanted to ask him about the FBI contact, but I didn't dare bring it up in front of a room full of cops. Ian was among them. He didn't say a word to me, however, so there really was a silver lining inside every dark cloud. I'd wondered.

The chaos that followed the incident rivaled that of an impromptu visit from the president. Streets were blocked off. Cars were searched. No idea why. News crews set up around the perimeter. And everyone within a five-mile radius was questioned ad nauseam.

"We need to go to that house thing."

I turned toward Cookie. "The house thing?"

"The mansion. But only if you're still up for it."

She was trying to get my mind off everything. To distract me lest I become depressed and start a round of self-mutilation treatment. "Let's go, then. We're getting pedicures," I said to Bobert in a lyrical, come-hither voice. "I'm pretty sure you want to join us."

"I'm pretty sure I don't," he said, matching my singsong voice. He leaned in and took my hand. "But if you need anything, Janey . . ." He left the offer hanging in the air and a slip of paper nestled in my palm. After giving that hand a quick squeeze, he stood and stretched. "You girls have fun."

We watched him go, and I put my head on Cookie's shoulder. "I like him."

"I do, too," she said.

Francie's voice broke into my musings. "Reyes! Are—? Is everything—?"

He strolled past her, ignored a scowling Ian, and made a beeline straight for me. At least he wasn't glaring. "Are you okay?"

"I'll be right back," I said to Cookie before taking hold of the hem of his shirt and leading him away from the melee amidst the scowls of Ian Jeffries. When we were in a relatively cop-free zone, I lifted my hand to his side. The side that had been soaked in blood.

He let me lay my hand on it, just barely, just enough to let him know what I would be referring to in my next question. He didn't move but watched me with the intensity of a cobra.

"I should be asking you that. Are you okay? And Reyes, what the hell happened today?"

"You and your friend foiled an attempted robbery."

"And that's it?"

"That's what I saw." He loomed over me. He'd showered and, from the feel of it, wrapped his wound.

I thought of what I'd said to him when time had stood still. Embarrassed, I lowered my head to nudge a piece of loose baseboard. "You didn't see anything else? Or, maybe, hear anything else?"

"Like what?"

I still had my hand on his side, careful not to press. He

reached out and hooked a finger into the belt loop on my jeans. It felt so natural, so fulfilling, to be there with him. To talk with him as if we did it every day. As if we'd been doing it every day for years. Not even the heat of Ian's fury could penetrate the warmth I was getting from Reyes.

He inched closer. I saw his inch and raised him a three.

"What should I have heard?" he repeated.

"Nothing. It's . . . dumb." I gazed up at him, pleading. "But I saw the blood." I grazed my thumb over his bandages. "What happened?" Could he have fought the angel? How would that even be possible? It wasn't like he had a sword hanging from his belt. But it was getting harder and harder to deny the fact that he was shrouded in darkness. It cascaded off him. Pooled at his feet. And looked exactly like the black smoke that had taken the woman from the storeroom. That had stopped the angel from slicing me into bite-sized chunks.

I had so many questions. Possibly most important of all, why the hell had an angel, a celestial being, tried to kill me? That was wrong on so many levels.

"Please tell me what happened."

A grin tugged at one corner of his mouth. "You first."

I dropped my hand and stepped back. I couldn't. There was still a chance that I was as crazy as a soup sandwich, and I had no intention of spending the rest of my life locked in the mental ward of a hospital. Or, possibly worse, downing a cocktail of psych meds everyday.

He let go of my belt loop, then put his fingers under my chin to tilt my face toward his. But he didn't say anything. He just perused. Studied. Ran his thumb over my mouth. Caused quakes of hunger to shudder through me.

"Reyes—"

"This is a crime scene," Ian said, his hand resting on his gun.

I snapped to my senses. Reyes dropped his hand but didn't look at Ian, almost as though he knew that would infuriate Ian more. Reyes could have argued. Hurled insults. Physically attacked him. None of those things would outrage a man like Ian more than being ignored.

And boy, did it work. Ian's anger shot out of him like a lightning strike. Reyes either didn't know or didn't care.

"If you aren't part of this investigation, you need to leave."

Francie was watching us, too. Well, pretty much everyone was watching us by that point, including Dixie. She'd been at the bank when everything went down and came back to a plethora of flashing lights and police units. That had to be a little disconcerting.

"Officer, he works here," Dixie said. "I asked him to come in to help me with some boxes out back."

Ian stepped closer to Reyes. "Then help."

"Thank you," Dixie said, tugging at Reyes's shirt.

Reyes winked at me, then obeyed the harried woman. She was genuinely worried about him, even though he wasn't.

I was still recovering from the wink when Ian walked over to stand beside me. He rested a puppy-dog gaze on me. An expectant one. I got the feeling he thought I'd fall into his arms with relief that the ordeal was over. That he'd come in on his day off to see about me. That I was now even more indebted to him and couldn't deny the fact that I owed him my life no matter how cra-cra he was.

"Excuse me," I said to him, a sharp edge to my voice.

I'd spotted Francie and wanted to know if any of that

did the trick. If she didn't fall for Lewis now, one of the bravest men I knew—and one of the only men I knew—then it just wasn't there. You couldn't force another person to like you. No one could. I took Ian as a prime example of that. But if she didn't see what was in front of her, she didn't deserve him anyway.

"What did you think of Lewis?" I asked Francie.

She was leaning against the drinks counter, tapping a text into her phone.

"Pretty brave, right?"

"Please," she said. "I know what you're doing. This doesn't change anything." She offered me her best smirk. It was really pretty. Right before she left me standing there, she whispered, "Game on, bitch."

Uh-oh. I had a feeling we just became enemies. Oh well. Every girl needed a harmonious balance of good and evil in her life. Otherwise, we'd take everything for granted. And if she thought she was going to wrest Reyes away from my hot little hands, the game was most definitely on. I couldn't fight a ghost, a lost love that haunted Reyes night and day, but I could fight a redhead who cared more about her hair than the environment, four-inch advantage or not.

Speaking of brave, I tried Erin next. We had yet to speak after the picture debacle, but she'd rocked that whole man-waving-a-gun thing. I thought she was going to tackle him for a minute. We might not have been on speaking terms, but nothing brought people together like tragedy.

I walked up to her, a timid smile on my face.

"Don't even," she said before I uttered a syllable. She turned and walked away with a roll of her eyes.

I let a sigh slip through my lips. Maybe it was two tragedies.

I wondered how Lewis was holding up and found him

in the storeroom, sitting on the cot, with a furious Shayla-fairy tending to his swollen elbow. He'd landed on it when he fell.

"I hope your arm falls off," she said, her feisty side surfacing under all the pressure.

The look that Lewis gave her had me believe that all things were possible. He was smitten in the worst way. I stood befuddled. It took something like this for *him* to see *her*? Who'd've thunk?

I could only hope he wasn't too late. She seemed pretty pissed.

Tears filled her crystalline blue eyes, eyes so light they almost looked clear. Add to that a tiny freckled nose and bow-tie mouth, and you had one gorgeous fairy. She was about two feet shorter than he was, but that would make their coupledom all the cuter. I saw good things coming from this.

"You want my arm to fall off?" he asked, wincing when she slapped on an ice pack.

Or not.

"Why? I won't be able to play anymore. Something Like a Dude needs me."

She turned and walked away from him, a bright spark of anger lighting the room. For me, anyway.

When she walked back to him, she hit his arm with a doll-like fist.

"Ouch," he said, rubbing the spot though it couldn't have hurt that bad. While he was confused, he was also hopelessly intrigued.

She hit him again. Then again, her punches barely making contact. It was all for show, an outlet to filter her anger. Her feelings of helplessness.

He held up a hand to stop her and said in his own defense, "I could've died today."

It was the wrong thing to say. Tears slid past their gilded lash cage and over her freckled cheeks. She slapped his hand away and hit him again, her frustration palpable.

In a movement that surprised even himself, he bolted up and pulled her roughly into his arms. She fought him at first, then buried her face in his chest and hugged him to her. Her shoulders shook softly, and he kissed the top of her head.

I stepped away, unwilling to taint this beautiful moment with fist pumps and whoops of success no matter how badly I wanted to celebrate that small victory. I'd take it. Victories were good no matter how small.

Dixie had really put Reyes to work. He was busy rearranging her office, the hussy, and I worried about his wound. About his darkness. And about the kiss I'd given him. Was he really frozen in time like everyone else? Was it all just an act? I would die if it was. I'd crawl under the table and wither away. I'd professed my love. Said I'd loved him for a thousand years. How amazingly lame was that?

I totally needed a girl's day. Cookie would understand. She was psychic, after all. Surely I could tell her about my . . . *gifts*. Surely she could help advise me on what to do with Mr. V. With his family. With Reyes.

I mean, I knew what I *wanted* to do with Reyes, but maybe she would know what he was.

Please don't be evil. Please don't be evil. Please don't be evil.

Thankfully, the cops hadn't taken my tip money as evidence. I took out my day's earnings to see how much I could spend and how much I needed to set back—that phone wasn't going to buy itself—and found the hundred nestled among the smaller bills. I fished it out, planning to break it, but realized it had writing on the other side. Someone had written across it in pencil, so light I could barely read it, so I raised it to the sun streaming in the window again.

There, written in French, were the words *Je t'ai aimée pendant mille et un. –R.*

I stilled. Read it again. And again. *Je t'ai aimée pendant mille et un. –R.*

I've loved you for a thousand and one. –R.

I spun around, rushed back to Dixie's office, but he was gone.

12

Signs you drink too much coffee:
Your eyes stay open when you sneeze.
—INTERNET MEME

Cookie and I did get pedicures and *mucho grande* mocha lattes. On her, though. She'd insisted. I wasn't sure I'd ever had one, but I knew damned well a pedicure was going to become one of my weekly routines. The phone might have to wait. Apparently I was made to be pampered.

After my toenails turned a pretty shade of Mocha, which bizarrely matched Reyes's eyes, we drove to the Rockefeller mansion. We'd been talking about going out there for two weeks, but the mansion only opened at certain times during the year. Thankfully, Cookie got us on a list, and when the caretakers were giving a special tour to a group of third graders, they'd called and invited us to join them.

Cookie was a little worried about the kids, but they were third graders. I assured her I could take them if it came to that. And I was certain I could. As long as they didn't gang up on us, we were good.

The mansion itself, a National Historic Landmark, was absolutely stunning. The Rockefellers had completed construction of Kykuit—Dutch for "lookout"—in 1913. Sitting north of Sleepy Hollow, it was a sprawling, forty-room stone mansion with gorgeous architecture and incredible gardens. Every room we entered wrenched a tiny moan of ecstasy out of me.

Thankfully, the kids were great. Besides a few odd looks, and one kid informing me that he knew how to satisfy a woman—Seriously? That shit started in the third grade?—we had a wonderful time looking at all the furnishings and artwork.

"I have to start saving my tips," I told Cookie. "I want this." I raised my arms and indicated my surroundings with the gusto of inspiration.

"You want this bathroom?" she asked me. We were in the bathroom at the time. "I know a good decorator. He could make your bathroom look like this one."

"No. I want it all. Someday."

"Right? This would rock, but I'm not sure it's really your style."

"Why not? You think I don't have enough blue blood?"

She crinkled her nose in thought. "I think you don't have enough of a competitive spirit. Or enough arrogance. I heard that John D. Rockefeller Jr. built it only because his brother built a 240-room estate nearby."

"Oh. I might have agreed with you if not for the pedicure."

She chuckled as she powdered her nose. "The pedicure?"

"Yep. You've spoiled me, introduced me to the finer

things in life. I need to be pampered. To have my nails done by someone else. To have my feet massaged."

"I think I know someone who would massage your feet free of charge."

A tiny thrill laced up my spine at the thought. "I don't know, Cook. I think he's pretty hung up on his ex."

"I get that, but he is so into you, it's unreal. Surely you can see it."

"Sure I can, but that doesn't make him any less hung up on his ex." I leaned closer to the mirror, wondering where the dark circles came from. Probably a product of my night in a car. With a cat. And Reyes's jacket. So it wasn't all bad. "I'm hoping she was an absolute bitch. That way he can get over her faster."

She shook her head and snapped her compact closed. "Okay, I am as hot as I'm going to get for the moment."

"Which is smoking."

"Aw . . ." We high-fived, ignoring the girl washing her hands who wore enough makeup to go clubbing with us.

"Are you sure these kids are in the third grade?" I asked Cookie.

"That's what they told me."

"Okay. Just checking."

"So, what now? I'm famished."

We'd finished up the tour and were about to head out. "Food good," I said, doing my best Neanderthal impersonation. "I just need to make pee-pee. I'll be out in a sec."

"You got it. I want to snap a shot of a table I saw in the great room. I'll meet you outside?"

"I'll be there with bells on."

Cookie left, and I entered one of two stalls they'd set up to accommodate the tourists. I couldn't imagine the Rockefellers had needed stalls.

When I stood to pull up my jeans, something nudged me. I fell back onto the toilet with a squeak and looked up into the mouth of a horse. I gasped as it pushed farther into the stall and nuzzled my neck. It was a gorgeous tan with huge brown eyes and eyelashes as long as my pinkies.

"Oh, my goodness," I said, petting its nose and hugging it to me. "Aren't you a pretty"—I looked out the slit on the side of the door—"girl? Yes you are."

She whinnied and nodded her head. "Yes you are. I'm going to pet you and nuzzle you and take you home. I have a ball of fur just vibrating with energy that would love to meet you."

I realized at that moment that there was a girl in the next stall.

"Misty," she said, talking softly as I kissed the horse's nose, "I think the lady in the stall next to me is talking to her vagina."

I sucked in a horrified breath. "Did you hear that? She called you a vagina. That's just wrong. So, so wrong."

She nodded in agreement again, huffing out a puff of air as though disgusted. She was absolutely adorable. And she was my first departed horse.

"Okay, I have to pull up my pants now." Standing in a tiny stall in which a horse was taking up the majority of the room was easier said than done. I finally got my jeans fastened and opened the door, where I came face-to-face with, you guessed it, a headless horseman.

My gaze rocketed past black riding boots, black pants, and a billowing black cloak to the rider's face. Or where his face should have been. The space above the collar where one usually finds a head sat empty.

I screamed and fell back. The horse reared up then retreated a few precious steps. It was enough for me to scramble past and run for my life. I sprinted through the gift shop and out the front door, asking no one in particular, "Are you kidding me? Are you fucking kidding me?"

The headless horseman didn't follow, thank God. I slowed my steps as I descended the outside stairs and forced myself to calm down. Glancing back every few seconds, I went to the car, a coppery crossover, to wait for Cookie.

"There you are," she said when she found me. "You seriously need a phone. I thought you were still inside."

"Nope." I shifted my weight from foot to foot waiting for her to unlock the doors. She did so, and I practically dived inside.

"You okay, hon?" she asked when she climbed in.

"Yep."

She really needed to hurry.

"Okay. Oh, did you hear a scream?"

"No. Someone screamed? That's weird."

"Yes, it is." Her tone was full of suspicion.

"I say we go somewhere far away to eat. Like Manhattan."

After a giggle, she started the car and backed out. "That would take a while. How about we go somewhere in Tarrytown?"

"Okay."

We talked all the way to the restaurant, which was a quaint little hole-in-the-wall with amazing food. We'd discovered it by accident one day while shopping for flip-flops. In the snow.

"So," she said to me, growing serious, "you gonna tell me what happened back there?"

I'd wanted to spend the afternoon with her, to tell her all my dirty secrets, but how could I do that to her? How could I introduce the world that I can see to someone who can't and then expect that person to be unchanged? Unaffected? Not that she'd believe me.

Even with all that, I'd started suspecting a few things myself. I bought the whole story about her friend Charley and how she disappeared, but I still felt like she was holding something back. Like she knew more than she was letting on. And if my suspicions were right, I was about to get a lot of answers.

There was one surefire way to get those answers: the threat of physical violence.

"I'll tell you what," I said, opting for negotiations first. If those didn't work, then violence. "I'll tell you everything if you'll reciprocate."

Anxiety spiked inside her, but she pasted on a bright smile and said, "What do you mean?"

I leaned closer. "You know something. About me. I can tell."

"What?" She smoothed her napkin on the table. "I don't know what you're talking about."

"I think you do." I raised my butter knife. "I will cut a bitch," I said through gritted teeth.

She gasped. Slammed a hand to her chest. Heaved her bosom. "No, please. I swear I don't know anything."

Damn it. I let out a lengthy sigh of disappointment. "You're not even scared."

"Yes, I am," she assured me with a nod.

"Oh my God, you're not." I dropped the knife on the table. "You aren't even remotely scared."

She hesitated. Chewed on her bottom lip. "Sure I am."

"You are, like, the worst actress."

She lowered her head in shame. "I am. I'm horrible. Always was. I once got booed off stage."

"Broadway?"

"Kindergarten."

"Goodness. That's . . . harsh."

"No, it was bad. My agent had to let me go."

"You had an agent? In kindergarten?"

"Yeah, well, she wasn't in kindergarten. It was my mom. She was a talent agent in Hollywood for years."

"Your mom was a talent agent?"

"Yes."

"And she let you go?"

"Yes. Not personally, just professionally."

"Cook, I'm so sorry."

"No, trust me." She patted my hand to appease my misgivings. "It was for the best."

"But why aren't you scared? I could be a serial killer."

"I'm pretty sure you're not a serial killer."

"You don't know that. Heck, I don't even know that."

"I know."

And that brought me back to my point. I leaned closer, let a stretch of several seconds pull the tension tight around us, then asked, "Do you know who I am?"

She pressed her lips together, an involuntary reflex, then relaxed them. "Yes," she said, her tone resigned, and a spike of electricity rushed up my spine. "You are my best friend."

She wasn't lying, but that wasn't what I'd asked.

"What is my name?"

With the gentleness of a doe kissing its fawn, she took my hand. "Today, you are Janey Doerr. But I can't tell you who you will be tomorrow. Who you'll be next week. I can tell you that no matter who you are or who you turn out to be, I will always love you."

Again she was telling the truth. I wilted under the weight of fallen hope.

"Honey, do you think I know who you are? Who you really are?"

I lifted a shoulder because I no longer had the energy to lift both. "Do you?"

"I know that you are kind. I know that you are a good person and that no matter who you were in your past, no matter who you'll become, you are incredible. You're special, Janey. God doesn't make someone like you for no reason. You are here for a purpose. A wondrous, beautiful purpose, and someday you will remember what that is."

I kept my eyes lowered as embarrassment heated my cheeks. I'd suspected this incredible person, the only person in my life that I truly trusted, and accused her of deception. She gave so freely of herself, and I hid and scurried and ducked my head every time I came across someone in need. Gawd, I sucked. I swallowed and faced her again.

"I'm sorry, Cook."

She squeezed my hand. "For what?"

"For interrogating you like that. I just thought . . ."

"You thought what, hon?"

"It's stupid."

"Janey, nothing you could tell me would surprise me."

I dropped my voice to a whisper again. "Okay, I'm just going to come out with it. Are you psychic?"

The shock on her face pretty much told me I'd gone in a direction she never saw coming. If she were a psychic, wouldn't she see everything coming? Maybe it didn't work that way.

She took a sip of her moscato, choked on it a little, then said, "Sweetheart, why do you think I'm psychic?"

"Because you work with the police but have no discernible skill set that would explain why."

She fought a grin. The grin won. "Um, thanks."

"No, I don't mean that in a bad way. It's just, nothing surprises you. It's like you know things. You see them coming."

"Or I'm just not easily surprised."

"But you are. I've noticed things that surprise you all the time."

"Like?"

"Like the time that man offered you a dollar fifty for a tryst. You were surprised."

"I wasn't surprised. I was insulted. A dollar fifty? Seriously?"

"Good point. But every time you spill water in men's laps, you're surprised."

"True."

"Yet when a guy tries to rob the place and shoots a gun, you're as calm as an anesthetized patient."

"Oh. That. Well—" She had to think about it. "I just have a high . . . danger threshold."

And she did. "So that's it? You really aren't psychic?"

She folded her hands over mine. "I'm really not psychic. I help the police, mostly Robert, with research."

"Oh." It was my turn to be surprised. "You're a research consultant."

"Yes. Though I wish I were psychic."

Her emotions turned on a dime and blurred. "Why?"

"I could help my lost friend if I were. And—" She hit me with her stern face. "—I would know more about you. You don't tell me anything. Even when you're hurting. I feel like you don't trust me."

That stung. "I'm sorry. My life is just really messed up."

"Oh, it's not you, it's me? That kind of thing? And of

course it's messed up. You woke up in an alley with retrograde amnesia. But if you opened up to someone, if you told someone what you're going through, it would help."

I wanted to tell her. I wanted to trust someone. But at the same time, would I lose her? Would she think me nuts and dump me like a bad date? "Cook," I said, shifting in my seat, "I'm different."

"Different how?"

"I don't know. It's just, there are some things in this world you don't want to know about."

"Sure I do."

"No, you don't."

She leaned into me, a grin on her pretty face. "Try me." When I still hesitated, she said, "Charley, you know you can tell me anything. I know we've only been friends for a month, but you are the best friend I've ever had."

Could I? Did I dare? Maybe if I started out small. "Okay, so, you know how some people can hear things others can't? Like they have excellent hearing?"

She nodded.

"And you know how some people can see things others can't. Like, one person might have 20/20 vision while another has 50/80?"

"Yes," she said, drawing out the word as though she were trying to figure out where I was going.

"Well, I can see and hear things others can't."

"Oh. Okay. So you have really good night vision?"

"Kind of. Not exactly." I sat back when the server brought our food. After he left, I took a bite, rolled my eyes in ecstasy, then continued. "I can see other things."

"Wait," she said, taking a sip of water to wash down her food, "are *you* psychic? Is that what you're telling me?"

I straightened my shoulders in thought. "Well, maybe, in a way."

"Wow. What kinds of things do you see?"

And we're off. "I see, you know, things like dead people."

She nodded, fascinated but not the least bit surprised. Either she didn't believe me, or she was way more open-minded than I'd expected. I pressed my mouth together. "You're not the least bit surprised. Either you don't believe me, or you are way more open-minded than I'd expected."

"Open-minded," she confirmed. "Janey, I might not be psychic, but it's funny you bring that up. I have a cousin who is, well, she's nuttier than almond paste, but she sees things, too. She's the real deal, and . . ." She lowered her head as a blush of shame crept over her face. "And no one believed her. No one stood by her. Even after she warned us of impending doom and her predictions came through, her parents put her in an institution. She practically grew up there. And now—now she has no social skills. No one she can really talk to. It's awful."

"I had no idea. I'm so sorry, Cook."

"No, it's okay. Thank you, but my point is, I will never doubt true talent again. If you can see dead people, you can see dead people."

"You really believe me?"

"With all my heart."

The weight I'd been carrying around vanished in an instant. She believed me. I could feel it to her marrow. Surprisingly, tears stung the backs of my eyes. I hadn't realized how much I'd wanted to talk to someone about all this until that moment.

"Oh, honey," she said, her own eyes tearing. She pulled

me into an awkward, over-the-table hug. "Now that this wall is down, tell me everything."

I blinked at her. "Everything?"

"Everything."

So, I did. I told her about how I felt the emotions of others. How I saw another world beyond ours. A volatile world where supernatural creatures really existed. I didn't tell her about Reyes. Or even Osh. I felt like that was their story to tell. Not mine. But I did tell her about the demon in Mr. P and the angel who tried to kill me. The smoke billowing up.

She seemed to focus on one specific aspect of my story. "Another world? Like you see it within our own?"

"Yes."

"And it's all around us?"

I nodded.

"Wow." She fell back in her chair, her forehead lined in thought. "That's new."

"What do you mean?"

"Well, you know, just in general. It's not something you hear every day." After a moment of contemplation, she asked, "Anything else?"

"Yep. I know, like, eight languages."

"No way."

"And," I continued, "I can stop time." That might have been pushing it, but she seemed cool. "And," I continued again, "apparently the departed can pass through me."

"Well, yeah, their ghosts."

"No, like through me through me. Like the chicken who crossed the road."

"To get to the other side," she said. "Janey, do you know what this means?"

I snorted. "I absolutely know what this means. Stay as far away from dead people as I can get."

"Well, that's not what I was going to say."

"That's because you've never had a dead person frolic through your brain."

"True. Not that I know of, at least."

"It is not something I ever ever ever want to happen again."

"Understandable."

"How are you so accepting of all this?"

"You make it all sound so fascinating."

"Even the headless horseman thing?"

Cookie's face softened further. "Even the headless horseman thing, though I doubt I'll get any sleep tonight."

"Sorry."

"No. I'm okay. I am a big girl. I have big girl panties. I'll put them on and be fine."

"I don't get it. Oh, you mean that metaphorically," I said as understanding dawned. Her expression deadpanned, and I giggled. Just a little.

"You know what this calls for?"

"Appletinis?"

"Apple pie."

I laughed softly. "Even better."

13

A dyslexic man walks into a bra . . .
—T-SHIRT

Cookie dropped me off at my apartment. I had to feed the fur ball before heading back to the café to use Dixie's computer. The only electronics I had were an old television that weighed as much as I did and a DVD player that got too hot after about forty-five minutes, at which time I had to stop the movie to let it cool down. Sadly, neither got the Internet.

I walked into my apartment and was immediately attacked by a furry gray cat and a gorgeous, though departed, Rottweiler. They were getting along famously. Who knew cats could see the departed?

After hanging up Reyes's jacket and turning up the heat, I offered Irma a high five to no avail, went to the kitchen, and poured goat's milk into a saucer for Satan's feline offspring. Just the way I knew so many other things in my life, I knew not to give her regular, store-bought milk. I knew how to work a DVD player. Turn on a clothes dryer. Cook macaroni and cheese. Everyday things were second nature. My life, however, was not. It made no sense.

I was up to the T's now, so I combed through some of those as Satana ate.

Tamara? No.

Tasha? No.

Teresa? No.

I continued through as many T's as I could think of while Artemis tugged on Irma's muumuu and I cleaned the kitchen. It needed a good scrubbing. Then again, so did I. But when I walked into the bathroom, I stopped short.

Something wasn't right. Someone had been there.

Last night, while freezing in the backseat of Mable's Fiesta, I'd realized that my landlord could've been the one who came in and changed the light bulb. So that could be easily explained. But this time my things had been moved in the bathroom. I always kept my toothpaste in the drawer to my right, but it was on the counter. The one bottle of perfume I had, which I kept in the right corner, was now by the sink.

Little things like that tended to set me on edge. I drew in a deep breath and tried to come up with a feasible explanation. It couldn't have been Ian. I'd taken the key. Then again, who knew how many he'd had made? Or maybe he had a tool to pick locks. Cops sometimes did. Still, my landlord could have come in and worked on the sink. It'd been draining slowly. Did he work on it and have to move my stuff in the process?

I tried not to get too worked up. There could be any number of reasons why my things were out of place. Heck, even Satana could have jumped up and . . . what? Spritzed on a little perfume? Brushed her teeth? Next she would be using my dental floss. Admittedly, it probably wasn't her.

Either way, enough worrying. Enough playing the scared victim of a potential stalker. I just had to be smart. Pay attention to my environment. Stick to well-lit areas. Hire a round-the-clock bodyguard. I'd have to look in the yellow pages for a discount bodyguard service.

I took a shower with the bathroom door locked and a chair shoved under the knob. It felt wonderful. The shower. Not the chair. Artemis chased streams of water. Satana meowed and complained about being locked inside after she was the one who insisted on coming in. Who had to smell every object in the room for two minutes before moving on to the next.

I wondered about calling the number Bobert had placed in my palm. I'd have to do it from the café, but I was going back anyway. Should I risk it? Did I have a right to? Clearly Mr. V didn't want me to get involved, but he was in danger. Frustration coursed through me.

After putting on fresh clothes, I checked all the windows to make sure they were locked, grabbed Reyes's jacket, and headed out the door.

"Be back soon," I said to Artemis and Satana. "Do not bother Irma. I mean it. You two play nice."

I ran the doggy bag I'd brought home from the restaurant over to James, then walked back to Mable's house. I hadn't planned on borrowing her car again, but it was so cold and I was so tired after spending hours in it the night before that I changed my mind.

Unfortunately, she was already in bed. I still had a key to the car, but I would never take it without her permission.

"Well," I said to the little girl who'd been following me ever since Cookie and I had left the Rockefeller mansion.

She had a tangle of blond hair hanging down her back and wore pajamas with Strawberry Shortcake on them. "I guess we're walking."

She cradled a doll to her chest and petted its bald head, her eyes wide as she studied me. I figured she'd talk when she was ready. Sadly, it didn't take her long to get ready.

"Jessica said you lost your marbles." She stayed about five feet back as though to give me a wide berth.

I looked over my shoulder. "She said that, did she?"

"Yes. But I've looked everywhere. I can't find them."

"Darn it. Thanks for trying," I said with a chuckle. My breath fogged around me in the crisp night. I made sure to walk on the side where the street lamps were and kept a close eye on traffic. The fancy black car I'd thought was following me the day before sat parked just ahead. Like the little girl, I gave it a wide berth. As I passed, however, I realized it was a Rolls.

Why would an immaculate Rolls-Royce be parked in this area?

"It's okay," the little girl said. "Jessica told me I have to think of others, too. So I do. I think how dumb they are or how ugly their shoes are or how they don't brush their teeth enough. Can I brush your hair?"

"Maybe later." I didn't have the heart to tell her she probably couldn't hold a brush, being dead and all. "Where's Jessica now?"

"At Rocket's place."

Rocket? I stopped and turned around, my chest cavity oozing with hope. "Is Jessica about yea tall with red hair?"

"Mm-hm."

My visitor from the storeroom. The one who was swallowed by the black smoke that might or might not have been Reyes Farrow. She'd been the only one who seemed to know who I was. If Reyes did silence her before she could tell me anything, then he would have a lot of explaining to do.

"Is she okay?"

"I guess. Where are you going?"

"Back to work for a bit. Can you go get her?"

"No. She won't come here anymore."

I stepped closer. "Why not?"

She stepped back. "He told her not to."

"Who did? Reyes?"

Her nose crinkled. "Ew, no. I don't think you should give food to that man anymore. He lives in a box and he stinks."

"Okay, well, first of all, that's not very nice."

"His smell is not very nice."

"And second, who told her not to come here?"

She blinked at me as though trying to understand the question, so I tried again.

"Do you remember who told her that? Did she tell you?"

She just stared ahead, her expression suddenly blank.

"Are you having a seizure?" I asked, coming up with no better explanation.

Her gaze slid past me, her eyes growing bigger by the second.

A heavy dose of dread crept up my spine. "Is there something behind me?"

She nodded and took another step back.

"Does it have wings and a sword?"

She shook her head.

"Oh, then how bad can it be?" I turned to see and stumbled, tripping on my own feet and landing on my ass beside the little girl. The headless horseman was staring down at me. Or he would have been if he'd had a head.

The horse reared up onto its hind legs. Her whinny echoed along the houses, and even though it wasn't pretty, I scrambled to my feet and ran. I thought about stopping at the motel and pounding on Reyes's door, but his windows were dark. So I ran all the way to the café, the sound of hoofbeats following close behind.

When I got to the café, my lungs burning and my legs boneless, I found Reyes in the kitchen. They were about to close up for the night. As long as I got there before they closed, Dixie let me stay as long as I needed to. We didn't have to use the key to lock the back door as we left. But he'd worked that morning. Why was he there now?

"Hey," I said, leaning against the door frame. Mostly so I wouldn't fall down.

He stopped and gave me a once-over before saying, "Hey, back." He'd pulled out one of the refrigeration units that was on the fritz and was working on it. Tools decorated every available surface. "What's going on?"

A fine sheen of sweat covered my face. So that was great. Someday I'd meet him when I looked normal and not sleep deprived or sweaty or on the verge of passing out. Sadly, today was not that day.

"Nothing. I was going to use Dixie's computer for a bit. What's going on with you?"

He lifted a shoulder. "I get easily bored, so I offered to do some maintenance work."

"That's funny. I get easily distracted." And now I was going to try to get some work done while the man voted most likely to cause spontaneous orgasms was lurking nearby.

He let a smile as smooth as aged whiskey soften his features.

I wanted to ask him, "So, did you give me that

hundred-dollar bill? And if so, did you hear me when I said I loved you today? And if you did, how did you write a response on a bill that I got before I spilled my guts?" What came out was "Want some coffee?"

His eyes glistened in the low light as he took in every inch of me. Mostly my boobs. "Sure."

"I'll make a fresh pot."

Brenda was the only server left, and she was spot-mopping the café. I didn't know her that well, but she'd always been really nice to me.

"Hey, Brenda," I said as I filled the pot with water.

"Oh, hey, Janey. Great shirt."

Shirt? I looked down and almost groaned aloud. I'd forgotten I'd put on a shirt that read SAVE A VIRGIN. DO ME INSTEAD! No wonder he was staring at my boobs. This shirt was another Scooter purchase. That man made a killing off me that day.

With humiliation warming my face, I went to Dixie's office and closed the door. I'd made up my mind about Mr. V. I had to at least try. To feel out this connection of Bobert's and see what he could do. What kind of guarantees he could offer.

I dialed the number and waited.

A female picked up. "Agent Carson." I hadn't expected a female. Actually, I wasn't expecting anyone to pick up. It was after hours. I figured I'd go straight to voice mail.

I panicked and hung up. Anything I said to her could potentially put Mr. V's family in even more danger. But the phone rang about thirty seconds after I hung up. Was she calling back? Was that even legal? Son of a bitch.

I cleared my voice and picked up the receiver. "Firelight Grill."

"Yes, this is FBI Special Agent Carson, and I just received a call from this number."

"Oh, right. Some girl came in, used the phone, then ran out the back. It was weird. But thanks for calling."

"Are you Janey?" she asked.

Damn it. "No."

"That's strange. You sound like a Janey."

"Seriously?" What would the odds be that Janey was my real name? It was sort of growing on me.

She chuckled. "You sound very much like a Janey. I've been expecting your call."

I let out a long sigh. "Look, I don't think this is a good idea. I don't want to get anyone hurt."

"By law, you have to report what you know, especially if someone's life is in danger. I could have you arrested, see how you feel about it then."

I gaped at her. Or, well, at the bobblehead Beatles Dixie had on her desk. "Are you threatening me?"

"I never make threats, Janey. I make promises."

This was unreal. "So you would really have me arrested? "

"If what Detective Davidson told me is true, then yes I would."

"What the hell did he tell you? I hardly said a thing."

"He . . . filled in the blanks."

"Great." I was so calling him Charley Bob. "Before I say anything, I want you to know that Mr. V practically begged me not to try to get help. His family is in real danger. Their captors killed their dog. They mean business."

"Mr. V? Is that a name or an initial?"

I wilted in defeat. "It's an initial."

"And you believe he and his family are in danger why?"

Here we go. "It was just a hunch at first. There were men digging a tunnel in his store."

"A tunnel to where?"

"The dry cleaners. Look, that's not the point. The point is that they stand guard and watch his every move. And his family hasn't been seen for days. And they have a plasma cutter."

"How do you know his family hasn't been seen for days?"

And that was how the conversation went. Me trying to explain my misgivings without sounding like a mental patient, and Agent Carson probing for more.

"I happen to be pretty good friends with the head of the FBI in your area," she said at last. "I'm flying out tonight. I'll try to keep you out of this unless I have no choice. Is there a way to contact you?"

"Not unless you have a can with a really long string attached."

"Can I call you at this number?"

"Sure. I work the morning shift, but if I'm not here, you can leave a message."

"Okay."

"Discretion is key," I said to her, my voice pleading. "If Vandenberg's captors suspect anything—"

"I understand."

By the time we hung up, a huge weight had been lifted from my shoulders. Agent Carson really did seem to understand the situation. And she was savvy. I could tell by her questions and no-holds-barred comebacks. I didn't know where she was coming from, but the fact that she was flying here meant a lot.

What it didn't mean, however, was that I couldn't still try to find out where the Vandenbergs were being held. I fired up Dixie's computer and did a search. Several articles came up about Mr. V and his store. I found a picture he'd been tagged in of a birthday party they'd had for their son. I couldn't find a photo that specifically referenced the cabin, although one showed them fishing in an area that looked like it might be nearby.

I did every search I could think of with every combination of words that might point me in the right direction. I finally found a county assessor's report on some property Mr. V owned, but it was his house. Nothing about a cabin.

One thing I did find out was who the Vandenbergs' closest friends were. If worse came to worst—and it really didn't get much worse—I could hit up one of them, maybe flirt with an acquaintance, to see if they could tell me anything about the mountainesque property. I wasn't above flirting.

Speaking of which, I decided to do one more search. Even though it was almost eleven o'clock, I heard tinkering sounds coming from the kitchen. Reyes was still there. My heart had been racing ever since I saw him earlier. With each passing moment, knowing we were the only two in the place, it accelerated a little more.

I typed in the name Reyes Farrow and then sat for another hour, reading article after article, taking an emotional hit from each one.

He'd been in prison for ten years for a crime he didn't commit. He'd aided in a prison riot, helping employees who would have lost their lives escape. He'd earned several degrees while inside, including a master's in computer science. And he'd bought a bar and grill in Albuquerque, New Mexico, after he was finally released, because the man he'd been convicted of killing was found very much alive.

There were even a few pictures of him. Some when he was younger. One from the day he was found guilty for murder in the first degree. His face stone. His expression blank, as though he'd expected them to find him guilty, to think the very worst of someone like him, even though he had done nothing wrong.

I put a hand over my mouth, the sorrow I felt overwhelming. A lump formed in my throat as I kept searching. I quickly realized that he'd been something of a celebrity in prison and out. While he was incarcerated, men and women from all over the country, all over the world, created what could only be referred to as fan sites about him. One seemed to be more popular than the rest, however. The woman who'd created it, Elaine Oak, claimed to have done personal interviews with him. Her blog revealed that they slowly formed a relationship until, about a year before he got out, they were married.

I closed my eyes. This woman had professed her love almost to the point of worship and then, when he got out of prison, left him? Had she broken his heart? Maybe she wasn't able to deal with the real thing. With him behind bars, their relationship was sporadic. Probably fun and exciting. But maybe having a full-time husband wasn't what she'd signed up for, so she dumped him.

She'd abandoned him, just like the judicial system. She hadn't done another post for over a year. One of her lasts posts included a copy of their marriage certificate. Even after all this time, he was still struggling to forget her.

My heart ached for him, but I fought it. I battled the sympathy threatening to overtake any misgivings I was still clutching. I had too many questions. Too many concerns. None of his history explained why he'd stopped that woman from telling me who I was in the storeroom. She'd known me. She was about to tell me exactly who I was. Exactly where I came from. Why would he stop her? What would he have to gain? And why had he called me Dutch when I fainted yesterday? Was that my name? Did he know me?

I cleared the history and turned off the computer. If Dixie wanted to know more about him, she'd have to do a search herself. So he'd been here, on earth, just like any other human. But he wasn't just like any other human, and it was high time to find out why. I just needed a little chloroform and a few cable ties.

Since I couldn't figure out where to get chloroform or cable ties this late at night, I decided to go another direction. He seemed fairly amenable to a physical relationship despite his hang-up over his ex. I simply had to seduce him. Or pretend to seduce him. Surely I could distract him long enough to incapacitate him.

I strode to the kitchen and stopped. He was on his back, halfway under the sink, his lean hips so inviting, his legs bent at the knees and slightly open.

Good and merciful Lord. The things He could do with a little clay and some spare time. And He'd done an exquisite job with this particular specimen. I could hardly look at Reyes anymore and not feel a sharp tug at my heartstrings.

He raised up, just barely, from underneath the sink. He stilled. Studied. I could feel curiosity radiate out of him. He let his gaze drop to my chest, but only for a moment.

"You're still here," I said, suddenly remembering what shirt I'd decided to wear. It was pretty much the only thing I had clean.

He rose to his feet, the movement effortless, a charming smile lighting his impossibly handsome face. "So are you."

I moved to the side when he reached for a tool I was blocking. His heat enveloped me, and I bit down, tried to ignore my own heat gathering in places it had no right to gather, assembling unlawfully.

I decided to make myself useful and marry the ketchups, a term I found hilarious. "Why are you still here?" I asked when he turned to examine his handiwork. He wore a black T-shirt stretched taut to accommodate his wide shoulders, and jeans that fit snugly over his hips and the curvature of his sextastic ass. The bandages around his midsection left a soft line across his waist, and I wondered how badly he'd been hurt. I also wondered how he'd been hurt period.

"I'm still here because you are," he said matter-of-factly.

Wonderful. Now I felt guilty. "I don't need a babysitter."

"That's good, because no babysitter alive should have the thoughts I have about you."

His admission stirred something deep inside me. I was pretty sure it was a little-explored area just right of my spleen called stark raving lust.

"You were married," I said, empathy and jealousy battling for world domination.

Surprised, he turned back. "I was, yes."

Standing close to him was like standing next to a jaguar. Well, a jaguar made of fire. Every move he made was powerful. Exotic. Hypnotizing. Or I was ovulating. It was a toss-up.

"I'm so sorry it didn't work out. She seemed so devoted to you. Almost like she worshiped you. And then she, what? Broke it off? It makes no sense."

His lids narrowed to glittering slits, as though he had no idea who I was talking about. "Who are you talking about?"

Nailed it.

"Your ex-wife. Elaine Oak." When he didn't respond, I added, "And I'm sorry about . . . about everything else, too."

He stepped closer. "Everything else?"

"Yeah, you know, like . . . prison."

A scorching heat wave slammed into me, and he closed the distance between us. "Where are you getting your information?"

My defenses rose. "I know what a Google is. I can use a computer."

He lowered his head, his jaw straining against the force of his bite.

I wanted to explain. I understood. "The articles said that you were there for a crime you didn't commit. That your conviction had been overturned. They weren't bad."

The next expression he graced me with was disappointment. But I felt something else radiate out. Pain. Had I hurt him? Surely a man of his experience couldn't be so easily wounded. "Then by all means," he said, his voice dangerously low, "find out what you can about me via the Internet. Because everything on the Internet is real. Except alien abductions. They're bullshit."

He turned away from me and lowered himself to the ground to continue whatever it was men did under sinks.

Awareness of him hummed through me, pulsed like a living thing, throbbed with a combination of fear and desire. He was so off-limits it was unreal. I needed to interrogate him, not pleasure him. And yet all I wanted to do was test those limits. To push them. To push him.

I wanted to play. To explore. But that would require him wanting to do the same in return. For some reason, I didn't want to give him that much control. Not now. Not over me.

Was there a way to keep him at arm's length while I, for lack of a better phrase, had my way with him? Would he let me? Would he want me to? Or would he be repulsed by my advances? Judging from what I took to be his extreme interest, I thought not, but one never knew. Men were weird. Especially men made of tempered steel and fire and perpetual darkness. Or men with penises. Either way.

I let the ketchups practice cunnilingus virtually unsupervised as I devised a plan. He was simply too big, too powerful for me to overtake him. To tie him up. I doubted even sex would distract him that much. No, I needed to incorporate the restraints. Men loved that shit. Also, I just wanted to see him tied up.

I sat beside him and watched him work. He stiffened, paused his efforts to twist the round thing onto the other round thing.

"Can I ask you something?"

He slowly resumed his work. "I'd rather you ask me than Google."

I snorted. "Please. You wouldn't have told me half of what I learned on the Web, and you know it."

He didn't argue. "What did you want to ask?"

"First, you have to promise you'll do it."

He ducked under the cabinet door-frame and sat up, one hand resting on a knee. We were mere inches from each other. "I don't trust you."

His admission surprised me. I blinked up at him. Tried to figure out why he wouldn't trust me, of all people. He was the powerful one, after all. "No offense, but what on earth could I ask of you that would be a great hardship?"

His gaze rested on my mouth before making its way to my eyes again. "You could ask for the world, and then where would civilization be when I conquered it and laid it at your feet?"

I stilled. He was dead serious, and I realized I'd greatly underestimated his power. He was a supernatural being, yes, but he was more than that. So very much more. I breathed in his emotion and realized he'd done it. He'd conquered a civilization. Possibly more than one. His confidence was not derived from conceit. He was not arrogant. Not in the least. He was . . . experienced.

That knowledge sent another shudder through me, but not of revulsion, as it should have. As it would have any normal person. It sent a shudder of awe rocketing through my veins, and my plan solidified right then and there.

I stared at him with a new determination, but I still needed a guarantee. "If I promise not to ask for the world, will you do as I ask then?"

It took him a moment, but he finally agreed with a curt nod of his head. Apparently he took his promises very seriously. I liked that.

Down to the wire. My nerves sprang to life, and I almost chickened out. Two things drove me forward. I was desperate for answers and, again, I really wanted to see him tied up.

I chewed on my lower lip a moment. He watched me.

Drawing in a deep breath for encouragement, I said, "I was wondering if, maybe, you know, if you weren't doing anything at the moment and you liked me—as in *liked me* liked me—if you might consider letting me tie you up and have my way with you. For fifteen minutes."

Gawd, I was good at this shit. I should've been a lawyer. When he only stared, I looked away and tried to force the heat that crept up my neck and face back down. Humiliated was not my best look.

"But I understand if you don't want to. It's kind of sudden."

I scrambled to my feet and was about one step from the threshold when an arm shot out to block my path. I didn't even hear him move.

He stood at my back, his breath stirring the hair I'd stuffed behind my ear, which was probably as red as the rest of me.

"What happens after fifteen minutes?" he asked.

A surge of adrenaline laced up my spine. The soft fire that bathed his skin reached out to lick over mine. To caress. To punish just a little. I watched for a moment as it brushed over my exposed skin. The flames lapped like a thirsty animal, stretching as though to further its reach.

Reyes stood waiting for an answer. As always, I felt many things from him, but desire topped the list. It was like a white-hot pinpoint of blinding light in a sea of absolute blackness. And yet he didn't make a move. He didn't reach for me. He didn't touch me.

Perhaps he didn't want to scare me off. Whatever the reason, I was glad for it. I would only have refused his advances. Not that I didn't want them. I wanted him as badly as he wanted me, but I didn't quite trust him, any more than he trusted me. Not with all of me. Not with control over me. And I most definitely didn't trust him with my heart.

But if we just played . . . Surely there was no harm in playing.

I turned to him but kept my head down, afraid that if I peered into the sparkling depths of his eyes, I'd be lost.

He had one hand braced on the door frame. He braced

the other on the counter at my side, locking me in. "What happens after fifteen minutes?" he asked again, his voice smooth and full of challenge. It tugged at something deep and primal. I fought my reaction to him. Tamped it down. Forced my bones to stay solid.

I craned my neck to look at him, but he didn't accommodate me by moving back. He stood his ground, and I stood mine. "Nothing," I said, both confident and drunk with anticipation. "You'll be completely spent by then."

The small, incredulous grin that lifted one corner of his full mouth sent every nerve in my body springing to life. He'd just presented me with a challenge I couldn't refuse.

"I'm not pubescent, darlin'. I'm pretty sure I can last more than fifteen minutes."

"And I'm not a giggling schoolgirl. I'm pretty sure you can't."

His features darkened with the challenge I threw back at him, anticipation like sparks of electricity in the air.

I nodded toward a chair in the corner past the prep counter. "That'll work. But I have one more condition."

Taking his time, he glanced at the chair over his shoulder, then turned back to me, one brow quirked in question.

"You can't touch me."

"For fifteen minutes."

"Right. For fifteen minutes," I said, praying the interrogation wouldn't last more than five. After that, I could hightail it out of there. After a kiss, of course. I had to fuel the fantasy. It would probably only take him a few minutes to get free, and I had to be long gone by then. I could face his wrath tomorrow. While some might consider my plan cruel and unusual, he started it. He was holding back information as to my identity. I had a right to get that information by any means possible.

I grabbed the chair and pulled it to the center of the kitchen. If Dixie came in to check up on things, this could get really awkward. "Okay, sit down."

He hesitated a few seconds before taking the seat I offered, his stiff movements evidence of his reluctance. "Is the clock ticking yet?"

"No. I'll—" I glanced around and found a kitchen timer on the shelf over the grill. "I'll set the timer."

I ran to the office and took the belt off Dixie's spare coat, a trench she kept there for emergencies. Hurrying back as though worried he'd change his mind, I stormed through the swinging door to find him still seated. He'd dropped his hands to his sides and gripped the back of the chair.

I walked over, my approach wary, and pulled his thick wrists together behind his back. Threading the canvas belt around them, I tied it as tight as I dared. I wanted his hands to receive a regular supply of blood, but I wanted more to survive the evening. My gaze raked over every inch of him as I worked. His muscles contracted. Ripples of light and shadow swept over his arms. His breathing, slow, methodical, lifted his wide shoulders ever so slightly.

When I was certain he was secure, I walked to the grill, took the timer off the shelf, and set it for fifteen minutes. Then I stepped forward. He looked up at me, his appraisal was filled with a dubious curiosity.

I straddled him and plunged my fingers into his thick hair. It was softer than I thought it would be. Silky. I tightened my hold and tilted his head back.

His breaths started coming quicker as blood rushed through his veins, spurred by anticipation.

I pressed my body into his, tilted my hips, felt his erection through my jeans. His solid form was like nourishment, as though I'd been starving to death and didn't know it. My energy leapt with need. Just like the fire that rose off him, that need reached out to caress. To stroke. To inflame.

When I spoke, my voice was hoarse. Distant. I was already at the place I'd wanted to be for a long time: on top of the world with Reyes Farrow succumbing to my will. But to do what I was about to do was almost unforgivable, and I doubted someone like the dark entity beneath me was the forgiving sort.

"I have to do this now. Once I'm finished, you'll never speak to me again."

"And why wouldn't I speak to you?"

"Because you are about to be a very angry man."

"I'm about to be a lot of things, love. Angry is not one of them." It was not a threat. It was a promise.

But I knew better. He was wrong.

I bent my head to his while I still could, hovered my mouth over his, our lips barely a centimeter apart. Then I kissed him. His mouth was like the rest of his body: blisteringly hot. He opened to me immediately, and I pushed my tongue inside. My hands curled into fists, entangling his hair further, holding on for dear life as his tongue grazed over my teeth.

A warmth coiled inside me. Pooled in my abdomen. Tightened my skin until it felt too small for my body.

After what might be the only action I'll have for decades, I broke the kiss to examine him. To assess his emotional state. He was so startlingly handsome, I lost precious seconds just staring at him. He stared back. Slightly drunk, he watched me with his jaguar-like intensity, on the verge of pouncing.

He was going to want to pounce even more in a moment, but for a very different reason.

I leaned my head back, took in a sip of cool air, then asked, "Who are you?"

"Whoever you want me to be," he answered without hesitation.

This was not going to be easy. "No," I said, inching off him. "What kind of being are you? Because you damned sure aren't human."

He stilled, but it didn't take him long to realize what I was doing. Once he caught on, the fire that danced across his skin grew brighter. Hotter. He lowered his head. Monitored me from beneath his dark lashes as the predator in him took over. I could only pray my knots held.

When he said nothing, I moved on to phase two. I found the biggest knife I could, dared to enter into his circle of reach should he break free, and held it to his throat. He had no way of knowing I'd never really hurt him, but I still had to convince him I gladly would.

I slid the razor-sharp edge under his chin and raised his face to mine. "Who are you?"

Anger glittered bright and hot in his eyes.

"Fine," I said. "Who am I?"

"You're wasting precious time, Dutch." He looked at the timer. "In twelve minutes these restraints are coming off one way or another."

"You stopped that woman from telling me who I was. Somehow, you're the smoke. It cascades off you in waves. You're fire and darkness and dusk."

"Eleven."

"And today you heard me. When time froze, you still heard me. You stopped that angel from killing me. Why would an angel, a heavenly being, want me dead?"

"Ten."

"I can see things others can't. I know a dozen languages. I can talk to dead people."

"Dutch," he said through gritted teeth.

"And you keep calling me Dutch. Is that my name?"

"Nine."

It wasn't working. He didn't buy it. Not for a minute. Either that, or he wasn't concerned for his own safety. Perhaps he'd be more concerned about mine.

Growing more desperate by the second, I stepped back and held the knife to my own throat.

He fought the restraints, but I'd tied the belt to it so he couldn't get up. Not without great difficulty.

And suddenly I didn't care. I almost welcomed the excuse to join the departed. They didn't have it so bad. Unless I'd been a horrible person in my previous life, I would either go up or stay put. I was good with either. And I was getting answers tonight if it killed me.

"You'll have two minutes to untie your restraint and get me to a hospital. Last chance." I pressed the serrated edge into my throat. Flinched when it broke the skin. This was going to suck on all kinds of levels. "Who am I?"

"Eight."

I closed my eyes, took a slow, steadying breath, tightened my grip, and pulled the knife across my throat.

14

Denial, Anger, Bargaining, Depression, Acceptance . . .
The five stages of waking up.
—BUMPER STICKER

Before I got even a quarter inch in, I was pinned against
the refrigeration unit, my airway cut off by a steely grip.
Though not by a human. Smoke surrounded me, and I
couldn't see anything, but I could feel the hand around my
neck, the body pressed to mine.

Then the smoke dissipated and Reyes Farrow materialized. He had one hand, the one holding the knife, pinned
at my side. His other hand was busy making sure I'd never
breathe again.

With his face a mere inch from mine, I could see into
the incredible depths of his eyes. Mixed in with the deep
bourbon brown were flecks of gold and green. They glittered, and the old saying "All that glitters is not gold" came
to mind. Just because something glittered did not mean it
was good. And Reyes defined that line between the two.

He bit down. I could see the muscles in his jaw flex as he worked them. But I was mainly having a hard time getting past the smoke thing.

Who could do that? What in this dimension or the next was capable of dematerializing into another state of matter?

With a final shove of frustration, Reyes let me go. I fell to my knees and coughed so hard I almost threw up. I still had the knife. I tightened my grip even though it would clearly do me no good.

He'd turned his back to me, and I took the opportunity to scramble to my feet and bolt. I hit the swinging doors to the hallway and didn't look back. He could have caught me. Easily. Yet he didn't. Either he didn't care what I did, who I would tell about him, or he was afraid he would really hurt me. I was leaning toward the latter.

I woke up the next morning sore and exhausted. How did I even go to sleep after what I saw? The impossible. The inconceivable. Even though I was pretty sure physics wasn't my strong suit, I knew that what he did defied the laws of . . . everything. Nature. Science. Man. Did that mean that everything we knew about the world around us was a lie?

My mind spun with all the possibilities. With all the implications.

When I dragged myself into the shower, I tried not to think of it.

I failed.

Since I'd run home without Reyes's, I had no jacket to walk to work in. As with many things in life, layering was the answer. I pulled on a T-shirt, then a button-down, then a thin sweater, and to top off my layer cake ensemble,

I found the biggest, bulkiest sweater in my admittedly sparse closet and wiggled into it.

If this didn't do the trick, nothing would.

I grabbed my bag, said good-bye to the crew, and stepped out into a world of glittering ice. And there on my porch, hanging from a hook that had once held a wind chime, was Reyes's jacket. He'd brought it to me. I wrapped it tightly around myself. He couldn't be that mad if he was concerned enough to leave his jacket.

With breath visible, I hurried down the steps, almost biting it on the last one, then crunched across my yard and to the café.

Mable peeked out her screen door and waved at me.

"Good morning, Mable!"

She seemed different. Upset, perhaps. Her wave wasn't so much a greeting as a device to get my attention. I glanced around, then walked up her steps.

"Is everything okay?" I asked her.

She nodded, then gestured for me to enter. Mable walked the fine line between being a messy housekeeper and a hoarder. Piles of mail and magazines sat on every available surface. Plastic bins of items she was saving for this grandkid or that cousin lined the walls. And a collection of old dolls sat in a glass hutch that hadn't been dusted in probably twelve years. She wasn't gross, just cluttered. And a little dusty.

I waited for her to put in her teeth, then questioned her with a quirked brow.

"Laryngitis," she whispered, a slight wheeze to her voice.

"Oh, I'm sorry."

She waved off my concern. "Doesn't hurt a bit. I just had to tell you the latest. Have you met Jeremiah Kubrick?

He's Dixie's ex-father-in-law. Lives down the street near the Denton house?"

"Sorry," I said with a shrug. I had no idea what the Denton house was.

"Well, we were texting this morning"—I swallowed back my surprise that she and an elderly man were texting—"and he likes to keep an eye on the neighborhood. Has a telescope and everything. Anyway, he said he saw someone in your house last night."

I let my surprise shine through that time.

"And the night before. But you weren't home either time, so he thought you should know."

"Did he get a look at who it was?" I asked from between teeth that had cemented together.

"Sure did. That Jeffries boy. The one who became a cop."

I knew it. He must've made more than one key. "I'm so stupid."

"You most certainly are not." She gave my shoulder a chastising whack. "That boy has leaned a little off center since the day his mama brought him into the world. Force must've been desperate to hire the likes of him."

"Thank you so much for telling me." I had started to leave when the deeper implication sank in. "So this Jeremiah was watching my house with a telescope?"

"No," she said, chuckling. "He was just seeing if you were home. You know, to try to catch you walking around in your skivvies."

A horrified yelp squeaked out of me involuntarily. "He's a peeping Tom?"

"Certainly not! A peeping Tom sneaks around houses and looks in windows. Jeremiah looks in windows from a distance."

I didn't know whether to laugh or press charges. Not that I really would have. Pressed charges. I now knew who was breaking into my house, and I had an eyewitness. Jeremiah Kubrick had just given me the proof I needed to report Ian to his superiors.

I had to be careful, though. He was clearly unstable. The best I could hope for would be formal charges for breaking and entering filed against him. But there was a chance he could just lose his job. Then I'd have an even angrier unstable man with a license to carry on my ass.

"Thank you, Mable. I knew someone was breaking in. I just didn't know who."

"Well, now you know. And Jeremiah has pictures."

"No way." I fought the urge to fist-pump. "Those will help. Can I get a copy?"

"Course."

"Thanks, Mable. I have to get to work, but—"

When I stopped midsentence, she asked, "What's wrong?"

"He has pictures?"

"Yes."

"Does—Does he have pictures of me?"

She laughed. "Where do you think his new wallpaper came from? You look good in that bronze bra and underwear set, by the way. It's his favorite."

That was so wrong. So, so wrong. Time to invest in shades. But first, Ian.

Seething to the very depths of my soul, I walked out without even asking if I could get her anything.

How dare Ian. The gall. I felt utterly violated, and he'd never touched me. Well, he had, but not in that way.

Bobert had been a detective. He could advise me on how to proceed. Filing a complaint was one thing. Filing a complaint against a crazy man who also happened to be a cop was another beast entirely.

I strode to work without feeling the cold, I was so mad. Also, I was layered out the ass, a fact that became supremely evident when I had to de-layer in the storeroom.

When I'd first walked in through the back door, I was met with the scent of heaven. Literally. One word hit me. A word I may or may not have worshiped in my previous life. A word that meant the difference between a life filled with meaning and joy and a life vexed with doldrums and thoughts of suicide.

Chile.

Having shed most of my outer coating, I started toward the prep station to get the coffee going. Cookie wasn't in yet or it would already be done.

As I passed, Reyes stepped out of the kitchen and settled his weight against the doorjamb, his lean body holding the swinging door back.

I stiffened and glanced at him only because it would have been more awkward not to.

He was wiping his hands on a towel. "Feeling suicidal today?" he asked, anger shimmering in his eyes.

"Maybe." Seriously, I had the best comebacks.

"At least I can remember my name."

I inhaled, appalled that he would use retrograde amnesia to score such a cheap shot. I stepped closer. "Oh, yeah? At least I'm human." I probably should have taken note of our surroundings before saying something like that, but he didn't seem to care.

We were in the middle of a bona fide staredown when he reached into the kitchen and handed me a plate. "Merry Christmas."

He'd made eggs and enchiladas, with both red and green

chile. Christmas style. My mouth flooded so fast, I almost drooled.

"Thank you," I said, feeling sheepish.

"Oh, and this, too." He reached back in and handed me a steak knife.

I frowned. I didn't need a knife to eat enchiladas.

"In case you want to finish what you started last night."

"It's perfect," I said, snatching the knife out of his hand. Another badass comeback for the record books.

Actually, I did want to finish what I'd started last night. In the worst way possible.

I was in love. I didn't realize just how much until thirty seconds ago. I knew it the minute my eyes landed on him. Even angry and hurt and volatile, he liquefied my bones and infused my heart with warmth and life and a sense of security. He was like a sanctuary. Like shelter from a storm. I knew, beyond anything known and not known, beyond the future and the past, that I could count on this being, on this man, to be there for me.

It was the whole rote memory thing. I'd woken up in that alley knowing how to talk. How to walk. How to search the Internet. And I woke up in love. It was ingrained in my DNA. I loved Reyes Farrow. I craved him, and there was nothing I could do about it.

This went beyond the fact that he'd saved my life. Then again, he did. He couldn't be evil. That angel had every intention of dismembering me. Reyes—and the details were still a bit hazy—fought it off. Somehow he fought a celestial being. For me. Was even wounded in the process.

But angels weren't evil either. Maybe it wasn't as simple as good and evil. Maybe there were an infinite number of grays in between.

It didn't matter. Nothing else mattered. What he was.

Where he was from. How he freaking turned into smoke, because damn. He was mine, fire, smoke, and all. I staked my claim right then and there.

"Sorry I'm la—"

Cookie had rushed in like a frozen tornado but stopped short when she saw Reyes and me. She cleared her throat and walked to the storeroom to de-cloak.

I took my prizes and continued to the drinks station to start the coffee, but not before sampling a bite. When Cookie walked up, I groaned aloud and took another bite.

"Is that what I think it is?"

"If you think it's authentic enchiladas, then yes."

"I caught a whiff when I walked in, but I thought I was dreaming."

"Here you go." Reyes handed Cookie a plate as well through the pass-out window.

She sucked in a soft breath and took the plate as if it were a delicate treasure. And so the morning passed with the two of us sampling Reyes's cooking—when he wasn't looking, of course—and waiting on tables. But only because we'd get fired if we didn't.

Mr. P and the dead stripper came in. Ordered the usual. Garrett came in. Ordered the usual. Osh came in. Ordered off the menu, thus the usual. And a plethora of women filled up every other seat we had. The words *morning rush* were taking on a whole new meaning. Reyes might have been good for business, but I had blisters from trying to outrun the headless horseman last night and then running all the way home after the Reyes incident. And now they throbbed like the fires of a thousand suns. Still, like Dixie had said, dude could cook. I could forgive a few blisters if it meant a steady supply of chile et al.

When Bobert came in, I asked him if he could look into

Mr. Ian Jeffries. Surely I wasn't his first crush. If he'd gone stalker on other women, there would be a record of some kind, even if he'd never been formally charged.

I also told him about the phone call I got from the FBI agent.

"She's really good at her job," he told me. "Said she'd get back to me if they found anything."

"Bobert, what if I just endangered them more?"

"Janey." He covered my hand with his. "You did the right thing. The fact that you noticed what was going on may save their lives."

I gave him an unconvinced nod.

By eleven, Francie and Erin had arrived and dined on the now-famous enchiladas. Francie's face turned bright red, and her nose ran for the next half hour, but she carried on like a trouper. Mostly to impress Reyes.

But it was eleven and past time for Mr. V's usual phone call. I waited for his order, but none came.

"I'm going on break," I told Cookie. She was on break herself, sitting with Bobert. They both looked like they'd just had sex, but it was only the enchiladas.

I wrapped myself in Reyes's jacket and headed out the front door toward Mr. V's store. I hadn't even gone halfway when I noticed a sign on the door. No. This couldn't be good. Practically sprinting the rest of the way, I read the sign. CLOSED DUE TO ILLNESS.

I threw myself against the plate-glass window and cupped a hand over my eyes. It was dark inside. And empty. I stepped back and glanced at the dry-cleaning store. If the men had tunneled in and stolen something from them, wouldn't there be cops and investigators? Their open sign flickered, and a woman walked out holding the hand of a young boy, a plastic-covered dress draped over her arm. So it was business as usual.

A plan formed in my mind. I stepped to the street and studied the buildings. If I was right, I might have a way into Mr. V's store that did not involve lock picking, which I was pretty sure I'd fail at, or breaking out windows, which I was pretty sure I'd fail at, too. Not the window-breaking part, but the stealthy, not-getting-caught part.

I hurried back to the café. The lunch crowd would be arriving soon. I didn't have much time. And I'd need help.

I hated taking Cookie away from the love of her loins, but people's lives were at stake. With an almost imperceptible nod, I motioned for her to meet me in the storeroom.

She squinted at me.

I motioned again, with a perceptible nod this time.

She shook her head and shrugged.

I gritted my teeth and pointed outright to the storeroom.

"Sweetheart," Bobert said, trying not to chuckle, "if you don't meet her in the storeroom posthaste, she's liable to stroke."

I probably should have tried to be discreet at someplace other than right beside his booth.

After kissing Bobert good-bye for, like, ever—PDA much?—Cookie followed me to my home away from home. "What is so secretive that you can't tell it to me in front of Robert?"

"I need your help breaking and entering."

"Okay, but I'm not sure how much I can help. I'm good with breaking things. Entering, not so much. Especially if it involves a rooftop and a rope. Just no."

"I just need you to be the lookout."

"Oh. I can do that." We walked into the storeroom and locked the door behind us. "Is this going to stress me out?"

"Probably. And I might need your phone."

"I'm just not sure I can handle more stress in my life right now."

I nudged a shelf with my body weight until it was closer to the corner that paralleled Mr. V's shop. There was an access panel to the heating and cooling system there. If I was right, the stores had once shared the system.

"Nonsense. You're like tea. The hotter the water and all. What's going on?"

"I don't know. It's just everything. New town. New house."

"New friend who sees dead people?" As Cookie held the shelves steady, I climbed up and lifted the access panel.

"Not at all. You're one of the best parts."

"Thanks. Can I see your phone?"

She handed it to me. "That's what's crazy. Everything is great. My husband is great. My house is great. I love the area. I mean, seriously, this town is beautiful."

"I agree." I turned on the flashlight. The panel gave repairmen access to the wiring and the sprinkler system. The lower ceiling was only made up of two-by-fours and Sheetrock. I hefted myself up. Kind of. I mostly stacked boxes on the top shelf and made myself a ladder. "But all change, even good change, puts stress on our bodies and minds."

"True. Wait, why are you doing this again?"

"Mr. V is out sick." I scanned the entire length of the buildings with the flashlight and found what looked like a cutout in the dividing bricks about fifteen feet from me.

"I don't think we should be taking advantage of his illness by breaking into his store."

"He's the one."

"Which one??

"The one I told Bobert about. The one being held hostage."

"Janey, really?" she asked in alarm. "And you're breaking into his store because?"

"I need to see exactly what they're doing." With only about two feet of clearance, navigating the claustrophobia-inducing space was proving tricky. "Also, I need to figure out where his cabin is. Do you know?"

"I have no idea what they're doing, but I feel awful for Mr. Vandenberg."

I placed a knee on one board, then a hand on another, crawling forward at a snail's pace. My break was going to end before I got halfway.

"No, I mean do you know where his cabin is?"

"Oh, no. But Robert could check into it."

Oh, yeah. I didn't think of that. I made it to the opening. Sadly, it was the size of a credit card. I swiped at a few spiderwebs, then slid through. It was touch-and-go where my ass was concerned. Took a little while and a lot of wriggling to get her through. Mr. V's ceiling was exactly like the café's. His access panel was closer to the opening, thank goodness.

The muffled tones of Cookie's voice wafted up to me, but I didn't respond. Partly because I couldn't understand her, but also, I didn't want to have to shout loudly enough to be heard. From what I could tell, the opening was somewhere above Dixie's office. I doubted she'd appreciate my creeping about her attic.

I army-crawled to Mr. V's access panel, ignoring the pain in my knees and rib cage where I lay across the boards. Who knew the edges of a two-by-four could be so painful? Prying the panel up proved to be harder than planned, but I finally got my fingernails under it and lifted one corner slowly.

It was still dark inside his store, so I lifted the panel and set it aside. Then, with the stealth of a drunk ninja, I lowered myself through the hole. Sadly, Mr. V didn't have any shelves conveniently placed under the panel for me to climb down, so I had to drop several feet to the floor. The second my feet hit the ground, I looked up and wondered how I was going to get back.

I'd worry about that as soon as I figured out exactly what the captors had been up to. Using Cookie's flashlight, I wound my way around antiques of every size and nature. There were simply too many breakable things. I'd never be comfortable working in a store that carried so many breakable things.

The plasma cutter sat on the side of Mr. V's desk. It was connected to an extension cord, so either they'd already used it or they planned to soon.

I finally found the door to the back room, held my breath, and opened it. If they had set some kind of guard to watch over their handiwork, I was dead. I could live with that. Thankfully, it was just me and a gaping hole.

The entire floor had been torn out. The whole thing. It was a small room, more like a closet really, but still. I felt they got a little carried away. The dark hole lurking beyond the battered floor was my main concern. More tiny spaces. Great.

I got onto my hands and knees and was shining a light into the tunnel when I heard a growl. A low, deep grumble right behind my left ear.

I turned slowly and came face-to-face with a snarling

set of teeth. The Vandenbergs' German shepherd. He growled and snapped at me. It was the cutest thing.

"Hello, pretty boy," I said to him. He was beautiful. "Aren't you the prettiest thing?"

Despite the growls, I raised a hand to pet him. He whimpered instantly and licked my face instead of ripping it off. We played tackle-and-roll a bit, and then I asked, "Do you know what they've been doing down here?"

He barked, then offered an apologetic whine.

"It's okay. It's not your fault. We'll figure this out together, okay?"

He barked again, and I took Cookie's phone and climbed down the rabbit hole.

15

I don't understand your specific kind of crazy,
But I do admire your commitment to it.
—T-SHIRT

Barely wide enough for one good-sized man, the tunnel extended only about ten feet, then stopped under another rabbit hole. Just as I thought, they were tunneling into the dry-cleaning business.

I reached up and felt the cool smooth texture of metal. The plasma cutter. They were going to use it to cut their way inside. Two questions came to mind immediately: Why would a dry-cleaning business need a metal floor, and what could they possibly be keeping in there?

Was it a vault of some kind? If so, it had to be massive. Like a bank vault. Or maybe it was a panic room. Or an old bomb shelter, though the metal had glistened a bright silver. It couldn't have been very old.

GS, for lack of a better name, whimpered again when I started to back out. He picked his way through the dirt, then bounded up into the shop. I didn't bound, but I did hoist myself up using the brute strength God gave me. And the frame of the door. My fingernails would never be the same.

GS and I searched Mr. V's desk for some clue as to where the cabin might be and found nothing. I glanced at all the pictures again, examining them closer this time, reminiscing about Mr. V's wonderful kids while looking for a house number or a street sign. Nothing again. Sadly, I just didn't know the area well enough for any of it to look familiar. Those pictures could have been taken in Nepal for all I knew.

Giving up, I took one of the pictures out of its frame, ran my fingertips over the kids' mischievous faces, then folded it and put it in my back pocket. Then I turned to the next challenge. How to get back up to the access panel. The answer presented itself by means of a massively tall ladder, the kind that looked like it would topple over at any moment.

After positioning it under the panel, I climbed it the way I imagined I would climb to my execution: slowly and reluctantly.

When I made it to the top, I clutched the opening and had little choice but to jump as hard as I could. The ladder would surely fall, but I had no alternative. I simply wasn't strong enough to pull myself up from that distance.

"Bye, sweetheart," I said to GS.

He barked and disappeared through an old chest on the wall opposite me.

With one final prayer, I shoved off the ladder as hard as I could and pulled with everything I had. Sadly, everything I had wasn't going to be enough. I heard the ladder crash into a myriad of fragile things. Mr. V was going to kill me. Now I had antiques to pay for along with my hospital bills. I'd never get a phone. And my arms were beginning to shake.

When I heard a bark above my head, I glanced up to see GS standing over me, his tail wagging as though we were playing a game. But my arms were giving out. I kicked to try to heft myself up, to no avail. Then GS took hold of my shirt at the shoulder and pulled.

It was working. I slowly ascended until I had enough leverage to pull myself up. Why on earth did people make ceilings a thousand feet high?

I crawled back as quickly as I could without falling through the ceiling, but my shaking arms weren't helping. Neither was GS's desire to play pounce-the-human. Basically, the next chain of events was the result of a combination of several key factors, the main one being a sudden and devastating lack of strength. Despite all the careful navigation, I fell through the ceiling. I know. I never saw it coming either.

And I had been *this* close.

Part of me landed on the shelves we'd dragged over, and the other part, namely my ass, did not. I executed this cool flip thing—I knew this because the ceiling was there, then it wasn't, then it was again—and landed face-first on the linoleum floor.

"Janey!" Cookie screeched and rushed to me. "Oh, my God, are you okay?" She pried me off the floor and helped me to my feet.

"I—I think so." I blinked and tried to fill my lungs. They refused to take more than a quarter of a tank. It would have to do for now.

She brushed me off, and then we turned in unison to the gaping hole in the ceiling.

"Think Dixie will notice that?" I asked Cookie.

It really wasn't that big. And it was right beside the original access panel. Now Dixie could have two.

"We can cover it up," Cookie said, panicking.

"That's going to take a lot of spackle."

"No, with the shelves."

"Oh, right." We pushed the shelves over until they were directly under the hole.

"Okay," I said, assessing our work. "As long as everyone stands right here, right in this very spot, they won't be able to see it."

"This sucks," Cookie said, suddenly despondent.

"Don't worry, hon. I'll pay for it. Dixie won't mind."

"Wait, maybe Robert can fix it. We can offer his services in exchange for us keeping our jobs."

"Cook, you are not taking the blame for any of what happened here. This is all on me."

"Let me at least try. I'll text him to see if he's still here. He can come take a look. You got my phone?"

I patted my front pockets. My empty front pockets. My eyes rounded, and fear shot lasers up my spine. Did I lay it down somewhere? I couldn't remember.

"Janey," she said.

This was not happening.

"Oh, Janey, no. No, no, no. You did not leave my phone in Mr. V's shop where any terrorist could find it."

"Cook, I never said they were terrorists," I said as I patted my back pockets. My fingers touched something square, and I almost fell to the ground in relief. But I'd already done that today, and once was good enough for me. I grinned.

"Oh, thank God," Cookie said.

I pulled it out and handed it to her, pretending not to notice the shattered screen.

"Oh," she said.

"I bet a little shipping tape will fix that right up. You'll hardly be able to tell."

She tried to stop a giggle from escaping and ended up snorting in the process.

"I'm sorry, Cook."

"Janey, do you think I care?"

"Yes."

"Well, you're right, but not at the expense of your safety. It broke your fall."

"That was my face."

"Was any of that worth the effort?"

I told Cookie what I'd found as we headed to the door and opened it to a sea of heads.

Dixie stood on the other side. Along with Reyes, Bobert, Garrett, Lewis, and Sumi, though I could only see the top of her head. They were all packed into the tin-can hallway like sardines. Osh was there, too, but he stood back a little, wearing his signature smirk. He would be the smart-ass sardine.

"Could you two be any louder?" Dixie asked.

"We could try," I said, my brows scrunched together with worry. "This was my fault. Cookie had nothing to do with it."

Cookie stood behind me, biting her bottom lip. "Yes, I did. It was my idea."

"It so was not."

"Was too."

I glared at her. "Cook—"

"What on God's green earth?" Dixie had spotted the ceiling. She stepped inside.

"It just fell," Cookie said. "It was crazy."

Dixie turned back to . . . Reyes? An accusing expression on her face. An expectant one.

He nodded, and she brightened. Like surface-of-the-sun bright. "No harm, no foul," she said, ushering us out. "That happens all the time. We'll get it fixed in no time. Herb Wassermann. Best handyman in town."

Cookie and I exchanged confused glances.

Wait. No we didn't. I exchanged a confused glance. Cookie didn't seem surprised in the least. Relieved, but not surprised.

"So weird how that happens," she said to Dixie.

Dixie nodded. "Water damage from the storm back in '22."

As in 1922?

"You mean '82?" Bobert asked.

"Yes." Dixie chuckled. "Sorry. Get my decades mixed up all the time. Back to work, girls. Place is hoppin'."

She practically pushed Cookie and me into the café. Everyone else either went back to work or sat back down. We were thoroughly glared at by Erin and Francie. Apparently they'd been handling the lunch crowd on their own and were none too happy about it.

I pocketed the keys I'd lifted while in the storeroom and went back to work. Dixie was right. The place was definitely hoppin'.

My first stop was a table with a single white female. Probably here for dinner and the show. If Reyes would learn to strip, we'd be set for life.

"Hey, hon. Can I get you something to drink?"

She glanced up at me, the barest hint of recognition flashing across her face, but only for a second. I'd learned not to get my hopes up. Everyone who'd seen me on the news thought I looked familiar.

"Hi," she said, giving me a quick once-over. She had a short brown bob and a pretty oval face, but the navy power suit said it all. She was someone important. Or she could have made paper airplanes for a living. Didn't matter. With that suit on, she could convince anyone of anything.

"Love the suit," I said. "Can I get you something to drink?"

She offered me an appreciative half smile, but what I felt from her was more like . . . relief? "I'd love water for now. And coffee."

"A girl after my own heart."

Before I left the table, the blond woman I'd met a day earlier walked in—or, well, stumbled in—and sat at the table across from my customer. I could only hope they knew each other.

"Hi again," the blonde said. Her hair was a bit wild and her cheeks bright pink. "Some weather, huh?"

"Yes, it is. Are you having a good vacation?"

"This is Kit," she said in lieu of an answer.

I stuck out my hand with a chuckle. "Hi, Kit."

"I'm Gemma."

"I remember." Clearly Gemma had issues. "Can I get you something to drink?"

"Sure." When I stood there staring at her, she jumped as though startled. "Oh, right, yes. Ummmm . . ." She looked at the menu. "How about a . . ." She tapped her fingers. "Oh, I don't know . . ." She bit her lip. It was a big decision. "Coffee?"

"Great choice," I said, latching onto coffee and running with it before she changed her mind.

I could practically feel the heat of Reyes's gaze on me. But better me than Francie. That was my motto.

The lunch rush was even worse than the day before, and it was only Reyes's second day. I thought about demanding Dixie hire more help, but since I'd just fallen through her ceiling, I decided against making demands for the time being.

Reyes glared but made sure I ate. Francie flirted and made sure I noticed. Erin glowered and, well, glowered some more. Cookie only assaulted one customer, and it wasn't nearly as sexually charged as her normal fare. And Lewis? Lewis was in love. Shayla didn't come in until five, but I could see him counting down the minutes. My heart wanted to burst little hearts out of its left ventricle for them both.

With only about thirty minutes left on the clock, I walked into the kitchen to see how Lewis was doing, but before I could talk to him, Reyes looked up and said, "It's been almost seven hours, and you're still alive. I'm impressed. Figured you would've abandoned all hope by now."

I let out a loud sigh, turned on my heel, and left. But I didn't go far. I went into Dixie's office, actually. She was out on a bank-slash-nookie run—I was pretty sure she was practicing the popular pastime referred to as an afternoon delight with a boyfriend she kept stashed somewhere— so I helped myself again to the belt from her canvas trench.

I rolled it into a ball, stashed it in the back of my pants, and went in search of a victim. I stormed into the kitchen so fast, the door ricocheted back and almost slammed into my face. It didn't. I caught it, but just barely.

Reyes arched a brow. I strode up to him and pushed, walking him back until we were between the prep counter and the walk-in unit. It allowed us a tidbit of privacy. I continued to push until I had him up against the wall. His dark irises sparkled with interest. Especially when I brought the belt around, gathered his wrists in front of him, and tied him up.

Tendrils of heat slid beneath my clothes as he looked down at me, and I wondered if he was doing it on purpose. How much control did he have over the heat he emitted, the energy he radiated?

He wasn't *that* much taller than me, not quite a head, but I grabbed Sumi's stepstool and placed it at his feet. Now we stood eye to eye, and his particularly mesmerizing eyes held both humor and intrigue.

I wrapped my arms around his neck and kissed him. He let me. It started out sweet and sensual, but it quickly escalated into a kiss more passionate than I dreamed possible. Then his arms were free and around me. Somehow he managed to reverse our positions so my back was to the wall instead of his, and still keep me on the stool.

He raised a hand to my jaw and lifted, exposing my neck so he could place blisteringly hot kisses on it. I gasped and tilted my head farther to give him more access. An arc of heat followed his trail, and I curled his hair into my fists, pulling him closer, begging him not to stop.

"I'm sorry, Dutch," he said, doing the exact opposite.

My body screamed in protest.

"For this."

I thought he was apologizing because he'd stopped. He was apologizing for the almost translucent bruises he left on my throat. They were barely visible, but he ran his fingers over the ones he could see. It caused the most amazing sensations to race down my spine and dart between my legs.

I refocused on him. On his full mouth. On his clenched jaw. On his serious expression.

"I claim you," I said, sounding silly, but I didn't care. After I ran my fingers over his mouth, I said, "You're mine."

"I always was. But what about your suicidal tendencies?"

"None of that other stuff matters right now." I tightened my arms around his neck.

He moved one hand to my lower back. The other rested on my rib cage. "It does if you were serious. Which you were."

"Temporary insanity. It's gone now."

"Is that a promise?"

"I don't suppose 'Cross my heart and hope to die' would be an appropriate response?"

He pulled me closer. "Only if you want me to tie you up next time."

The thought sounded way more appealing than I let on. "Okay, then I promise."

Dixie walked in, and I stiffened as though I'd been caught making out with the quarterback during recess.

"What'd I miss this time?" she asked.

"She tie him up," Sumi said, her voice forlorn. And she had a tiny speckle of drool at the corner of her mouth.

"Janey, would you stop tying up my cook and get back to work?"

After offering Reyes a whispered apology, I bounded past him and out the door, mumbling another apology to the woman who signed my paychecks along the way. All fifty-six dollars' worth.

By the time I got off work, my body was thrumming with excitement. Reyes was mine. Mine, all mine. I did a little hip twitch and ran to get his jacket. While I would have killed to spend the afternoon with him, there was a whole other place just begging to be broken into. And I had the keys.

"What are you making?" I asked him before heading

out. Officially, he was off the clock, too, but he seemed to enjoy the heck out of cooking. And keeping busy in general.

"Posole," he said, flashing me a crooked grin that dissolved my kneecaps.

His hands were busy chopping stuff, so I rose onto my toes and whispered into his ear. "You are so trying to win my heart through my stomach."

"Is it working?"

"Hell, yes." Then I put my mouth squarely on his.

I jumped and whirled around when a plate shattered behind me. Francie was standing there, her mouth open in shock. Embarrassed, she turned and ran out.

"Crap," I said. "I'll go talk to her."

"About what?" he asked, and the fact that he was genuinely confused made me fall down the rabbit hole of crazy-for-Reyes just a little bit farther. "Do you know what you do to people?"

He lifted a powerful shoulder. "I guess. But what are you going to tell her that will make her feel better?"

He had a point.

"I have no idea, but I have to try."

His expression turned to astonishment. "You're still so—"

"What?" I asked when he didn't continue.

"You're so caring, even when people don't care about you."

"Clearly you know next to nothing about me. I bought a Rolex from this guy named Scooter in the Walmart parking lot and it was a fake. I don't even like him anymore. Seriously."

A dimple appeared on his right cheek as he tried to fight a grin. "But if he were in trouble and needed your help with something?"

"Oh, well, I might help him. But only if he gave me a refund. Two bucks is two bucks."

He released a breathy laugh that was part bewilderment and part admiration.

I'd take it.

"I'm sorry, Francie," I said, walking into the storeroom. "I didn't mean to just flaunt that in front of you. I wasn't thinking."

She scoffed. "Like I care." She finished applying lip gloss and started out the door. "I could get a date with a different guy every night of the week if I wanted to."

I wanted to say, "If you wanted to look like a ho?" What I said was "I know. I didn't mean it that way." But Francie was already out the door.

I felt the sting that rocketed though her when she saw us. It wasn't what I wanted for her.

Erin stood a few feet away. "You're just a ray of sunshine, aren't you?"

"I can be," I said, defensive. "And what the hell, Erin? I took a couple of extra shifts you'd asked for. It's not like you can work both shifts all day every day."

"Is that why you think I can barely stand the sight of you?" she asked.

"Pretty much."

"You're so clueless."

She turned to leave, so I rushed to say, "Then what?" I stepped closer. "What did I do?"

After releasing a sigh of annoyance, she said, "When I was little, I went to a palm reader set up at the state fair."

An alarm sounded in my head with the words *palm reader*.

"She told me I'd have three children and all three would die before they were a year old."

The clanging got louder.

"The first would die when all the land became water. Hailey died after a huge flood five years ago." She stepped closer to me. "The second would die after my mother's heart broke. Carrie died two days after my mother had a massive heart attack."

"Erin, that doesn't mean—"

"The third one would die after a girl with no past showed up. No past! I thought, everyone has a past. Surely we can have a baby now. But no. In walks a woman with no. Fucking. Past."

She turned and stalked away. I stood in shock, trying to breathe air that had vacated the room. This sucked on every level imaginable.

I had to figure out what was going on, and I had to do it now. Then I planned on hunting down that bitch palm reader and asking her how she lived with herself, saying shit like that to a little girl. Who does that?

I picked up a couple of sandwiches, said hey to Mr. P and the stripper, who'd come in for a late lunch, then started for home. And, naturally, the man and his trusty steed followed me. I pretended not to notice the thousand-pound animal or the headless guy atop it. Mostly because I had too many blisters to run from them again.

"I can do this all eternity," he said. In perfect English. "Follow you around. Fuck with your head. Speaking of which, did you know there's an old guy with a telescope watching you?"

How the fuck was he talking? And his vocabulary was

way more modern than I would've expected. If he was really the man from Mr. Irving's story, he'd adjusted well to modern life.

"I'm not kidding. All. Eternity."

I finally stopped but refused to turn around. To acknowledge him. "Look, I'm sure your story is tragic, but I don't know where your head is."

He started laughing. "I think I have that covered. Would you just face me?"

With the reluctance of a food taster for a king hated by all, I turned toward him, but I only looked as far as his black riding boots.

"Look up."

I raised my gaze to his black pants.

"A little farther."

I finally focused on where his head should have been. Or where one would expect his head to be. The man talking to me was actually in the coat.

"It's a costume," I said. I hadn't thought of that.

"That it is."

"So you don't want me to find your lost head?"

"Seriously, I could do so much with that. Have you ever met a man?"

"Oh, right, sorry. But then why are you following me?"

"Firstly, because you are who you are and—"

"Wait, you know who I am?"

That tripped him up. "No. Not really. I just know you can see people like me."

"Yes, I can." I walked up and nuzzled his horse before restarting my journey to James's place. "And secondly?"

"Secondly, I need a favor."

Headless guy followed and explained as we went, so that by the time we arrived at James's cardboard palace,

I knew that his name was Henry, that he'd been an actor re-creating a scene from "The Legend of Sleepy Hollow" for Halloween a couple of years ago, and that he and the horse, Gale Force, were killed when the bridge they rode across gave way. They ended up falling into the frigid water, and Henry couldn't get out of the costume. The fall broke Gale's neck on impact. Henry drowned. It was a tragic freak accident. Nothing more.

"That's awful," I said, oddly enough a little more sad about the horse than the guy. I nuzzled her again.

"I need a favor."

"I'll try."

"My best friend designed the costume, and he's blamed himself for my death ever since."

"Oh, no, he couldn't possibly have known."

"I know. I just want him to know it's okay. That I'm okay."

I couldn't just show up and tell him his best friend was okay; it probably wouldn't go over very well. "What if I wrote him a letter?" I asked.

"Honestly, I don't care how you do it. He isn't doing well. He needs to know that I don't blame him."

"I think I can do that." Gale Force whinnied and nudged me when I stopped stroking her neck. I laughed and asked, "Anything else?"

"Oh, yeah, just one more thing. Stay away from that cop you're seeing."

"What?" I asked, surprised. "Why?"

"I don't like him. Never have."

Sounded legit. "I'm not seeing Ian. So you don't have to worry."

"Yeah," he said with a scoff. "That's what the last girl said."

"What last girl?"

Gale Force reared up. I gasped and stepped back. She was so beautiful.

"Tamala Dreyer," he called out as he turned and spurred her forward. "Look her up!"

"Wait! Why did you let me run from you yesterday? Why didn't you say anything?"

"Dude, I'm the headless horseman. I live for that shit."

He took his job way too seriously. But he pulled it off well. As they galloped down a side street, black cloak billowing out behind him, he looked as headless and creepy as ever.

16

*Coffee has given me unrealistic expectations
of my productivity.*
—T-SHIRT

I dropped off a sandwich at James's box and listened to his version of "Don't Fear the Reaper" for a while before taking the other sandwich to Mable. She had to tell me the latest on her great-nephew, and I was suddenly glad I didn't have a drug problem. He'd have to spend a lot of money if he was going to cover the tat of a vagina he got on his neck during a three-day binge. On the bright side, he was now in rehab and feeling pretty stupid.

I borrowed the car and drove to Erin's house. I knew her husband had similar hours, so after knocking, I took the key I'd stolen and opened the door. The house was small, but neat and tidy. I started in the living room, and sure enough, almost every picture there was of the old creepy lady. Her eyes were solid white, and her toothless mouth hung open in a scream or a laugh, I couldn't tell. She did seem angry, though.

The only pictures that didn't feature the old lady were of Erin and her husband or other family members. One, an older one of a young girl with teased bangs and laser lights shooting behind her, had to be her mother. The eighties were a scary time. Another one of a young girl with cat's-eye glasses and a bouffant, could have been her grandmother. Or possibly a beloved great-aunt. But for the most part, the Clarks were living in what I would consider a house of horror. Every picture was disturbing on new and escalating levels.

Then I realized they might not all be of baby Hannah. Some of them could be of Erin's first children. Was someone or something haunting Erin? Was a ghost targeting her children for some reason? And if so, for what reason? What would a ghost have to gain by killing children?

I wish this seeing dead people had come with a manual of some sort. Or a diagram. A flowchart would have been nice. I might have to go to the library and look up *Fifty Reasons Ghosts Kill*. Or *How to Tell if You Have a Poltergeist in Ten Simple Steps*.

Poltergeist. Could that be it? Weren't they different from, like, regular dead people? I wracked my amnesic brain. What did I know about honest-to-goodness poltergeists? They were angry. I knew that. They often attached themselves to a place, an object, or a person. They lived, in a manner of speaking, for scaring the crap out of people.

But if that was the case, Headless Henry fit the definition as well.

Wait, no he didn't. He wasn't angry. He wasn't using his power for evil. He had an evil sense of humor, but that didn't make him a bad guy. This woman, the woman targeting Erin and her family, was bad.

If I were being the least bit honest, I would have admitted that I had no idea whether a ghost could actually kill. It seemed wrong in the grand scheme of things. But it was the only explanation. Other than the obvious one that any normal person would adhere to: Erin's children died of SIDS. Plain and simple and what I considered one of the most tragic of all losses. Pretty much any bad event that happened to a child made no sense. Everything from kids with cancer to the ones who'd been abused or abandoned. The mere thought ripped at my heart. And the idea of Erin losing another child squeezed it like a vise.

Why? Did the child really have to pay for the sins of the father? And if so, what the bloody fuck? Why should my kid have to pay for my mistakes?

I was so never having children. They'd be doomed.

A male voice sounded from behind me, and the adrenaline that dumped into my system caused me to jump so high I almost bit it on the landing.

"Hey!" he yelled. "What are you doing?"

Reflexively, I picked up the poker from the fireplace and turned to him, aiming it like a sword. "Stay back! I mean it."

He stood just outside the kitchen, wearing only a towel and holding a . . . frying pan. Really? An entire kitchen at his disposal and he chooses a frying pan? Admittedly, it was cast iron. It'd kill if wielded properly, but I didn't think this guy was a killer.

"You're in my house," he said, holding the skillet with both hands in the exact manner I was holding the poker. I honestly didn't know who was more frightened. But he did have a good point. I was the trespasser, he the trespassee.

"Who are you?" he asked as he took a wary step back. He looked to the side and spotted something.

All my dreams of living a life free of sliding bars and crappy food vanished when I realized he was going for his phone.

"Wait!" I yelled before he picked it up. "I think your house is haunted!"

He picked up the phone anyway but didn't do anything with it. Not yet.

There was still hope. I took one hand off the poker and raised it in surrender. "I know how this is going to sound, but I think your baby's in danger."

"That's what my wife keeps saying. Do you know her?"

"She told me your first two children passed before they were a year old."

He lowered the pan. "Yeah, but they weren't mine. She and her ex divorced after their second child died."

That made sense. Not many couples lasted after losing a child.

"And now she keeps going on and on about this bitch at work and how she now believes Hannah will die, too, no matter how safe we are."

"Yeah. I hate to be the bearer of bad news, but I'm the bitch."

His muscles tensed.

"Did she tell you about the palm reader?"

He nodded. "I know it sounds crazy, but I think I'm starting to believe her. Either that or it's like those cults where they brainwash their members into believing aliens are going to take them to their home planet."

"Right? What's up with that?" I wracked my brain trying to remember his name.

"That still doesn't explain what you're doing in my

house. Unless, like Erin said, you are here to kill our baby." His hand tightened around the pan again, and he started pushing buttons on his phone.

"What? She said I would try to kill your baby?"

"Not in so many words, but she said just the fact that you're here has put her in danger."

It finally came to me. "I'm here to try to save her, Billy. To try to figure out what's going on."

"Mm-hm." He held up an index finger to put me on pause, then scrolled though his phone. I heard elevator music in my mind until he said, "Yes, I'd like to report a break-in."

My jaw dropped open. "Billy!" I whispered, rushing toward him. Prison orange did not look good on me. "Just give me a chance. I can see things others can't. I can see a woman in the pictures of your daughter. An old woman with white eyes and—"

"Never mind," he said into the phone. "I thought someone was breaking in across the street, but they were just leaving a note." His entire demeanor changed in a heartbeat, and he went from scowling at me to gaping at me, only in a really cute way. Seriously, the kid could have been a supermodel. "Yes. No, yeah, I understand. I'll keep an eye out. Sorry about that."

He talked his way out of the call and put his phone down.

"You've seen her, too?" I asked. "In the pictures?"

"No. In the house."

Fuck. I was right. She was here.

"Okay, tell me exactly what you saw."

He'd grown a little pale and had to sit down. We walked back into the living room and sat on their very used but terribly comfy couch. It was probably a hand-me-down.

They clearly couldn't afford much. Their decor was sparse but prettily placed.

They worked hard for what they had, and I admired them both.

"So, I got up one night about a week ago to check on Hannah. Just this weird tug inside me."

I wondered if he might be a little touched as well.

"I was half asleep, but when I got to Hannah's room, I could have sworn I saw someone standing over her. An old lady. I asked her what she was doing in my daughter's room, and she—" He stopped as though gathering himself. "She turned and just came at me. I fell back, but when I looked again, she was gone."

"That's awful." I wanted to share. I wanted to tell him about being chased by the headless horseman and how this customer at work had a demon tucked inside him, but now was not the time for group therapy. "What did you do?"

"I ran to Hannah and picked her up. I thought . . . I was worried she'd done something to her. By the time Erin got up, I'd decided I'd dreamed it all."

"I'm just glad Hannah was okay."

"But when you said the part about her eyes . . . This woman's eyes were solid white. That's all I saw, and I haven't slept well since."

While I was totally glad not to be handcuffed, I was still at a loss. What if the woman really was haunting Erin? What if she really killed the babies? What then? Could one really hire an exorcist? If so, how? From what I understood, the Catholic Church tended to drag its feet about these things. Hannah was in danger now. Especially since I—aka the girl with no past—showed up.

"Where's the baby now?" I asked.

"With Erin's aunt."

I nodded and walked over to the pictures on the mantel. "Are these all of Hannah?"

He stood. "No, these two are of her first two babies, Hailey and Carrie."

All I saw was the creepy old lady. It was like a horror film on pause.

"What exactly do you see?" he asked me.

"In every picture of the children, I only see the old lady. In the others, though, I see you guys and other assorted family members."

"Are you sure?"

"What do you mean?"

"I mean, how would you know? You can see past the woman, right?"

"True."

"Okay, then point to the ones where you see the old lady."

I pointed to the first one. He nodded. The second. Another nod. The third, and so on. Erin was so into family, it was charming. We walked to the pictures on the wall. She had them artfully arranged and all framed in white.

The babies were only in two pictures there. I started again and pointed to the one closest to me.

Billy frowned. "You see her in this picture?"

When I nodded, he shook his head. "This is Erin's great-aunt Novalee. She died in the thirties or forties."

Surprised, I pointed to another photo. He shook his head again. "This is Novalee, too."

"All I see is the crazy ghost chick. Why does Erin have pictures of relatives she's never met?"

"She's just like that," he said. "She loves old pictures and antiques and stuff. And Novalee's story is tragic. I just think she always felt a connection with her even though they never met. All her older relatives say Erin looks just like her."

"How is Novalee's story tragic?" I asked, suspicious.

"From what I understand, she was a nut. Like certifiable. Set fires. Tore up any paper with pictures for no reason. Spent almost her whole life in an institution."

Sadly, that could have meant any number of debilitating mental diseases. Or it could even have been a result of a childhood injury or illness.

"You know what?" he said, heading to the hallway. "There might be something up here." He pulled the ladder to the attic down and had started to climb up when he remembered he was wearing a towel. "Maybe I should put on some pants first."

"Maybe," I said, chuckling.

It was a shame. He looked really nice in that towel. I needed to get Reyes a towel. Everyone needed a towel. It wouldn't look too desperate.

Billy went to change, so I perused the pictures along the walls there. Erin had an incredible ability to decorate combining both old and new. Some of her heirlooms looked so fragile. So delicate.

I came across a drawing and stopped. It was very old, from the early 1900s judging by the dress the woman was wearing in it. But it was her.

"Billy!"

He ran out while pulling on a shirt. "Did you find something?"

"Is this her?" I asked him. "Because this woman could be Erin's twin."

He squinted. "Oh, yeah, I think it is." He took the drawing off the wall and looked at the back. "Yep. Erin labeled all of the pictures. This one is from 1910. Novalee Smeets."

I studied the drawing, but she was too young in it. I couldn't tell if that was the crazy lady or not.

"You can see her in this, right?"

"I can. What were you going to show me from the attic?"

"Oh, when Erin was a kid, she used to draw a lot. I think she copied a lot of the old pictures she had. She might have drawn another one of Novalee."

"Did she draw any of Novalee when she got older?"

"Let's find out."

I started up the stairs, and the situation seemed eerily familiar. It gave me flashbacks. "I just fell through a ceiling. I won't fall through, right?"

"Nah, it's finished."

"Okay."

After some rearranging, Billy found a box of Erin's old drawings. She was an incredible artist. She practiced hyperrealism. Her drawings looked so real they could have been photographs.

"Does Erin still draw?"

"Unfortunately, no. I mean, look at these. We could be rich," he joked. "She stopped after her first baby died."

"She's amazing."

We pored over each drawing, checked names, and searched for other photographs she'd used as reference.

"Here's one," he said, holding it up for me. "The original is downstairs."

I could see why she used that picture. Erin had focused mainly on the face and let the other details in the picture fade away. The woman in it was old with fragile cracks along her skin and eyes that didn't quite look right. She was staring off into space; then I realized why.

"This is a mourning portrait," I said to him.

"Wow, how'd you get the time of day?"

"No, mourning as in grieving. Novalee had already passed when this picture was taken."

He lurched back as though suddenly afraid to touch it. I fought the urge to chase him with it while screaming, "Death cooties! Death cooties!" Sometimes my thoughts led me way too far astray.

"Well, mystery solved."

He stared a moment, then asked, "This is her? The woman I saw?"

"Unless there are two ghosts hanging out here, that's her."

"What the hell? I mean, is she trying to kill Hannah?"

I chewed on a fingernail in thought. "I'm not sure."

"Then what do we do? How do we stop her?"

"I have no clue." He gaped at me, so I explained. "I see her, plain as you see me, but I don't know what to do about her. I'm not exactly an expert, but I do have connections."

"What kind of connections?" he asked, his brows knitting in suspicion.

"The, um, noncorporeal kind. I'll ask around."

He stared again, then snapped out of it and looked at my hand. "You know, you can put that down now."

I looked at the poker I still held. The one I'd climbed to the attic with. "Oh, right. Sorry." After I laid it on the floor beside me, I said, "Look, Erin and I don't exactly . . . get along. If you could, maybe, not mention that I broke and entered?"

"Don't worry about her. She's a pussycat."

To him, maybe. She wanted to kill me with a tire iron.

"How did you get in here, anyway?"

I fished the keys out of my pocket. "I stole them from her purse."

"Nice."

"Okay, I'm going to do some research, check with my connections, and I'll get back with you the minute I know something."

I drove back to the café. Reyes was gone, but he'd left the posole unattended. Crazy man.

I scooped up a bowl and went to kick Dixie off her computer.

"I'm playing online strip poker," she said, pretending to be annoyed.

Knowing better, I scooted her out of her chair with my butt.

"Fine. I have to get home anyway."

"I know."

"Oh, yeah? How?"

"That special ringtone you use anytime you get a text from your secret lover? It dinged three minutes ago."

She gawked at me for the better part of a minute, then gave in and let excitement shimmy through her.

"Oh, by the way, your ex-father-in-law is taking pictures of me in my underwear."

"Really? He's good. You should get some nudes while you're at it, too."

"Will do. Have fun." I waved her off and brought up Google.

Before I went into the whole poltergeist thing, I decided to check up on the name Headless Henry gave me: Tamala Dreyer.

The search garnered dozens of hits about a girl who died under suspicious circumstances. Her death was eventually ruled a suicide, but her friends and family disagreed and openly accused her high school sweetheart, who they claimed was stalking her after a messy breakup, of killing her. One article showed a picture of the grieving family. In the background was Henry.

The article listed him as a second cousin. He protested the loudest, swearing she was killed by the stalker. And then he named him. Called him out. Challenged him.

"I have nothing to hide, and I will not be quieted by an incompetent police force."

Ouch. That couldn't have helped their cause.

"Tamala was killed by Ian Jeffries."

Wow. The guy had balls. I wondered what he could have done with his life if it hadn't ended so young. I soon found myself searching every inch of the Internet for information on Mr. Ian Jeffries. A couple of years later, there was another suspicious suicide of a woman he'd claimed to be dating. When Henry heard Ian was a person of interest but nothing ever came of it, he protested again, and the proverbial shit hit the fan.

I read further. *A close friend of the deceased says the woman never said yes to Officer Jeffries's proposal. "He wouldn't take no for an answer."* Ian was claiming to be the fiancé of the woman, but her family denied that vehemently.

And the million-dollar question? Was Henry's death really just a freak accident?

And the ten-million-dollar question? Was Ian planning a similar fate for me?

I looked at all the facts. Ian had been a person of interest in the suicide deaths of two women. I was a woman. He had access to my house. He knew my routine and the fact that I had no phone. No way to call for help. Time to change the locks and get a stupid phone once and for all. I just hadn't really needed one since I knew no one on the planet when I woke up.

I called my landlord immediately, told him someone was breaking into my house, and asked for a complete lock change. He grumbled a little but said he could get to it in a couple of days. So as long as I didn't become suicidal over the next two days, all should be right with the world. I could borrow Mable's car tomorrow and see about getting a phone. Hopefully tips would rock.

I remembered the hundred-dollar bill. No way was I spending that. Surely I'd earn enough for a cheap Trac-Fone, if nothing else.

That settled, I opened a new Google and searched poltergeists, to no avail. Actually, to too much avail. There were hundreds of thousands of hits, and the more I read, the more convinced I became that I was crazy. I was just seeing things.

But wait! There's more!

Billy saw her, too.

Okay. I felt better. From what I gathered, poltergeists were the entities believed to be responsible for physical disturbances, like moved objects and loud noises. But I couldn't find anything about a poltergeist that actually killed people. Nothing legitimate. There was tons of fiction, but I needed real answers.

Then I found another interesting tidbit. One researcher believed they could definitely attach themselves to people or objects and become obsessed with them. I knew that, but it was nice to have it confirmed.

Erin had gotten off work some time ago, so I hated to do it, but I had to call Billy. He'd given me his number before I left so I could let him know what I'd found out.

"Hey, it's me," I said, whispering. Not sure why.

"Oh, hey, Tommy," he said. Then he yelled, presumably to Erin, "It's Tommy. From work."

"I am well aware of where you know Tommy from, hon." She laughed, but it was the baby sounds in the background that brought on the attack.

The edges of my vision blurred, and a sadness took hold, the force of it seizing my lungs. I had to sit down. To catch my breath. To try to fill the emptiness that was drowning me.

"You there?" he asked.

"Yes. Yes, I'm here." I closed my eyes. Focused.

"So, I got more of the story from Erin. About her great-aunt."

Alarmed, I asked, "You didn't tell her, did you?"

"About us? No, baby, we're good." His voice was full of humor, and the situation struck me as ironical as well. If there were a list of reasons for a guy to sneak around, to exorcise a poltergeist would not have been at the top. "So, what are you wearing?"

His teasing helped. I filled my lungs, confounded by the panic attacks I'd been having. Just another day in the life, I supposed. "What did you find out, Romeo?"

"Prepare to be blown away."

I bounced around and lolled my head from side to side like a prizefighter. "Okay, totally prepared."

"Erin's great-aunt killed her own daughter, then spent the rest of her life in an insane asylum, telling everyone who would listen that the doll was her deceased kid. How's that for creepy?"

"I'd give it a solid 9.8." The thought of a mother killing her own child disturbed me way more than I let on. I knew it happened. I just liked to be kept in the dark about it.

"Okay, does Erin have anything of Novalee's? Perhaps a piece of jewelry or a blanket? Anything?"

"Besides those pictures, I'm not sure. Wait. Now that she's told me the story, I wonder if that doll in the attic was hers."

"What doll?"

"There's this really creepy doll in the attic. Come to think of it, it does look like the one from the picture."

"There wasn't one in the picture."

"Not in the drawing, but there is in the picture Erin used to draw it."

I perked up. "And Erin has it? What does it look like?"

"You know, one of those old dolls that looks dead. Its face is cracked, and its eyes are solid white."

"Billy, can you get to it?"

"I guess. I think it's still in the attic. Why?"

"I need you to get it out of your house."

"And do what with it?"

"I'm not sure. For now, just bring it to me. I'm at the café."

"I'll try. I'm not sure how I'll do it without Erin finding out."

"You'll think of something."

"Is it the doll?" he asked, as though it suddenly all made sense. "Janey, Erin's aunt Noreen gave her that doll the very first time she got pregnant. Noreen had tried to have kids for years but miscarried several times. Then when she finally did carry all the way, her baby died two weeks later in its sleep."

"Just like Erin's."

"Exactly."

That fact only reinforced my belief that this was

somehow connected to that doll. "Billy, get that doll out of the house. Now. I'll wait for you here."

"I'll be there as soon as I can."

We hung up, and I started a new Google. Good thing they were free. This time I looked up how to destroy a possessed item. From what I could tell, I'd need holy water, the heart of a dragon, and the nail clippings from a canonized saint.

17

Ahhh, Friday . . .
My second favorite F-word.
—T-SHIRT

A little while later, Billy knocked on the office door.

"Come in," I said as though I had a right to.

He walked in with a brown paper bag. "It's in here. You think this will stop her?"

I took it. Opened it. Shivered. "I hope so. What did Erin say?"

"Nothing. I told her I was meeting my mistress. She told me to make sure I wore clean underwear, 'cause she'd rigged the brakes and it would be awkward if the EMTs had to cut off dirty boxers."

"She plans ahead. I like that."

He nodded, suddenly nervous. "What if this doesn't work?"

"Then we'll keep looking. I won't give up, Billy."

"Thanks. I can't imagine why Erin hates you so much."

"Boggles the mind, right?"

Billy left, and I let myself acknowledge the heat that I'd begun to associate with all things Reyes Farrow. I tucked the bowl I'd used to confiscate a sample of his posole against my side and hurried to the kitchen sink.

I rinsed it out, hiding the evidence, then turned toward him. "You're here again."

"You're here again," he said. He was leaning against the prep table, watching me.

I was busy thinking, *My God, that man defines the word "smoldering,"* when he asked, "What'd you think of it?"

With a snort, I said, "It was freaking awesome. Seriously. Like, mind-blowing. What are we talking about?"

Humor deepened the dimples he sported whenever he wanted any woman within a fifty-foot radius to melt into a quivering puddle of girl jelly. His dimples were just too sexy, too delicious, not to have an ulterior motive.

"The posole," he said.

"What? I didn't take any of your posole. I have my own posole at home. Like, a gallon."

"Ah. So, that hint of red chile on your blouse?"

I gasped and checked out the front of my shirt.

A breathy laugh escaped him. "Busted."

After closing my lids, I said, "For the record, it was incredible. You should become a chef. Or buy a restaurant. You'd make a killing. And only partly because you draw crowds of ovulating women."

He sobered and dropped his gaze. "I don't mean to."

I'd meant it as a compliment. Apparently it wasn't one. "I'm sorry."

"Don't be. It doesn't suit you."

Having no idea what he meant by that, I went back to

my earlier thoughts of all the words in the English language that he defined. *Beautiful. Alluring. Provocative. Captivating. Charming. Sensuous. Dark. Brooding.* And somewhere in there, as always, the word *bad* popped up. I got the feeling that when Reyes Farrow wanted to be, he could be very, very bad.

I realized he was letting me take him in. Giving me a moment, as it were. I dropped my gaze and asked, "Want to go for round two?"

I felt the tension in the air tighten like a bowstring being pulled between us.

"With the same rules?" I added.

"And what rules were those again?"

"Can I have you? For fifteen minutes?" Humiliation surged through me. He was a tad angry the last time we did this. It would serve me right for him to say no.

"Right," he said softly. "I remember now. I can't touch you for fifteen minutes."

"Yes."

He was in front of me. I felt his heat but could not bring myself to look at him. "And what happens after fifteen minutes?"

The arrogance I'd used to my advantage last time had fled me. I had no clever comeback. No promise of what I could do to him in that fifteen minutes. I just knew that I wanted him. Plain and simple.

"After fifteen minutes, all bets are off."

"And I can touch you?"

A warmth washed over me. The prospect of him touching me caused both excitement and anxiety. The mere thought made me feel vulnerable. Exposed. At his mercy. But a deal was a deal.

"Yes."

"And no thoughts of running a blade across your throat while I'm tied up?"

I looked up at him at last. "Like it would do me any good."

"Exactly."

He reached behind himself, took off his apron, and ripped off its strap. "If we do this, will you finish what you start?"

He asked it while holding the strap out to me, giving me permission to tie him up. For some reason, the thought of him tied up gave me a hit of confidence, even though I knew it would do absolutely nothing to stop him should he want out.

"And if I don't?" I asked. I wasn't a tease. I was pretty sure about that, but if something happened . . . I wanted a guarantee of some kind that he would not become the bad boy I knew he could be.

"Like I said before, Dutch, I'm not pubescent. I'll survive if you want to stop, but just barely. I might need CPR."

I let out a soft laugh.

He showed me those dimples again, then fetched the chair, sliding it to the center of the room. He sat down and crossed his wrists at his back, a challenge glittering in his eyes. The width of his shoulders became all the more evident in that position, and I had to take in his form for a moment before walking around to the back of him.

I knelt down and wrapped the strap over his wrists. He let his fingers slide over my hands as I tied. The movement, so small and seemingly inconsequential, sent tiny shivers up my arms. When I finished, I bent forward and kissed his palms. His long fingers glided over my cheek and neck.

When I stood, I walked to the timer, set it, then turned back to him. "I only have fifteen minutes," I explained as

I peeled off my boots, jeans, and underwear. I had to save every second I could.

The sweater I wore hung past my hips, so he didn't really see anything, but he gave a low growl and let his head fall back as though he now regretted being tied up.

I straddled him like last time and drove my fingers into his hair. He focused on me, his glistening gaze sharp, his sleek muscles hard. I kissed him, softly this time, the act unhurried and intoxicating. When he opened to me, he tasted like storm clouds and rain. I settled on him, and he drew in a cool breath of air between our mouths. His erection teased and tempted me, and I pushed into him a little harder. A whispery moan escaped him, and he tilted his hips into me. The friction caused a jolt of electricity. I clutched his shoulders, and he did it again, rubbing my clitoris, sparking a fire deep inside me.

Unable to hold the swirl of arousal in check any longer, I reached between our hips and yanked up his T-shirt to reveal the rungs of his stomach, before returning to his face. His fire had grown even brighter, but I focused. Saw past it. Concentrated on the man behind the inferno.

Scooting back, I brushed my mouth over the smooth skin of his chest. Grazed my teeth over a nipple. Flitted my tongue and suckled.

The strap creaked against the strain of his hold, but he kept his word. He stayed tied to the chair, but I felt the struggle raging inside him. The rise of temperature. The tightening of muscle.

I let the shirt fall and turned my attention to his jeans.

Every move I made caused a burst of adrenaline to spike inside him. That, in turn, caused the exact same reaction in me. Every point of contact, every nuance of desire sent a ripple of ecstasy shooting to my core.

After I unfastened his jeans, I pushed them over his hips. He lifted off the chair for me, and I slowly lowered them to reveal his erection, swollen and rigid. To say I was impressed would have been an understatement. I pushed his jeans past his knees and wedged myself between them. I wanted to taste him. To graze my teeth over the length of him. To swallow his excitement until need gripped him so hard he had no choice but to come in my mouth.

But I didn't. I wanted him inside me even more, and I was running out of time.

Instead, I leaned forward and ran my tongue from the base of his cock to the tip. He stiffened, his muscles tensed to the consistency of marble. When I crawled onto his lap, took his erection into my hand, and slid the entire length of it inside me in one smooth effort, his groan caressed my senses. Pushed me higher.

I wrapped my arms around his neck, grabbed handfuls of his hair, and moved. Slowly at first. Rocking my hips ever so slightly. Stoking the embers inside me, giving them time to ignite. Then faster. Letting the pressure in my abdomen grow with each stroke. With each driving thrust.

Then I felt it. The first quiver of orgasm. Just a tiny tremor, a spark in the deepest nether regions of my body like a white-hot pinpoint of energy.

He felt it, too. I could tell when he stilled. When he closed his eyes. When he clenched his jaw.

It grew with the speed of a lightning strike. Spread. Pooled in my abdomen like molten lava until the pressure exploded and spilled over me with the sweetest sensation known to mankind.

The strap broke, but Reyes kept his word. He wrapped his hands around the back of the chair, his knuckles solid white as his own orgasm rocketed through him. He groaned as the sting washed over him. Bucked as the last remnants pulsed through him.

I held him to me so tightly I feared he might suffocate, but he didn't seem to mind. Then I realized I'd heard a sharp crack. I leaned back. He'd broken the chair. The metal chair. That was going to be difficult to explain.

The timer dinged, and he dropped the back of the chair and wrapped his arms around me. It surprised me at first. His hold was tight but tender, his breaths hoarse and ragged. I held his head to my chest for a long time, and I didn't want to let go. I never wanted to let go.

If not for Sumi sneaking in to turn the slow cooker down as we sat entwined in the broken chair, then leaving without making a sound, pretending she didn't see us, I might never have. But we both started laughing when she left, and the time had come for me to let him breathe again. I shimmied off him, scooped up my things, and headed to the bathroom to clean up while he pulled his jeans over his hips.

After grabbing his jacket, I waited as he turned off the kitchen lights. We walked out the back door, locking it behind us.

"I guess I'll see you tomorrow," I said as he walked me to Mable's car. He slipped his fingers into mine and we walked like high school sweethearts, hand in hand.

He had what I realized was his black truck parked across the street or I would've offered him a ride.

"Why didn't you want me to touch you?" he asked, his voice sincere.

Even though it was embarrassing, I told him the truth. "Partly because that would be giving you too much control over me."

He nodded, not the least bit offended. "And the other part?"

"Because I don't deserve your touch."

"What do you mean?"

I dismissed it with a laugh. "Never mind. I don't know."

"Please, tell me."

Even more embarrassed, I scraped my foot along the pavement. "I think I'm a bad person." When he started to argue, I said, "I know this is going to sound crazy, but I can tell when a person is bad just by looking at them. I don't know why and I don't understand how and I don't expect you to believe me, but I can tell when a person is bad. And trust me when I say I'm a bad person."

"You're wrong."

"You know I'm not. You have good instincts as well. You have to sense what kind of person I am. Why else would I be here? Why else would I forget everything if not because I'd done something very bad?"

When we got to Mable's car, he turned me to him. "You're wrong."

I was about to argue again, but he dipped his head and kissed me. It was soft and demanded nothing, and I fell another notch.

I heard yelling in the distance. High pitched. Angry. The tone telescoped until it was right in my face. I was back in my apartment and had jumped Denzel the minute I got home. So was I dreaming? Having another nightmare? I pried my lids apart to see an elderly woman in my face, a decomposing elderly woman, her eyes solid white, her mouth open as she screamed at me.

"Where's my baby?" she asked over and over.

Bolting upright, I scrambled to get away from her and fell out of bed. The wooden crate that served as my nightstand slammed into my shoulder. Before I could get up, a coffee cup whizzed past my head and shattered against the wall on my right.

I crawled on my hands and knees to stay clear of the flying debris. My apartment had exploded, and at the epicenter was a very angry, and very powerful, lady.

The bathroom seemed like the safest place. I armycrawled to it and tried to kick the door closed. Instead, I cut my foot on shards of broken glass. I lifted my gaze to see hundreds of pieces of broken glass hanging in the air around me.

She'd shattered the mirror, and what little moonlight there was glinted off each hovering piece. The second she dropped them, I dived out of the bathroom. They showered the floor with tiny, musical clinks.

Since she was using Denzel as a battering ram and aimed him straight for my head, I scrambled to the living room. My bed crashed into the wall, shaking the whole house. I stood and started for the door and was busy praying Mr. Kubrick wasn't taking pictures when a glass rocketed past me. It swam through Irma's head and struck the wall on the opposite side. Pieces of it hit Satana, who'd been hiding under Irma's feet. She hissed and darted off.

Anger exploded inside me. I bit down and glared at the woman destroying my most prized possessions, like the glass. It was my only real glass.

I glanced at Irma. "Stay put. I have this." Then I was in front of her. I grabbed the woman's throat mid-scream. I could barely understand her anyway. All I knew was that she wanted her baby.

"First of all," I said, pointing in the direction Satana had run, "that is my cat." She tried to blind me with her nails, so I grabbed her hand with my free one and pulled her closer. "Second of all, I'm not as easy to kill as an infant, but keep trying. We'll see how many babies you kill after tonight."

She calmed instantly and blinked. "What?"

I blinked back.

"Why would I kill you?" she asked, her voice suddenly soft. Confused. "Why would I kill a baby?"

I blinked again. "Because that's what you do?"

"I have never!" she said, appalled. She slapped my hands away.

I dropped them and stepped back.

"I would never do something like that. I've tried to stop him every time."

A dread the weight of the planet crept over me. "Who, Novalee?"

She pressed her lips together. "The man who killed my daughter. The one who had me locked away in an asylum for the rest of my life when I tried to tell people he'd done it. My husband, Delbert Smeets."

An eerie silence settled about the room. Novalee's blank eyes watered as she thought back.

"He killed my precious Rose and told everyone I'd done it."

"And they just believed him?"

"He was The Mayor," she said, matter-of-fact. "No one questioned The Mayor. He had half the town in his pocket."

I crunched over to a rickety dining chair, cursing when I stepped on a Lego. No idea. "Novalee, I don't know what to say. We thought it was you."

"No." She sat in the other dining room chair.

If only I had a dining room. Or a dining table, for that matter. As it was, we just sat in the chairs, facing each other.

"I would never harm a child."

"But a grown woman?" I asked, indicating my poor apartment with a nod. What was I going to tell my landlord?

"No. Never. I was just trying to scare you."

"Well, it worked. Holy rusted metal, Batman."

The smile she flashed seemed so rational. So . . . sane. If not for her solid white eyes and that touch of decomposition.

"Do you still want your doll?"

She lowered her head. Twisted her hands in her lap. "It's not my baby, is it?"

I shook my head.

"They told me for years it was her, and I began to believe them."

"I'm so sorry, Novalee. But I need to know, did your husband kill Erin's first two children?"

She lowered her head farther. "Yes. I tried to stop him.

"But why?" I asked, saddened and sickened.

"My sister. She was the only one who stood by me after what happened. She tried to get me released. Tried to convince the authorities that Delbert had killed our child. Tried to get people to come forward with all the atrocities he'd done to them. Because she defied him, because she dared to stand up to him, he vowed to kill her daughters, too. And all of her son's daughters. And so on. He's been doing it ever since. Only the girls and only until they reach a full year. If they survive that long, he leaves them alone."

"Damn. He really hated girls."

"He was an evil man."

"No need to convince me of that. You've been trying to stop him?"

"Yes." Her shoulders wilted, as though she were exhausted from the effort. "I've been successful three times in all these years. With Erin's mother and her twin sister, and then with Erin herself."

"What about Erin's aunt? She had a baby—"

"Yes. It was Delbert. I couldn't hold him back any longer. He's getting stronger." She raised hopeful eyes to me. "You have to stop him. Once and for all."

This went way beyond what I'd signed up for. I shook my head. "Novalee, I don't know how. I can't even imagine."

"But you have to," she said, panicking.

She was right. I had to try. What was my life worth if I didn't even attempt to save a child in danger? "Okay. I'll try. How do I stop him?"

"Don't you know?"

"I haven't the slightest."

She smiled sweetly. "You just have to see him." Then she leaned forward and placed her cool hands, soft with age, on either side of my face. "Your light will do the rest."

"My light? Like, my flashlight? I might need to put new batteries in it, then."

She patted my cheek and stood as if to leave.

I followed suit. Pointing to the doll that now lay on the floor under Irma, I said, "I'll give her back to Erin."

"Thank you." For a moment she just stared at it, and I thought she was going to cry. Maybe I shouldn't have told her it wasn't her baby. Sometimes ignorance was bliss. She sniffed and refocused on me. "But you must hurry. I can hold him off, just not for very long, and he's almost there."

Alarm coursed through me. Without asking her anything else, I grabbed the doll, then the keys to Mable's
car, and ran.

By the time I got to Erin and Billy's house, I was shaking uncontrollably. Probably because I was wearing a tank
that read I'M PRETTY SURE MY GUARDIAN ANGEL DOES
CRACK and a pair of scrubs I'd taken home from the hospital, and the temperature was somewhere between holy-
shit and it's-cold degrees below. I'd torn out of Mable's
backyard, risking her reporting the car stolen, but I didn't
have time to explain. Or, apparently, grab a jacket. I hadn't
realized how badly my foot was cut until it kept slipping
off the gas pedal, so blood loss could have been a contrib-
uting factor to my convulsive quivering as well.

I skidded to a stop in front of their well-cared-for home
and sprinted to the door.

"Billy!" I yelled, pounding as hard as I could. "Erin!
Open up! Hurry!"

After about two minutes of disturbing the peace at the
most irritating time possible, I'd managed to get everyone
in the neighborhood to turn on their porch lights except
Erin and Billy.

"Billy!" I screamed, shoving all my weight against the
door. If I couldn't get them to come to me, maybe I could
go to them. But the door was made of some kind of super
wood. The harder I shoved, the more stuck it seemed to
become, until finally, like a light shining down from
heaven, their porch light flickered on.

Erin cracked open the door as far as a chain latch would
allow, her brows drawn from both sleep and fury. "What
the fuck, Janey?" she asked, her voice thick and groggy.

"Open the door," I said.

"Fuck you."

Once again, I didn't have time to explain. "Sorry about this."

I drew in a deep breath and threw all my body weight against the door. The chain broke, and Erin stumbled back with a scream.

"Erin!" Billy said, scrambling down to help his wife up.

I tossed him the doll. "It's not the doll. I was wrong," I said, as I shot past him and up the stairs.

"Janey!" Erin screamed. She hurried up the stairs behind me, but I soon lost track of her movements. The minute I crossed the threshold into her daughter's room, I stopped short.

Delbert was there, and he had Novalee by the throat, his meaty hands choking her. She slowly sank to the floor. Could he really hurt her? She was already dead.

She looked over at me. At least I thought she did. With no irises, it was hard to tell.

Yep, she was definitely looking at me, and she appeared none too happy with me. Then I realized why. She was keeping him distracted, and I was rubbernecking.

"Billy, get your daughter out of the house," I ordered.

"What the fuck are you doing here?" Erin asked, demanding an explanation. Unfortunately, Delbert had lost interest in choking his wife to death and had whirled around to face me.

Billy—God bless him—didn't hesitate. He ran for Hannah and scooped her up. "Where do I take her?"

Erin stood appalled and more than a little confused. "What is going on?" she asked him, alarm raising her voice an octave. She rushed to join Billy as he grabbed Hannah's diaper bag.

I honestly had no clue where he should take her, but surely a place with holy ground would keep evil away.

"To a church," I said. "Or a cemetery. Anywhere with consecrated ground."

He nodded and bounced Hannah as she began to cry.

Her cries caught the undivided attention of The Mayor. His eyes glittered with appetite.

"Now!" I yelled at him, then to Billy. "Get them out!"

Again, he didn't hesitate. He latched onto Erin's hand and bolted down the stairs with both of them.

Anger flared to life around Delbert like electricity when they left. I took it. Siphoned it off him. Absorbed it and molded it to my will. He was strong, though. And I'd forgotten my flashlight. I wondered if any light would do.

I searched for a light switch and realized Erin had come back. "Erin, what the hell? Get out."

She shook her head. "No. Billy is taking Hannah to safety. I need to see the end of this." She knew. Somehow she knew that there was something supernatural upsetting her life.

I didn't know what she could see, but I was pretty certain the earthquake that shook the house would leave an impression.

Novalee found her footing and stepped back, arms crossed and a satisfied expression on her face. I wanted to tell her about the flashlight, but Delbert was growing both angrier and weaker by the moment.

His energy, evil or not, felt wonderful. I blinked in surprise. He was like a drug. Like heroin or extacy or 3 AM coffee. I stepped closer, unable to get enough as though suddenly parched. I drank him in. Reveled at the high it gave me. Inhaled him until he was completely drained of energy.

Novalee placed hopeful hands over her chest. Delbert groaned. And the house shook to its foundation.

Pretty soon, Delbert was holding his arms over his eyes. He squinted as though blocking light.

"I'll kill your daughter, too," he said in a desperate attempt to stop whatever was happening to him.

I curled a hand into the lapel of his dusty jacket and pulled him closer. "I don't have a daughter."

"I'll be sure and tell her that when I steal the breath from her lungs."

Though I knew his threats were hollow, the walls shook even harder. Pictures fell and crashed to the floor. Erin screamed but held her ground. I couldn't say I would have done the same in her position.

Delbert began convulsing. His skin cracked and bled darkness. His head shot back and his spine bowed.

"Down, boy," I said, giving an order I didn't quite understand.

But a shadow appeared beneath him. It grew, spreading in all directions under his bodyless soul, until he melted into it, his eyes like saucers, and the darkness took him. He wanted to be evil. He could do it down there.

The moment the shadowy portal closed, everything stopped and a silence settled around us. Novalee fell to her knees and cried. Erin stood in shock.

She found her phone and called her husband. We heard sirens in the distance. She didn't tell him what had happened. She just told him to bring Hannah home. It was safe.

"That's so weird," I said, turning to Erin when she hung up. "We keep having the strangest earthquakes." Though this one I was pretty sure was caused by Delbert.

"You're bleeding," she said.

"Oh, shit." I'd left a large puddle of blood on her carpet. "I'm so sorry," I said, lifting my foot and bouncing to the doorway.

"Wait. In here." She led me to a bathroom down the hall.

I kept my foot in the sink as Erin ran to the door to greet her family. When a police cruiser rolled up, Billy dealt with them—while I prayed Mable hadn't reported the car stolen—and Erin saw to the gaping hole in my foot. I sat on her bathroom counter gazing at Hannah as she slept in a basket beside me.

"She's so beautiful."

Erin nodded, then poured more peroxide on my foot. I got the feeling she enjoyed that part.

"Are you okay, hon?"

She nodded again, her lips pressed together as though she were trying desperately to keep calm. She shook worse than I did, though, and I realized she'd been traumatized. Thank God she didn't see Delbert. She'd be in therapy for years.

"Erin," I said, ducking my head to meet her tear-filled gaze, "she saved you from him. Your great-aunt Novalee. She saved you and your mom and your aunt."

Her expression showed both surprise and understanding. When she could finally talk, she said, "I've always felt a connection with her. Like I knew she was watching out for me."

"Now you know why. And I think she'll be around for a long time to come."

"I hope so," she said, looking around as though trying to talk to Novalee.

The elderly woman heard her. She was standing right beside me, gazing lovingly at Hannah. "I'm sorry about stealing your extra shifts at work," I said.

She shook her head and drew in a cleansing breath.

"You were right. I could never have kept it up. Not working that much with a baby. Billy's great, though."

"I agree. And he looks fantastic in a towel."

"Right?" she said with a soft giggle.

"Erin, you don't need more hours at work. You're an incredible artist. You need to go back to school. Become a graphic designer or an interior decorator. Your house is amazing." I scanned the area. "Or, you know, it used to be."

"If you hadn't come when you did . . ." Unable to hold her emotions back any longer, she broke down. Her shoulders shook.

I put a hand on her arm, and she tackle-hugged me, almost knocking me off the counter. I held her tight, struggling with the whole thing myself. Her emotions were overwhelming, and I couldn't tell where hers stopped and mine began.

"I'm just glad I got here in time."

"Me, too."

We stood like that while Erin grasped at the tattered edges of her composure. After several long moments, she hiccupped and asked, "When did you see Billy in a towel?"

18

If only one of my personalities liked to clean house.
—T-SHIRT

There was nothing like a wrecked house and a poltergeist to rob a girl of a good night's sleep. In lieu of draping my body across Denzel, chasing rest I knew I'd never get, I cleaned. Swept. Scooped. I didn't have that much furniture to begin with. Now my apartment was downright pathetic. And I needed a new glass.

When I'd done the best I could, I showered and retaped my foot. It was still early, like dark-out early, but I decided Reyes needed coffee, and I needed Reyes. I stole Mable's car again and hit the local twenty-four-hour convenience store.

Osh was there in his signature top hat, buying several packages of extra-large condoms. He gave me a conspiratorial wink. I tried not to snort, though I didn't doubt he had no problems with the ladies. The kid was pretty. Those dimples and shimmering bronze eyes were going to get him into trouble.

When I got to Reyes's motel, his windows were dark. I parked and walked to his door. Holding two giant cups of the good stuff, I knocked softly. If he really was sound asleep, I didn't want to disturb him. The door opened almost immediately, and a groggy, gorgeous specimen of a man in desperate need of a shave and sporting hooded lids and mussed hair answered. Also, he was shirtless.

I gave him a sheepish smile. "Were you awake?"

He opened the door farther in a silent invitation.

"Do you look this good when you wake up every morning?" I asked as I stepped into the warm room. "I look like I died in my sleep."

He closed the door and took the coffee I handed him. "I'm glad you didn't."

"You made your bed?" It was perfectly made up. He'd answered the door immediately. How did he have time to make his bed?

"Nah, I just slept on top." The last time I'd been in this room, the covers were mussed from him lying on it. That bed had not been lain on. "Are you okay?"

I stood looking at the collection of books piled on his nightstand. "Sure. Why wouldn't I be?"

He sat at the small table and watched me. Like always. "Just making sure. You seem tired."

Crap. I knew it. "I didn't get much sleep."

He leaned back, tilting his chair against the wall, and folded an arm behind his head. "Anything wrong?"

I turned and sat on the side of the bed. "Not at all. Are you okay?" I asked because, on the way home from Erin's, I could've sworn I saw him across the street from her house. I did a double take and he was gone. Like always.

"Peachy," he said, and I almost laughed. I would never have pictured him using the word *peachy* to describe anyone, much less himself.

We talked for about half an hour. It was nice, but he had to get to work soon. I checked my watch. "I'll let you get ready for work. I have the day off, so—"

"You don't have to go." He stood and started for the bathroom. "I'll just be a minute."

"Um—Okay."

His sexy mouth tilted sideways as he unbuttoned his jeans without closing the door between us. I froze, my gaze laser-locked onto his crotch, before sucking in a sharp breath and whirling away from him. I heard a soft chuckle. Pants hitting the floor. Shower water coming on. I peeked over my shoulder. He'd pulled the white curtain closed. Damn it. I stared hopefully at the opaque curtain, but nooooo. I had to be gifted with time travel instead of x-ray vision.

I finished my coffee and walked to his kitchenette, which was oddly not that much smaller than my kitchen. And he had glasses. Like four. I thought about stealing one, but what kind of person would that make me?

A few minutes later, he strolled out with one towel around his waist and another around his shoulders. He was using that one to rub his head, obstructing his line of sight, so I took the opportunity to gape in honor of women everywhere who'd never get the chance.

When he dropped the towel back and shook his head, my knees almost gave beneath me.

"Oh, you already have one," I said when he looked at me.

He glanced around. "One what?"

"A towel. I was going to get you one for Christmas."

He chuckled. "Yeah, well, it's not really mine. The motel frowns when I steal them."

"Good. They should. I frown when you steal them, too. But what about the glasses? Are they the motel's? I hear the penalty isn't as harsh for glass thieves."

He sobered. "Do you need glasses?"

"Nope. Five by five, baby." When his mouth thinned, I said, "Mine broke last night."

"All of them?"

"Oh, no." I laughed. "I only had one."

"You only had one glass?" he asked, taking all four off the counter.

"Yeah. It's not like glasses grow on trees." He searched for something to put them in. "Reyes, I was only kidding. I don't need your glasses. I have two plastic cups. And coffee cups out the ass. Not sure how that happened."

He looked down at them. "These aren't that great anyway. I'll get you some at the store today."

I chuckled. "Really. I can get a couple of chipped ones from Dixie. It's all good."

He'd grown serious. The glass thing really seemed to bother him.

With head still lowered, he said, "I have to let you find your way."

I felt guilt waft off him. Guilt and frustration.

"What do you mean?"

He worked his jaw. "You have to understand, it goes against every fiber of my being. But I have to let you navigate the terrain on your own."

What was he getting at? That he knew more about me than he was letting on? That he was following me but couldn't interfere? "Were you there last night?" I asked him point-blank. "Were you at Erin's?"

He put the glasses back and said without turning to face me, "No."

He was lying. He had to be. I saw him. "I have to get Mable's car back."

"Wait," he said, but I was already out the door. He'd been there. And if not him, then Garrett or Osh. They'd been tag-teaming, following me around. They knew more than they were saying.

I gulped huge rations of icy air when it hit me in the face. It was like plunging into the Arctic Ocean. I hurried to climb into the driver's side, fumbling in Reyes's coat pocket for the key.

Before I could slide it into the ignition, a knock sounded on the window.

Reyes stood outside. In the towel. With soaking wet hair.

Sure he was barefoot as well, I jumped out. "What are you doing?" I asked, pushing him toward his door. Not that he moved. Not even an inch. And, yes, he was barefoot. Darwinism at its finest.

"You're not what you think you are," he said as I shooed him back. That didn't work either.

"I know," I said, throwing my weight into it. I put a shoulder against his midsection and heaved-ho. Nothing. "I've known for a long time. Duh."

He finally took a voluntary step back. I was making progress.

"You know?" he asked.

"Yes. I know what I am."

"You—you do?"

"I'm a time traveler."

All progress came to a screeching halt.

I leaned against him, panting. "I think I'm from the future."

"Okay."

"My question is, where are you from?" I faced him again and poked him. In the chest. With my finger. "What are you?"

He lowered his head, examined said finger, then said, "I'm part of an interdimensional time investigations unit."

"Shut the fuck up. Are you for real?"

"No," he said with a snort.

I deflated. "Oh, that's messed up." I pushed again. This time he obeyed. The sun was just cresting the horizon, and his eyes sparkled like fire in the glowing light.

"Get inside. I have errands to run, and you have to go cook shit."

"I thought you were taking Mable's car back."

"I am. Then I'm going to ask if I can borrow it again."

He nodded. The frozen ground, the frigid air, none of it fazed him.

Just before I climbed into the car, I said, "Save me some posole for breakfast. I'll be in later."

He chuckled. "How 'bout I make you breakfast."

"Okay, but it better be as good as that posole."

"You have my word."

On the way home, I made another stop at the convenience store and bought a cheap, pay-as-you-go phone for emergency use, then stopped by Mable's, told her I'd stolen her car last night, gave her the last of my tip money to cover the expense even though I'd filled it up, and drank another cup of coffee with her.

She didn't say anything about Mr. Kubrick. I took that as a sign that he hadn't gotten any shots of last night's events. Too bad. He could have sold them to a tabloid. Made a little extra cash. But it did help me out a lot that he hadn't. No idea how I would've explained that one.

"I hate to say this, but I may need the car again today. I'm . . . investigating."

"Oh. Sounds intriguing. Anything I can help with?"

I perked up. She might know where the cabin was. Then again, she could talk to the wrong person and . . . I couldn't risk it.

"No, but thanks."

"Well, you know you can take it anytime you want to. I'll have to call the police and tell them to cancel that APB they put out on you last night."

My eyes rounded. "Really?"

"No." She cackled with delight. "Gotcha."

Apparently it was National Punk the Amnesiac Day. I walked back to my apartment to plug the phone in to charge for a bit—the battery was low when I activated it—and decided I'd try to catch Mr. P at the café when I went in for breakfast. He'd been a detective. Not here in the Hollow, but he'd lived here long enough to know people. Maybe he'd know about the cabin. Or at least the area. I hadn't been showing the picture around that I'd lifted from Mr. Vandenberg's shop because when I took it, I was breaking and entering. *Breaking* being the key word. A lot of breaking.

But if I had to fess up, I had to fess up. I hadn't heard back from the FBI agent. She'd sounded competent enough on the phone, but she could've been dealing with political red tape.

I had no red tape. I didn't even have any clear tape or duct tape or electrical tape.

Nope. I lived a tape-free life and liked it. Unless, you know, I needed to tape something.

I lay across Denzel and fantasized about plunging my fingers into a head of thick black hair. Of running them over the top of a damp white towel wrapped around a backdrop of dark, sinuous muscles. Of pressing my lips against a full mouth that defined the word *sexy*. I'd barely gotten my legs around Reyes's waist when a knock sounded at the door.

The fantasy incarnate stood on the other side when I opened it.

Guilt consumed me. "You can't read minds, can you?" I asked, suddenly aghast at the thought. He was otherworldly. Who knew what he could do?

He flashed a set of blindingly white teeth. "Not that I know of."

"Swear?"

After settling his tall frame against the doorjamb and crossing his arms over his chest, he said, "Pinky swear."

Good enough for me.

He wore a beige sweater with the sleeves pushed up and dark, loose-fitting jeans. He looked like a model for some expensive cologne.

"I thought we could go to breakfast instead."

Elation bounced through me like a rubber ball. "Wait, won't you be late for work?"

"I don't think Dixie will care."

"Do you know Dixie?" She was all kinds of wonderful, but forgiving of tardiness was not her strong suit.

"I've gotten to know her pretty well. I think I can risk it."

"Okay," I said, adding an it's-your-funeral tone to my voice. "Just let me get your jacket."

He stepped inside to close the door against the cold wind rushing in and seemed to take special note of the surroundings. Until that moment, I'd never noticed how dreary my apartment was. Or how much the floors creaked. Or how the wind whistled through the ill-fitting windows.

Then again, he lived in a motel. A dive motel at that. How much greater could he have it? Not a lot. And that made me feel better.

"Where were you thinking?" I asked when I walked out of my bedroom with his jacket.

He was checking out the kitchen. My massive supply of coffee cups, all five of them, and my two plastic cups sat on a dish towel. I'd had to put a piece of cardboard over a broken pane over the sink. Something else I'd have to explain to my landlord. My coffeepot was one of those tiny hotel types that did single serve, but that was cool. At least I had one. And a cupboard that was missing a door showed the extent of my food stores, which mainly consisted of saltines, peanut butter, half a box of cereal, and a tube of eyeliner that I'd been looking everywhere for.

His demeanor had changed. He seemed . . . upset. Angry even.

"Reyes?" I followed his gaze. "What's wrong?"

He pushed the sleeve of his sweater down to cover his Rolex, the one I was pretty sure was genuine. Did he feel sorry for me? Need I remind him that he lived in a motel? A dive motel? And that the Rolex he was now wearing could probably pay for a fairly decent house? Or at least put a nice down payment on one?

I took a deep breath and chastised myself for judging him. I didn't know his financial situation or his family situation. He could've still been married. Had a kid even. Or several. Who knew? Maybe his dad gave him that watch or his grandfather on his deathbed. Who was I to question him? To speculate?

"You're amazing," he said, and that certainly wasn't the direction I'd expected.

I snorted. "Because I live in squalor? I have it a thousand times better than James over there." I pointed in the homeless man's general direction.

I pulled the sturdier of my two chairs to the center of the room, a challenging grin sliding across my face. "Ready for round two and a half?" Since our first round didn't quite go as planned, it still deserved half a mark for effort. Luckily our second was pretty fucking spectacular.

The hungry look that overcame him told me that he most definitely was. He let his gaze wander the length of me before sitting down.

Reaching down into his pocket, I said, "I don't have a timer." I took out his phone and set his timer for fifteen minutes.

"I can't wait to get my hands on that ass," he said.

I straddled him and wrapped my arms around his neck. "I'll finish you first."

One corner of his sensuous mouth lifted into a lopsided grin. "Not this time, sweetheart."

Oh, it was on.

19

I don't like making plans for the day.
Because then the word "premeditated" gets thrown
around the courtroom.

—INTERNET MEME

After the most incredible breakfast I'd had in ages, I untangled Reyes's limbs from mine, crawled off the bed, and sought out his phone. It was still in the kitchen, the timer still going off. I hit the STOP button right when a text dinged. The message flashed across the screen, so it wasn't like I was snooping. It was from Garrett Swopes. The same Garrett Swopes that came into the café?

It read simply, *You need to check this guy out. He's the only unknown in the area.*

Intrigued, and now truly snooping, I tapped the message. It brought up a picture of a half-fallen storage shed with cardboard boxes inside. It was James's place right across the street.

I looked toward the bedroom. Toward Reyes. Why would they be checking out a homeless guy?

*   *   *

An hour later, after we'd made a picnic of crackers and peanut butter on top of Denzel—aka, the second most incredible breakfast I'd had in ages—we headed to the café.

"Is Erin working today?" Reyes asked me.

"I don't know," I said, curious about the inquiry.

We walked in, and Reyes had been right. Dixie wasn't the least bit concerned at how late he was.

I glared at him. "Are you trading sexual favors with our boss for special consideration and advancement opportunities you are underqualified for?"

A lopsided grin spread over his face. "No."

"Oh. I was going to say that if that's what it takes, I'd do 'er."

"What about Cookie?"

"I'd do her, too, but I don't think it would get me very far with Dixie. Unless, you know, she was into that sort of thing."

He let out a soft laugh. "I meant, is she working today?"

"Oh, right. Looks like it." She walked out of the bathroom, a mortified expression on her face, her blouse splotched with dark espresso. "Short controlled bursts," I reminded her.

She gave me a murderous glare worthy of Lizzie Borden.

"That color looks great on you," I said, trying to help.

That time, she flipped me off. I decided to stop while I was ahead.

Reyes wrapped his arms loosely around me and pulled me closer. "You need to come back for lunch if you can."

"I bet I can," I said, intrigued.

"I think you'll like what I have in store for you."

"Okay, but it can't be better than posole for breakfast."

"You might be surprised."

"I can hardly wait. And looks like she is."

He turned to see what I was talking about as Erin walked in, looking both haggard and . . . at ease. Reyes gave me a sweet kiss, just enough to get my juices flowing, then went to the kitchen to start his day. Erin walked over to me. Francie was already there, and she watched us with a certain kind of bloodlust in her eyes.

When, without saying a word, Erin hugged me, I thought Francie's jaw would fall off it dropped so hard.

Erin set me at arm's length but again said nothing, and I realized she couldn't. She was too choked up. Too grateful.

"You're welcome," I said, giving her hands a squeeze. "I'm so happy for you, Erin."

"I am, too," she said with a hiccup of emotion. "I can never repay you."

"What? Erin, no. Please, please, please, don't ever feel like you owe me."

"Okay." She sniffed. "I'll try, but just so you know, Billy has vowed to build you a gnarly hog when he gets the money to."

I burst out laughing.

"He loves motorcycles."

"Well, tell him thanks, but he needs to save that for Hannah's college fund. I have a feeling she's going to be incredibly artistic."

Just as I was about to lose all hope of seeing Mr. P today, in he walked with the stripper in tow. Or, with Helen in tow. I'd gotten to know her a little more over the last few days. She had a great sense of humor and offered me some tips from her hooking days. I'd used one on Reyes last night, and he almost came unglued. I totally owed her.

"Hey, Mr. P," I said as he sat in a booth. "I was wondering if I could ask you a few questions."

"Well, hello there to you, too, and of course. Sounds serious."

Francie took his order as I settled in across from him.

"Do you know the Vandenbergs?"

He nodded. "Not well, but I do know William from the club."

"The country club?"

He snorted. "No, the strip club. The one in Tarrytown."

Helen suddenly made a lot more sense.

"Mr. V goes to strip clubs?" I asked, trying not to look too surprised.

"Only with his wife. It's her idea, I think."

When I had an even harder time getting past that, he added, "Don't worry. They're not swingers or anything. Just like to appreciate what God put on the earth every once in a while. And I promise you me, that woman did not leave him."

Finally, someone immune to the gossipmongers. "I don't think she did either. Do you know if they have a cabin?"

"Oh, gosh, I just don't know, hon."

My hopes fled the scene like a parolee at a busted meth lab. I took out the picture I'd grabbed out of Mr. V's store.

"Does this area look familiar?"

"Looks like it might be up at Blue Mountain Lake, but I can't be sure."

"It's Lake Oscawana," Helen said, taking a look herself. "That's Doc Emmett's place. I been there plenty. Lots of floor space."

"Sorry I can't be of more help," Mr. P said, and I got the bizarre feeling that he wasn't. "Why are you asking?"

Excitement swelled inside me nonetheless. Helen knew. "Oh, I just love the area," I said, lying through my teeth. "And I thought if this was their cabin, I might ask to rent it for a weekend."

"Good idea, Janey. Get out of the city. Get some fresh air."

"Exactly. Well, thanks anyway."

I got up and motioned for Helen to join me in the little *niñas'* room. She did, and five minutes later, working from her verbal directions, I had a crude map of the area. I also knew that while Helen was her first name, her stage name was Helen Bedd, and that Mr. V's friend Doc Emmett liked fine whiskies, lap dances, and hunting. He'd gone hunting, in fact, last week, and nobody had seen him since.

Using Helen's map, I took the Taconic State Parkway for about forty-five minutes to Lake Oscawana, where Doc Emmett's cabin sat nestled on the waterfront. I drove around the lake to the northeast shore, taking this turn and that, until I finally found Chippewa Road. The cabin I sought was somewhere on that road, but it was broad daylight. Well, cloudy-with-a-chance-of-rain daylight. I couldn't just drive up there and ask if the Vandenbergs were home. I'd been hoping an idea would magically pop into my head as I drove. Sadly, nothing popped, magical or otherwise. I'd just have to do some recon and see what I could see. Hopefully, without getting anyone killed.

I parked the Fiesta and hiked up the road, passing by a house now and again, but nothing that looked like the cabin in the picture. I was beginning to worry Helen had been wrong when I spotted a canoe I'd seen in one of Mr. V's photos. The cabin looked different. It could have been the starkness of the forest as compared to the lush greens of the summer camping pictures they'd taken.

Either way, this had to be the place. By the time I found the cabin, I was too close. They would look out a window and spot me, if they hadn't already. I didn't see any vehicles, but they could have had them all parked out back. I walked until I could no longer see any part of the cabin, then doubled back, taking a trail that led farther inland. If I circled around, I might spot cars or other outbuildings where they could have stashed cars.

I fought the cold with my evolved powers of shivering. As I got closer, every twig that snapped under my feet, every branch that broke as I picked my way through the brush, seemed to echo across the land to announce my arrival. I was scratching the heck out of Reyes's jacket. Maybe he'd like it even better. It now had a cool "worn" look. People paid out the ass for that crap.

Hidden by a hill behind the cabin sat two vehicles. The pickup they'd used the other day to bring in the equipment and an older-model PT Cruiser. That had to be Mr. V's. It just looked like him.

Without having thought to hunt down a pair of binoculars, I had no way of getting a closer look. So I squinted really hard and saw no movement. Their vehicles were not proof that the Vandenbergs were out here. I needed something good to give Agent Carson. I took a couple of pictures on the phone, then used the camera to zoom in. The picture was so blurry, I still couldn't make out anything.

I did, however, notice a man sitting in the brush south of the house. He looked like a hunter. Great. Now I had to worry about being mistaken for a deer. If only Angel were here.

"What are we looking at?"

I squeaked and jumped thirty-seven feet in the air. Angel had appeared beside me and was now laughing at my reaction. I held one hand on my chest, the other over my mouth so as not to squeak again.

"You are so jumpy, *chica*. People like you make life worth living."

"This coming from a dead kid," I said in a loud whisper.

"True. We looking for dead people again?"

"I'm hoping, if the Vandenbergs are in there, they are very much alive. Can you check?"

"What's in it for me?"

"Your ability to talk in a normal voice."

"I don't get it."

I grabbed his arm, clawing at it, digging my nails into his skin as hard as I could.

"I get it. I get it," he said, falling to his knees.

I let go, and he cradled his injured arm, blowing on the marks I'd left.

I glanced at him. "People's lives are at stake, Angel. And all you can worry about is your angle. Your cut."

"I'm thirteen."

He had a point. "Look, I'm sorry, just go see if the Vandenbergs are there." When he glared back at me, I added, "Please."

He disappeared. I tried to calm down, but I was cold and tired and hungry. And more than a little worried about Mr. V, Natalie, Joseph, and Jasmine.

Just then I heard a low thud. Nothing too spectacular, but the energy that hit me almost bowled me over. A wall of fear hit me head-on, and I knew before Angel got back that Mr. V and his family were in there. Was the sound a gunshot?

I stood and started for the cabin. Soon I was sprinting.

I would have run right up to the door and burst through it if Angel hadn't tackled me to the ground.

We rolled in the brush, and I fought him, trying to get to that family. To those kids.

"Stop it, damn it," Angel said, pinning me down.

I kicked out and tried to claw at him again.

"They're okay, Janey. They're alive."

"What was that sound?" I asked, frantic.

"Mrs. V dropped a pan. The bad guys got mad. They're okay."

I stopped struggling and lay in his arms, trying to calm my breathing. Then I realized how stupid what I'd just done really was. I could've gotten them all killed. I put a hand over my eyes as they stung with emotion.

Angel pulled me tighter. I let him.

Now I had another big fat dilemma. I'd gotten too close to the house. If they hadn't seen me already, they very well could when I got up. At the moment, I was hidden by the tall vegetation, but I couldn't stay there until nightfall. I needed to get them help.

"Are they okay?" I asked Angel. "Even the kids?"

"They're alive."

"If only I had a way to—" My eyes flew open. I had a phone. I could call . . . who? I didn't have anyone's number, and it wasn't like there was a directory for cell numbers. Not that I knew of.

We were close enough to the house to hear yelling. I cringed when a man's voice speaking Farsi wafted toward me.

"I don't know what to do, Angel."

"Me neither."

Just when the voices in the house quieted down, my phone rang. At first, I didn't recognize the sound. Then

I realized my pocket was ringing. I scrambled to answer it, hoping the captors hadn't heard. Who would be calling? No one had this number.

"Hello?"

A woman spoke into the phone, her voice calm, soothing. "Janey? What are you doing?"

I blinked in thought. "Um, nothing."

"You're not lying by a cabin that may or may not have the Vandenbergs held hostage inside?"

I bolted upright, but Angel tackled me to the ground again. He was right. That was a bad move. Damned reflexes.

"Agent Carson?"

"The one and only. And where are you supposed to be?"

It took me a moment, but I answered, "Anywhere but here?"

"Brava. You get to move on to the bonus round."

"Where are you?"

"In a very well-thought-out covert position. Unlike, say, you. I had two units that were ready to move until you showed up. I can guarantee, you will also be arrested the minute I can get my hands on you." She was so testy.

"What do you mean, ready to move?"

"They were getting ready to do covert surveillance so we could get eyes in there."

"In broad cloudy-with-a-chance-of-rain daylight?"

"They're very good. It's what they do."

"Just hold on. Angel, where exactly are the Vandenbergs being held?"

"They're all in that corner bedroom," he said, "except for Mrs. Vandenberg. She's cooking for them."

"Is there a guard with the family?"

"No. There are three men. Two in the living room and

one in the kitchen. The family is tied up, so they aren't going anywhere."

I nodded. "Look, I have inside information." I told her what Angel said. "If we can distract them somehow once Mrs. Vandenberg is finished cooking, we can get them out. They aren't guarding them."

"How do you know that?"

"I saw it. Through my binoculars."

"What binoculars?"

"The ones I dropped. And no longer have."

"Well, thanks to you, the first thing we have to do is try to get you out of there so you don't get everyone killed."

Guilt ate through the lining of my stomach. "I know. I'm so sorry."

"Can you see them now?"

I was just about to say no when Angel nodded. Of course, he could be my eyes.

"Yes. Yes, I can."

"Do you think you can get out of there if we provide some kind of distraction?"

"No!" I whisper-yelled at her. "No, two distractions in one day? It isn't like they're not a tad suspicious already. They're bad guys. They were born suspicious. I can see them."

Angel gave me a thumbs-up, then disappeared.

"I'll know when to run."

"Janey, if you are wrong and they spot you—"

"I have this. Just get ready to move."

"What? What do you mean?"

"You said your guys were ready. Are they or aren't they?"

"They are, but this isn't a game, Janey."

"I have this. Once the Vandenbergs are all in that back

bedroom, I'll provide a distraction, and you and your men secure that room and get them out."

"Janey, I refuse to authorize you to do any such thing."

"I'm not asking permission. I'll give you the okay sign when it's time to move. Or I might get shot in the head. If either of those happens, move."

"Janey, I am ordering—"

I hung up before she talked me out of doing something stupid. Truth was, I had the advantage over all of them with all of their equipment. I had a dead teenaged gang-banger with an attitude and, well, not a whole lot to lose.

Angel appeared beside me again. He lay down in the brush, ducking his head as though they could see him. "There's one guard on the window at all times. I'll have to do something to draw his attention away."

"I have another idea. A really good one. I just need a sharp stick and a lot of blood."

I was so nervous, I wanted to throw up. My stomach roiled as I lay on the ground, waiting on word from Angel.

Agent Carson called back a third time. I told her they were finally letting Mrs. V go back with her family, so it was almost time and she should get her team ready.

She had reluctantly agreed to let me distract the captors so her men could secure the room. I hadn't given her much of a choice, but despite that, no agent alive would just let some stranger waltz into her sting operation and "be the distraction." No way. Absolutely not. There had to be more to that story than met the trained eye.

"Janey," she said, growing somber, "these are very, very bad men."

"I know. They're holding a whole family hostage."

"The Vandenbergs never stood a chance of survival. These are not the kind of men that let their hostages go."

That got the blood pumping. "Got it. They're super bad."

"Are you sure about this?"

"Positive."

"What exactly are you going to do?"

"I thought I'd play it by ear." I hung up and glanced at Angel. "Here goes nothing."

Angel had found me something better than a stick, but if I didn't get killed in the crossfire that was sure to come, I would probably die of tetanus or a flesh-eating virus. This couldn't be sanitary.

I took the piece of rusted metal he'd found a few feet away and started cutting along my scalp line. My first try wasn't deep enough. I needed more blood. This had to look convincing.

"Maybe you should stab me with it," I said to Angel.

"Fuck that. I ain't stabbing you. I ain't cutting you. This was your idea."

I closed my eyes and tried again. This time I thought of Joseph and Jasmine and how scared they had to be. The metal sliced through several layers, and blood gushed down my face. I rubbed it into my scalp and shook my head to disperse it, then scraped the metal along my cheek, neck, and chest, making deep—and hopefully convincing— gashes.

The phone rang again. Agent Carson was probably not liking my plan. Sadly, part of that plan was to smash my phone. I raised the metal and slammed it into the phone over and over.

"You're one angry chick," Angel said.

I put my hand on his arm where I'd scratched him. "I'm sorry, Angel. I didn't mean to hurt you."

He stared a moment, then laughed it off. "Please. I'm an asshole. I know that."

"You weren't being an asshole. You were being a thirteen-year-old boy." I leaned in and kissed his cheek. He lowered his head, embarrassed. "Okay, tell me when he's not looking."

He nodded and disappeared. About fifteen seconds later, I heard the single word "Go."

I hopped onto my feet and sprinted as fast as I could to the tree line that circled the house. Once there, I skidded under some brush and waited.

After another few seconds, I heard another "Go."

This time, I ran in the same direction I'd just come, only I stumbled a lot, falling all the way down and having to drag myself back up. I weaved to the back door, knowing they were probably all three watching now, and slammed my palms against it.

"Is anyone home?" I yelled, my voice hoarse.

I didn't wait for them to actually answer. I just wanted them to think I was out of my mind, trying to get help. I walked the perimeter of the house, yelling for someone, anyone, to help my husband. When I got to the front door, I pounded on it.

"They checked the room, just to make sure nothing was up," Angel said as he followed me. He disappeared and re-appeared again in the blink of an eye. "Now they're all three up front, watching you. Their guns are drawn."

I fell against the front door and pounded, leaving bloody palm prints all over it. "Please, I need to use your phone. Please."

"Tell them to go now," Angel said.

I dropped one hand to my side and gave Agent Carson the okay signal, praying she saw it, because the door opened. The man had put his gun aside and was studying me.

It was the same man who sat at Mr. V's desk for at least two days, but I'd mussed my hair and bled all over my face. Surely he wouldn't recognize me.

"Please," I said, swaying as though I were about to lose consciousness. "My husband. He's in the car." I pointed toward the lake then held out my busted phone. "Do you have a phone? Please. He's trapped."

When they did nothing but watch me, I bent at the waist and vomited on their floor. The vomit was real. No way to fake that shit. The fact that one of them was holding an AK-47 on me—I'd seen it through the slit between door and jamb—proved to be all the motivation I needed to empty the contents of my stomach. Then, in a dramatic twist even I didn't see coming, I fell to my knees and passed out in my own puke. Or, well, I pretended to. I lay as still as humanly possible as one of the men brought his gun around and pointed it at my head.

20

Life ain't all burritos and strippers, my friend.
—TRUE FACT

Trust hadn't exactly been my strong suit, but I was putting my life in the hands of an FBI agent I'd never met and her team. Hopefully, they would live up to their reputation of being excellent shots.

The men started to panic. They spoke in frantic Farsi, trying to decide what to do with me, arguing among themselves, giving the team precious time to save the Vandenbergs. One of the men shoved another. He wanted to put me in the shed out back. Surely I wouldn't live long, especially in this cold. The other wanted to bring me inside and put me in a room so they could keep an eye on me. The third just wanted to shoot me in the head. They were too close. They were going back to Mr. V's store and getting the package that evening, and risking it all by keeping me alive when they were only going to kill me anyway would be stupid.

I didn't dare open my eyes, so Angel relayed to me their every move.

"They keep looking outside to see if anyone saw you come up," he said. "But none of them have thought to check on the Vandenbergs yet."

We just needed a few minutes. Just long enough to get the family untied and out the window.

"Be right back," he said, then, an instant later, "Okay, they are all untied, and the team is lifting the children out now."

I fought the spike of elation and found I didn't have to fight it too hard. One of them kicked me in the gut. He was trying to get me off the porch. They'd decided to tie me up and put me in the shed to die, but no one wanted to pick me up, probably thanks to my inspired decision to pass out in my own vomit. It was also an excellent rape deterrent.

My hair was a mess of tangles. And, sadly, the afore-mentioned vomit. It stuck to the blood on my face so that even if I'd wanted to see, I couldn't have. The man kicked me again to roll me another couple of feet. Tears pushed past my lashes as the pain ricocheted through me. He finally gave up and picked up one of my booted feet to drag me across the wooden porch.

"He's going to pull you off the edge," Angel said. He started to panic. "The side of the porch is at least a five-foot drop. The fall will break your neck. Hold on." He must've done his disappearing act again. He came back almost in-stantly with "They're coming down the hall." He sounded more excited than afraid. "Get ready to run."

But did the FBI have all the Vandenbergs out? I needed to know.

"The big one is turning around," he said, the panic filtering back into his voice again. "I think he heard something."

I groaned and pretended to come to for a moment. I gave a halfhearted kick at the man trying to wrench my foot off. It gave me the perfect excuse to protect my head when he pulled me off the porch. I landed with a thud that knocked my breath away, but I'd curled up a little and protected my head from hitting the side of the porch and my neck from being broken, landing on my shoulder instead.

"You did it," Angel said. "You got their attention."

Then, in an act that defied my imagination, it was so fast and so decisive, three shots were fired almost simultaneously through suppressed rifles. I opened my eyes and scraped at the hair in front of them in time to see the one next to me crumple into a heap. Through the porch slats, in my peripheral vision, I could see the other men crumple at the exact same time, as though the whole thing had been choreographed.

The team had killed them. A sniper in the trees across the road took out the one closest to me, and the team who'd entered from the back got the other two. All headshots. All perfect.

I scrambled away from the guy closest to me and, yep, threw up again.

A female agent brought me a bottle of water as Angel played with the Vandenbergs' German shepherd and an EMT saw to my self-inflicted wounds.

"Agent Carson?" I asked.

She nodded and sat beside me on the back of the ambulance.

I laughed softly. "We've already met."

"Yes, we have."

"You came into the diner yesterday. Why didn't you introduce yourself?"

She shrugged one shoulder. "I couldn't have told you anything anyway. And I didn't need anything else from you at that moment, so . . ."

"I get it. Love 'em and leave 'em."

"That's the kinda girl I am."

It was nice talking to her. Comfortable. Like an old pair of jeans—

"But I still have to arrest you."

—that had been rolled in a cactus plant. "No shit?"

"No shit. You interfered with an ongoing investigation—"

"Yeah, but you were only investigating because I told you to."

"There is that. I'll talk to my superiors and try to get your charges reduced."

I was hoping for dismissed.

"You cut yourself up pretty bad," a man said from beside me.

I turned to see Bobert there. He handed me a cup of coffee, and I kind of wanted to make out with him.

I took a sip, then asked, "What are you doing here?"

"Giving Agent Carson a hand."

"Can you convince her to drop the charges?"

"Drop them?" he asked, taken aback. "I was going to see if she'd pile on a few more. Obstruction of justice."

"She has that one."

"Endangering a law enforcement agent."

"I didn't mean to."

"Unlawful use of a . . . sharp, rusty object."

"You know what?" I said, stopping him while I was ahead. "I'm good with her charges. It's okay."

He chuckled. "Wait till you see Cookie. She is not happy."

It was my turn to be taken aback. "You told her?"

"Only because I want to continue being married to her."

"Yeah, well," I said, mumbling to myself. "The name Cookie does not strike fear into my heart. How bad could it be?"

The moment I said it, a loud shriek that carried over the land far and wide and made children of all ages cringe and dogs whimper sounded from my left.

"Janey Doerr!" it said. It knew my name.

Cookie came stomping up, and for the first time I was a little afraid of her. "What the fuck?" she asked, her eyes filling with tears. "What—? How—? I can't even—!" Then she pulled me into her arms, unaware of how painful it was.

I looked at Bobert. "What the heck did you tell her?"

"The truth," he said, the turncoat.

"Janey," she said, holding me at arm's length, then pulling me back in for a bone-crushing hug. Literally. She was crushing my bones, and I was pretty sure she was doing it on purpose.

Agent Carson spoke again. "You'll have to thank Mr. Pettigrew for me, Detective."

"I sure will," Bobert said. "He gave it his best shot."

I straightened my shoulders and tried to speak. It was a pretty good effort, given that no air would pass through my windpipe. "What about Mr. P?"

Bobert grinned. "He was trying to put you off coming out here."

I gasped. For a really long time. "He was in on it?"

Cookie let go, then questioned her husband with an arch of her brow, equally curious.

"Yes, he was," Bobert said.

I felt so used. So betrayed. So utterly out of the loop.

"I have to admit," Agent Carson said, "we didn't even know about this cabin until you asked Detective Davidson to look into it. You led us straight to them."

"So you're dropping the charges?"

"Not on your life."

We watched all the activity while the EMT finished bandaging my wounds and gave me a tetanus shot. The cut on my foot from last night was already healing. Hopefully this would heal just as quickly. Must've been a vitamin freak in my previous life. Probably ate green shit. Stuff that rhymed with *ale* and . . . *ettuce.*

"Hey," I said, elbowing Cookie to get her attention.

It was her turn on the oxygen mask we found in the ambulance. She pulled it off with a sucking sound and a questioning shrug.

"That's the guy." I stood and walked slowly forward, stunned to my toes.

"You're just doing this because it's my turn," Cookie said.

"No, really. That's the guy." I pointed. Among the plethora of officers and agents roaming the area both outside and inside the yellow tape stood the massive bald-headed hulk that worked at the dry cleaners. "Hold it right there, mister!"

He turned to me and flashed a nuclear grin. I thought about tackling him to the ground. Instead I just stormed up, all stormy like. About that time I realized he was wearing Kevlar. Did bad guys wear Kevlar?

Before I could say anything, he asked, "Vy you are here?" Then he threw back his big head and laughed.

I was still processing his presence when Agent Carson walked up with the woman from the dry cleaners as well. She also wore Kevlar.

She looked at her comrade. "Vy she is here?" Then they both threw back their heads and laughed. It was so bizarre, like a bad laugh track for a sitcom.

I was in the Twilight Zone. And not the good one the dentist puts you in.

The woman stopped first and pointed to my head wound. "You have balls," she said. "I am Klava Pajari, and this is my partner, Ilya Zolnerowich. Ve are retired FSB agent. Ve vork—" She considered how to put it. "—job on side."

"Oh, so this is a side job?"

Ilya nodded. "Because of you, ve sleep together. Vith our minds."

"You're psychic lovers?"

Klava gave a nervous chuckle while glaring at Ilya. "His English is not so good. Vat he means is our minds are rest knowing how you have help us. Ve clean your coat for free, yes?"

They laughed again. It echoed through the tilting fun house that used to be my brain.

After they got over teasing me—which took forever—they told me the story of how they had been on the trail of a Russian arms dealer for years. They'd tracked him to America, but he moved around a lot, and they couldn't get a lock on his location. The only thing he did religiously, no matter where he went, was bet on street fights. He grew up fighting on the streets of Russia and was addicted to the life.

So when the US ignored Russia's application for extradition, they set up a sting operation involving an illegal street-fighting organization that had been going on for a few months. The metal that the Vandenbergs' captors were going to plasma-cut through was a panic room, but one set up to keep someone in instead of vice versa, if they should ever catch him. He had a lot of muscle around him. They needed to keep him both hidden and unattainable.

"Is called extraordinary rendition," Klava said. "Is to kidnap and force transfer of a criminal to another country for prosecution."

"Ve are like Dog," Ilya said.

"Dogs?" I didn't get it. "Like bulldogs?"

"No, Dog the Bounty Hunter. Only I have better hair, yes?" He smoothed a hand over his bald head and laughed again. It was growing on me.

"Is Dog even a thing anymore?"

He pounded his chest. "He is big thing inside me."

I could have gone so many places with that.

"Ilya is good fighter," Klava said. "He vin much of money."

I didn't doubt it. "You've been after this guy for two years? Is he in the area?"

"Da. Ve grab him last veek, but have to keep him in box until papervork is coming through."

Considering the guy's illicit hobbies, I shouldn't have been alarmed, but I was. "You've been keeping him in a metal room for a week? He'll freeze to death."

"Ve are Russian. Ve can handle ten of your vinters. Also, is heated and cooled and have little toilet."

This was the craziest story. One that I wouldn't have pictured if it had been a paint-by-numbers.

"But how do these guys fit in?" I nodded toward the

cabin, or, more pointedly, toward the body bags on the ground by said cabin, and shuddered.

"They vere his best customers. Al Qaeda. They vant him back. Mostly, they vant his money and veapons cache."

"Sucks to be him."

"Yes!" Ilya slapped me on the back. "Totally."

I resisted the urge to call him a Valley Girl. Mostly because I used that word way too often myself. And I was afraid of what he'd do to me if I called him a girl.

"Janey?"

I turned to see Mr. V standing there and straightened my shoulders. "Mr. Vandenberg, I thought you were with your family." They had been taken to the hospital immediately. I'd wanted to see them so bad, but the children were suffering from dehydration and a massive need for therapy for the rest of their natural-born lives.

"I'm on my way," he said, his voice cracking. "I just—" He stopped and shook his head. "They told me . . . I don't know how to thank you."

I walked up to him and put a hand on his arm. "You could thank me by not pressing charges." I still had a crap-load of antiques to pay for, but if he'd just hold off on the breaking-and-entering snafu . . .

His brows slid together. "I don't—"

"It doesn't matter right now. I'm just glad your family is okay."

He wrapped long, thin arms around me. I motioned Angel over. I wanted him to be a part of this. Without him, I could never have done what I did. I took Angel's hand, pulled it to my mouth, and kissed it. He lowered his head, suddenly bashful.

"My daughter was right," Mr. V whispered into my ear.

"You're an angel." He set me at arm's length. "She saw you outside the window. Said you were an angel and you had come to save us. And she was right."

I shook my head. "She must have me confused with someone else."

He shook his, too. "Seriously, where do you keep your wings?"

Bobert and Cookie followed me all the way back to Sleepy Hollow. Like right-on-my-tail followed. Like they expected me to do something crazy. Like they didn't trust me. So weird. I drove straight to the café, and they followed me there, too. It was becoming an issue.

They'd told me Cookie ran out of the café, screaming like a banshee, with no explanation and no forwarding address when Bobert called her. She needed to explain to Dixie what happened. I needed to explain why I missed lunch with Reyes. And to see if he wanted to have sex with me again later. I could pencil him in.

We stormed into the place as if we worked there, and even though it was well past Cookie's scheduled shift, Dixie put her to work. She was apparently short-handed.

Reyes gave me odd glances, and I wondered if he knew about the Vandenbergs. Or was upset I'd missed lunch with him. I would have called if I hadn't crushed my phone.

Drawing in a lungful of air, I started toward the back. Shayla stepped in front of me before I got too far.

"Hey, sweetie," I said before I really looked at her. When I did, I kept the smile on my face because I didn't know where else to put it.

She gazed at me wide-eyed. Her cute, freckled nose and

huge, almost colorless irises made her look utterly fairy-like, but now she had a grace she didn't have before. A gentleness that enraptured me.

Still, in the grand scheme of things, I'd rather have had her as she was. Sweet, caring, and full of life.

I stumbled back a step.

She held out a hand. "It's okay. I'm okay. I promise."

She blurred as my vision became flooded with wetness. This wasn't possible. I'd just seen her the day before, and she was the picture of health. She was happy and vibrant. She fairly glowed. How could that change so fast? How could she become one of the transparent gray departed?

I turned from her and leaned against the checkout counter. Fought to breathe. Struggled for an explanation. After Erin's baby. After the Vandenberg children. This? Now? Was life really so meaningless? So fragile? So easily lost?

She touched my arm. "Janey, I just stayed for him. For Lewis. Can you get a message to him?"

A tear pushed past my lashes when I looked at her again. Did death really target the innocent? Did it zero in on the purest, most radiant souls?

"Can you please tell him I've had the best two days of my life?"

"I don't understand," I said at last.

A few of the customers had turned toward me. Dixie stepped out from behind the prep station, wiping her hands on a towel, her expression curious. Cookie stopped what she was doing and stilled.

"I had asthma and severe allergies. It was no one's fault. I ate a corn dog from Whips. I've eaten a hundred. They must've switched to peanut oil."

A soft cry wrenched from my throat, and I sank onto

my elbows. If not for the desk, I would've crumpled like the three men earlier today. This was not happening.

"I just want Lewis to know how wonderful a person he is. He really has no idea. He needs to know, Janey. And he needs to know how much I loved him." She stepped closer.

I couldn't look at her. In spite of all the bravado today, I was a coward after all.

"Promise me," she said, her tone harder than before, probably to get me to focus.

It was one thing to see the departed as being other. As almost not being real. It was another thing to know on a visceral level that they were once alive and dynamic and worthy of all that life had to offer.

I nodded, agreeing at last, and she smiled. "Thank you." Without another word, she slipped to the other side.

I clutched the counter, digging in my nails as her life flashed before my eyes. I saw the first time Lewis noticed her. Or kind of noticed her. She'd dropped her books in high school, and as a group of kids beside her laughed, he hurried over, picked them up, handed them to her, then kept jogging as he tried to catch up to his friends. It was the everydayness that captured her. He didn't do it for accolades. He just did it. It was simply in his nature. She was invisible until that day. That day, that very minute, she decided to be seen.

I saw her watch him at a talent contest in middle school where his band played a Fall Out Boy song. He was lead guitar, and the entire event won him a trophy and a lot of female admirers. Yet there wasn't a jealous bone in Shayla's body, because she loved him even then. She was happy for him. Wanted only the best.

I saw her during an asthma attack at her fifth birthday party. It was so bad, she had to be rushed to the hospital. She wasn't mad that she missed the party or the cake or the time with her friends from the hospital. She was mad because she spilled red Kool-Aid on the dress her mother stayed up all night making for her. It broke her heart, and she cried for hours, so her mother stayed up all night again and made her a shorts set out of what was left.

I saw her the day she was adopted. After she was tossed around a series of foster homes as an infant, her parents finally found her when she was three. She was thin and sickly and had an oxygen tube looped under her nose and around her ears, but they'd recognized her anyway. Said they'd been looking everywhere for her. Even though she was pale with blue eyes and freckles, and they were dark and tall and beautifully exotic, she recognized them, too.

I saw her in the neonatal ICU, shaking with the effects of the drugs, so weak she couldn't breathe on her own, her heart couldn't function on its own, so they connected her to a machine that lulled her to sleep with whirring sounds for ten days. The nurses told her to fight with everything she had, so she did.

I saw her come into the world on the filthy floor of a crack den. Her mother had OD'd and was already dead. No one noticed her at first. No one called the police. But it wasn't their fault. She'd been born invisible. It was a miracle one of the dealers saw her. Not wanting anything to do with the cops, he wrapped her in a shirt stiff with dried blood on it and left her in front of an all-night liquor store.

She turned back to me, a Cheshire smile on her face. Only then did I notice the tattoo she had on the inside of her wrist. INVISIBLE GIRL, NOW SHOWING.

I stood in the present, still clutching the counter, shaking so hard with anger and indignation and outrage that it vibrated. Small clear drops landed on the Formica under my face. Tears had dripped off my chin. The fury inside me took on a life of its own.

"Charley." Cookie walked slowly toward me, her hands up, her voice soft.

Reyes watched me from the kitchen entrance, his head bowed, his expression one of warning.

Too late.

I released the furious thing inside.

21

I see dead people.
No, wait. I take that back.
I see people I want dead.
—ECARD

It was like in those movies when the misunderstood girl gets so mad she suddenly develops superpowers and blows out the windows of her high school, showering all the kids who were awful to her with shattered glass without meaning to.

It was like that, only I'd meant it.

The world exploded. Everything from the plate-glass windows to the coffee cups that lined the tables splintered into a million sharp, lethal torpedoes. People flew back, their faces frozen in a variety of horrified stages when time slowed to a full stop. Cookie stood before me, reaching out, her face sad. Knowing.

Then I saw Reyes. The anger simmering beneath his steely surface went way beyond what I'd expected. He stood deathly still. His fire blazed around him, the flames reaching all the way to the ceiling and fanning out.

We both turned toward the front door. With fists clenched at my sides, I watched as the angelic being I'd seen before walked toward me. The slivers of glass that hung in the air parted slowly, moving out of his way, tinkling as they bounced off each other. It sounded like ice crackling on a winter's day.

His wings spanned the entire width of the café before he folded them at his back.

Though Reyes was across the café, the angel addressed him first. "Rey'aziel."

"Michael."

The angel faced me, his movements stiff. Formal. "Elle-Ryn-Ahleethia—"

I frowned and stepped back. "Is that my name?"

"—I am sent by the Father Jehovah, the one true God of this dimension, to end your mortal life so that you may ascend to your rightful place of omniscience and duty."

My anger dissipated, and shock took its place. "I don't understand."

"You are Val-Eeth. You are too powerful for this world in this condition."

I glanced at Reyes. His flames had died down a bit, and he studied Michael with a new curiosity.

"I don't understand even more."

Michael eyed me, assessing me with one quick sweep. "Can you imagine what would happen if the detonator for an armed nuclear device fell into the hands of a child?"

"I'm guessing that's bad."

"Now imagine that same child holding the detonator for a hundred trillion of them."

"Since I'm assuming I'm the child in this scenario and I have a detonator of some kind?"

"You *are* the detonator, Elle-Ryn, and the nuclear devices, all one hundred trillion of them, are inside you."

I looked down at myself. "I have a bomb inside me," I said, trying desperately to understand.

"Your inability to comprehend the situation is a rather large part of the problem."

"How is something like that even possible?"

"And you prove me right again."

"Quit being a smartass," I said, taking a step closer. The glass trembled and closed in around him. "I get it. I'm an idiot. Now answer my question. How is something like that even possible?"

"It shouldn't have been," he acquiesced. "You should not have come into your powers before your corporeal form expired. You learned your name too soon, and as such, absorbed your powers too soon. As you can see, it was too much for you to regulate. Now you can't remember your name. Any of them. And you can't control your anger. You just tried to kill every person in here with a single thought."

"No." I stepped back until I hit the counter. "That wasn't what I was doing." I glanced around the café. At Dixie and Mr. P and Cookie. "I would never hurt them."

"What is this, then?" he asked me, indicating the glass that hung like sparkling crystal around us. "And this was just the barest hint of a thought. One infinitesimal inkling that didn't amount to a single grain of sand in your Sahara. Can you imagine what you'd do with more forethought?"

Reyes was only a few feet away now, slowly advancing, gaining ground.

"So you've come to kill her?" he asked Michael.

The air pushed out of my lungs as if I'd been punched.

"It cannot be helped."

"I'll make you a deal," he said. "Get off this plane now, and I'll let you live."

But we weren't on a plane. I glanced around just to make sure. Nope. No plane.

"I have been sent, Rey'aziel."

"Then you have been sent to your death."

"I would've thought after the nick I gave you last time—"

"Funny. Most of the blood on my shirt was yours."

Michael rolled his eyes. Did angels really do that? "We could be at this all day."

"What does He want, exactly?"

"The Val-Eeth to do her job. It is why He allowed her onto this plane in the first place. To stop the fallen one."

Reyes tilted his head. "And here I thought He allowed it so she could be the portal. His portal."

He lifted a shoulder. "That, too. But, as it were, there is a loophole in the original agreement with your father."

"Ah. So killing two birds with one stone."

He didn't disagree. "But, alas, it would seem two gods is one god too many." He gave him a chastising scowl. "Five is an invasion."

Reyes took another step closer to me. "We know about the three gods of Uzan. You're strong, Michael, but you're not that strong. I've seen how they fight. And, you know, there is the matter of them being gods. You're going to need our help. We can get all three of them off this plane for good."

He stilled, his lids narrowing. "You can get them off? All three gods of Uzan?"

"Yes."

He thought a moment, let his piercing vision rake over Reyes. "And you're going to cast them out?" He sounded thoroughly unconvinced.

"You of all angelic asshats should know what I'm capable of."

Michael lifted his sword, slowly, nonthreateningly, and placed the tip at my throat. He raised my chin with the cool blade. Studied me. Judged me. "Will that be before or after she collapses the universe with her temper?"

The dark smoke that cascaded over Reyes's shoulders and pooled at his feet materialized into a black robe. He pulled a sword from underneath it and did the same thing, lifted his sword until his blade rested across the angel's throat. "It will be sometime before she collapses the universe with her temper and after I collapse your lungs with my blade."

Unmoved, the angel shot him a sideways glance. "He'll come after you if you fail. Personally."

"I doubt that."

The angel lowered his sword, but Reyes held his steady. He clearly had trust issues. "I have your word?" the angel asked. "You will cast out all three gods from this plane?"

"You have my word."

"No matter the cost?"

"No matter the cost."

I suddenly got the feeling Reyes was being played. The barest hint of a smirk lifted one corner of Michael's mouth. He was pleased with the bargain he'd just struck. A little too pleased, in fact, and I couldn't help but wonder what Reyes had gotten himself into.

Before Reyes could react, Michael raised his right fist and slid his wrist along the razor-sharp edge of Reyes's blade. Then, as though self-mutilation were a sport, Reyes did the same. He dropped the hilt into the palm of his left hand and sliced his right wrist open on his sword.

My hand shot up to cover my mouth. Blood gushed out of the deep opening and ran in rivulets over his forearm. They stepped toward each other and started to shake on it, but Michael paused, holding back for one last assurance.

"Your word. All three gods of Uzan will be banished from this plane and will never, ever return."

Reyes knew something was going on. Had known from the first. I could feel the turmoil bubbling inside him. He lowered his head and watched Michael from underneath his dark lashes, his eyes glittering, his brows knitting in thought. After a moment of contemplation, he gave one quick nod.

Michael grabbed his forearm close to the elbow before Reyes could change his mind. Reyes followed suit, and their mutilated wrists touched in what amounted to a blood oath.

With an archangel.

What were the odds?

I felt the need to ask one burning question. "So there's more than one god?"

They didn't answer. As soon as the deed was done, Michael took on an expression way too smug for the direness at hand. "The bargain has been struck, Rey'aziel. The blood exchanged. You cannot, for any reason, back out."

Reyes stepped closer to me. "I don't plan to."

"I am well aware of this . . . uncommon sense of honor you've gained while here in His realm." He sheathed his sword. "Just don't forget where you came from."

Reyes didn't take the bait. He watched and waited for the angelic asshat to leave.

Michael turned to go, then stopped and said, "I just

thought you should know, I couldn't have killed her either way."

I felt Reyes still.

"She dematerialized her human form. She fused it together with her celestial energies. Now, even her physical body is immortal. Only another god can end her life. Father was on his way to do just that, but now that we have an agreement . . ."

Oddly enough, Reyes seemed more confused than upset. "You did it on purpose. Why? We would have agreed. It is to our advantage to cast out the gods. You didn't have to threaten her." He took a bold step, closing the distance between them. "Why?"

"Some bargains are just too good to pass up."

An unsatisfied growl rumbled out of Reyes's chest. Giving up for now, he said, "You need to fix this."

Michael admired the surroundings once again. "Clean up your own mess."

"For old time's sake," Reyes said.

In an instant the world was back where it belonged. The windows stood fully intact. The coffee cups rested on their respective tables. People sat talking and laughing as though their cook hadn't just sealed a blood pact with an archangel to cast gods out of their world.

I glanced around for Reyes, then looked through the pass-out window. He was behind the grill, cooking, as if nothing had happened. My mouth formed a perfect O. Had I just hallucinated everything?

When Reyes glanced at me from underneath his lashes before reaching up to the spice rack, I knew that it had all been real. A huge gash ran the length of his arm. I hadn't imagined anything. I inched backward to the front doors as what I'd done came rushing back.

I'd gotten angry and risked the lives of my best friends? I was some sort of time bomb that would eventually collapse the universe? God—*the* God—wanted me dead? What kind of monster was I? Reyes stopped what he was doing. Gauged my emotions. Saw the fear in my eyes. Just as he started after me, I burst out the door and took off.

I thought of nothing but running. Nothing but getting away from people before I hurt someone. The otherworld raged around me as I ran. Its wind blistered my skin and scorched my lungs. I shook out of it and fought to stay in the tangible world, where it had just started to snow.

I kept running, my legs pushing forward as though they had an unlimited source of energy. The last time I tried to run, I got half a block and almost keeled over.

This was not me. This was the being Michael wanted dead. The one God wanted off His planet.

Slowing to a stop, I fell to my knees and panted. My breaths made puffs of white fog in the air, and my jeans were wet from the snow.

Then the wind scorched me again. I looked down at my arms. At my hands. Blisters started to bubble on my skin. The wind began to peel it off my muscle. I let out a quick scream and scrambled back. I forced myself to snap out of it, to find the snow again, the snow and the freezing wind that I'd complained about for weeks. But something dive-bombed me, and I couldn't tell from which world it came. It happened again, and I huddled on the ground. Was it a bird? A spiritual being?

I squinted and focused on the sparrow trying to protect its nest. I seemed to be teetering on the razor's edge between two worlds, unable to get a foothold in either.

I felt a hand on my shoulder and flinched.

"Janey," a male voice said. "What's going on? Did you take something?"

Ian. It was Ian.

"I need to go home," I said, near panic.

He stood and looked around. "How did you get up here?"

"Where?" When I took in my surroundings, I realized we were on top of a mountain peak, looking down at the city. "I need to get back to town. I need to get home." When he didn't say anything, I asked, "Can you take me?"

He helped me to his patrol car. "Are you working?" I asked him. He was in uniform.

"Just got off. Hold on."

He went to his trunk, rummaged around, and came back with a bottle of water.

"You're dehydrated."

We started down the steep and curving roads, over the Hudson and toward Sleepy Hollow.

"What were you doing up there?" he asked me for the tenth time.

I was getting a better grip on the worlds around me, more able to keep one on one side and the other on the other. I just needed sleep. The edges of my vision blurred, and by the time we hit the highway, I was out.

I awoke to cabinet doors banging and a cup breaking in my kitchen, but I was in my empty bathtub with all my clothes on and no memory of how I got there.

"You don't have a drop of alcohol," Ian said as he stormed into the minuscule room. "What the hell?"

"Ian, what are you doing?" I put my hands on either side of my head to try to stop the room from spinning. Or at least I tried to. They flopped past my face and fell to my lap. I had zero muscle control.

I tried to look at Ian but couldn't lift my head.

"What were you doing up there?"

"I went for a run. Ended up at the top of that mountain. Why? Do you own it?"

My words were slurred, but he seemed to understand me okay.

"I have . . . friends up there."

"You don't have any friends." I giggled, an embellishment he did not appreciate.

"You're just like all the other fucking bitches."

I might not have known a lot about my previous life, but I was pretty sure I didn't like being called a bitch.

"You're all just teases and whores until you get what you want, then you're on to the next sucker that you can stand to fuck long enough to get what you want."

"We never had sex," I reminded him. He didn't appreciate that either.

He knelt beside me. "If I could knock the shit out of you, I would, and trust me when I say I'd enjoy it."

"I'm having trust issues today."

"This is where I made my mistake with Tamala. Nobody gets it right the first time, you know. They hesitate." He made tiny marks on my skin, some shallow and a couple much deeper. "They chicken out. Then . . ." He sank the knife into my wrist.

The pain cut through to my marrow. Blood dripped down the side of the tub and onto my pants. My head lolled back, and I hit the spigot.

He grabbed a handful of my hair. "Be careful," he said with a hiss. "Any other mark will cast doubt on a suicide ruling."

"Sorry," I said. Whatever he'd given me made this entire situation seem a little funny. This would make the third time today someone, or something, had tried to kill me.

I snorted as he worked on my other wrist. He made fewer marks on that one because he said once they make the first cut, their adrenaline is going and they're better with the second one. So that was good to know for future reference.

"My first one is up there," he told me. "On the mountain. I go up there to talk to her sometimes."

"That's so nice."

He finished slicing into my wrists and sank on the floor beside me. "Her name was Janet. I didn't try to make hers look like suicide or anything, so I had to bury her. The constant weight of that, of someone finding her body and some stupid little mistake I made leading the investigators back to me . . . It puts a lot of stress on me."

When my head lolled back again, he pulled it forward. "Careful, damn it. I told you, any other mark will cast suspicion."

"Any mark?"

"Any mark."

"Like this?" I asked and lifted my arm.

The look of utter disbelief on his face when I showed him what I'd scratched into my skin made me burst out laughing. His mouth did a fish thing when he read, *Ian was here,* and I doubled over.

Seriously, this day just got better and better.

He grabbed a handful of my hair, twisted his fingers into it, then—in an act I felt was a bit much—slammed my face against the rim of the tub. My head bounced back, and a blindingly sharp pain shot through me. He did the face-slam thing a few more times. Eventually it stopped hurting, so there was that.

"Not laughing anymore, are you, bitch?" he said into my ear. He wrenched my head back, and the irony of it all—that there would be a soulless man in a trench coat and fedora standing behind my captor and attempted murderer—struck me as hilarious.

My shoulders shook, and I thought Ian was going to come unglued.

He wrenched me closer until we were nose to blood-red nose and asked, "What?"

I looked past him and tried to raise an index finger to show him, but before Ian could turn around, the man placed his hands on both sides of Ian's head and twisted. Ian's neck snapped with a loud crack. Then he went completely limp and fell to the side.

The man grabbed a towel off my counter, tore it into strips, and wrapped them around my hemorrhaging wrists. "Can't lose all of this," he said with a flirty wink. "We're going to need at least a couple of drops." He frowned down at Ian. "I have to say, he was the easiest human to manipulate I've every encountered."

"He was a douche," I said, trying not to giggle.

"I agree."

He lifted me out of the tub and carried me to the place where he would kill me.

No, really this time.

22

Every girl wants to be swept off her feet.
It's when you put her in the trunk that she starts
*   to freak out.*

—INTERNET MEME

"Thankfully, it takes a lot to kill you now," he said to me as his driver took us through the streets of Sleepy Hollow in a black Rolls-Royce. "That Jeffries kid could have beaten you for days. Would not have made the slightest difference."

I was worried about getting blood on his seats, since it was gushing out of my nose and from a gash over my left eye, but he didn't seem to mind at all.

"You're the nicest man who's tried to kill me all day," I told him.

"Thank you." He turned toward me. "I appreciate that. So many people, mostly humans, don't understand what goes into preparing something like a political assassination or a mass suicide or a ritual sacrifice. It's exhausting."

"I hear that."

"And then take somebody like you," he said, waving a dismissive hand, "a god, no less. Talk about prep work. One word: years. That's all I'm saying."

I gave him a horrified expression. That was dedication.

"Oh, and I won't even go into how horrible the record keeping was back in the 1400s."

"Dude, they didn't even have computers." I rolled my eyes. "I don't know how they got anything done."

"Amen."

I was busy trying to spit hair out of my mouth when he started humming the Blue Öyster Cult song "Don't Fear the Reaper." I socked him in the arm. "Oh my God," I said, floored. "You're James."

He tipped an invisible hat, as he'd taken off the afore-mentioned fedora. "If you want to get technical, this human's name was Earl James Walker. He was your husband's . . . well, I don't know what. He raised him, if you want to call what he did raising. That guy was a crude piece of work. Anyway, just thought it would be a nice twist."

"I'm married?"

"Oh, sweetheart, you really don't remember, do you?"

I shook my head, causing another rush of blood to ribbon over my eye.

"Well, you won't have to worry about that much longer."

That made me feel better. I closed my eyes and drifted off to sleep. But I'd barely managed a few nonproductive Z's when my eyes fluttered open again. I was tied to a rather comfy chair in the middle of a gigantic warehouse with a fire blazing behind me in a stove.

My face had stopped bleeding, and James was wiping it with a warm towel.

"I just want you to know this isn't personal."

"Thanks, James."

There were several men working on this or that, all dressed casually in an array of light jackets and jeans, and a handful of departed stood sprinkled about, probably acting as lookouts.

One of the departed was a man who'd come into the café quite often. He never spoke to anyone and never sat in my section. I took that as a sign that he wasn't into small talk. The lanky man towered over most of the others and looked like he ate a lot of roughage when he was alive.

James finished up, the towel that was once white now dark red, then went to supervise the unloading of a massive trunk.

The departed man disappeared from his spot and reappeared next to me. He knelt beside me and used my body as a shield from James's line of sight. "Charley," he said in a soft whisper, "you have to snap out of it. This is the real deal, hon."

I was busy doing the head-bob thing, fighting the urge to drift off to sleep again. "Is that my name?" But he'd disappeared.

James glanced over his shoulder, so I acted natural. Lolled my head back to check out the ceiling. Lolled it forward to examine my blood-encrusted nails.

When he turned back to the box, Dead Guy appeared beside me again.

I tried to focus on him. Did I really have an ally? "Can you . . . Can you get Reyes?" I asked. "Reyes has a sword."

"No," he whispered sadly.

"What? Why? You're like the worst ally."

"He can't see this. No one can see this. Not yet. Not until you're ready."

"No, I'm ready. Really. I was born ready." I'd started to

panic and raised my voice enough to get James's attention. Dead Guy had disappeared again and reappeared at what I'd suspected was his post in a far corner by a huge garage door.

James walked back over and turned my chair around. "You have got to check this out. Remember the 1400s quip? Well, this is why."

I looked at the trunk they'd brought in. It was a massive wooden box with cogs and gears all around it. "Nice wood."

"Finding that box, which was hidden in the 1400s, was one thing," he said. "Finding the key to it was another story altogether."

Okay, I was intrigued.

One of his minions inserted a huge iron key that looked like it had been on the bottom of the sea for centuries. He twisted it, and the cogs and gears started rotating.

"If this works, and I like to think it will, that box will open, and inside will be an object that is literally the only one of its kind. As in, there isn't another like it in any dimension in any universe anywhere. This'll blow your mind. And it will trap you in a hell dimension for all eternity. But still . . ."

While I could laugh death in the face, being trapped in a hell dimension for all eternity was a tad more disconcerting. Either that or the drugs were wearing off and shit was getting real.

I glanced over my shoulder at my ally. He completely ignored me. Unlike Cookie, that guy could act.

The box continued to groan and shift. Panels slid over others and then disappeared. Cogs rotated, then sank into the center. Each movement revealed layer after layer of mechanical devices, which then slid over to reveal more mechanical devices and intricately carved wood. It was like a giant mechanical Russian nesting doll, each layer revealing a new box inside.

James stood admiring it, a fascinated smile on his face. "According to talk around the universe, Lucifer stole the portal from its maker and used it for his own nefarious purposes, because, let's face it, it's Lucifer. And when he was finished, he gave it to a priest who used it to be the judge, jury, and executioner of his parishioners and, eventually, the entire countryside. If any of them went against his wishes or did something he felt was wrong, he would use this device to banish their souls to a hell dimension."

The more the box worked, the smaller the final product, until all that was left was a tiny wooden trinket box. No way was I fitting in that.

"But only their souls would be banished. The people he stole souls from became catatonic, as the host cannot live without the soul."

He walked over and picked up the box.

"He did this for almost two decades, until a group of very brave monks figured out what he was doing and set a trap."

He carried the box over, displayed on his palm, very Vanna-esque, so I could get a better look. Adorned with carvings and iron fastenings, it looked both delicate and hardy.

"One man volunteered to send the priest through the portal, knowing what would happen to him when he did."

He pocketed the box in his trench coat, then took the massive iron key and threw it into a fire they'd been stoking.

"Legend has it that once a soul or being is sent through the portal, the only way that entity can be brought back is if the person who originally sent him opens the portal and says his name."

He took a poker and nudged the key slowly turning red in the fire, flipped it as though browning it on both sides for a more even, enjoyable dining experience. While James and his minions stood transfixed by the orange and yellow glow, I nodded to the departed guy, basically telling him to go fetch.

He appeared beside me again, pretending to want a better look in case James were to turn around. "I can't get Rey'aziel," he whispered. "He can't see this. Not until you want him to know the truth, Charley. There's a lot you don't know."

I didn't know anything. That was the problem.

"So, just to be safe," James continued as he roasted the key around a campfire and told ghost stories, "the volunteer sent the priest through the portal to the hell dimension—not Lucifer's, by the way—and then the monks, normally a nonviolent bunch, beheaded the brave man so he could never open it and speak the priest's name again."

"Snap out of it," Dead Guy whispered.

I scowled at him. "I can't," I said through gritted teeth.

"Of course you can. Stop overthinking it and just remember. It will take everything you have in your arsenal to take on Kuur."

"Kuur?"

He nodded toward James. "He's an emissary from Lucifer's army. An expert assassin of any type of being in any of the known dimensions."

"Well, his name is very manly."

Dead Guy clenched his jaw. My humor wasn't for everyone.

"Snap out of it before it's too late."

"Then what? It's not like I can fight them."

He stepped even closer. Cupped my chin and lifted my face to his. "Once you remember who you are, you won't have to."

"Got it!" James called out as he retrieved a small piece of metal from the fire.

He turned back to me, and Dead Guy appeared at his position across the room, staring into space as dead guys were wont to do. If James did see him near me, he didn't seem to give a rat's ass.

"And in their infinite wisdom," he continued, because this was apparently *The James Show*, "the monks made this box to hold the portal. To keep it safe." His expression changed to one of frustration. "Then they buried the box under a thousand feet of dirt and neglected to tell anyone where it was. Fuckers."

I gave him a dubious frown. "That little box is holding a portal to a hell dimension?"

"It is."

"Is it a hell dimension for tiny people? Because I promise you, I won't fit."

"Ah," he said, understanding my doubt. "Your human mind has limited you to a certain way of thinking. Things don't always work the way you believe they should. There are dimensions with creatures that fly from star to star, feeding off their energy. There are worlds with pebbles the size of your fingernail that could power this entire planet for all eternity. There is a galaxy with a world where the oldest living creatures are slowly melting and flooding the lands, drowning millions. There is so much you could have seen." He held up a small silver key, formerly a big iron one, he'd fished out of the fire. "But hell dimensions can be fun, too."

"Have you seen it?" I asked, growing more nervous by the heartbeat. Sadly, my heart was racing.

"Not this one." He pointed to the box. "Only one way in or out of the dimension you're going to."

James put the key in the lock and turned. The lid opened with a soft sigh, and a light shone out of it. He reached in and drew out a beautiful round pendant. It was really a locket, but the top piece was clear glass. Inside was a smooth jewel, the likes of which I'd never seen before. My vision laser-locked onto it like a homing beacon. I sat transfixed. Wherever it went, my gaze went.

James laughed, delighted with my reaction. "It's called god glass. And if you just happen to be a god, like you are, you will see the untold treasures of a dimension accessible only through this glass." He seemed almost jealous of the things I saw. The dancing light. The shimmering water.

"It's beautiful," I said. "How can that be a hell dimension?"

"There are many kinds of hell, love."

The pendant emitted a soft glow of colors. "Why send me there? Why not just kill me?"

"Someone didn't pay attention in God Composition 101. You're a god. Gods cannot be killed except by another god. But they can," he said, holding up an index finger, "be trapped. Especially one that has amnesia and can't remember that it's a god. But even then, there are rules. A set of conditions that must be met for the transport to take place."

"Which are?" I asked to keep him talking. I squinted, gritted my teeth, made grunting sounds, all in an attempt to stop time. I finally gave up. Clearly I had a faulty timer.

"The only way to trap a god is if it takes physical form first. It can be anything from a houseplant to a kangaroo, but once the god chooses its form, one drop of its life force—in this case your blood—and the recitation of the god's name, and that god is trapped for all eternity. Unless, of course, the being who put it there, and only that being, decides to set it free. There is no other way out."

"If you put me in there and then you die, what happens then?"

"No more mocha lattes for you."

"So it really is like hell. Only worse."

He laughed softly, then took out a handkerchief and polished the glass.

I gave him a blurry once-over. "I guess you have nothing to worry about, then, being soulless and all."

"Not true." He tapped a corner of the kerchief on his tongue and continued to polish." I am a sentient being. I have an essence, an aura, if you will, just as you do."

"But it's not like a human soul."

"Neither is yours," he said, seemingly offended. "And thank goodness. Human souls don't tend to fare well. They were not created to survive the psychological atrocities of a hell dimension. The priest brought a soul back once. A young girl from a French village not far from where he lived. He'd fallen in love with her, and when her father refused the priest's offer of marriage, citing age as the main reason—the priest was in his forties and the girl was twelve—"

"Ew."

"—the priest sent her soul to hell."

"To punish her. And her father," I said, knowing how men like that thought.

"Very likely. But obsession is a tricky thing. Her family

took care of her catatonic body, but she was no longer the vibrant girl he remembered, the one he fell in love with, so for the first time, he opened the portal again and called out her name."

I eased up in the chair, my curiosity growing. "What happened?"

"She woke up at home in her body, but according to his writings, she came back . . . different. He called her a berserker, most likely because she knew what he did to her and she screamed every time he came near." He leaned in, his voice full of intrigue. "But she became quite famous for a gift she'd received thanks to her time in a hell dimension. The gift of sight."

"Like psychic?"

"Indeed. She went by many names, but you know her as Joan of Arc."

Astonishment sent a pulse of electricity over my skin.

"Read the history books. There's a reason she refused to give out her real name to anyone ever again." He straightened his shoulders and said, "Enough. Let's get on with it, shall we?"

He turned to give the box to one of his minions. In that instant, Dead Guy appeared beside me and whispered into my ear. "I'm sorry, sweetheart. I have no choice but to leave you now."

Alarm clutched around my heart. "You're leaving me?"

"Be ready." And then he was gone.

James turned back, took the pendant in both hands, pushed the latch on one side, then let it fall open in his palms. It was about that time I lost all control over my bodily functions.

* * *

"Be ready," Dead Guy mouthed again from across the room.

I barely saw him. I was much more concerned with the lightning strikes that burst from the pendant. The ones that lit the entire warehouse, that branched out and crawled across the ceiling, leaving sparks and burn marks in their place. I winced as a hot wind rushed over my skin, causing it to bubble and crack, the acidic sand peeling away at the reddened layers.

And yet none of that concerned me. Lightning, hot wind, acidic sand blasting away at my skin—that part I could handle. It was the other part that had me doubling over.

James's minions stepped back to a safe distance. All but one. Of course, he was the one with the knife.

James yelled over the noise, delighted with the events. "No human, unless gifted with sight, would ever have seen any of this! The priest could never have known the true power he'd held in the palm of his hands." He watched the swirling clouds and the lightning bursts and laughed. "I never imagined it would be like this."

Apparently the people inside the dimension screaming in terror did not compute. For me, it was agony. I didn't just hear their screams. I felt them. I felt flesh rip and bones crunch. I smelled burned hair and rotting wounds. I tasted old blood and fresh bile. This was not a place built to hold human souls. These people were not sent there because of the choices they made while alive. They were sent there because an asshole of the worst kind decreed it so.

My hands gripped the chair so tight, my fingernails started breaking at the quick. The captives' suffering sliced into me until my entire body felt like a mass of raw nerve endings. I had to get them out. I had to set them free.

I looked over at Dead Guy, my vision blurring and growing dark at the edges.

He was turned toward me and had hunkered down as though preparing for a race. "Now," he mouthed. Then he took off.

He sprinted toward me, and suddenly I realized what he was going to do. He was going to cross. I didn't feel it was the best time, but when several minions noticed and tried to tackle him, he dodged them. Zigzagged around them. Hurdled an arm here, a leg there, until with a last desperate glance, he dived inside me.

James looked on but seemed more confused than worried. And then it was silent.

The first thing I heard was a steady, solid tone that stretched on forever, and I knew the sound was not good. I looked over at a man in hospital scrubs. He sat on a stool, his shoulders shaking with grief.

Then I was in his arms and he was smiling down at me. Through the agony I felt to my core, through the utter sense of loss, he smiled.

"Looks like it's just the three of us," he said, and another bout of sorrow ripped through him. It shuddered through me as well.

It was Dead Guy. My father. And he sacrificed our time together to cross so that I could snap the fuck out of it. So that I would remember who I was. What I was. My life through his eyes rushed at me like a film on fast-forward, including the wife he lost and the daughter he gained on one fateful night. He deluged me with memories of myself through his eyes, of all the things I did growing up, of all the abilities I had, of the good I did by helping him solve crimes—he'd been a detective—and put bad men behind bars. Of all the things he did wrong and a few he did very, very right.

He showed me the time he taught me to ride a bike, pretending I was doing it all on my own, holding a finger on the back of the seat for good measure as he ran beside me cheering me on.

He showed me the time he held me in his arms as I cried for hours because a little boy I'd befriended crossed through me, and I saw how his stepfather had killed him. I felt it. For weeks, I felt the sting of that man's fists. The agony of his kicks. Together we put the man behind bars, but it had been a powerful lesson for my father. He saw what I went through when I helped him with his cases. He saw what the memories of others could do to me.

He showed me the regret he often felt at having married a woman who could not love me, no matter how hard she tried. Despite everything, I grew up okay. I wasn't a perfect kid by a long shot, but he loved me beyond measure.

And then he was gone. He was killed, and he saw the celestial part of me for the first time. My light mesmerized him. It beamed out of me as though I were made of glass to become a blinding beacon of hope.

He'd had no idea. He knew I had gifts, but this was different. This was world changing.

He also saw what Reyes was. The darkness. The danger. But by then he knew enough about me and my world to see Reyes as a protector. A warrior who would give his life for me. A husband.

And he saw Beep coming from a light year away.

Beep.

I stilled, put the flashbacks on pause.

Beep. I had a baby. Reyes and I had a little girl, and she was made of stardust and light and warmth. Because of me, because of my light, because of who I was and what I was made of, we had to send her away to live with some very good people. There were beings after her, and my light would lead them straight to her.

He showed me crumbling when they took her away. He'd been there when I cracked. When my powers reached nuclear meltdown levels and I exploded and vanished, only to end up here, in Sleepy Hollow. And now I knew why.

Earl James Walker. Kuur. He'd found the god glass and he knew how to use it. With the intention of sailing to the other side of the world and dropping the box into the ocean there, the monks' ships sank off the coast of what would become New York.

They rowed ashore with the box, traveled as far inland as they could before exhaustion and disease overtook them, then spent the next month burying it as far underground as they could in a little spot off the Hudson River.

Dad vowed to do everything in his power to help us keep Beep safe, so—a cop to the core—he went undercover. He infiltrated Satan's ranks and learned everything he could. And now he was relaying everything that he'd learned to me in astonishing Technicolor.

He'd been spying on the emissaries for Reyes, trying to locate all twelve. And he sacrificed himself, his mission, and any more time he could have with me to force me to snap out of it. To save myself and, in turn, my daughter. The one destined to destroy Satan. The tiny creature the emissaries called the Ravager.

But I called her Elwyn.

Elwyn Alexandra.

My heart swelled with all the emotion coursing through it. When they'd taken Elwyn away, it was simply too much to bear. After everything Reyes and I had been through, after every obstacle we'd overcome, that was the straw that broke me. The one that sent me here to this town with no memory.

When the replay stopped, I sat there in astonishment. I would never see him again. After everything he did for me, for us, he was just . . . gone.

James was staring at me, not sure what to think. Why that man had crossed. He nodded to his minions, and they reluctantly continued with their task, which was basically to hold my arm so James could get a drop of blood onto the pendant. It was that easy. One drop of blood. The unfortunate's name spoken. And the soul would be transported to a dimension of eternal torment.

James studied me. Deciding his men had secured me, he lowered the pendant, and one of the minions sliced my finger. I wrenched my arm away and slapped James on the face, raking my nails across his cheek.

"Hold her!" he shouted over the winds, angry for the first time that evening.

They wrenched my arm and held it still as he pushed a drop of blood onto the glass. A bolt of lightning shot out of it, but I held steady.

His expression changed from wary to elated. He lifted the pendant to the sky and spoke my name.

"Elle-Ryn-Ahleethia." Of course. My celestial name. He said it softly. Lovingly. And then he waited.

And waited.

He glanced at the blood on the glass and said it again, louder this time. "Elle-Ryn-Ahleethia!"

Nothing.

He shook the pendant in his palms. Looked at his minions, confused. Then let his gaze wander to me. And he stilled.

He was sharp. I'd give him that. He caught on faster than I thought he would. He snapped his hands together to close the pendant, but a microsecond before it shut, I said it.

"Kuur."

Thankfully, he had a short name. The locket clicked closed, and silence blanketed the area. He waited with bated breath, realizing I'd stolen his blood when I slapped him and put that on the glass in place of my own.

I heard a series of sharp thuds. Someone was pounding on a metal door. Then I heard a sharp bang and, in my peripheral vision, saw a sequence of struggles. I didn't dare take my focus off Kuur, but I could just make out the smooth, deadly shape of my husband as he snapped neck after neck to get to me. Another skirmish, just as short as the first one, involved Osh and three minions. Garrett took on two more when they tried to run.

But Kuur's eyes were glued to the pendant. He was just about to release a sigh of relief when a lightning bolt reached out and grabbed him. Tiny branches like spider legs crawled around him. Ripped at the beast inside. Closed like a fist.

And he was gone.

The pendant hung in midair for several seconds, then dropped. I reached out and caught it. Then, so that word of this did not leak, I obliterated every departed present with a single, devastating thought.

23

We are the granddaughters of the witches you
weren't able to burn.
—UNKNOWN

I packed up what few earthly possessions I had, which mainly consisted of a dozen or so articles of clothing, a tube of mascara, lip gloss, hair bands, and a killer collection of boots. Even amnesiac me had had a thing for boots. I also packed the trinket box, but the pendant I kept in my pocket. I still had some work to do in that area. I was going to get those human souls out of there if it was the last thing I did.

At first I thought James's minions had taken Ian's body and cleaned up the place, but Reyes, who hadn't left my side since he lifted me into his arms and carried me out of that warehouse, informed me that he and "the guys" had done it.

Exhaustion had overcome me after the fight. There were bodies scattered across the warehouse floor. Reyes snapped one last neck and pushed the minion aside before sprinting toward me and sliding on his knees to kneel before me. And I looked into the familiar—and painfully handsome—face of my husband. My beautiful, surreal husband.

"Dutch," he whispered, scanning my face for injuries. His dark irises shimmered with relief that I was alive and relatively unharmed, considering the situation. Then he saw my neck, and the flames that forever sheathed him grew slowly. Steadily. Lethally.

"That was fun," Osh said as he walked up to assess my condition for himself.

Garrett followed him, an impish grin tugging at one corner of his mouth. "I'm thinking you should take up a new hobby."

Osh nodded in agreement. "One that doesn't involve people or supernatural entities trying to kill you."

I let out a breathy laugh, my relief complete, absolute. I knew who I was. I knew who they were. I was no longer floating in a sea of uncertainty. Not about my identity, anyway. I glanced at my husband and fought the concern that threatened to draw my brows together. He didn't notice. He lifted me into his arms and left Osh and Garrett to discuss the cleanup of the warehouse.

I didn't say anything when I nestled further into his arms in the back of an SUV that Garrett had rented. Having apparently come up with a plan, Osh and Garrett got in, and we headed to my apartment.

Reyes watched me the entire time. His fingers slid over my face, leaving a soft flame in their wake. It was the last thing I saw before falling into a deep, tranquil sleep.

When I jerked awake at three the next morning, still cradled in Reyes's arms, we spoke little and loved a lot. A really lot. We made love more fiercely than I ever remembered. And yet, for some reason, I didn't tell him that I had gotten my memory back. Not just yet. I didn't want to ruin the moment. And I suddenly wanted to savor the anonymity of Janey for a few hours more. To stare at him and re-remember every curve of his face. Every line of his mouth. Every contour of his sculpted body.

And as ready as I was to go home, I had a few things to see to first, so I convinced him that it was okay for him to go to work, that I'd be there shortly—not that we wouldn't be hours late. He set Osh out front to watch over me, no longer trying to hide that fact, and left with the reluctance of a man walking toward the executioner's noose as I fought a grin behind him. And then I packed.

I looked down at my box of earthly possessions. I'd already said good-bye to Mable. She took Satana and offered to sell me the Fiesta. It was tempting, but I really didn't want to drive it all the way back to Albuquerque, New Mexico. I left everything I owned—in the state of New York, anyway—in a box by the front door, said good-bye to Denzel, then turned my attention to Irma, the woman hovering in my corner.

I crossed my arms and leaned my head against the wall so I could see her face.

"Aunt Lil," I said, trying not to laugh. Or burst into tears. I knew what she was doing. I'd had a tiny Asian man hovering in the corner of my apartment in Albuquerque for years. He turned out to be the equivalent of an archangel and had left to watch over Beep, so I figured Aunt Lil was going to take his place for a while. Perhaps to give me something familiar. Perhaps because Beep's absence left her just as sad as it had the rest of us.

Playing her part to the end, she didn't answer me.

I let out a soft giggle and hugged her to me. "I'm okay now, Aunt Lil. You can come back to me."

She hugged me back. "Hey, pumpkin head," she said, her sweet, toothless smile heavenly.

"Sorry I called you Irma."

"Why? I like it. Might change my name permanent."

We hugged for a long time, and then I told her I'd meet her in Albuquerque. She nodded and vanished before my eyes.

I got ready to leave for what would amount to my last day at work. Sadly, I would leave on a bad note. I was beyond late. Everyone would already be there. And boy, would I give them a morning they would not soon forget. I wanted to scream with happiness and a sad sense of regret, but I didn't want to leave Denzel with a bad impression of me. We'd had some lovely nights, Denzel and I. Our parting would be such sweet sorrow.

With Osh following me from a distance, whistling as though he hadn't a care in the world, I made a quick pit stop at Headless Henry's best friend's house and explained the situation. He looked at me as if I were the headless one, but I was okay with that. I felt calmness come over him as I spoke, as though he finally had permission to forgive himself for something he never actually did.

There were flowers on the doors of the café and a note saying the Firelight Grill would be closed for a funeral in two days. Shayla's death would be felt for a long time to come. A somberness blanketed the café. Even those who didn't know her well felt the loss.

I was well aware of how I looked. I healed fast, more so now that I was officially a god, but I still had fresh bruises, cuts, and scrapes across my face. So the concerned glances didn't surprise me when I walked in and strolled straight to the kitchen, where a certain son of evil incarnate was making huevos rancheros.

He stopped, a coffee mug halfway to his mouth, and focused all his attention on me. I felt a languid appreciation roll out of him, and my chest contracted.

It was time.

I grabbed Sumi's stool, set it before him, and stood to face him eye to eye.

"Are you going to tell me another lie?" I asked, my voice soft.

"I wasn't aware that I had."

I fought to keep a sad grin at bay. "Are you or are you not married?"

He put the cup on the prep table. "I am."

"So, what? You've been having trouble? You're not in love with her anymore? You're separated? What lie are you going to give me next?"

"No lies," he said, stepping closer.

I heard Dixie walk into the kitchen, felt the warmth she felt at seeing us. She knew. She'd known who I was and had been in on my wonderful family and friends' plan for some time now. Reyes must have told her everything.

His expression softened, and his dark gaze flitted over my face with such appreciation, such admiration, my heart ached for him. But there was also a wariness, and I realized he didn't know what I was thinking. He could no longer feel my emotions. So he didn't know exactly what was going on, but he suspected. Or—perhaps—he hoped.

"I've loved her for centuries," he said. "And I will love her until the stars burn out."

"Well, okay then," I said, leaning into him. "That's all you had to say."

He stilled when he realized for certain that I knew. That I had all my memories back. The relief I felt from him melted me. His emotions were overwhelming, but he schooled his features as always, ever the poker player.

"Welcome back," he said, wiping at the wetness sliding down my cheeks.

I reached up and did the same to him.

Then I remembered a conversation we'd had a couple of days ago. "Did you really think that when I learned my celestial name, I'd leave? I'd forget all about you?"

"You did leave. You did forget all about me."

"That's different."

"The pain was just as real."

I couldn't argue that. He wrapped his arms around me and squeezed as though his life depended on it.

"I'll need to know what happened to you," he said from behind the hug.

"Only if we can go home."

He set me back. "Yes, ma'am."

Cookie walked in then, and she seemed to be the only one who didn't care that my husband and I were having a moment. "Where have you been?" she asked. "And why do you look like hell on a stick?"

I released Reyes and turned to her. She'd jammed her fists on her hips and was glaring. A real glare, too. Not one of those fake, pansy ones.

"I think I met your friend Charley."

"You . . . did? When?"

"When I looked in the mirror this morning."

She stood in disbelief for a moment. Then

astonishment. Then doubt. Then hope. Then wariness. Aka, the five stages of Cookie.

She whispered, almost as though she didn't want to get her hopes up too high, "Charley?"

I nodded.

An elated cry wrenched from her throat, and she ran to me.

And that was pretty much how the morning went.

"You know," Osh said, when he came in, "you could have marked a few of these people for me. I'm starving here. That asswipe after Erin's kid? I could've lived off that guy for months. But no. You send him downstairs. What are they gonna do with him? Let him burn in hell, that's what. Doesn't benefit anyone. Just sayin'."

Garrett was a tad more grateful I was back. He pulled me into a long, warm hug and didn't end it until Reyes growled. As far as Ian and the other bodies were concerned, they implemented a strict don't ask, don't tell policy. I was down with that.

I did a quick exorcism-hug combination when Mr. P came in. I wasn't sure why that demon had targeted him or why it was lying dormant, but all that really mattered was Mr. P. I gave him Helen's message, the one about her son and how grateful she was to him for how much he was helping.

"It's not out of the kindness of my heart," he said. "Helen was a good kid growing up."

Of course, she was sitting right beside him. "He knew me?" she asked, surprised.

"She was one of my best friend's daughters. It never set well with me, the way they treated her. I think she ended up on the street because of her father."

"I did," she said. She put a hand over her heart, appreciation for him evident.

"Always felt like she deserved another chance."

"Then you *are* helping her son out of the kindness of your heart."

"Partly. But also the love of her mother. She was a good woman who died entirely too young. If Helen'd had her for just a little longer . . ."

"See?" she said, leaning over and laying her head on his shoulder. "Told you he's the greatest."

Dixie had called in another crew to work our shifts, and I found out that Reyes had been paying them to stay at home all along. "He told me you'd get your memories back. He just wanted you to have a job while you were here, and them to still have jobs when you came to your senses."

Holy cow, I would miss her. "I don't know what to say, Dixie. I owe you so much."

"Nonsense," she said as she pulled me into a hug.

We stayed for a while, eating Reyes's huevos rancheros and chatting. I really wanted to say good-bye to Lewis, but I wasn't sure he would come in. Francie and Erin had made it, though. They were both still grieving, but Francie seemed different. Completely taken aback by what happened to Shayla.

Erin had done a small drawing and presented it to me in private. It was of Reyes, and she'd captured him with stunning accuracy. That was one of the longer hugs of the day.

Lewis eventually dragged himself in, looking haggard and distraught. Red, swollen eyes and a broken heart will do that to you. I explained that my memories had come back, and he was genuinely happy for me despite his sorrow.

"I just want you to know," I said to him, "Shayla told me she'd had the best days of her entire life with you. She loved you and wanted you to know how great you are."

He lowered his head, and his shoulders shook a couple

of times before he got his emotions under control. I pulled him into a hug, and he broke down completely, crying into my hair. It was okay. I cried into his as well.

When he couldn't take it anymore, he tore away from me and went to work. At one point, Francie tried to console him. I felt genuine concern from her. Affinity and compassion and empathy. Lewis all but ignored all of it. Ironically, it seemed to crush her.

"I never saw him," she said to me when I went to talk to her. "And when I do finally see him, it's too late."

"Give him time, hon."

She gave me a quick hug. "I always liked you even though I didn't always show it."

"I always liked you, too."

By the time Bobert walked in, aka, my uncle Bob, I couldn't hold back. I ran to him, threw my arms around his neck, and burst into tears. How he got an entire month off work, I'd never know, but I owed him everything. He'd coordinated my round-the-clock surveillance. He'd made sure I was being watched almost every second of the day. Too bad none of those seconds were when Ian or Kuur had showed up. We might need to discuss the holes in his administrative skills.

"I missed you, Uncle Bob," I said, and the sudden wetness in his eyes said he'd missed me, too.

I pretty much stayed glued to his neck for the next half hour until it was time to go home at long last. After another round of hugs and a promise from Reyes that we would drop in at the funeral home to say good-bye to Shayla, we left the Firelight Grill.

We swung by for my stuff and packed up the few belongings Reyes had in the motel room, and then Reyes and

I sat arm in arm in the back of the rented SUV. He seemed relieved. Happy.

"Have you heard anything?" I asked him, and I didn't have to elaborate.

He placed a powerful gaze on me. "Only that she's healthy and doing well."

I nodded. That was enough. It had to be. For now, anyway.

I nestled closer as we left the lovely town of Sleepy Hollow and wondered when I should tell him what my dad had found out. Namely about him. About when Lucifer had stolen the god glass from none other than God Himself. He used it to trap a god just as James was going to do with me. Only Lucifer, because he's Lucifer, had ulterior motives. Craving the power of a god for himself, he had trapped one only long enough to harness its energy and create his only son with it, Rey'aziel. His plan all along had been to take over Reyes's body, and with the power of a god at his fingertips, he could finally challenge the God Jehovah. He would finally have a shot at taking over heaven.

When Michael tried to kill me, he had talked about casting out the three gods of Uzan, very pleased with himself at the promise he'd gotten from Reyes. That we would do it. We would cast them out. All three of them. Problem was, one of them was the god Lucifer used to create Reyes. And of the three, the Razer, as he was known across the span of dimensions, was the most violent. The most bloodthirsty.

His name said it all, because that's what he did. He razed. He demolished. He destroyed. And I was married to him.

I squeezed the god glass pendant in my pocket. My father was right. It could come in very handy one day.

Read on for an excerpt from the next book by
Darynda Jones

The Curse of Tenth Grave

Available in hardcover June 28, 2016
From St. Martin's Press

Chapter One

Charley Davison:
Maybe she's born with it.
Maybe it's caffeine.

Ignoring the dead girl standing next to me, I crossed my bare feet on the cool windowsill, took a sip of piping hot coffee, and watched the emerging sunrise from my third-story apartment window. A soft yellow scaled the horizon and stretched across it like tendrils of food coloring suspended in water. Ribbons of pinks and oranges and purples quickly followed, the symphony a slow, exquisite seduction of the senses. Or it could have been if there wasn't a dead girl standing next to me.

She jutted out a tiny hip, anchored a fist onto it, and let loose a lengthy sigh of annoyance for my benefit. I continued to ignore her. There were few things in life more irritating than other people's children. Hell, perhaps. Been there, done that. But for the moment, the only thing complicating an otherwise serene morning was a tiny blonde-haired, blue-eyed beast in Strawberry Shortcake pajamas.

"Are you going to read it to me or not?" she asked, referring to our recent ventures into Harry Potter land.

I stopped what I was doing, which was basically trying not to drool into my cup. As a master mixologist, I felt the need to experiment from time to time on my morning elixir. To liven it up. To create new concoctions of greatness to which others could only aspire. This morning, however, I'd done good just to push the right button on Mr. Coffee. At least I think I pushed the right button. I could have started a nuclear war for all I knew.

"I've already read it to you seven thousand, eight hundred, forty-three times."

She pursed her bowlike lips, causing dimples to emerge on either side of her mouth. But these weren't happy dimples. They were dimples of disappointment. Dimples of frustration and irritation and fury.

I hung my head in shame.

Just kidding!

I turned back toward the window and ignored her.

"You've read it twice."

"Which is two times too many in my book," I said,

focusing on the spectacular display before me, realizing that, to the everyday passerby, my apathy toward the tiny creature might've seemed cold. Aloof. Cruel even. But I'd just come from an all-night stakeout that involved a woman, aka my client, who swore that her husband was sneaking out at night and meeting his personal assistant for some *very* personal assistance. She wanted proof.

After showering, the only thing I wanted was to drink the key to life itself, enjoy the colors bursting before me, and figure out how to tell my client that her husband was not cheating on her with his personal assistant. He was cheating on her, in a sense, with the college kids that rented their above-garage apartment. He snuck out to play video games and enjoy a little plant-based, medicinal stress relief. After getting to know his wife, I could hardly blame him. She turned high-maintenance into an extreme sport.

Now, I just had to figure out how to tell her what her husband was up to. Even though there was nothing sexual about her husband's exploits, a woman like that would still feel betrayed. If, however, I could put just the right spin on it, I could lessen the sting when I gave her the news. So, instead of my original plan of saying, "Your husband is escaping you for a few blissful hours of recreation because you are cra-cra and he needs a break," I figured I could say something like, "Your husband is sneaking out to tutor the struggling college kids who rent your apartment. He counsels them on how to stay focused no matter what life throws at them (or who throws it), advises them on how to shake off a bad day (or a bad marriage), and push through. He even cautions them about the dangers of illegal drug use."

Yeah. I nodded my head, quite proud of myself. That's

the ticket. By the time I was finished with her, she'd see her husband as a paladin of the pawn. A defender of the downtrodden. A savior of the suffering.

A HERO!

I took another sip, ignored yet another sigh coming from the irreverent beast beside me, and let myself slip. Just a little. Just enough to see the other side. The supernatural one. Because there was nothing more spectacular than watching the sunrise in the mortal world, the tangible one, from the vantage of the immortal world. One seemed to affect the other. The raging, powerful storms of the supernatural realm grew even more vibrant. Even more brilliant. As though somehow our sunlight spilled into the domain of the preternatural.

Made sense. Preternatural inhabitants tended to spill into our world as well. On occasion.

The marvel that I could shift from one realm to the other was not lost on me. For a month, I'd lived on the crux between the two worlds, having no idea I could control where I stood in each.

In my own defense, I had amnesia at the time. Had no idea who I was. What I was. The fact that I was a god from another dimension who'd volunteered to be the angel of death in this one, to be its grim reaper, was the furthest thing from my imaginings, and even as an amnesiac I was pretty darned imaginative.

Now that I had all my memories back—both good and bad—I saw my mission as a celestial version of the Peace Corps. Volunteer work for the good of another people and, in turn, for the good of all.

That was a week ago. I'd been back in Albuquerque a week. I'd had my memories back for a week. And still I felt disoriented. Unbalanced. Like a Weeble that wobbled but wouldn't fall down. That *couldn't* fall down. I had too much to do.

My best friend-slash-receptionist, Cookie, was worried. I could tell. She put on a happy face every time I walked into her office or strolled into her apartment unannounced, an action my Uncle Bob, aka her new husband, did not appreciate. But one of the advantages—or disadvantages, depending on one's point of view—of being from the supernatural side of things was that I could feel others' emotions. And I could feel the worry that ate at her every time she looked at me.

She was right. I hadn't quite been the same since I got back, but for good reason. Three, actually. Three main ones, anyway.

First, my daughter had been taken from me when she was barely two days old. It was for the best. To keep her safe, we had no choice but to send her away. But that didn't make it any easier. Probably because the fault lay at my feet and my feet alone.

I was apparently made of this bright-ass light that lured the departed, those who did not cross when they died, to me. Cool beans, right? I'd always considered the light a pretty nifty side effect of being grim. But that was before I had a child who was destined to defeat Satan and save the world. Now that same light worked only to lead our vast and powerful enemies straight to me. And in turn, straight to my daughter.

Thus, it wasn't so much that we had to send Beep away to be safe. It was more that we had to send her away from *me* to be safe. Her mother. Her matriarch. The woman who bore her. At the bottom of a well, no less. Long story. So the torment of heartbreak I felt was a constant weight on my chest and, unfortunately, my mood.

Second, in an attempt to restore my memories, my departed father crossed through me. When people cross, their lives flash in my mind. When my father crossed, I was flooded with memories of myself through his eyes. I saw the love he felt every time he looked at my sister and me. I felt the pride that swelled his heart to twice its normal size. But as wonderful and surreal and life-affirming as all that was, I still lost him. He was now safely tucked on the *other* side of this dimension, a realm to which I had no access. None that I knew of, anyway.

But his crossing was only the predecessor of the second reason for my melancholy state. When my father's life flashed in my mind, he also made sure I saw what he'd learned since he'd died. In an instant, I learned secrets of an underworld I never knew existed. Spies and traitors. Anarchists and heretics. Alliances lost and nations won. And wars. A thousand wars that spanned a million years. But the most salient thing he wanted me to see was the fact that Reyes—my husband, my soul mate, and Beep's father—was a god as well.

A god.

But not just any god. He was one of the three gods of Uzan. Three brothers who knew only death and destruction. Who devoured millions. Who ate worlds like others ate corn chips. Worse, he was considered the most dangerous of the three, the most bloodthirsty, before Satan tricked him, trapped him, and used the god's energy to create his son, Rey'aziel. Otherwise known as Reyes Alexander Farrow.

So my husband was a god—an evil god—who'd destroyed worlds and obliterated life wherever he went. Known across a thousand dimensions as the Razer, he was by far the worst of the three. And I was married to him.

But there was still so much I didn't understand. I'd had no idea I was a god. Not really. Not until I learned my celestial name. When that happened, all of the memories I had as a god came rushing back to me. I wasn't supposed to learn my celestial name until my earthly body passed. Until I died and took up my reapery duties. But an unfortunate series of events forced a friend to whisper my name into my ear. Now I had the power of creation itself at my fingertips and only an inkling of what to do with it or how to control it, a fact that set Jehovah, the God of this dimension, a little on edge. This according to His archangel Michael.

Michael and I don't really get along. He tried to kill me once. I refuse to be friends with anyone who's tried to kill me.

But Reyes has heard his celestial name. He's even met the other two brothers. Was loaned out by his father to fight with them side-by-side during a particularly nasty war between two realms. Does he know he is a god? Does he know the most important ingredient his father used while creating him, the one that made him so powerful, was a god? Even if he doesn't, how much of the god Razer controls Reyes's actions? How much of him is god? Demon? Human?

In a nutshell, is he good or evil?

All evidence would point to the latter, but he was forged in the fires of sin and damnation. Did that affect him? Did the evil that forever burned in his home dimension leech into him as he grew up? As he fought to survive the cruelties of being raised in hell by a bitter fallen angel? As he rose through the ranks to became a general in his father's army? To command legions of demons? To lead them into war and sacrifice?

After all this time, after everything we'd been through, I thought I knew my husband. Now, I wasn't so sure.

One thing I was sure of was the fact that I needed to learn his true godly name. It couldn't be Razer. That term had to be an interpretation of his true name. Or perhaps a nickname. If I knew Reyes's godly name, I could do what Satan did. I could trap him, if need be, in the god glass I kept with me always.

I shifted back onto this plane, patted the pendant in my sweats pocket, and turned to the girl beside me. The one who clearly had no intention of leaving.

After forcing my biggest and brightest fake smile, the one made of irritation and paint remover, I asked, "Why don't you have Rocket read it to you?"

Rocket was a mutual friend who'd died in a mental asylum in the fifties. He was also a savant who knew the names of every human being on earth who'd lived and died. Ever. Strawberry crashed with him and his sister, Blue, though I'm not sure the departed actually sleep. I hadn't seen Rocket in weeks, and his place was first on my list of places to hit for the day, now that my one and only case was almost over.

Strawberry crossed her arms over her chest. "He can't read it to me."

"Why not?"

I was expecting her to say, "Because he's dead and he can't turn the pages." What I got was, "Because he can't read."

I finally leveled a semi-interested gaze on her. "What do you mean he can't read? He writes the names of the departed all over the walls."

That was his main gig. Rocket scratched thousands and thousands of names into the walls of the abandoned asylum, all day, every day. It was fascinating to watch. For about five minutes, at which point my ADHA kicked in and I'd suddenly have places to be and people to see.

She rolled her eyes. "Of course he can *write* names. Duh. It's his job. Doesn't mean he can *read* them."

That made about as much sense as reality TV.

"They aren't there for him to read anyway," she added as she picked at the sleeve of my T-shirt that read *My brain has too many tabs open.* "They're for her."

As intrigued as I should've been, intrigue was not as intriguing as one might imagine at six o'clock in the morning. Especially after pulling an all-nighter. I took another sip. Studied the steam rising out of the cup like a lover. Wondered if I should use my powers over the next twenty-four hours for good or evil. Evil would be more fun.

Finally, with the patience of a saint on Xanax, I asked, "For who, hon?"

Her large irises bounced back to mine. "For who what?"

I shifted toward her. "What?"

"What?"

"What did you say?"

"For who what?"

I fought the urge to grind my teeth into dust, and asked, "If not for Rocket, for who—whom—are they written?"

She pursed her lips and went back to lacing tendrils of my hair into her tiny fingers. "For whom is *what* written?"

I'd lost her. And I suddenly had a raging desire to sell her on the black market. It would do me little good, though. Poor thing drowned when she was nine. Not many on earth could see her. My luck I'd have to take her back and give the buyer a refund. Then I'd have to mark the perv's soul for hell for trying to buy a child on the black market. Seriously, what the fuck?

I took another sip for strength, then explained as simply as I could. "The names Rocket writes on the walls of the asylum. If he can't read them, who are they for?"

"Oh, those!" Suddenly excited, she tried to disentangle her fingers and took half my scalp with her. She spread her arms like wings and began running in circles around the apartment making engine sounds. No idea why. "Those are for Beep."

I paused mid-scalp-rub. "Beep?" I asked, a tingling sensation racing over my skin. "My Beep?"

She stopped just long enough to shoot me a look of exasperation before flying around the apartment again. Not literally. "How many Beeps do you know?"

I blinked at her for a solid minute with my mouth slightly agape. Drool slipped from one corner as I tried to wrap my head around what she'd just said. If only I had more brain cells at 6 AM. They didn't even begin to amass until around 7:12, and the all-nighter didn't help.

As I sat pondering Strawberry's statement, the son of Satan walked in from our bedroom wearing only a gray pair of pajama bottoms and a sleep-deprived expression. The bottoms rode low on his lean hips. The expression darkened an already dark face. Black hair sat at charmingly unnatural angles. Thick lashes hooded sparkling brown irises. The boy defined the popular phrase *sex on a stick*.

But I had to remember what he was. It was bad enough that his father was public enemy number one, but to be an evil god from another dimension? That was a lot of evil to pack into one body, no matter how succulent.

I should have guessed long ago that he was more than met the eye. Even barely awake, his stride was powerful.

Sleek. Graceful. Like that of a big cat. I slipped into the outer edge of the supernatural realm and saw the darkness billowing out of him like a cloak to cascade over his shoulders. To wash down his back. To pool at his bare feet.

The fire that bathed him in yellows and oranges and blues licked over his smooth skin like a layer of sin. It dipped between the valleys of hard muscle. Shifted with every move he made. As though it were as alive as he.

Strawberry noticed none of that. Her harried little mind, like her body, spun in circles like she hadn't just dropped a bombshell on me. Why would those names be meant for Beep? It made no sense.

"What do you mean, hon?" I asked her, suppressing a giggle when Reyes spotted the little beast coming in for a landing near his rubber tree plant. It wasn't like she could actually knock it over.

Instead of answers, I got, "I love cotton candy. I'd marry it if I could." She came in for a landing, taxied just long enough to catch a second wind, then took off again. "I can smell it sometimes. There was a house on fire once, but I couldn't smell it. I can't smell perfume or paste or oranges, but I can smell cotton candy. Only sometimes, though. All pink and fluffy. Do you like cotton candy?"

I'd been busy watching my husband head for the kitchen, trying not to let the soft grin he tossed me ease the turmoil roiling inside me.

"Cotton candy daiquiris," I said, unable to take my eyes off him.

We had fallen into a continuous series of short conversations and awkward silences. And I had no idea why. No idea what I had done. For a man who could barely keep his hands off me a week ago, this new form of torture was disconcerting.

Did he know that he was a god? More importantly did he know that I knew that he was a god?

That could certainly put him on edge. Then again why? I was a god. Why shouldn't he be one as well? Maybe there was more to this than I knew. Or perhaps his recent disinterest had nothing to do with any of that.

Maybe it was due to the fact that I had done exactly what he had predicted I would. I forgot him. When I learned my celestial name, I forgot him. He'd said I would. No, wait, he'd said I would leave him, and then I would forget him. Two for two. But amnesia was a really good excuse for not remembering someone. And it's not like I'd done it on purpose.

The fact that he was so drop-dead sexy did not help anything. The pajama bottoms did absolutely nothing to hide the fact that he had the most perfect ass I had ever seen. Steely. Shapely. Deep divots on either side. Solid, rock-hard muscle. The kind of ass no heterosexual woman could resist. Damn him.

I craned my neck to watch him walk into the kitchen and pull the carafe out from the coffee maker.

"I just made it," I said, referring to the coffee.

"What do you think brought me in here?" There was a softness to his voice despite the darkness surrounding him. A humor. It was nice and more reassuring than it should have been.

"Sometimes I eat it for breakfast," Strawberry added, then pointed to Reyes from the space between a slate coffee table and a creamy sofa. "Does he ever eat cotton candy for breakfast?"

He stepped around the counter to face us, lowered his gaze, and took a sip from the black mug in his hands.

"No," I said. "He's very much like the big bad wolf. He eats little girls for breakfast."

He spoke from behind the cup, his voice deep and as smooth as butterscotch. "She's wrong. I eat big girls for breakfast."

A tingling sensation fluttered in my stomach.

Strawberry stopped at last and crinkled her nose in thought, our playful banter going over her head, thankfully.

"Did you catch the bad guy?" Reyes asked, pinning me with his powerful gaze.

I turned around in the chair I'd pulled up to the window and sat on my heels to savor the last few drops of nirvana. "No bad guys this time. Just a man trying to make it through the day."

"Aren't we all?" he asked, and I paused to study him.

He studied me back, his lashes narrowing as he took me in, and I wondered if he really understood, on even the basest level, what he did to women. A man just trying to make it through the day? Uh-huh. Right.

Strawberry landed again, plopped onto the coffee table, and let her feet dangle beneath her. "I like what you've done with the place."

Reyes grinned and ducked back into the kitchen, hopefully to make me the breakfast of champions, whatever that might entail. I took the opportunity to once again scan the vastness of what used to be my microscopic apartment. I hadn't seen it for over nine months, eight of those having been spent at a convent—long story—and the other one spent as an amnesiac waitress at a café in upstate New York.

At some point during our recent adventures, Reyes had renovated the apartment building. The entire thing. The exterior remained relatively unchanged. A few fixes here and there, a good cleaning, and it was good to go.

The interior, however, had been completely overhauled. Each apartment had been updated as students graduated or long-term residents moved into one of the newly renovated ones while theirs received the same treatment. But the third floor, the top one, had received a little extra attention.

It now had only two apartments, ours and Cookie's, each consisting of over 13,000 square feet of absolute luxury.

The rooftop storage units had been opened up so the ceilings in half of the apartment were now over twenty-four feet tall. Metal rafters zigzagged across our ceiling. Two adjoining gardens sat on the flat part of the roof outside, complete with lights and a pond and real plants. The whole place looked positively magical.

Reyes kept only one room locked and had refused to open it when he brought me home for the first time in months, but locked doors were never much of a problem for me. The day after we'd arrived home, I took advantage of the fact that he left earlier than I did and broke in. I'd flipped the light switch and stopped short. The room had been decorated in mint green stripes and pastel circus animals and equipped with a basinet. It was Beep's room, and the fissure in my heart had cracked a little more.

"I'm going to see if Blue wants to play hopscotch."

She disappeared before I could get out a good-bye. Or good riddance. Either way.

I looked past where she'd been sitting toward Reyes's plush cream-colored sofa. He didn't get it at a garage sale like I'd gotten my previous sofa. Her name had been

Sophie and I often wondered what happened to her. Was she lamenting the days away at a dumpsite? Sure she'd only cost me twenty bucks, but she'd been with me a long time. I hated the thought of her being destroyed.

Then another thought hit me.

Speaking of discarded items, "Hey," I said, suddenly concerned, "where did you put Mrs. Allen and PP?"

PP, aka Prince Phillip, was an elderly poodle that had once fought a demon for me, doing his darnedest to save my life. He and Mrs. Allen had been living down the hall since I'd moved in, and if anyone had a right to live here, to have one of these sparkly new apartments, it was those two.

Reyes lowered his head. "Her family had to put her in a nursing home."

My spine straightened in alarm. "What? Why?"

He bit down. "A lot's happened since we've been gone."

"You should have told me."

"It happened last month. You wouldn't have known her."

I paused to absorb that. He was right. Didn't make it any easier to swallow. "Where is she?"

"At a retirement home in the North Valley."

I made a mental note to visit her. "What about PP?"

"PP?"

"Her poodle. The one that saved my life, I might add."

He fought a grin. "He's with her. The home where she's at allows animals."

"Oh, thank goodness." I slumped in the chair and put my chin on the back. Reyes was right. A lot had changed. Including the state of my cup.

"I'm going to make another pot if you want more after your shower," I said, hopping up and heading that way.

He lifted a wide shoulder, studying his own cup. His

bare feet were crossed, his other shoulder propped against the opening to the chef's kitchen, and I slowed my stride to take it all in.

"I'm not sure I want to shower today," he said.

"What? Why?"

A panty-melting grin as wicked as sin on Sunday slid across his handsome face. "Your Aunt Lillian keeps . . . checking in on me."

I stopped mid-stride, finally becoming intimately acquainted with true, paralyzing mortification.

He stifled a chuckle as he set his cup aside and started for the bathroom.

"Aunt Lillian!" I yelled, summoning her to me instantly. Aunt Lillian had died in the sixties. She'd been elderly at the time, but she didn't let that stop her from enjoying the flower-child generation, complete with love beads and a floral muumuu. I'd always figured a hit of acid at her age could not have been good.

"Pumpkin head!" she said, her tone as hollow and insincere as her dentureless mouth. She wasn't even looking at me. Her gaze instantly sought out the son of evil. Locked onto him like a laser-guided missile.

He tossed her a wink as he strode past, and I thought she was going to melt right then and there.

"Aunt Lillian," I whispered accusingly. "I thought you didn't even like my husband that much."

"Oh, pumpkin, I've seen him naked. What's not to like?" She wiggled her brows and I gaped, appalled. Appalled that, for once in my life, I had no argument. No sarcastic comeback. No snippy comment. Because she was right as rain on a scorched desert.

I looked my husband over once again. Watched his back muscles ripple with each step he took. Our apartment was much bigger now, so it took a lot of steps to get to the bathroom now. A lot of rippling.

One of those ripples was inside me. A ripple of unease. Reyes was right. Way more had changed than I was comfortable with. Which brought me to the third, but far from final, reason for my gloom. My husband hadn't touched me in days. Since we got back, in fact. Normally, he had trouble touching anything *besides* me, but he hadn't offered his services in over a week. A very long, very lonely week, made even lonelier when I'd been blindsided by a receipt I'd stumbled upon. He'd made a payment to the Texas Child Support division.

He was paying child support.

He had another child.

I closed my eyes again, trying to figure out if I ever really knew the man I married.